PHILLIPA ASHLEY writes warm, funny romantic fiction for a variety of world-famous international publishers.

After studying English at Oxford, she worked as a copywriter and journalist. Her first novel, *Decent Exposure*, won the RNA New Writers Award and was made into a TV movie called *12 Men of Christmas* starring Kristin Chenoweth and Josh Hopkins. As Pippa Croft, she also wrote the Oxford Blue series – *The First Time We Met*, *The Second Time I Saw You* and *Third Time Lucky*.

Phillipa lives in a Staffordshire village and has an engineer husband and scientist daughter who indulge her arty whims. She runs a holiday-let business in the Lake District, but a big part of her heart belongs to Cornwall. She visits the county several times a year for 'research purposes', an arduous task that involves sampling cream teas, swimming in wild Cornish coves and following actors around film shoots in a camper van. Her hobbies include watching *Poldark*, Earl Grey tea, Prosecco-tasting and falling off surf boards in front of RNLI lifeguards.

🐦 @PhillipaAshley

Also by Phillipa Ashley

The Cornish Café Series
Summer at the Cornish Café
Christmas at the Cornish Café
Confetti at the Cornish Café

The Little Cornish Isles Series
Christmas on the Little Cornish Isles: The Driftwood Inn
Spring on the Little Cornish Isles: The Flower Farm
Summer on the Little Cornish Isles: The Starfish Studio

The Porthmellow Series
A Perfect Cornish Summer
A Perfect Cornish Christmas
A Perfect Cornish Escape

A Surprise Christmas Wedding

The Falford Series
An Endless Cornish Summer

A Special Cornish Christmas

Phillipa Ashley

avon.

HarperCollins*Publishers*
1 London Bridge Street
London SE1 9GF

www.harpercollins.co.uk

HarperCollins*Publishers*
1st Floor, Watermarque Building, Ringsend Road
Dublin 4, Ireland

A Paperback Original 2021

1

First published in Great Britain by HarperCollins*Publishers* 2021

A catalogue copy of this book is available from the British Library.

ISBN: 978-0-00-837166-1

Typeset in Birka by Palimpsest Book Production Limited, Falkirk,
Stirlingshire

Printed and Bound in the UK using 100% Renewable Electricity
at CPI Group (UK) Ltd

For my mum and dad

Chapter One

Falford, Christmas Eve

'Happy Christmas Eve!'

Bo Grayson's pulse rocketed as two arms encircled her unexpectedly in the twilight outside the Boatyard Café. She'd just given the padlock on the door a final tug to check it was secure before the festive break.

'Oh my God, Hamish! You scared me.'

'Sorry,' he said, freeing her so she could turn around and look at him face to face. 'Didn't mean to make you jump.'

'It's OK – you just took me by surprise.'

'Well, I'm a good surprise, I hope?'

Bo hesitated, but only to keep him on tenterhooks. Hamish MacKenzie had made her heart pound far too often over the past few months, and it was fun to see him unsure about her feelings for a change.

'Yes, you are a good surprise,' she conceded.

A satisfied grin spread over his face and his eyes glinted. 'Cade not around?' he asked, scanning the terrace area next to the café beside the estuary. Birds called as dusk fell and lights already twinkled in the windows of the cottages of Falford village, which straddled both sides of the creek.

'No. I sent him home half an hour ago. He wanted to help me clear away and close up but he deserves some time with his family on Christmas Eve. He's worked so hard all season. Neither of us has been able to have a proper break.' Cade was not only Bo's assistant but also one of her regular partners at the Falford Flingers, the dance group of which she was a member.

'You've worked bloody hard too. You're a saint,' Hamish said, then raised one of his eyebrows suggestively. 'Though not too much of one, I hope.'

Suddenly he swept into his arms and kissed her, the soft wool of his scarf tickling her nose and making her laugh so that the kiss ended sooner than she'd really have liked. Then again, it was always too soon to end one of Hamish's kisses.

'Sorry,' Bo said, wrinkling her nose and trying not to sneeze, which would have been most unromantic. 'Your scarf got in the way.'

'In that case, I must remember not to wear it again.' His eyes glinted with promise. 'I wouldn't want to let anything get in the way of kissing you.'

With a tingle of excitement, Bo tucked the scarf deeper into the open neck of his Barbour jacket. He looked more delicious than anything she'd served up in the Boatyard café over the past six weeks. Bo could still hardly believe that this year, for the first time in many, she wouldn't be waking up alone on Christmas Day. She'd always enjoyed spending the day with her parents, sister, brother-in-law and little niece and nephew, but it would be lovely to wake up with Hamish and share breakfast in her own place; open their presents together before heading off to visit her family.

She'd had his present wrapped up and hidden away in the back of her wardrobe for weeks now, and she couldn't wait to give it to him. She'd ordered a beautiful hip flask – sterling silver with his initials engraved. As they hadn't been together for too long, she felt confident this was just the right sort of gift: a playful nod to his Scots heritage, but also something personal – a keepsake from her.

Bo smiled to herself, thinking how lucky she was to have found Hamish. It wasn't easy meeting new people in a small village like Falford and, though Hamish was working in nearby Helston, it was fair to say he'd caused a stir for miles around. He was tall and hunky with curly brown hair and a Highlands accent to-die-for and – God love him – he was a vet.

He was single too, which had seemed like a minor miracle. He was also a keen sailor and had been given use of a colleague's yacht which was kept at the boatyard. After a few visits to Bo's café and a lot of chat, he'd asked her out for a drink and a meal at a local pub. That had been back in September and, it was safe to say, they hadn't wasted any time since.

'You managed to get away from work, then?' Bo said, knowing the vet's surgery where he worked always planned to close at three on Christmas Eve, but that was never usually the case with people rushing to make last-minute appointments for their pets ahead of the holidays.

'Remarkably, aye. I castrated a male cat and emptied the anal glands of an elderly spaniel but that's as wild as it got. Luckily I'm not on call for a few days so we can make the most of our lie-in tomorrow.'

'I can't wait,' Bo said. She'd always loved Christmas morning, and spending it with Hamish would be the cherry on top of the icing on a very large and delicious cake.

'Come on, let's go home and I'll have a shower before we go over to the Ferryman.'

'You'd better plan on inviting me to share that shower . . .'

At thirty-five, Bo had thought she was past the age of blushing, but the prospect of getting hot and soapy with Hamish brought a glow to her cheeks despite the damp evening. He'd warmed her nights as the weather turned cooler, and her days off had been filled with walks, pub lunches and afternoons in his bed. She'd even persuaded him to call in at a Falford Flingers social night once, but he'd drawn the line at joining in with the dancing.

He was solvent, single and thirty-seven. On their first date Bo had known he was perfect for her, and she tried in vain not to fall too hard for him. She'd woken up one morning next to him and, watching him as he slept, realised that, despite her best efforts to keep things casual and keep her cool, she was in love. Deeply, madly in love – was there any other kind?

He tucked his arm around her now and they walked up to the car park where he'd left his mud-spattered Land Rover. Bo heaved a sigh of relief. She loved the run-up to Christmas but she was mighty glad she'd served her last turkey and cranberry wrap, festive brownie and spiced latte until after the New Year.

She was looking forward to two weeks of snuggling up by the fire, watching trashy TV and lie-ins with Hamish until he headed home to Scotland for Hogmanay. Now she could relax, put on her dancing shoes and cherry-red frock and head to the pub with Hamish to celebrate with her friends from the Flingers.

Hamish drove up the hill towards the bridge that crossed the head of the creek and across the water then back down into

Falford village. The lane was narrow and ran in front of the cottages and the shops until it turned sharply upwards again and out of the village.

Bo's little cottage was situated in the centre of the village on the opposite side of the creek to the boatyard.

Falford itself was a sheltered offshoot of the main Fal estuary, which gave way to the open sea on the eastern side of the Lizard. Its creeks were dotted with villages and hamlets, havens for watercraft of all kinds. Coloured fairy lights adorned the terrace of the Ferryman Inn and the Falford Yacht Club which faced each other on opposite sides of the water. The art gallery and folklore gift shop, Cornish Magick, had closed for the holidays, but their windows were still aglow with festive displays.

The post office-cum-village store near Bo's cottage was still open, though, and would be for a while, catering to locals and holidaymakers scurrying in for cranberry sauce, tinfoil or an extra bottle of prosecco.

Hamish parked next to Bo's small van in the village residents' car park and, with his arm around her, they walked through the clear Cornish air to her cottage. Bo's fingers trembled in anticipation as she unlocked the door, then led Hamish straight upstairs where he made good on his offer to join her in the shower. Getting clean after her long day at the café and his at the vet's turned out to be the last thing on their minds – getting dirty was a more accurate description – but at last, fresh and steamy from the shower, they made it downstairs where Hamish lit the wood burner and they snuggled onto the sofa to relax and talk about the busy week they'd had in the run-up to Christmas.

Prior to buying the café, Bo had trained as a chef, learning her trade in various restaurants and pubs in the area before travelling and working abroad. She'd finally come home to Falford five years previously and found the Boatyard Café had come up for sale. It had been little more than a shack by the slipway, where the height of sophisticated cuisine was an egg on your sausage butty. The roof was leaking, the paint was peeling and the plastic chairs and tables were cracked.

Back then, it catered almost exclusively to boat workers and fishermen – it did the job, but Bo had always thought it held so much more potential, particularly as Falford Boatyard was becoming a trendy place to keep your boat as well as a practical one.

In the spring through to the autumn, Falford was bustling with visitors who gravitated to the water's edge. All kinds of waterfowl feasted on the low-tide mudflats and sometimes seals and even dolphins popped up in the deeper parts of the estuary. The café was the perfect spot for watching all the action, and Bo had long cast a wistful eye on it, fantasising about how she'd transform it and keep customers coming all year round.

When she got the chance, she pounced.

She still served breakfast butties, but she offered them on bread from the local bakery rather than cheap loaves from the cash and carry. A few customers grumbled that she had to put up the price but most had forgiven her when they tasted the result, made from fresh Cornish produce.

The old-timers rolled their eyes when she added smashed avocado on sourdough to the menu, but they didn't have to eat it and she knew the second-home owners and London holiday cottage visitors adored it. Over the summer, she'd been open seven days a week from nine until four, with the help of a couple of part-time staff who enabled her to have a rare day off. She'd done shorter hours and fewer days from October with another surge of six-day weeks in the run-up to Christmas. It was high time for a break and she'd never looked forward to it more.

Hamish had her feet in his lap and was massaging them. Closing her eyes, Bo sighed in ecstasy.

'I could stay here all evening,' he said.

'Me too, but everyone's expecting us and I need to get changed.'

His fingers encircled her ankle and slid higher up her leg. 'Don't see why.'

'Because I can't go to the pub wearing a fluffy bathrobe and no knickers.'

'Again. I don't see why not?' He gave the cheeky grin that drove her wild.

Laughing, she extricated herself from the sofa, forcing any thoughts of lingering to the back of her mind.

'I won't be long.'

With an exaggerated sigh, he picked up the TV remote. 'I'll just have to amuse myself, I suppose.'

Her wardrobe was bulging with vintage pieces in her favourite 1950s style. She picked out a cherry-red velvet dress, which was nipped in at the waist with a sweetheart neckline and three-quarter-length sleeves. She added a black cropped cardigan she'd found on a vintage stall, black seamed tights and black patent shoes with chunky heels.

None of it was practical for a December night by the river but she didn't care. It was only five minutes to the Ferryman and, although it was a damp night, it was still ten degrees in this mild corner of Cornwall, where camellias and magnolias were already in bloom thanks to the sheltered river valleys and micro-climate.

Hamish was sprawled on the sofa watching *Die Hard* when Bo entered the sitting room. He let out a whistle. 'You look bloody amazing.'

'Thanks. I'm probably overdressed for the Ferryman but it is Christmas Eve.'

He muted the sound and beckoned her closer. 'As long as you're underdressed later, I don't care.' He lifted the hem of her dress. 'Are those stockings?'

'That's for me to know and you to find out.'

'Well, that would only take me a minute . . .' Hamish said suggestively as he started to run his fingers up from the back of her knee to her thigh.

Bo playfully batted his hand away, saying, 'Not now! You'll have to wait, but I wouldn't get your hopes up.'

Trying not to think about how much she'd like to take Hamish up on his offer, Bo shooed him out of the house. He unhooked his battered Barbour from the hall stand and they stepped into the night air. The light mist was rising off the estuary and cast halos around the fairy lights adorning most of the homes and shops. The Ferryman was no exception, with strings of coloured bulbs that hung from the eaves and over its terrace. Even some of the yachts moored in the estuary and at the yacht club opposite had lights on their masts. Caught up in the festive excitement, Bo couldn't wait to start the celebrations.

When they reached the Ferryman, some of the revellers had spilled out from the bar and onto the waterside terrace above the jetty. Waving at various locals, Bo and Hamish threaded their way through the drinkers, looking for the rest of the Flingers. The group's leaders, Hubert and Sally Jaye, were sitting at a table by the fire with some of the other older members.

Cade was their son, but he'd be spending Christmas Eve at home with his wife and new baby.

After a quick hello to her fellow dancers, Bo and Hamish went for a table in the corner where a bright-eyed middle-aged woman sat with a glass of Coke in front of her.

'Hello, Angel! Happy Christmas!' Bo said.

Angel Carrack sprang up and hugged her. 'Happy Christmas! I saved you both a space – it's packed in here.'

'Thanks, Angel,' Bo said.

'Hello, Hamish. Happy Christmas,' Angel said.

'Happy Christmas,' he replied, giving her a peck on the cheek.

Hamish popped to the bar while Bo and Angel chatted. Bo decided on a glass of mulled wine but Hamish wasn't drinking, saying he'd had a skinful at the vet's Christmas do earlier that week.

Bo shrugged off her coat, draping it over the back of her chair.

Angel gave a sigh. 'Oh, I love that coat. You look amazing.'

'You look fabulous yourself! Is that a new dress? What a gorgeous colour.'

Angel beamed as she smoothed out the skirt of her emerald-green satin dress. The style fitted her petite form like a glove and the colour perfectly complemented her auburn curls and green eyes. 'It is! In fact, I made it.'

'Wow. You're so talented.'

Angel wrinkled her nose. 'Tommy said it makes me look like a Christmas tree.'

'You don't! He's rotten!'

'He was only joking, I expect. He did also say it really suited me.'

'I should hope so,' Bo said, picturing Angel's gruff husband and feeling quite cross with him for teasing her friend.

'He's coming to pick me up tonight. It'll make a nice change for him not to be at sea and for me to have a lift rather than collecting him from the pub.'

'I'm glad he's home for Christmas,' Bo said. Angel's husband was a fisherman and often at sea for days on end. He also liked a drink or two but that didn't seem to be an issue for Angel, who tolerated Tommy's quirks with remarkable good humour. Bo wasn't sure she would have been so forgiving.

Hamish was engaged in a conversation about worming treatments with one of the other vets who'd stopped at their table so Bo chatted to Angel about their preparations for Christmas dinner, and the Christmas shopping triumphs and disasters. Bo had done some of hers at the Country Stores, which was stocked with gift ideas as well as more mundane essentials like horse feed and compost.

She loved hunting out the perfect gift for friends and family; knowing you didn't have to spend much if you planned in advance and put some thought into the ideal present. As a businesswoman herself, she also liked to stick to smaller local shops as much as possible – even if her purchases from the Country Stores helped to line the pockets of Kelvin, Angel's boss, who'd taken on the place after his great-uncle had retired. However, tonight wasn't for wasting time thinking about Kelvin, and Bo soon moved on to chatting about the Flingers.

'Is Ran coming tonight?' Angel asked.

Bo shrugged. 'I don't know. He didn't say.'

Ran Larsen was a relatively new face in Falford and the Flingers' latest – and rather enigmatic – member. He was Norwegian by birth but had lived in the UK most of his life, moving from London the previous spring. He'd joined the Flingers in early October, but not to dance – he had been sent along by Cookie, their usual DJ, who couldn't make it at the last moment.

Cookie knew Ran as a regular customer in the vintage record shop he ran in Falmouth. He'd mentioned Ran was renting a cottage by one of the narrow valleys that branched off from the main Falford estuary and Bo knew the house – a solitary place almost hidden under the trees at the very head of the romantically named Smuggler's Creek.

Ran had turned up that night at the Flingers rehearsal, knowing no one and appearing anything but a rock and roll enthusiast, dressed in black jeans and an anonymous grey T-shirt as opposed to the quirky vintage gear favoured by most of the men. He'd played some great tunes, many they hadn't heard before but they had got everyone bopping away enthusiastically. However, in contrast to Cookie's amusing patter, Ran had largely let his music do the talking. Apart from chatting to Hubert briefly, he hadn't hung around. The more charitable members of their group might describe him as 'quiet', the less forgiving members as 'aloof'.

'Maybe he's just shy,' Angel, generous as ever, had remarked to Bo. 'After all, he doesn't know anyone. I wonder what Ran's short for? I think it's a Viking name. He looks like a Viking.'

'Well he certainly doesn't look like the rock and roll type,' Bo had said. She simply couldn't imagine him with sideburns and crepe-soled shoes anyway, and the thought made her want to giggle.

'I think he looks like a younger version of that chap from *Tarzan* . . . my kids still love that film even though they're grown-up.'

Bo knew exactly what her friend meant, and sneaked a look at Ran, who'd been setting up the decks and sorting through

11

records. 'You must mean Alexander Skarsgård? Hmm, I *can* kind of see the resemblance.'

Sideburns or no sideburns, the music he played was fantastic. He clearly had a passion for the sounds of the era and an impressive set of equipment, record decks, and amps. Even so, Bo hadn't expected him to come along again and had been surprised when he'd turned up with Cookie the following week. When Cookie had confessed he was too busy with his business to DJ any longer, Ran had become a regular fixture.

Hamish returned from the bar and, a moment later, Ran himself emerged from a laughing group of locals. He made for their table, a half pint in his hand.

Bo and Angel exchanged glances, as if to say: 'What timing!'

'Oh, hello, Ran! I didn't see you walk in,' Angel said.

'I came up from the terrace. I've had a word with the others en route.' He kissed Angel on the cheek. 'Happy Christmas, Angel.'

She beamed.

'It's good to see you,' Bo said.

Ran gave one of his enigmatic smiles that might have meant anything.

'So, how are you liking Falford?' Angel asked. 'Now you've been here a few months.'

'It's been eight months, actually,' he said.

'So long?' Bo was genuinely surprised. 'Time flies!'

'I'd been here a while before I joined the Flingers,' Ran said.

'You're almost as new here as me,' Hamish said. 'So, what's your verdict on the locals?'

'Everyone's been very welcoming so far,' Ran said evenly.

'You can say that again. I've certainly had a *very* warm welcome from the locals,' Hamish said as he kissed Bo's lips

12

briefly. 'Especially from one in particular. Phew, talk about hot.'

'Ooh errr.' Angel let out a squeak.

Bo felt the heat rise into her cheeks and squirmed, feeling embarrassed.

Hamish's hand crept over her thigh under the table. Bo shifted in her seat. His fingers slid underneath the hem of her velvet dress and rested above her knee. It would have been sexy in private or possibly in a quiet corner of a pub, but *here*? The Ferryman was packed with people, many of whom she knew, and Angel was only two feet away on the opposite side of the table, with Ran standing next to her. She hoped no one could see and gently moved his hand off her leg. 'Later,' she mouthed with a smile.

'Are you staying in Falford for Christmas, Ran?' she asked, sure her voice was rising higher in pitch but trying to deflect attention away from her red face.

'I am,' he said.

'No plans to see your family?' Angel said, sounding a little surprised.

'My sister's lot will be going to see our parents in Surrey. I don't mind staying at home and, anyway, I'm on duty over the festive period.'

'On duty?' Hamish asked.

'I occasionally volunteer for the Marine Divers Wildlife Rescue,' he said. 'And besides, Thor needs me.'

'Thor?' Hamish burst out laughing.

'My cat.' Ran smiled. 'Although I call him the Beast of Bodmin. He's a terror to the local wildlife.'

'You love him really,' Angel said. 'I'm so glad you could take him.'

'He's certainly got his paws under the table, and I was glad to give him a home.'

'A wildlife rescue diver with a rescue cat? I approve,' Hamish said, miming applause.

Ran smiled politely.

'This is the first I've heard about a cat,' Bo said.

'I've only had him a couple of weeks. A customer of Angel's died and the family couldn't take him so I was persuaded.'

'A customer from the Country Stores?' Bo said. Angel worked at, or rather, virtually ran, the local country supplies centre a few miles away and got little thanks for it, from what Bo could glean.

'Yes, Thor belonged to a lovely old chap who lived on his own and had no relatives. I mentioned it to Ran and he said he'd take him.'

'For my sins,' Ran said solemnly.

'You didn't need much persuasion!' Angel said. 'You told me you love cats.'

'No, well, who could possibly have turned down Thor? I think we make a formidable pair, too – Thor and Ranulph.' Ran smiled.

'Ranulph's an unusual name. I went to vet school with one. He was from Orkney. Viking stock, are you?' Hamish asked.

Bo sipped her wine, hoping to hear more about the mysterious Ran.

'My mother's Norwegian so it's pretty likely. My father's British and, like I said, they live in Surrey now. Not many Vikings there.'

'How exciting,' Angel said. 'Christmas in Norway sounds like it would be magical.'

'Magical, but also very cold and very dark.' He smiled. 'My family are from Tromsø, in the north.'

Hamish grinned and put his arm around Bo. 'I'm personally happy to stay in warmer regions for Christmas.'

'We're planning to have a quiet Christmas together but we're going round my mum and dad's for Christmas dinner tomorrow,' Bo explained, squirming a little at his innuendo and wanting to move the conversation on. 'Hamish has yet to experience the full effect of my sister and her kids.'

'Don't worry, I'm escaping for Hogmanay,' Hamish said and they all laughed. Even Ran smiled.

Bo was a little nervous about introducing Hamish to her family for the first time but it felt like the right step given he was becoming a regular fixture in her life. Whether that fixture would be more permanent remained to be seen. The atmosphere in the pub warmed as the landlord amped up the festive tunes. Having exhausted the more modern mix tapes, some vintage tunes came on.

'Oh, I love this one!' Bo cried, instantly recognising 'Rockin' Around the Christmas Tree'.

'And it's the original by Brenda Lee!' Angel cried in delight.

'Thank goodness,' Ran said archly. 'If it had been the Kim Wilde version, you wouldn't have seen me for dust.'

Bo tapped her fingers on the table to the beat. 'I feel like dancing right now.'

Hamish winced. 'Not in here, surely?' He rolled his eyes. 'This stuff's out of the ark. It's my grandad's era.'

'I know . . . but I love it,' Bo said.

Hamish turned to Ran as he said, 'I keep telling Bo she's too young for this sort of thing. You too, if you don't mind me saying, mate.'

'Hamish . . .' Bo said, playfully, but a little annoyed at his teasing her friends. 'There are all ages of people at Flingers.

Some are in their early twenties. You don't have to be old to enjoy vintage music.'

'Bo's right,' Ran said. 'You don't have to be two hundred years old to enjoy reading Jane Austen or born in the nineteenth century to appreciate a Monet painting.'

'I suppose not,' Hamish replied, sounding unconvinced. 'But come on, it's hardly cool.'

Ran sipped his pint before replying. 'I don't listen to it because it's cool. I listen to it because I enjoy it.'

Bo sensed the tension ramping up between the two men but, before she could interject, Hamish said, 'Right . . . I still can't imagine you bopping along to this.'

'Actually, you don't need to imagine me bopping along to anything. I stay strictly on the other side of the decks.'

'I wish you would dance,' Angel said. 'You'd love it.'

'Thanks, but I have two left feet. I am more than happy to play the music while you all enjoy the hard part.'

'Well, if you ever do, there'd be plenty of people who'd teach you and be your partner,' Angel said. 'You too, Hamish.'

Hamish smirked. 'I'm more than happy to stay in the twenty-first century, thanks. I'll leave all this old fogey business to you lot.'

Angel's eyes widened, though if she was hurt by Hamish's comment, she covered it with a smile.

Bo wondered if Hamish felt left out because they were all talking shop, but he could at least have shown an interest and not been quite so combative with Ran. If he was worried Ran was some kind of rival, he was wrong – she barely knew him.

'I love Brenda Lee,' Angel went on, presumably sensing the atmosphere and wanting to defuse the situation. 'Hard to believe she was only thirteen years old when she recorded this.'

'Incredible, isn't it?' Ran said. 'I've got an early pressing of this one in my collection.'

'Oh, you never mentioned that before!' Angel squeaked in excitement.

'I'd love to hear it,' Bo said.

'I'll bring it to the next Flingers meet. We could dance to it at the New Year's Eve party,' Ran said.

Hamish blew out a breath. 'I'm even more glad I'll be in Scotland now. You can say what you like, I really don't get this obsession with vintage songs. They're so cheesy and trite.'

Ran smiled to himself. 'Actually, rock and roll has a great cultural history that everyone ought to know about, though I'm no expert. You should ask Hubert and Sally about that. Hubert's grandparents came from Harlem where some of the dances such as Lindy Hop and swing originated.'

'Don't worry, I'll take your word for it.' Hamish smiled and mimed a yawn. 'Actually, I think it's time we headed off. After all, Santa won't fill my stocking if I'm not in bed early.'

'Hamish! The evening's barely begun.' Bo blushed again, annoyed at him for making fun of her music and her friends. 'Why don't you grab us another round of drinks? Here, take my card.'

'OK,' he said, grinning. 'But I'll get them in this time.'

Bo watched him leave, all smiles as he greeted people he knew on the way to the bar. He was smiley enough but she thought he was on edge and not in the best of moods. She put it down to nerves and, perhaps, feeling out of his comfort zone among all her friends and the dance group.

While he waited to be served, a load of vintage tunes came through the speakers and had Bo and Angel – and the rest of the Flingers nearby – tapping their feet and humming. There were classic Christmas songs from the Ronettes, the Crystals and another of her favourites, 'Here Comes Santa Claus' by Bob B Soxx and the Blue Jeans.

Before long, the unmistakeable sound of Elvis Presley's 'Blue Christmas' blasted out from the speakers.

'Oh, this one always makes me cry,' Angel said. 'It reminds me of a boy I was mad on at school who dropped me at the Christmas disco. I spent most of the holidays moping around and driving my mum mad.'

'Oh no,' Bo said. 'But at least you met Tommy.'

'Hmm . . .' Angel said. 'Though sometimes I can't help wondering what might have been . . .'

Bo was taken aback by her friend's wistful tone. Angel had been married to Tommy for almost thirty years and they had two grown-up children. Their marriage didn't sound perfect, but something must have gone right for them to have stuck together that long. She tried to imagine being with Hamish for thirty years . . .

While Elvis warbled about missing his ex, Hamish returned from the bar with a tray of drinks, shaking his head. 'Not *another* one?' he said, groaning as he put the tray on the table. 'When are they going to roll out the good old Pogues?'

Bo laughed but wished he wasn't quite so obvious about his dislike of her favourite sounds in front of her friends.

She knew some people thought they were harking back to a 'simpler time' and maybe wanting to ignore the fact that there were many things wrong with the past. It wasn't true in her case, or for most of the members. They took time to learn about the context of the dances and their history, some of it rooted in a time of racial inequality and injustice, as Ran had pointed out.

Hubert and Sally, the founders of the club, were always happy to explain the origins of the music. Bo enjoyed being educated about the different dances and how they'd developed. To her, the cultural background added richness and a powerful sense of being part of history to their pastime. Most of all, like the rest of the Falford Flingers, Bo simply loved the joyous feeling of moving her body to great sounds.

They had another round of drinks and chatted to more of the Flingers, as more locals squeezed into the bar. The volume of chatter rose and the landlord turned up the music. Bo was well and truly infused with Christmas spirit, although she was also aware that the time was creeping on.

To her relief, Hamish seemed more at ease and was chatting to Angel about a donkey he'd treated which had ended up being part of a living nativity scene at the local farm shop. She was laughing out loud and Bo could tell he loved his work.

The wine and the festive spirit were flowing warmly through her veins, and she was ready to snuggle up in front of the fire and see Christmas Day arrive. She might even hand over Hamish's gift this evening, once the chimes had struck midnight.

With her business doing well and Hamish in her life, this Christmas was shaping up to be her best one ever.

Chapter Two

'I think we'd better be going,' Bo said, squeezing Hamish's hand discreetly under the table.

'Hmm, it is getting late. It's past ten,' Angel said, glancing at her phone.

Bo picked up her bag and got up from her chair. Hamish finished his Coke and waited by the table as she said her goodbyes.

'Have a lovely Christmas.' Bubbling with happiness, she hugged Angel and, impulsively, gave Ran a peck on the cheek. 'Merry Christmas, Ran.'

To her surprise, his eyes lit up with pleasure and he smiled. 'Merry Christmas, Bo.'

'Come on, or we'll be on Santa's naughty list.' Hamish put his arm around her, steering her towards the pub doorway, with the sound of Bing Crosby crooning 'White Christmas'.

'We don't want that to happen,' Ran said, an amused glint in his eye.

Angel murmured something Bo couldn't catch but caused Ran to laugh out loud. This evening she felt she'd learned more about him than she had in the past few weeks, although he was still largely a mystery. Maybe Angel could enlighten her after Christmas.

As the cool night air hit her lungs, Hamish put his arm around her and held her close. They walked up the lane towards her cottage, the buzz of chatter still ringing in her ears.

'Have I socialised enough?' he said. 'Dare we go home to bed without arousing further scandal?'

'Oh, I should think so,' Bo said, wondering if she'd overreacted to his risqué comments earlier. She had to admit the prospect of getting between the sheets with him was a delicious idea.

'Angel seemed shocked.'

'No, she wasn't,' Bo said and giggled. After a couple of glasses of mulled wine and a large G&T she was feeling less inhibited about his teasing and more ready to forgive his sarcastic comments about the music.

The scent of woodsmoke greeted them when they walked in, the ashes in the hearth stirred by the draught from the front door. Bo turned on a lamp and started to instruct her smart speaker to play some soothing sounds, but Hamish put his finger to her lips. 'Shh. No more music, please. I don't think I can take it.' His tone was light but his eyes held a genuine plea. 'I've had enough Christmas schmaltz,' he said, pulling her into his arms. 'The artificial kind, anyway. I'd happily have skipped the entire evening in the pub to spend it with you.'

'You don't want a coffee, then?' She said it teasingly, almost to provoke him.

'I only want you.'

He sat on the sofa, gently pulling her down onto his lap. Moments later, she was lying on top of him and making short work of his shirt buttons.

'Damn, tights,' he said.

'Maybe stockings tomorrow – a Christmas Day treat.'

They lay there afterwards, covered by a fleece blanket that Hamish had pulled over them in the cooling air. The clock on the hearth chimed the half hour and its tick was the only sound in the house as Christmas Day approached.

Bo lay with her head in the crook of his arm, tracing circles in the hair on his chest, enjoying the rise and fall of his torso. The tree lights glimmered, the tinsel shimmered as Hamish stroked her hair. A wave of happiness swept over her, something between joy and contentment. It lifted her up, gently but sweetly, and sent her spirits soaring.

'I love you,' she whispered.

The words slipped out naturally – nothing heavy, just lightly, part of a stream flowing down the valley to the estuary. No big deal.

Hamish stiffened in her arms. Bo hardly dared to breathe, waiting for him to say something.

Three words.

Two would do: *You too*. But Hamish had far more to say.

'Look . . . Bo . . . I don't want to let you down or give you the wrong idea. I'm having a great time and you're gorgeous and funny and smart, but I hadn't . . .' He sat up and swallowed hard.

He couldn't meet her eye – a sure sign of guilt, Bo thought, already regretting her impulsive declaration and knowing it was too late. Those three little words were about to ruin more than Christmas.

'Hey, it just slipped out.' She almost said she didn't mean it but the words stuck in her throat. She *had* meant it. 'It's no biggie.'

A heartbeat ago, she'd felt her world had sparkled brighter than the Christmas tree, but now felt tawdry and fake.

Hamish had moved a few inches away from her. 'It's lovely of you to say it. It's just . . . it was unexpected. I hadn't thought of anything serious . . . not yet, not with . . . anyone.'

'Hamish. Like I said, no biggie. It must have been the wine.'

'Sure.'

Bo pushed herself up, acutely aware she was naked. 'Look, let's forget about it.' She smiled, even though she felt on the edge of blurting out the truth: that his reaction had left her feeling embarrassed and hurt.

'Yeah . . .' He found it impossible to meet her eye. He pushed off the blanket and found his boxers from the sofa.

'Right then,' Bo said as lightly as she could, finding her knickers on the carpet.

So many words were unsaid now, not just the three important ones. Both of them were brimful of unspoken emotions. How could she have misjudged him so much? Mistaken great sex for something much deeper? She'd thought she was a good judge of people's feelings; she saw so many people every day at the café, hiding their emotions – some needing a kind word with their coffee, someone to take an interest in their life. With her regulars, she thought she could tell by now the ones who were holding back heartache or needed a shoulder to cry on. Oh yes, she was such a good judge of character, but she'd got Hamish totally wrong.

With no fire and wearing only her party dress again, Bo shivered. She put her cardigan on while Hamish struggled into his jeans, seeming to have trouble with the fly buttons.

'Where's my bloody shirt?' he muttered.

Bo spotted it behind the sofa. 'Here.' She handed it over.

'Thanks.' He took it and started buttoning it but fastened it wrongly. 'Feck. What's wrong with me?'

Bo couldn't answer a question that went so much further than not being able to fasten his shirt. The evening seemed to be growing colder and less festive by the second.

'Shall I make us a coffee?' she said with a brightness as artificial as the tinsel on the tree.

'Actually, it's late,' he said. 'Probably best if I don't stay after all. I've got an early start tomorrow.'

'Hamish, it's Christmas Day . . .' Bo said. 'You're on holiday.'

'Yes . . . but I need to go to Scotland.'

'What?'

'Scotland. In fact, I need to go now. Right now.' He snatched up his wallet and keys from the coffee table.

'Scotland? I don't understand.'

'No . . . neither do I, except I *do*.' He raked his hands through his hair. 'Look, I'm really sorry, Bo . . . I'm probably out of my mind and I know I shouldn't have done this to you. Shouldn't have even started anything . . . I should thank you really. I'll never forget what you've done.'

'What are you talking about?'

'My fiancée. Leonie.' He said it as if Bo was the one who was out of her mind.

'What fiancée?' She was in danger of thinking she was in an echo chamber but none of his statements made any sense.

'Ex-fiancée, technically – well, actually, I suppose. We split up in the summer. That's why I took the job in Helston, to get as far away from her as possible. I thought it would help to get over her: new place, new faces, a fresh start. All that stuff.'

'You mean . . .' she said, rapidly processing the meaning of his garbled words. 'You *used* me to help you get over a broken engagement?'

'No! Not *used*. I really like you, and I fancy you like crazy. You're amazing but I was lying to myself and lying to you – I thought you wanted some fun, I didn't think you were serious about me. I should have realised you were. Maybe I didn't *want* to realise but that's no help now, is it?'

'It's what I said after we'd had sex, isn't it?'

'No. Yes. Probably, but it started in the pub, earlier, with that stupid music. Bloody Elvis and his "Blue Christmas", wailing about life not meaning anything without his ex. I realised then, I suppose, but I didn't want to admit it, I need to go home to Leonie and give it another try. I should never have left in the first place. We had a row about the future and whether we should stay in Scotland or move south or even abroad. She had a job she loved as a midwife but I wanted to spread my wings. The whole thing blew up, it seemed to expose fundamental differences between us.' He heaved in a sigh. 'Now since I've been here, since I met you, I've realised that I want to be with her more than anything else. She might not have me back and I don't deserve her forgiveness, but I have to try. Right now.'

'Scotland's at the other end of the country, and it's almost midnight,' Bo said, still shellshocked that he'd admitted to a fiancée and had hooked up with her on the rebound. Suddenly she was Bo the café owner again, and he was a customer, using her as a shoulder to cry on; a convenient and temporary comfort pillow.

'I can be there for breakfast if I get a shift on. I have to give it another chance. You made me realise that.' He groaned. 'Sorry. Didn't mean it like that. Shitty thing to say. I know I've been a total wanker.'

Bo's disappointment mutated into anger. She felt used and discarded. She'd been a means for him to realise how little he felt for her and how much for his ex. He clearly didn't think he was being cruel and hurtful, just honest. She could barely move. If she did, she feared the motion itself would bring the tears spilling from her eyes. She'd been so wrong. Who can predict who we fall in love with? And more terrifyingly, if they would fall in love with us?

'Thank you for everything you've done for me.'

'I'm not your therapist,' she murmured.

His outstretched hand was inches from her, ready to offer consolation. 'One day, I promise, you'll find someone who lo—'

'Hamish. I think it would be better if you just fucked off.'

His lips parted briefly, perhaps in shock or to offer another platitude, but, wisely, he took her advice and a moment later the door closed behind him.

Bo stood in the centre of the room, still in shock. She thought of Hamish's gift, still wrapped up in her wardrobe, and felt slightly sick. What a fool she'd been; a romantic, sentimental idiot expecting Hamish to deliver some kind of fairytale Christmas – the kind you only ever came across in glossy magazines or Hallmark movies.

The kind that simply didn't exist in real life.

As the door had shut on her dreams, she'd thought she might cry, but instead, all she felt was crushing disappointment: in Hamish, in herself, in the whole idea of Christmas, which now seemed nothing more than shiny packaging wrapped around an empty box. She'd built up her expectations; she'd put her hopes in Hamish to provide the dream.

She curled up on the sofa and wrapped her arms around her

knees, trying not to cry over a man who didn't deserve it, even as her festive plans lay in ruins. Outside, she heard the church clock strike midnight, heralding the day she'd looked forward to for so long.

'Great,' she murmured, angrily wiping away a rogue tear. 'Happy bloody Christmas to me.'

Chapter Three

Eight months later

'So, who's going to be brave and go first?' Bo said as she queued with Angel and Ran outside the faded tent tucked away in a corner of Falford showground on a sweltering August Bank Holiday.

The tent must have been brightly striped once, but it was long past its heyday, with tattered pennants fluttering in the breeze blowing off the water. The Falford Festival was being held on the waterside recreation field outside the village. The sea shimmered in the afternoon heat as scores of boats ploughed up and down the estuary. Bo loved the sunshine and heat. It was such a shame that summer was coming to an end.

This year, she wasn't in any hurry for autumn – and especially Christmas – to come round again. In fact, after the last one, she'd be happy if the festive season was cancelled for the foreseeable.

'Brave?' Angel's brow furrowed. 'I don't think there's any reason to be brave. I'm quite excited! I've always wanted to have my fortune told.'

'I haven't,' Ran said with shake of his head. 'I can't understand all this eagerness to part with your hard-earned cash on a load of hokum. If I got a crystal ball and a tatty tent, I could do the job myself – and cheaper than Madame Odette too. Ten pounds to have someone tell you you're doomed? No thanks.' Despite his stern expression, there was a glimmer of mischief in his eyes, a hint that he was joking. Or not, Bo thought. You could never tell with Ran. Although she saw him every week at Flingers, he was still a closed book in many ways.

'Madame Odette would never tell anyone they were "doomed".' Angel sounded horrified. 'Real fortune tellers don't give people horrible news like that these days.'

'I'm sure Angel's right,' Bo soothed, sensing an air of tension brewing. 'Madame Odette's not going to say anything awful and, after all, we're only here for a bit of fun. Besides,' she slid a glance at Ran, 'you won't have to find out because you're not going to have your fortune read, are you?'

His eyes met hers, inscrutable as ever. 'No, I'm not.'

'I wish you'd change your mind,' Angel said eagerly to him. 'You might be surprised what you learn. The fete organiser says Madame Odette is very good and she really does have "the gift".'

'Thank you, Angel,' Ran said, 'I respect the fact you think there's something in all of this psychic stuff, but I'm afraid I think it's a bit of a scam.'

'They can be scarily accurate, though,' Angel said. 'I remember when I saw one a few days before I found out I was pregnant with Adam . . . I'd no idea. Me and Tommy weren't even trying but she told me I was expecting "a little surprise". The next morning, I threw up over Tommy's fried breakfast, did a test and, lo and behold, it was positive.'

'But a "little surprise" could have meant all kinds of things,' Bo said, not wanting to say outright that she thought it was a complete coincidence. 'Were you and Tommy trying for a baby?'

'Not really . . . but I suppose we weren't trying very hard *not* to have one.' Angel giggled and Bo laughed out loud.

'Maybe there is something in it . . .' Bo said, not wanting to burst her friend's bubble. Angel had talked of little else when they'd last met for a dance session in the Falford village hall. Ran stayed silent, perhaps not wanting to upset Angel, Bo thought.

Angel was rocking a pair of pink capri pants teamed with a fitted white blouse knotted at the waist. She fanned herself with a programme and Bo was also feeling the heat despite her light cotton tea dress. She'd always thought a dress was much cooler than shorts – though Ran's toned calves certainly looked good in his.

They all stopped to watch a red-faced man emerge from the tent, mopping his brow.

'Wow. He looks shellshocked,' Bo said.

'No wonder. It's probably forty degrees inside that tent,' Ran replied. 'And I saw that guy earlier at the bar.'

'Actually, I know him,' Angel murmured as the man weaved his way through the crowd towards the beer marquee. 'He's one of our customers at work. He's a pig farmer . . . I never thought he'd be the type to visit a fortune teller.'

'Maybe it was a dare?' Bo remarked as a group of men with pints slapped their friend on the back.

'Nextttt!'

Everyone jumped and turned to see the flap of the tent lifted. They could see nothing but a hand, beckoning them inside, and a voice intoned from its depths, 'Madame Odette will see you now.'

'Jesus Christ,' Ran muttered.

Angel let out a squeak. 'Eek!'

'It's your turn,' Bo said, trying not to giggle. 'Go on!'

Angel hesitated. 'I'm not so sure now . . .'

'You'll be fine,' Ran said. 'Ask Madame Odette if she bought her crystal ball from eBay or Argos. That'll break the ice.'

'You're very wicked, Ran,' Angel shot back, laughing. 'OK. I'm going in. Wish me luck!'

A few seconds later, she'd vanished inside.

'I hope she'll be OK,' Ran said. 'She seems to have high expectations.'

'I'm sure she will, it's only a bit of fun, but she's right, you *are* very wicked, Ran. You may think it's all a load of rubbish but Angel loves horoscopes and all that tarot stuff.'

'I don't mean to be wicked; I'd prefer to call it healthy scepticism.' He turned his gaze on Bo and, not for the first time, she had cause to marvel at the deep cornflower blue of his eyes. 'Come on, you can't possibly believe in all that stuff?' he said.

'Like you, I'm a sceptic and, personally, I think these fortune tellers are simply good readers of people. They tell someone what they want to hear or are so vague that you can make almost anything that happens in life fit their predictions.'

'True.'

'I've heard friends talk about visiting them and it's obvious to me that what they've been told has been a catalyst for them. It's nudged them into doing what they'd considered doing anyway. Then again, I have a friend – who I trust – who claims she's received some uncannily accurate and very specific predictions. So . . .' Bo shrugged. 'I'll keep an open mind.'

'I wish I had your tolerance but I think they can be dangerous. At worst, they can frighten gullible people and, at best, they're taking money for basically making stuff up and offering advice that has no basis in fact or evidence.' He smiled. 'Or maybe that's the analyst in me talking.' His phone buzzed. 'Excuse me.'

Stepping a few yards away, he took a call on his mobile while Bo watched the comings and goings of people around her. Even so, her thoughts wandered back to Ran. It was one of the rare times she'd heard him refer to his life before he came to Falford, and possibly the only time he'd ever been specific about his job.

Although he'd become more relaxed over the past few months, he still revealed very little about his past. Rumour had it he'd worked 'in the City' but all attempts to find out the details had been deflected. Bo had never pressed him. Many people came to Cornwall to get away from the 'rat race' of expectations and the daily grind . . . or to escape.

Hamish sprung to her mind then, once again intruding into her thoughts, reminding her of the disappointment and misery of the previous Christmas. She hadn't seen or heard from him since he'd walked out of the cottage, although she knew he'd resigned from the veterinary practice and had his stuff sent back to Scotland by a removal company. Angel had found that out from one of the vet nurses when they came into the Country Stores to order some supplies for the practice. He was probably married to the mysterious Leonie, having wed at some castle with everyone in kilts and sporrans while a piper skirled.

She'd tried to deny how much it had hurt at first. Happy-go-lucky, sensible Bo – the cheerful face of the Boatyard Café – could not afford to get down and give in to her unhappiness. She literally couldn't afford to let it show. Café customers came to her business not only for the fresh, delicious food and great coffee, but she knew they used it as a sanctuary, too.

For her customers, Bo's Boatyard Café was the place to go to sit in the sunshine, even when it was raining. To warm up when the coldest wind was blowing off the sea. To be cheered up when the darkest storm had descended on your life. With a cuppa, a friendly smile and a kind word, Bo had the ability to bring a tiny shaft of light into your day or make the dazzling scene in front of you shine even brighter.

That was the theory anyway. The reality was, of course, that Bo had her own storms, moments when she longed to have someone to turn to cheer her up, to comfort her . . . She'd simply become good at hiding her feelings over the years of presenting a professional face to the public. Perhaps too good at it.

She risked a glance at Ran, who was finishing his call, bidding a farewell to someone whose name Bo recognised from the dive school. He was good at hiding his real feelings too, although she suspected his were hidden under a veneer of cynicism – and yet, who knew for sure? Her judgement of people hadn't been the greatest of late.

He greeted her with an apologetic smile. 'Sorry. That was work. We have a party who want to go out to the Runnel Stone wreck the week after next and Luke wants to know if I can take them.'

Bo wrinkled her nose at the thought of plunging into the deep over the notorious reef. 'Rather them than me.'

'It's a great dive spot. There's so much sea life, anemones and wrasses before you even get down to the wreck itself. As long as you go at slack water with experienced divers and minimise the risks, it's fine. Though you do have to watch for the currents . . .'

She put her hands over her ears. 'Enough! I'm terrified even hearing about it.'

'I can't imagine you'd be scared of anything,' Ran replied.

Bo was taken aback. 'Oh, I can be scared. Sometimes. Not often, but jumping into the sea in one of the most dangerous coasts in Cornwall . . . That would do it,' she said, then added, 'I'm not scared of what a fortune teller might have to tell me, though.'

'Touché. I suppose if you put it like that, I should have nothing to fear either. I can't imagine she could possibly say anything that would surprise me.'

'Why don't you give Madame Odette a try then?' she asked, enjoying teasing him. 'If you're so sure. Then you can tell us how unsurprised you were and how rubbish she was.'

'Now that sounds like a challenge . . . or a dare?'

'I suppose it is.'

'Hmm.' He eyed her carefully. 'It looks like I'm damned if I do, and damned if I don't. Either I'm a wuss, or I've fallen into your trap and been goaded into seeing her.'

'It wasn't meant as a trap,' she replied hastily.

'I know.' He smiled. 'And don't worry – I'd never do anything I really didn't want to. In that case, I will visit the Amazing Madame Odette. If only to satisfy myself of what a load of rubbish it all is,' he softened, 'because it's for a good cause.'

'And do you promise to tell me what she said?'

'Yeah . . .' He held Bo's gaze. 'If you promise to do the same.'

'I won't back down from a challenge like that,' she said, thinking – not for the first time since she'd known him – how attractive he was. It would have been so easy to let herself fancy him quite a lot actually, if she hadn't been off men and he hadn't been exactly the sort of man she wanted to steer well clear of: closed-off and quite probably laden with emotional baggage.

'Do we have a deal?' he said.

'We do.'

They chatted about the Falford Flingers for a while, and the upcoming autumn schedule that Angel, as club secretary, had helped to draw up. In addition to their weekly meeting, they had some public demonstration events planned and a surprise organised for a member's birthday party at the Yacht Club. There was a Hallowe'en social, a Bonfire party with a dance afterwards, and then of course Christmas.

The Flingers were already booked in for two main festive performances. The two main events were a display at Trewhella House, and the Vintage Christmas Spectacular in Falford village hall in December.

Trewhella was a stately home with grounds nestled in a sheltered offshoot of the estuary which would be illuminated for Christmas. Bo had been before and been entranced by the experience. It was magical to wander around with individual trees, statues and arbours lit by coloured lighting. The Flingers would be dancing in the ballroom of Trewhella House which was going to be set up for a Christmas as it would have been in the late fifties.

Normally she couldn't wait for the festive events, but her memories of the previous year were tainting all that was to come this Christmas. After Hamish had left, she'd spent a long and lonely night on her own before dragging herself to her parents' and having to explain to the family why she was alone.

However much she'd tried to put on a brave face, the rest of the holidays had been pretty miserable. One thing she had resolved was that love – and romance of any kind – would be off the agenda for the foreseeable future.

Hamish's reaction to her declaration had hit her hard. It had shaken her confidence and made her dread another Christmas that would inevitably drag up unpleasant, hurtful memories. Even now she looked back she couldn't wish the words 'I love you' unsaid because, sooner or later, she would have let her true feelings slip and he'd have revealed his. She only wished she hadn't said them on Christmas Eve and soured her favourite time of year.

'Christmas seems a very long way off . . .' Ran said, as the sun beat down on them. 'I must admit I can't imagine bopping to festive tunes yet, even if we need to plan the music.'

'I know exactly how you feel,' said Bo, wishing she didn't have to hear Elvis's bloody 'Blue Christmas' ever again.

'It'll come round soon enough,' Ran said. 'Don't forget we have our first planning meeting for the Christmas performances next Friday.'

As if to reinforce the fact autumn was on its way, a yellowed leaf floated past them and landed on the toes of Bo's sneakers.

'I can see that taking quite a while,' she said, knowing it would be impossible to avoid the festive plans. She'd just have to try extra hard to pretend she was enthusiastic. Christmas music or not, she didn't want her heartache to taint her love of music and dancing. It wasn't Elvis's fault that Hamish had turned out to be a total git.

'Yes. I think there'll be a *lot* of debate over which tunes to play and which dances to do.' She turned. 'Oh look! Angel's on her way out.'

Angel emerged from the tent and joined them, though if Bo

had been expecting any clues from her face, she was disappointed. Unusually for Angel, her expression gave nothing away.

Bo pounced immediately. 'What did she say, then? We're dying to know.'

'Oh . . . a few things. I didn't understand most of them.'

Was Bo imagining it, or did Angel sound slightly disappointed?

'It was general stuff, a bit like a horoscope, telling me I have a hectic lifestyle and change is on its way that I might not appreciate at first but will benefit me in the long run. That always makes me worry, because I think something awful is about to happen first.'

'That's so vague, it could mean anything . . . and Angel, you don't really think Madame Odette can see into the future, do you?' Bo offered, trying to reassure her friend.

'No. I suppose not.' She glanced at Ran, who'd remained diplomatically silent.

'None of us has ever heard of her, despite the fete organiser saying she's gifted,' Bo added.

'She might just be a local amateur. Did you think you recognised her?' Ran asked.

'No. I really tried but she had a big scarf over her hair and these funny blue-tinted glasses. She had a weird voice too.'

'Weird how?' Ran asked.

'Dramatic, deep. Not local, I don't think . . . but I s'pose she could be disguising it of course.'

The tent flap opened and the voice beckoned them inside again. 'Nextttt!'

Ran raised his eyebrows. 'Uh-huh, looks like it's my turn.' His eyes widened in mock horror. 'Woo! Spooky.'

Angel glared at him in amazement. 'You said you weren't going to do it!'

He grinned. 'I changed my mind. I want to see what all the fuss is about, and now I'm intrigued to see if I can work out her identity.'

'I doubt you will,' Angel said firmly. 'I've lived here all my life and I'm pretty certain she's not from Falford.'

He nodded. 'I'd still like to try, and it'll be a laugh. Wish me luck.' He held up crossed fingers. 'If I don't come out in half an hour, look after Thor for me, will you?'

Bo rolled her eyes and Angel giggled. Thor was well able to take care of himself, judging by the constant tally of wildlife Ran claimed he brought into the cottage.

'Tommy's allergic to cats,' Angel said.

'I'll have him, then,' Bo said. 'But I don't think I'll need to.'

With a 'brave' smile, Ran ducked inside the tent.

'This is going to be interesting,' Bo said. 'I'd love to be a fly on the wall in there.'

'Me too. I wonder what she'll tell him?' Angel replied.

'I'm more intrigued by what he'll have to say to her.'

'Oh yes . . .' Angel glanced at the tent again nervously and lowered her voice. 'Now Ran's not here, I'll tell you more about Madame Odette's predictions.'

Chapter Four

'I suppose you want me to cross your palm with silver.'

Ran squinted at the woman sitting in deep shadow on the other side of the table. A single lamp, the old-fashioned kind with a large candle protected by a glass shade, provided the only light inside the small tent.

'Actually, I insist on contactless these days.' The woman's bracelets jingled as she pushed a payment terminal towards him. They were golden and numerous. She wore a dark purple scarf over her head, and her face was concealed by the shadows. There was no sign of the tinted glasses that Angel had mentioned.

'Very wise,' Ran said, half amused, half annoyed that he'd been persuaded to take part in this ridiculous charade. Still, it was all for a good cause. Madame Odette's proceeds would help to swell the coffers of the Falford Community Fund.

'I can tell you don't want to be here,' Madame Odette said.

He laughed. 'It doesn't require a fortune teller to work that one out.'

'In fact, you'd rather be anywhere else, wouldn't you, my dear?'

Ran rolled his eyes. He wished Madame Odette would at

least dispense with the fake accent, which was reminiscent of the Wicked Queen from *Snow White*. In fact, this whole set-up reminded him of a Disney film. An elaborate mirror was strung up on tentpole behind her, a sickly scent of incense emanated from the joss sticks and richly coloured drapes were hung around the tent. While shabby from the outside, she'd gone to town on creating an atmosphere inside.

'Well, frankly, yes I would, Madame Odette. I don't wish to be rude but I'm here purely because I've been persuaded – or rather,' he smiled, '*bullied* by friends into joining in with the general festivities and, more importantly, contributing to a good cause. Now, how much is your fee? Once I've paid up, you needn't trouble yourself with the actual fortune telling. I'll leave and tell everyone you said I'd meet a tall, dark, handsome stranger in the new year and shortly be travelling across water.' He laughed. 'At least the latter is likely . . .' He stopped in the nick of time, before he revealed his profession.

Congratulating himself on a lucky escape, he whipped his debit card from his wallet.

Madame Odette placed her hand over the pay terminal. Her nails were painted a crimson that reminded him of blood. He almost shuddered, despite the stifling heat.

'I'm sorry, sir. I can't accept payment without delivering my predictions.'

'It'll save us both a lot of time,' he said as charmingly as he could. 'You can move on to your next—' He almost said 'victim' but changed it just in time. 'Your next client. And besides, surely the money is the important part of the transaction? I honestly don't require anything else from you.'

'You may not require anything, but I think you *need* something.' Madame Odette's red lips parted in a smile, which was more of a smirk and quite a disturbing one at that. He felt a bead of sweat on his forehead and almost gagged at the scent of incense wafting through the tent, intensified by the oppressive heat. Sweat trickled down his back.

However, he was reluctant to let his imagination run away with him and Madame Odette obviously wanted to create an effect. This whole situation was ridiculous but he didn't want to be rude. For all he knew Madame Odette might be the local vicar's wife, or chair of the parish council. He was a relative newcomer to Falford so he'd better not cause offence.

'I can't think what,' he said. 'But if you feel more comfortable with it, you may as well go ahead.'

She smiled and Ran caught a glimpse of perfect white teeth. It was his first clue that Madame Odette wasn't quite as ancient as she probably wanted people to think.

His eyes widened as she pulled a black cloth from a glass sphere on the table.

'Now, I require silence while I gaze into my crystal ball.'

There was no need for her to ask for silence. He was speechless that she actually *had* a genuine-looking crystal ball. When she proceeded to wave her hands over it and then rest them on the globe, he almost gasped at the clichéd horror of it all. The scent of incense seemed stronger and the heat almost overpowering. As Madame Odette started to speak, he found himself frozen with fascination and quite unable to leave the tent, even if he'd wanted to.

Chapter Five

'It's not that I don't *trust* Ran,' Angel said, once they were sure Ran wasn't coming out. 'He's lovely but I was too embarrassed to give you all the details before.' She ushered Bo a few metres away.

'I'm sure he wouldn't have laughed,' Bo said.

'I'm sure he would and really, it *was* pretty cheesy.' Angel hesitated. 'You see, she mentioned a man – a tall, dark man – crossing my path.'

Bo giggled. 'What a surprise!'

'Yes. My heart did sink because it's such a cliché and it was one of the first things she told me. I thought she must mean Tommy, though he's not very dark now, he's totally grey and he isn't *that* tall . . . but when we met, he had almost jet-black hair.' Angel hesitated. 'Though maybe she meant someone else? The man who delivers the bags of logs to the shop is dark.' She stopped, and fanned herself again. 'It was so hot inside that tent.'

'I bet,' Bo said, feeling sorry for Angel who was very red in the face. At the same time, Bo was also eager to hear the rest of the prediction. 'Um . . . what was this tall, dark man supposed to do after he'd crossed your path?'

'Well, that's just it. What she said floored me and I didn't understand . . . she said that the tall, dark man would "let me down but I'd get over it in time".'

'Then it can't be Tommy,' Bo said firmly, seeing that Angel was genuinely worried. 'You two are so happy together. It's far more likely to be your horrible boss, not that there's a shred of truth in any of it.'

'Yes . . . although Kelvin's ginger . . . but he is tall and you're right, he lets me down a lot.' Angel gave a rueful smile although Bo was annoyed on her behalf as she often was. Kelvin put on her all the time. Angel practically ran the place and he was always asking her to work late but, from what Bo could tell, never paid her any extra and blamed her unfairly when things went wrong. It was thanks to Angel that the business did so well; she worked incredibly hard and the customers loved her.

'I do miss old Mr Jennings,' she said.

'I bet. It's a shame he decided to give up the business.'

'He was over seventy and I expect he thought Kelvin should take over. He is his nephew, after all.'

'He's pretty useless at running the place, though. Mr J must have known what kind of a man he is,' Bo said.

'Yes . . . but his mother is Mr J's big sister and she's always dominated him, from what I can tell, even when they were kids. I think she bullied Mr J into letting Kelvin take over. I don't think the old man dared say no to her. Some of the other staff tried to hint to him but old Mr J was too tired and weak to protest and it is his business, after all.' Angel put her hand over her mouth. 'Do I sound horrible for saying that?'

'Not at all. From the gossip I hear at the café, I tend to agree. Can't you team up with anyone to stand up to Kelvin?'

'Not really. While Jake Trencrom was working alongside me, I might have. He tried to work for Kelvin for a few weeks but he couldn't stand it and found another job managing the Lizard Craft Centre . . . and he's glad he did.' Angel smiled. 'I spoke to him the other day about a problem with their firewood order. We supply it to the café and bakery and Jake went to school with Tommy, you know.'

'I didn't know that.'

'Hmm. They were best mates at one time but they don't have anything to do with each other now. They lost touch, according to Tommy, though I think there's more to it than that.'

'Really?' Bo was intrigued, although not terribly surprised. Tommy could be volatile. He wasn't violent, thank goodness, and Angel adored him, but he did have a reputation for blowing up over small things, usually after a night at the pub.

'Tommy doesn't know I'm in touch with Jake, so I'd rather you didn't mention it,' Angel said.

'I won't say anything. I've no reason to tell him but it's always best to be forewarned.' Bo was puzzled and a little disturbed. She rarely spoke to Tommy and didn't see him that often. He was away at sea a lot and the fishing vessel he worked on was based out of Falmouth.

'She also said something else,' Angel went on. 'She seemed really adamant about it but I didn't understand how it could be relevant to me.'

'Go on . . .'

'Well, it sounds a bit corny and cheesy.'

'I'm sure it isn't. Get it off your chest while Ran's not here.'

'Well, she said that I would "be with the love of my life by Christmas".'

'Okayyyy . . .' Bo filed this with the 'tall, dark man crossing your path', comment.

'That can't be true, can it, because I already *am* with the love of my life. You know me and Tommy will be celebrating our thirtieth wedding anniversary on Christmas Eve, so I'm not sure what she means by me being with the love of my life by Christmas?'

Bo was equally foxed. 'I don't know. Maybe she meant you would "be with the love of your life *at* Christmas"? Could you have misheard?'

'I suppose so but I was sure she said "*by* Christmas".'

'She might have meant to say "by" . . . I wonder if Madame Odette could see you're wearing a wedding ring so she knows you're married. It's not much of a jump to assume you and your husband will be spending Christmas together, and while you didn't recognise her, she might even know you or Tommy. If she does, then she'll also know he's often away at sea so she only meant he'd be at home for Christmas with you.'

'Ah. Of course, I suppose she *could* be one of the customers at the Country Stores or even your café?'

'The Boatyard? Yes. Yes . . . she might keep a yacht there.' Bo giggled. 'Though I can't imagine a fortune teller sailing on a yacht for some reason but it makes sense that she's someone local, surely?'

Angel laughed. 'Ran will work out who she is. I can't wait to see his reaction when he comes out.'

'Nor me.' Bo tried to imagine the scene inside the tent again and smiled. She didn't know who she felt most sorry for, Ran or Madame Odette.

Angel smiled but then fanned herself. Bo thought she looked pale and a little clammy despite her summer tan. 'You know, it's so hot and it was roasting inside that tent. Goodness knows how Madame Odette copes with her jingly scarf and robes. I need a cold drink. I'm off to the refreshment tent but I'll be back as soon as I can.'

She hurried away, promising to bring back bottles of water for all three of them. Bo watched her, hoping she'd be OK and wasn't about to faint from the heat. She also wondered if she'd said the right thing.

Although Bo hadn't wanted to make Angel feel embarrassed, she felt she had to allay her fears by saying that Odette's 'predictions' were probably based on guesswork and psychology, perhaps even insider knowledge.

It was all 'hokum' as Ran had joked, but then again, Angel *had* been rattled by her experience with the fortune teller – and, Bo thought, with an unexpected shiver of apprehension, it was *her* turn next.

Angel had just arrived back with the drinks when she let out a little squeal of excitement. 'Oh, look, here's Ran!'.

Ran emerged from the tent and, unlike with Angel, Bo had no trouble judging his reaction to his visit to Madame Odette. Despite the sunny day, his face was like thunder. He stalked out and Bo thought he probably wasn't going to stop, had Angel not spoken to him.

'So, how did it go?' Her eyes were bright with excitement.

'Load of rubbish. As I could have told you from the start.'

'Oh, come on, tell us.'

'I wouldn't insult your intelligence,' he muttered. 'I need a cold drink. It was stifling in that tent.'

'I got you some water . . .' Angel said holding up the bottle, but Ran was already metres away, striding towards the crowds of people mingling around the beer tent.

'Oh dear. I wonder what she said to him? I hope it wasn't something awful!'

Bo peered into the crowd, after Ran's retreating back. 'Well, he keeps insisting it was all a load of rubbish so I'm amazed he took any notice.'

'Me too . . . but Madame Odette is very charismatic. I found her quite intimidating. I almost walked out but couldn't.'

Bo laughed. 'I can't imagine anyone intimidating Ran.'

'Hmm. She certainly told me some things she couldn't have guessed by chance. She knew I had two kids, a girl and a boy, and that they'd moved out.'

Thanking Angel for the water, Bo sipped it gratefully.. It seemed more likely than ever that Madame Odette was someone local and knew of Angel even if she'd never actually spoken to her.

'Of course, she might be someone who's been to one of our performances . . .' Angel said.

'Nextttt!'

Bo jumped. That sonorous voice from the gloom made her heart beat a little faster. It was ridiculous . . . this was fairground entertainment and meant to be a joke. There was no way she was going to take it seriously and certainly not be afraid. She would go inside and be extremely careful not to give Madame Odette any clues whatsoever.

Although, she mused, ducking under the flap, as one of the most recognisable faces in Falford, it was pretty impossible that any local person *didn't* know at least something about her.

It took a while for Bo's eyes to adjust to the dim light inside the tent and, even then, the woman sitting behind the small table was an indistinct figure. The heat was stifling and the air thick with exotic perfume. How the woman could stand the dark scarf over her head, Bo had no idea.

'Welcome, my dear. Please, sit down.'

After Angel's comments, Bo was attuned for any hint that the voice was familiar. Having lived in Falford for over five years she was sure she'd detect a Cornish accent so she resolved to say as little as possible herself while encouraging Madame Odette to do all the talking.

'Good afternoon, my dear.'

'Good afternoon, Madame Odette.' Bo perched on the edge of the chair. Madame Odette rested her hands on the chenille tablecloth. It was violet and reminded Bo of one her great-grandmother used to have on a table in her veranda, beneath a potted aspidistra. A black cloth concealed an item in the centre of the table that could only be a crystal ball. Imagining what Ran's face must have looked like when he'd entered the tent, Bo tried not to giggle. Then again, he'd seemed pretty upset on the way out, shaken in fact. Gosh, what was she in store for?

'Please, relax. There's no need to be nervous, my dear,' Madame Odette said.

Bo tried to sit back on the chair, a wooden one painted antique gold.

'Thanks, but I'm not nervous. I'm more . . . intrigued to hear what you have to say.'

'Good. I do like a receptive client.'

Receptive? That wasn't what Bo had meant to imply but she already felt she'd said too much.

'I'm going to consult my crystal ball,' Madame Odette said, tapping the item covered in the black cloth, 'but first do you have any questions for me?'

'Um, not really. I hadn't thought of asking you anything.'

'Nothing that's troubling you?'

'Only the performance we're doing later this afternoon. Will someone trip up? Will I get the moves right or will I end up bashing into someone or smacking into my partner?' Bo rolled her eyes, leaving Odette in no doubt that she was taking the whole thing with a large pinch of Cornish sea salt.

Madame Odette regarded her from behind the blue-tinted glasses. 'I'm afraid I can't tell you that,' she said, sounding as if she'd taken the question seriously.

Bo shifted in her seat. She'd at least hoped Madame Odette might have a sense of humour but fortune telling was clearly a very serious business. 'In that case, no.'

'Then, I'll proceed to the ball.'

She pulled away the black cloth to reveal a glass ball. It seemed like smoky glass to Bo, reminiscent of a giant paper-weight or doorstop. Nothing fancy – in fact, it was rather disappointing, but then what had Bo expected? Swirling mists and looming faces? Glitter?

Madame Odette curved her hands and held them over the ball. Bo glanced at them. Even though the fortune teller wore lacy fingerless gloves, Bo was sure they were the hands of a woman not that much older than herself. The crimson nail varnish also seemed vaguely familiar. Wasn't it the same shade that she used herself from time to time? A vintage red called Rockahula Ruby?

'The mists are parting and I can see something . . .'

In spite of herself, Bo leaned forward, transfixed.

Madame Odette inhaled sharply. Bo's pulse rocketed. 'What?'

'You will be with the love of your life by Christmas.'

Bo exploded with laughter.

Madame Odette glanced up sharply from her globe and Bo saw her face full-on. It was definitely a reasonably young face – younger than Angel – and yet there was nothing definitively familiar about it.

Madame Odette held her head down. 'You find that idea amusing?' she said silkily.

'Well . . .' Bo didn't want to admit that Angel had been given the exact same prediction. She didn't want Madame Odette to know they'd been swapping stories. She smiled. 'I'm sorry if I've offended you but I find the idea of me meeting "the love of my life" improbable.'

'Why "improbable"?'

Bo felt like a fish who'd been attracted by a shiny lure, or a fly twitching on the surface. Whatever she replied would give Madame Odette an indication of how she felt about the idea of falling in love.

'There's no one in my life of that kind at the moment and I'm definitely not looking for anyone.'

'Why not? Is it so outlandish that an attractive young woman like you might be romantically involved?'

Bo laughed, while trying to get a grip on the fortune teller's accent, which swung from vaguely eastern European with a tinge of Cornish to a bit 'posh' in an upcountry way. Bo glimpsed a camping cooler next to her and several empty glass bottles of luxury mineral water, plus a blue gel pad. So that was Madame Odette's secret. She was probably sitting on a chiller pad and changing them.

'Of course, you're young! Plenty of time.'

'Christmas is less than four months away . . .'

'Like I say, plenty of time. You might already know the person,'

Madame Odette said, 'or pass them in the street tomorrow. He might even be here at the fair.'

'How do you know I'm not looking for a "she" or a "they"?'

'I don't . . .' For the first time Bo thought a hint of doubt had crept into Madame Odette's voice. 'Apologies for the assumption. The vibes I was getting tell me that it will be a man, however . . .'

Bo smiled. 'If I were to meet someone romantically – and it's a big "if" – it would be a man. You're right about that, but I honestly can't think who it would be. I know everyone in Falford.'

'Yes, I'm getting a very strong feeling that you work in the public eye . . . you're a very sociable person, positive . . .'

Bo pressed her lips together, trying not to laugh. Madame Odette must know her – or of her – from either the café or the dance club, possibly both. The way she kept her head even lower over the crystal ball made Bo think she was trying to hide herself after her momentary lapse.

'That's reasonably accurate,' she said.

'And I'm also getting the feeling that while you present a positive face to the world, deep down, you're hiding a deep hurt.'

'What?' Bo was taken aback, a little embarrassed, but she didn't want to bite.

'Aren't most people?' she murmured. 'That could be true of everyone who ever walks in here. If you don't mind me saying.' She paused. 'Even you, Madame Odette.'

Her hands hovered over the cloudy sphere. 'But we're talking about you, my dear. You're the important one here.'

Deftly done, thought Bo, feeling the heat even more. She wanted to leave. Ran was right, this was all hokum.

'Am I right in thinking you have great trouble trusting people, after what happened last Christmas?'

Bo gasped and unintentionally did her best pilchard-landed-on-a-trawler expression.

'I seem to have startled you, my dear.'

'Startled? No. I'm just . . . surprised.'

'It did happen last Christmas, didn't it? The end of the relationship.'

'Well, yes. There was someone and we did split up not long before Christmas but it was my decision. Sort of. A joint decision.' Bo knew she was lying but there was no way she was going to admit it to Madame Odette. In fact, that was the story she'd told everyone, including her own family: that the sudden split with Hamish had been at her instigation. If they hadn't believed it, that was their problem. 'It was the only thing to do.'

'Of course, it was your decision, certainly you'll come to believe that, but he still let you down badly . . .' Madame Odette closed her eyes, her fingers fluttering over the crystal ball. 'He wasn't what he seemed. I'm sensing you felt betrayed . . .'

'Not betrayed. He hadn't given me the full story . . . He hadn't realised how he felt himself . . . that he hadn't moved on as much as he claimed, but yes, I did feel let down.' Even though she'd vowed not to reveal more, she couldn't help herself. 'Very let down.'

Madame Odette's fingers fluttered over the surface of the ball. Bo could see nothing but dark glass and, no matter what Odette said, she couldn't possibly see any of the stuff she'd mentioned by looking into a glass globe. Surely, she must know Bo – or at least enough snippets about her life to make her 'prediction' sound convincing. People knew she'd split up with Hamish and they'd probably gossiped about it for a while.

Anything and everything pointed to it all being a scam. A

bit of fun – not that this felt like fun, having her deepest secrets unearthed and exposed.

'This person hurt you deeply . . . but as I said, you're very good at hiding it and so no one realised how you felt. Last Christmas was a trial, you went home and cried many times, but to the world you seemed fine so not even your closest friends guessed how much you were hurting – how much you still are, deep down.'

Bo felt hot and slightly light-headed.

'I'm getting a picture of this man. He's tall, dark and good-looking . . . you fell very hard for him. I think his name began with an "H" or a "G" maybe . . . the clouds have come down again.'

'How do I pay, please?' Bo cut in, horrified. 'I can see you have a card reader,' she added. 'It's very warm in here and I need some fresh air.'

'Of course. Do you feel faint? I've got some bottles of chilled water.'

'No thanks. I've got one in my bag. If we can just get the payment done, because I really have to be going . . .'

'I haven't quite finished . . .' Madame Odette said. 'The signs are very positive going forwards.'

'I'm pleased to hear it, but I have to get back to my dance group. We have a demo this evening and we need to have a meeting before the performance.'

'Of course, if you really feel you *must* leave before I've finished my reading.' Odette pushed the payment terminal towards Bo. 'Here you are.'

'Thanks.' After tapping her card and seeing the payment go through, Bo jumped to her feet, desperate to be out of the tent.

'Wait a moment! I hope I haven't upset you. It's only that I saw such heartache in the ball in your past but, from now on, the road ahead looks so much more promising. In fact,' Odette smiled as Bo thrust her card back in her purse, 'you might think it's impossible now but by Christmas I think—'

'I'll be with the love of my life?'

'Well, yes. That's exactly the vibe I'm getting.'

'Great. Thanks for the good news but I don't expect to meet the love of my life. More importantly, I don't *need* to meet him. I'll be perfectly happy to be single this Christmas!'

With a pounding heart and a rising tide of irritation, Bo turned away and barged through the tent, desperate to escape the heat and overpowering scent. The sunlight was bright but had changed from when she'd gone in – not as intense and the air was thick and muggy. There was a distant roll of thunder from over the sea where dark clouds were marshalling. A storm was brewing.

Angel pounced on her. 'How was it, then? What did she say?'

Bo forced herself to laugh. 'Oh, exactly as you'd expect. A load of old rubbish. It was so vague it could have meant anything and been about anyone.'

Angel's face fell. 'Oh dear. What a disappointment.'

Bo felt guilty at fibbing to Angel. 'To be honest, it was so stuffy in there that I was desperate to get out and maybe I wasn't listening properly. I've got a headache starting . . .' she said, kindlier, and reached for her water. 'Maybe it'll all mean more to me when I've had time to cool down and think about it. Now, shall we go and find Ran and join the rest of the Flingers? The performance will come round soon enough.'

Chapter Six

'Well done, everyone! Great work.'

Bo congratulated her fellow dancers as she helped to hand out water bottles after the performance. The group of eight couples had danced six dances between them, including three involving Bo herself, all to high-energy tunes.

Drinking from her own bottle, she felt wrung out with legs like spaghetti – keeping up with Cade's kicks and flicks during their jive was a huge challenge; enjoyable but exhausting. Maybe the heat had got to her, or she'd wasted too much nervous energy on Madame Odette's predictions. At six p.m., the festival was winding down. The beer tent had served its last pint and visitors were drifting away bearing candy floss, helium balloons and carrier bags of purchases from the retail stalls.

The Flingers were glowing and pink-cheeked, but the dance display had gone well. Even Ran was smiling as he accepted a bottle from Bo.

'I feel like a limp dishcloth,' Angel said. Her red curls were escaping from their bandana and her skin was glowing with effort and the high of exercise. 'But that was brilliant!

'I think it went well,' Bo said, before sipping from her bottle. 'The audience were singing along and tapping their feet. I bet we get some new recruits, or some enquiries at the very least.'

'Dorinda was collecting names and handing out leaflets,' Angel said, nodding at the woman in cropped jeans chatting to a young couple by the edge of the temporary dance floor. It had been used for other performances during the day including a fisherman's choir and a local gym club.

Dorinda Morvah owned the local boatbuilding business at the boatyard where Bo's Café was located. Even though Dorinda was twenty years older than Bo, the two women had a firm friendship. Bo had even dated both her sons – separately and very briefly – a few years back, but they'd all decided to stay friends. Finn and Joey Morvah now had long-term partners, and Bo was genuinely delighted to see them so happy and settled.

Even so, watching them find and commit to the 'loves of their life' had given her a pang of envy amidst her happiness for them. It seemed impossible to her that she could make the same commitment to someone – and, even if she did, that he could feel the same way. The chances of two people coming across each other in a tiny place like Falford and feeling that same level of passion and commitment seemed vanishingly rare.

Angel drained her bottle of water. 'I'd better be going. I need to get Tommy's dinner. He's coming back on shore for a few days.'

'He won't mind you being late, will he?'

'No, but I haven't seen him for days. They were out fishing for hake on the *Briar Rose*.'

'In that case, off you go.'

'I can spare a few mins to help you tidy away all the stuff into the van?'

'Thanks, but we've got plenty of willing hands, honestly – off you go!'

With a grateful wave, Angel hurried away, leaving Bo to reflect on what made a long-term relationship work, and work *well*. Angel seemed devoted to Tommy but Bo didn't know him closely enough to make a judgement on whether he felt the same. He spent so long at sea, which was part and parcel of the job for a trawlerman. It was hard on families in so many ways and Angel didn't even have her kids around to focus on these days. Now in their late twenties, Adam and Emma had jobs and partners of their own.

Bo was happy to stay, musing that she didn't have anything to do that Saturday night anyway. Cade also hung around, helping to shifting the heavy amps and kit. It was tiring work on top of a day in the heat and the dancing but it was also a great opportunity to see if Ran might reveal more about his encounter with Madame Odette. Bo had been intrigued by his reaction, and even more so now she'd had a dose of her own medicine with the mysterious fortune teller.

'You really shouldn't feel obliged to help,' Ran said when Bo arrived at his van carrying a box of records she'd collected from the stage area.

'I don't mind,' she said, slightly discouraged by his attitude.

He softened. 'You've more than done your bit, jiving in this heat.'

'Do I look as if I'm ready to keel over?' she joked.

'Not at all. You looked fantastic. You always do. On the dance floor, I mean.'

Surprised at the compliment, Bo didn't know how to reply and Ran had already turned away to lift some kit from the grass into the back of the van.

'Thanks, though I'm sure you're flattering me way too much,' she said, then added, 'Don't you ever think about joining us on the floor?'

'No chance. Like I said, I've two left feet,' he said. 'And I'm not fit enough.'

'Rubbish. You're super fit.' Immediately Bo realised how her comment might be misconstrued and an extra layer of heat rose to her cheeks, but Ran didn't seem to have noticed, or at least chose not to tease her about it. 'All that diving, carrying the weights and tanks, I mean. It must keep you in shape.'

'In some ways it does but dancing is another thing. It needs a different kind of flexibility and stamina . . .' He took the box from her and loaded it into the van.

'That's the lot. Thanks for your help.'

'You're welcome.'

Ran was distracted by something across the sports field. Bo followed his gaze to the corner where the striped fortune telling tent lay crumpled on the ground. It must have been dismantled while they were dancing. There was no sign of its owner and it looked rather sad: empty stripey fabric, flattened and very ordinary.

'I wonder who she was,' Bo murmured.

'No idea.' Ran turned his back on the field and closed the van doors firmly.

'Are you OK?' Bo asked him.

'Of course. Why wouldn't I be?'

'I don't know . . . you seemed quiet after we visited the fortune teller. I don't blame you. I thought Madame Odette was a bit . . .'

'Bonkers? A complete charlatan?' he snorted.

Bo smiled to show she wasn't being too serious. 'Intrusive was more the word I was looking for.'

His eyes bored into her. 'Intrusive . . . how? What did she say to you?'

'Well, pretty much the same thing that she said to Angel. In fact, it sounded as if she told me the *exact* same thing.' Bo shook her head dismissively, unwilling to reveal the exact words. 'Sounds like she trotted out the same old rubbish to both of us.'

'Yes . . .' Ran's lips were pressed together, and Bo waited to see whether he'd reveal exactly what Madame Odette had said to him. 'Well, none of the guff she spouted made any sense at all, and I certainly didn't think it had any relevance. I did try to go in there with an open mind.'

'Of course, you did,' said Bo archly.

'OK, maybe my mind wasn't *quite* as fully open as it ought to have been but Madame Odette didn't alter my opinion of fortune tellers and all their ilk. She's a ham – a fairground entertainer – but seeing as the money goes to a good cause, I'll overlook that.'

Clouds covered the sun and Bo shivered in a gust of wind from the water. The air finally felt cooler and a few goosebumps popped out on her bare shoulders. The sun was sinking towards the horizon faster these days and the nights were definitely cooler, which would be welcome after today's heatwave.

'You're cold.' Ran's brow crumpled in concern.

'I'm glad it's fresher, to be honest, though I think there's a storm blowing in,' Bo said with brisk cheerfulness. 'So I'd better get back to the car and go home. Um, do you still want to meet up to discuss the music for the Christmas events?'

He nodded more enthusiastically, perhaps relieved to be on safer ground. 'Sure. Would it help if I put together a few choices so we can present a fait accompli? I don't want to dictate to the group, of course,' he added hastily. 'Only I thought it would save time.'

'Excellent. Otherwise, we could be here until Christmas trying to accommodate everyone's wishes. Do you have time, though?'

'I always have time for music, though I'd like your opinion before we present the set lists to the group.'

'Sure . . . if you think it would help.' Bo hesitated. There would be no escape from Christmas, no matter how much she'd rather avoid it this year, though she was surprised by the invitation to help from Ran. Early evening sunlight filtered through his messy honey-coloured hair and his eyes glinted. Not for the first time, she recalled Angel's remarks about him being a Viking and Hamish's sarcasm. In hindsight, she'd wondered if Hamish had seen him as a rival, which was pathetic considering Hamish hadn't even wanted her for himself.

She certainly had no designs on Ran, Viking god or not.

'I'm always interested in your opinion on music,' Ran said. 'And I can't say that about everyone in Falford.'

Bo's cheeks flushed again with an unexpected pleasure that slightly annoyed her.

Ran smiled and his lips parted. For a moment, Bo wondered if he was going to ask her round to the cottage.

'I'll WhatsApp over a few set lists so you can give me some feedback. How does that sound?'

'That would be great. Look forward to it. See you at the next Flingers meet?'

'Yes. Sure.'

Now that the fete was over, the crowds had melted away and only the stallholders and organisers were left.

· While she drove home, the identity of the mystery woman and her 'prediction' wasn't the only issue disturbing her peace of mind. She was perturbed by how pleased she was that Ran wanted her opinion above other people's and how physically attracted to him she was.

Ran's reaction to Madame Odette had also reinforced her view that he was a very private man, unwilling to open up to anyone in Falford about his private life – including her. Madame Odette had torn a plaster off a healing wound, and it had hurt. In another way, perhaps that was a good thing? It had reminded her of how easy it was to misjudge someone's feelings and to be far more wary in the future of anyone's feelings – especially her own.

Chapter Seven

'Thor? Where are you, you beast?'

Ran called to his cat as he pushed open the door to Creekside Cottage. The kitchen was in deep shade and the flagstones soothingly cool. Thor had found the only pool of light, a small patch on the mat by the back door where he was curled up nose to tail in what Angel called a 'kitty croissant'.

Feline sleeping postures aside, Ran couldn't imagine a less croissant-like cat. Croissants were fluffy and sweet and Thor was neither. He was a sleek, honed predator . . . Ran had nicknamed him the Beast of Bodmin due to his penchant for catching any kind of creature from wood mice to frogs. He smiled to himself. Thor was a softy, really – when he wasn't in killing mode.

Hearing Ran enter the kitchen via the sitting room, Thor opened one eye, saw that the visitor wasn't worth chasing, and went back to sleep.

'Welcome home to you too, buddy.'

Thor ignored him, not even blinking at the clatter as Ran threw his keys on the kitchen table. Ran stood and allowed himself to take a breath. The stillness was absolute. No breeze, no traffic buzz, only the cheeping of birds in the trees and waterfowl from the creek below the cottage. He'd been here well over a year now and still hadn't got used to the quiet, often stopping to listen to it and marvelling.

Creekside Cottage was situated a mile out of the village in a deeply wooded valley at the very end of the amusingly named Smuggler's Creek. Ran doubted if anything more exciting than ducks had ever hidden away on the creek, where there was only a trickle of water carving a path through mudflats foraged by waders and ducks.

Admittedly, it was a secretive, hidden-away spot where paths would wind from the cottage through the woods and over duckboards and footbridges, to Falford village itself. He'd often been glad to melt away into their shade and privacy while he forgot his past regrets.

Even so, regrets had stalked him all the way home.

He wished he hadn't been so quick to deflect the opportunity to invite Bo to the cottage in person to discuss the music for the festive schedule. Most of all, he wished he hadn't lied to her about Madame Odette's comments.

To be fair, it wasn't only the guilt he felt at lying that had made him reluctant to invite her. Conscious that he wasn't the best company at the moment – if ever – he didn't want to inflict his gloomy self on her. Madame Odette had probed at some raw wounds, and he had enough on his plate.

For a few hours at the festival, he'd managed to distract himself with lively company and great music but now he had to face up to what awaited him at home.

Even at Creekside Cottage, he couldn't escape from reality.

He'd chosen the house as a bolthole from his former life

in London the previous spring, though in many ways it was an impractical house for a man several inches over six feet. The thatched cottage and thick walls were charming but meant that the two bedrooms had been slotted in under the eaves.

The beamed lintels over their doorways had been padded to prevent occupants from doing themselves a serious injury. Even so, Ran had been caught out many times before he'd learned to duck instinctively when entering the master bedroom, which overlooked the cottage garden and the water's edge.

Downstairs, there was a reasonably sized sitting room and a dining kitchen with a bright blue AGA which had taken Ran almost as long to get used to as the doorways. On the upside, it was a favourite napping spot for Thor.

In spite of its quirks, Creekside Cottage did have one major feature that had caused Ran to pay his deposit almost on the spot. The sitting room and the adjacent snug boasted floor-to-ceiling bookshelves and several built-in alcoves where he could stack his vinyl records.

Seeing his music lining the walls had given him a pleasure he wouldn't admit to anyone other than another collector. He hadn't been able to keep many in his London Docklands flat, apart from a small selection which were deemed to look stylishly retro on the white plastic cube units by the TV. The rest had been boxed up and moved into a storage unit.

In the solitude of the cottage, Ran wracked his brain, searching his mental files for where he might have seen Madame Odette before.

Was she someone from the diving club – a former customer? People tended to look very different in a full wetsuit and hood to their everyday clothes. She wasn't one of the Flingers, that was for sure. Even if he hadn't recognised her, Bo or Angel surely would. They knew everyone for miles around.

The woman was either very clever or completely bonkers. He'd told himself that a hundred times since he'd left her tatty tent and yet . . .

'A woman whose name began with "P".'

He cringed. That was too close for comfort, not that anything in connection with Phaedra's name gave him much comfort. But why did the reminder of his past make his stomach clench and flood his mind with regrets?

He'd thought he'd moved on; he'd carved out a new life in Falford and had found solace in his music and diving. Hell, he'd even made new friends and started to trust people – was beginning to imagine growing closer to one of them.

Then Madame-bloody-Odette – whose real name was probably something sensible like Rachel or Sarah – had ripped off the scab and made him bleed again. That shocked him.

There was still no breeze to speak of but the rear patio was in deep shade so he took a pint of iced water out there and sat on the low wall that separated the garden from the bank of the creek. The tide was coming in, and eddies of brown water crept over the mudflats, filling in the shallow gullies and indentations.

Midges buzzed in the evening air as the sun sank lower. September was only around the corner, the nights drawing in despite the hot days. Ran needed something stronger than tap water but he wasn't ready to go back inside and face opening the official-looking envelope that had arrived before he'd set off for the fete. It remained on the table, propped up against the empty teapot.

He tipped the glass to his mouth, as the rain started in earnest.

He had enough self-awareness to recognise that the reason he'd been so angry with Madame Odette was that her comments had struck a raw nerve. He did not expect to 'be with the love of his life' by Christmas because he'd already met her – and lost her. And it was no one's fault but his own.

Chapter Eight

The first week of September roared in, in complete contrast to the cloying heat that marked the end of August. During the week, storms had blown in from the Atlantic, sending temperatures plummeting by ten degrees, with squalls and rough seas. Summer was over and Bo's clientele at the café dwindled with the start of the school term and other holidaymakers turned to the indoor cafés.

Originally, the Boatyard Café had been a one-room stone building built on the side of the slipway that was once the boatyard manager's office. That was until the previous owners had turned it into a rough and ready café with a small kitchen area and a staff cloakroom.

They'd also built a wooden lean-to which worked as a serving area with room for the coffee machine and a glass cabinet for cakes and bottled drinks. A counter area ran along one side of the lean-to where a couple of customers could perch on stools. There was enough space between the end of the building and the quayside for three bistro tables, though when it was busy people would park themselves on the edge of the quayside too, dangling their feet above the water. Some even sat on the slipway, much to the annoyance of the boat owners and despite the big 'Keep off the slipway; this is a working area' signs.

Bo had carried her passion for the fifties into the Boatyard Café, which had taken some of its inspiration from an ocean liner, with vintage bunting. She would have loved more inside space for wet days and a customer loo – with access only through the kitchen, using the staff cloakroom was out of the question.

She didn't want to move from the boatyard itself, though. She loved the daily bustle, and the fact the ebb and flow of the tide outside matched the ebb and flow of her customers. Boatbuilders, craftspeople and sailors in the morning, then a flow of tourists and walkers making their way around the estuary, stepping off boats and desperate for a cuppa or, in the warm months, an ice cream or cold drink. Yachties and second-home owners in the summer, and tour parties visiting the folklore shop – Cornish Magick – on the opposite side of the estuary.

In the shoulder seasons outside the big school holiday, she'd done deals with Oriel, the woman who ran Cornish Magick. Oriel had set up a series of tours to the mythical and ancient sites of Cornwall the previous summer and Bo had been providing afternoon teas as part of the package.

The shift from summer to autumn made Bo think more seriously about expanding the café. The terrace area had a few umbrellas but it really needed a sturdier and more permanent shelter from the elements so she could lure in more customers, whatever the weather.

Money was tight as always but she'd hit on the idea of getting an old canvas sail from the Morvah boatbuilders and stretching that over the decking. She also thought she could add an extra wooden counter and more stools against the wall that separated the terrace from the current boatyard office. Again, that was something the Morvahs might help her fix up as a favour in return for some bacon butties. She'd be able to take more bookings from groups, confident in the knowledge her customers could stay dry, no matter what the Cornish weather delivered.

Making a mental note to ask the Morvahs the next time she saw them, she came to the realisation she also had to start making some firm plans for the Flingers Christmas events. Ran had sent over two separate playlists, which would cover the bookings at the Illuminated Gardens and the Christmas Spectacular in the community hall.

It was a wild and wet Saturday evening when Bo scuttled into the Ferryman, shaking raindrops from an old-fashioned brolly she'd bought from a vintage store in Falmouth. She'd arranged to meet Angel but arrived slightly early so ordered a spritzer and found a corner seat to wait for her friend. The air was rich with the aroma of hot food and beer, as locals and tourists tucked into fish and chips and steaks.

She'd only been there a few minutes when Angel messaged to say she was running late because Kelvin had asked her to stay on at work to help him sort out a problem with the ordering system.

While feeling sorry for Angel, Bo took the opportunity to have a chat with Joey and Finn Morvah, who'd come into the pub after their cricket match had been washed out.

They were keen to help with her sail project and, soon, plans were being made to make the additions to the café terrace.

Buoyed by the news, she scrolled through her phone, looking at other cafés and what they'd done to maximise their outdoor space. Having already eaten, Bo was content with a spritzer and a chat with her friends but, as the minutes ticked by, she began to grow concerned that Angel would be kept behind by useless Kelvin for the rest of the evening. Bo felt doubly lucky to be her own boss, even if it could be lonely to know the buck stopped with her.

Half an hour after Angel was due to appear, Bo had a further text to say she'd popped home to change and would be at the pub as soon as possible. The Morvah brothers left and Bo ordered another drink, hoping her friend would appear soon. A gust of wind rippled the curtains at the window as the door opened. Bo glanced up expecting to see Angel, but it was Ran stepping in from the porch.

He strode in, carrying his Berghaus jacket and rubbing his wet hair.

Spotting Bo, he made a beeline for her table. 'Evening.'

'Hello. I wasn't expecting you. Bet you've had a wet walk.'

He grinned. 'You could say that. One of the footbridges over the creek is almost underwater. I hope I can get home again. It's a grim night, that's for sure.'

Bo hadn't had far to scurry from her place but she knew Ran would have a mile to trudge under dripping trees and sodden ground. 'You'll be wishing you had your wetsuit with you.'

'True.' He nodded at her half-empty glass. 'Can I get you another?'

'Thanks, but I was waiting for Angel to come. She was meant to be here a while ago but Kelvin has kept her late again.'

He scrunched up his face. 'Poor Angel. That man is a complete tool.'

'I know . . . she's on her way now, though.'

'Good. I'll get a drink.'

He went to the bar and chatted to one of the other guys from the dive school. Bo was a little surprised when he rejoined her, sitting on the chair opposite and resting his pint on the table. Rain lashed the windows.

'I won't bother opening up the café if it's this rough tomorrow,' Bo said.

'I think it's forecast to blow over by mid-morning but we had to cancel the dive trips for yesterday afternoon and all of the ones today.'

'That's a shame,' Bo replied, secretly thinking that any excuse not to jump off a boat was a good one. 'Where were you going?'

'We'd hoped to go and see that wreck that went down at the Runnel Stone off Gwennap Head – the *City of Westminster* steamer. She hit the rock and broke in two in dense fog in 1923. She knocked six metres off the top of the rock and that's why it's even more dangerous now you can't even see the reef at any state of the sea or tide.'

Bo suppressed a shudder. She knew of the notorious reef near Land's End that had wrecked the ship. Nowadays there was a large buoy tethered to the reef to warn vessels. In even moderate seas, the swell caused it to give off a howl that could be heard for miles.

'I know the Runnel Stone, of course – from the land. The noise the buoy makes always gives me the creeps, especially in the fog. It's so eerie, like someone moaning from the depths.'

'It's pretty loud when you're close up,' Ran said wryly. 'The wreck's fascinating though, and there are loads of anemones and wrasse feeding. That's even before you reach the boat herself.'

Bo shivered. 'I enjoy a swim off the beach, but the thought of descending into the depths, especially in rough seas, is scary. I'll leave you to it!'

'You do have to be careful. Safety is everything. Even in calm conditions, it's possible to flip the RIB over in the surge on that reef. There was no way we were going out yesterday. In the end we decided to err on the safe side and cancel everything.'

'It's been a quiet day at the café too. Most of the tourists would rather hunker down inside a cosy teashop in this weather. I've actually been thinking about how I can cater to customers throughout autumn and winter, though. I fancy a nice big sail stretched over the terrace. I've been chatting with Finn and Joey and they're going to let me know if they find one that's suitable.'

'Sounds like a great idea.'

'Thanks. Oh, here's Angel.'

Angel joined their table and threw off the hood of a cherry-red raincoat. 'Oh, sorry, I've dripped on you, Ran.'

'It's fine,' he said good-humouredly. 'I'm still damp from my walk here.'

'You walked?' Her eyes widened in horror. 'That was brave. I drove. Sorry I'm late, but Kelvin did something to the computer system that lost all the orders! Luckily, I managed to reset it and get them back. I could kill him sometimes.' She pulled off her coat, spattering raindrops on Bo and Ran. 'Gah!'

'I don't blame you being angry. You sit there and I'll fetch some drinks.' Ran got up. 'What are you having?'

Bo ordered another spritzer, while Angel asked for a Diet Coke.

'Are you OK?' Bo said. 'Kelvin is really out of order, keeping you so late at work. I hope he's paying you overtime.'

'I wish . . . it's so bloody annoying when you were waiting for me. If I've nothing planned, I don't mind staying a bit late when Tommy's at sea because on days like this I'd only spend my time at home worrying.'

A squall of rain rattled against the panes. Angel grimaced.

'When's he due back?' Bo asked.

'Couple of days. Can't be precise. You know what fishing's like. They'll stay out a bit longer if the catch is good but they'll have to time it right to make sure they get the fish back fresh for the market at Newlyn.'

A customer opened the door from the terrace, bringing a blast of cold air with him.

'It was so rough on the way here. The lane was littered with twigs and the brook was very high when I drove over the bridge outside of our village. I can't help worrying about what it must be like out at sea.'

Bo patted her arm, thinking of Ran's comments about cancelling all the dive trips. She really hoped he wouldn't resume the conversation about wrecks while Angel was around. 'I'm sure they'll be fine. You've always told me what an experienced skipper his boss is.'

Angel held up crossed fingers and Ran arrived back at the table.

To distract her friend, Bo turned the conversation to the music for the Christmas special again, hoping Ran wouldn't mind Angel being part of the conversation. Luckily Angel mentioned Tommy was at sea again and Ran seemed to realise that Bo wanted to steer the talk away from the rough weather. He produced the print-out of the set list and, together, they discussed it, making a few tweaks and suggestions.

Time flew by and Bo began to think about heading home, a little concerned that Angel would have to drive along dark lanes littered with debris and surface water. Ran also had a fair walk home, but Bo knew he wouldn't thank her for fussing over him. Now the meal service was over, the bar was much quieter and, despite some background music, you could certainly hear the wind gusting off the estuary. A couple of men walked in through the French doors from the waterside terrace and just stopped the doors from smashing back in the wind.

'Oh dear,' said Angel. 'I ought to be setting off. Do you want a lift, Ran?'

'Thanks, but it's miles out of your way and it would be safer for all of us if I walk.'

'But all those trees . . . and the creek. It might be flooded.'

'I won't take any risks,' Ran said with a grin.

Bo wasn't too sure, although Angel's attention was now drawn to the two men who'd recently entered the pub. They returned from the bar with foaming pints and sat down at the table next to theirs. Their faces were vaguely familiar as two fishermen who occasionally called in at the café.

Angel was reaching for her jacket when the men started discussing the weather.

'Terrible night to be out. Heard it's force eight out there. I wouldn't like to be out on a vessel tonight.'

'No.'

'Did you hear the *Briar Rose* is in trouble?' the man with a beard said.

'No? Where d'you hear that?'

'My mate at the *Galleon* on Falmouth harbour. He saw the RNLI go out an hour ago. The *Rose* is drifting onto the reef, apparently.'

'If she strikes that, she's a goner,' his mate said.

Angel's face drained of colour. She turned round sharply. 'The *Briar Rose*? My Tommy's aboard her. What have you heard?'

The bearded man's lips parted in shock then he spoke more quietly. 'Only that she's had engine trouble and the lifeboat's gone out to her.'

74

'Oh God, no. I have to find out . . .' She pulled her phone from the bag and it clattered onto the slate floor. 'Oh shit!'

Angel never swore so Bo knew she was upset. Ran picked it up from where it had skidded to his side of the table.

Angel fumbled with it. 'I turned it off when I left work to stop my boss from calling me. I wish I hadn't. What have I done?'

'Angel, hold on . . . Are you sure it's the *Briar Rose?*' Bo asked the man.

'I think so, my love.'

'Oh my God!' Angel paled when her phone flared into life with a series of loud beeps. 'There are three WhatsApp messages on here!'

By now, some of the other drinkers were looking their way, wondering what the fuss was about.

While Angel scrolled frantically through her messages, Ran exchanged an anxious glance with Bo. She knew he was thinking the exact same thing: if the *Briar Rose* had engine failure, Tommy and the rest of the crew were in serious danger.

'Oh . . . oh . . .' Angel squealed. 'Oh . . .'

Bo's stomach tensed. Poor Angel . . . 'Anything?' she asked gently.

'No. Nothing.' Angel turned to her with a desperate expression. 'Nothing from Tommy or from Abigail – that's the skipper's wife. I'd have thought she'd have been straight on our WhatsApp group if she'd heard anything.'

Angel's face drained of colour and Bo didn't blame her. She must be terrified.

'Oh, my love. I'd drive you home if I hadn't had wine.'

'Me too,' Ran added. 'Can I call you a taxi or ask someone from the pub to take you?'

'I need my own car!' Angel cried. 'I might have to go down to the harbour.'

'Look, let me at least come home with you?' Bo offered.

Angel hesitated. Bo thought she might burst into tears but she said, 'Yes, please. I'd feel so much better with you with me.'

Bo now knew the meaning of white-knuckle ride as Angel hurtled home. She clutched the edge of her seat and closed her eyes at one point. Conditions were awful, with the wipers swishing at top speed, water streaming down the lanes and twigs crunching under the tyres. There was no street lighting most of the way and while it was only a couple of miles to Angel's house in the next village, it was one of the longest journeys of Bo's life.

The house was one of a pair of semi-detached cottages near to the local pub. Bo pulled onto the driveway. Everywhere was dark, however when Angel unlocked the front door, there was a loud bang from upstairs that made Bo utter a little 'Oh' of shock.

'It's that bloody window,' Angel said. 'Tommy keeps saying he'll fix the dodgy catch but it will work itself loose from the frame. I hope it hasn't blown open and smashed the glass.' She scurried upstairs while Bo went into the kitchen and filled a kettle. She had to do something. How strange it was to focus on the mundanities in the midst of such a terrible time. She hoped against hope that Tommy would be home to fix the catch himself.

A sewing machine stood on the kitchen table, with fabric neatly folded next to it and a large plastic workbox, which Bo assumed was full of reels of cotton, pins and trimming. An apron hung from the peg next to a pot holder and some tea towels. They were clearly all made by Angel in her distinctive style with tiny repeated prints of seagulls, flowers and wildlife. Bo wondered where she got the fabric and patterns from – they were so cute and different to anything Bo had seen in the shops.

Angel was back very quickly. In the harsh light of the kitchen, her face was whiter than ever and her mascara was smudged. Bo's heart went out to her while she checked her phone again. It beeped several times as more messages came in now the phone had reconnected with the cottage WiFi.

'Any word?' Bo asked.

'Only from Kelvin moaning about the computers, as if I care right now. There's nothing about Tommy! Nothing on the landline answerphone either, just a call from our Adam about his dad's birthday present. The three of us were clubbing together for a new tablet for Tommy's birthday.' Angel let out a howl and tears flowed. 'What if he never makes it? What if he's out there now, on a sinking vessel or smashed on the rocks? What if – he's already gone? The sea's a terrible mistress, he's always saying it. So fickle, so cruel.'

Bo fought back tears herself at her friend's distress but knew if she panicked, it would only make things worse.

'Sit down for a minute,' she said, gently taking Angel's elbow and guiding her to the sofa. 'Let me make you a cuppa while you try to calm your mind and we'll find a way to find out what's happening. If the *Briar Rose* is in trouble, we'll be able to get some information. Have a think of who else might know and then we'll sort it.'

Angel took a juddering breath in and nodded.

'Please try not to worry yet. Maybe the situation's not as bad as those men made out if you haven't heard anything. I'm sure the skipper's wife would have been on to you and the other crew's families straightaway. You know how fast news travels round here.'

'I hope you're right. I don't know what I'd do without him.'

Angel nodded and Bo handed her a packet of tissues, already suspecting she might have to stay the night with her friend. She made two mugs of tea and took them into the sitting room where Angel was up again and pacing the room, despite Bo's suggestion.

She encouraged Angel to sip hers. 'Right, let's set about trying to track down some up-to-date info. We could try calling the RNLI station, maybe?'

'I thought of that but I don't want to bother them, even with something so important. They'll be flat out dealing with the rescue operation . . .'

'I could phone Finn Morvah to see if he's heard anything,' Bo said. 'They know everyone in the boating and fishing community, they're sure to be able to find out.'

'Thanks. I've messaged Abigail and a couple of the other crew's families,' Angel said. 'But nothing so far. I'll try Abigail's landline too.'

'Good idea.'

Bo called Finn while Angel called Abigail from her landline. As expected, Finn went into action immediately and said he'd see what he could find out. Bo could tell he was very concerned about the conditions, and if an expert sailor like Finn was worried, things must be bad. Even a couple of miles inland, the wind was howling around the house, so goodness knew what it would be like out at sea.

Bo heard a shriek from the hallway and her stomach lurched. Angel walked in, tears running down her face.

'It is the *Briar Rose*. She had engine trouble and she's drifted onto the reef at Devil's Point. They've launched another big lifeboat but what if they don't make it in time? If the *Briar Rose* hits the rocks, she'll be smashed to pieces.'

'Oh, love. I'm so sorry, but they'll get there in no time. They'll take the crew off and keep them safe.' Bo squashed down her worst fears.

'I hope so. I do hope so. I can't bear to lose Tommy. I can't help thinking it was a bad omen to see that fortune teller. She said I'd be with the love of my life at Christmas but what if I'm *not*? What if her prediction was tempting fate?'

'Now listen,' Bo said. 'That charade had nothing, absolutely *nothing*, to do with this. Madame Odette is a fairground entertainer. She told me exactly the same thing as you, remember? Don't you give her a second thought. You will be with Tommy; the RNLI will make sure of that.'

Bo put her arm around Angel, soothing her, despite being deeply worried herself. She'd heard far too many horror stories from her boating and fishermen customers to ever want to venture to sea herself.

Angel's mobile rang out, like a fire alarm.

'Oh, Jesus,' Angel said. 'It's Abi!'

Bo's heart was in her mouth. She wrapped her arms around herself, the suspense was unbearable.

'Abi . . .' Angel's voice was crackly and raw. Bo could feel her fear. She stood by, her body taut with anxiety. Angel listened. Her brow furrowed deeply, mascara smudged under her eyes. 'What? No? I don't understand . . .' she kept repeating the words.

She dropped her phone on the coffee table, next to the mug of tea she'd barely touched.

Angel was too shocked to speak for a moment. Bo was ready

to explode with tension. She reached out to take Angel's hand. 'Angel, hun. What's happened?'

'The *Briar Rose* has gone down.'

'Oh, my God!' Bo cried and threw her hands up to her face.

Angel, however, seemed amazingly calm. She had to be in shock. 'It's OK. The crew are safe. The lifeboat took them off.'

'Oh, thank God.' Bo could have wept tears of relief, but her friend was standing stock-still, not even looking at Bo, simply staring into space.

'Yes . . . but I don't understand. Abi said that Tommy wasn't on board. He never even joined the crew yesterday morning.'

Chapter Nine

Bo took a few seconds to process what Angel had said. 'He wasn't even on board? How can that be?'

'I don't know. Abi was in a bit of a state herself given what's been going on, but she was adamant. Tommy never set sail at all.'

'Then . . .' Bo hardly dared to utter the words. 'Where is he?'

'Abi doesn't know. She hasn't been able to have more than a few words with Skip after he was rescued by the lifeboat. They're on their way back to port now and I expect I'll find out more when they get here.'

'You're sure he said he was going to join the *Briar Rose* yesterday morning?'

'Yes. I heard him leave. It was in the early hours so he didn't disturb me to say goodbye. He never does. But I heard him close the door and his car's gone.'

'Have you spoken to him since he set off for work?'

'No. I had a text shortly after they were due to leave port. He usually does that while he has a signal but I don't expect to hear much if he's only away a few days. They can use the radio on board but you know . . . he doesn't like to get all lovey-dovey when he's working. I wouldn't want him to.' Angel's face crumpled. 'I want to phone him now. What if something happened to him on the way to work?'

'If he hadn't turned up as planned, then the skipper or Abi would have phoned you, surely?' Bo said gently, as a host of scenarios – none of them good – tumbled through her mind.

'Well, exactly!' Angel's voice rose in a wail. 'I need to speak to him now. He must have heard that the *Briar Rose* is in trouble too . . . wherever he is.'

She snatched up her mobile again and stabbed at a number which Bo presumed was Tommy's. Bo wondered if she should leave. This seemed like an intimate conversation to listen in on, yet she didn't want to abandon her friend.

'There's no answer.' Angel tried again and sent a message. 'What if he's done something?' she said, a thought that had also slipped into Bo's mind.

'I'm sure he hasn't,' Bo said.

'What other explanation could there be for him not turning up to work?'

'I don't know . . .'

'I'm going down to the RNLI now and I'm going to make Skip tell me what he knows,' Angel said, grabbing her coat.

'I'll come with you,' Bo said, following Angel, who had already made it to the front door.

When they reached the harbour, the big orange all-weather lifeboat was alongside the quay. The *Briar Rose* crew were being helped off the boat by their rescuers who were patting their backs in comfort. Bo had heard that losing a vessel felt like losing a close friend, and even though the crew would be relieved that no human lives were lost, they would now be realising how near they'd come to perishing and what the sinking of their livelihood would mean.

The devastation was written all over the crew's dejected faces. The skipper was openly weeping and Abi, his wife, ran to him in tears of relief. She threw her arms around him and they stood there, clinging to each other like limpets to a rock.

Angel watched, and Bo guessed she must be wishing and wondering why she wasn't there herself, greeting Tommy like that, instead of in a terrible limbo.

The other crew followed on, patting their skipper on his back. They trudged up the quay, past Angel and Bo. When Skip approached, Angel lunged at him.

'Skip!' He stared at her. 'I'm so glad you're safe. I'm sorry about the *Briar Rose* but I have to ask you: where's my Tommy? Why didn't you tell me he wasn't on board? I've been going out of my mind worrying about him and he isn't answering his phone. Where is he?'

'I'm sorry, Angel, love . . . but you can stop worrying. He's not been hurt. I'm more than certain he's safe but as to where he is and why . . . well, you'll have to ask him that.' Despite his exhaustion, Skip quickened his step, joining the crew. It was obvious he didn't want to speak to Angel.

'I'm sorry,' Abi said.

'What does that mean? I can stop worrying about him? I've been going out of my mind, Abi! What do you know?'

'I don't know where he is. Skip hasn't told me – we've barely had time to speak. If I knew, I swear I'd share it with you.'

Bo intervened. 'Angel, hold on. I know this is horrendous for you but you'll find out soon enough. Why don't you try calling him again?'

Ignoring Bo, Angel marched up the ramp into the lifeboat house where the crew were shrugging off their orange kit under fluorescent lights.

Bo followed her, unable and unwilling to interfere.

'Will none of you tell me why Tommy didn't get aboard the *Briar Rose*?'

She was met with a wall of blank faces from the half-dressed lifesavers.

'Come on. He wasn't on board!'

One of the crew, a man in a turban but no trousers, stepped forward. 'I'm sorry, love, we haven't a clue. Your husband wasn't listed as ever being on board. Wherever he is, he never got on the *Briar Rose* according to the skipper.'

Angel let out a wail before turning away and storming out, with Bo at her heels. She stood on the slipway, hugging herself, while the rain lashed down.

'They've closed ranks. That's what they do. They're all the same.'

'I genuinely don't think they know . . .' Bo said. 'And we ought to get out of this rain.'

'He could be lying in a ditch somewhere.'

'The skipper said he was safe.'

Angel rounded on Bo. 'What does that mean? Is he with the police? Why hasn't he told me?'

Bo had no answer other than to persuade her back to the car before they both looked like drowned rats. They drove home, with Angel speculating on what could have happened. The rain had eased a little though the roads were littered with small branches and water had swollen the creeks as they made their way back to Angel's house. Bo didn't dare voice her thoughts out loud.

As they turned into the driveway, Bo said, 'Would you like me to stay?'

'I don't want to put you out.'

'It's no trouble.' Bo undid her seatbelt. 'Until you find out he's OK, I'll stay.'

Angel nodded and dissolved into floods of tears again. Bo didn't blame her. 'What will I do without him? We've been married for almost thirty years. We're like an old pair of slippers together. Tommy has his faults but I love him.'

They made it inside where Bo hung their dripping coats over chairs, turned on the heating and put the kettle on again. It was past midnight but she didn't expect to get any sleep for some time.

'Has he ever gone missing like this before?' she asked, leaning against the worktop while Angel sat at the table, fiddling with a pair of pinking shears.

'No. Not really. He was back late from a fishing trip once before, a couple of years ago, but only by a day.'

Bo's ears pricked up and her skin tingled with foreboding. 'What happened?'

'They'd unloaded the catch and he was supposed to come home but his car wouldn't start so he had to sleep an extra night on board. His phone had packed in so he wasn't able to tell me until the following morning – he said everyone else had gone home – so I was worried, but that was different. I knew he was OK, and where he was. He always comes home.'

Bo wondered why Tommy hadn't asked one of the crew or a friend in the port to contact Angel but didn't say. She suppressed a shiver.

Bo poured hot water onto the coffee granules and the air filled with the aroma. She topped the cups up with milk and pushed one across the table to Angel. 'Sip this, you need to stay warm and hydrated. I've added sugar.'

Angel pulled a face. 'Look at us. We're soaked. I am sorry for dragging you out.'

'It's no problem.'

Ignoring the coffee and Bo's order to drink something, Angel pushed her chair back roughly and the scrape echoed around the kitchen, making Bo wince. 'I'll go and get changed and find you a dressing gown. I'll be back in a mo.'

Bo heard the thump of Angel hurrying upstairs and creaks from the floor above. She looked around the small kitchen and her heart sank further at the signs of Angel's life with her husband, which had seemed happy enough – to the outside world at least. There were photos of Angel and Tommy pinned to a corkboard, magnets of the kids on the fridge door, a small vase of pinks in the window.

A heart-shaped pot stood by the hob while a mug with 'Tommy – World's Biggest Catch' rested upside-down on the drying rack. A blue driftwood frame on the dresser held a photo of a much younger Angel and Tommy, arms entwined, in front of a fishing boat. Angel sported an eighties bubble perm and Tommy looked lean and handsome, blinking into the sun from a face tanned mahogany, the light glinting off the earring in one lobe. They were both grinning and hopeful. Bo wondered if it had been taken before their kids had been born.

She heard a thud and a cry from above and tensed up.

Bo lowered the mug to the table and crossed the kitchen to the foot of the stairs. Muffled sobs came from above.

'Angel! Are you OK?' she asked, already knowing that her friend was almost certainly not OK.

Bo hurried up the steps and stopped in the doorway of Angel's bedroom. The bed was metal-framed with a white cover and a padded garland of hearts draped over the frame.

Angel was sitting on the edge of the bed, a letter between her fingertips.

She looked up, her face a picture of pure misery. 'I f-found this under the d-dressing table. I didn't see it until I looked for my slippers under the stool. It must have blown off the bed or table with a gust of wind. That sash has never closed properly.'

Bo's gaze flicked from the sheet of paper to the large silver box on the dressing table. A make-up box, not unlike her own, one she used to get ready for dances, events, parties and all the joyful pleasures of life – the fun, happy, exciting times she shared with Angel and the rest of her friends.

She had an idea of what the note might say, even without having to take it from Angel and read the words in Tommy's rough scrawl.

Sorry, babe. Really sorry.

By the time you've found this, I'll be gone.

I'm no writer and I know this note can never make up for how sorry I am. You deserve more after all these years but I just can't put my feelings into words.

Staying would be wrong. I'd be lying to you and that's not fair, babe, but I can't do this any more. I have to go. I never meant to hurt you.

Please believe me. I'll always care for you but it's not enough. Don't worry about me. I'm all right. But best if you just forget me.

Tom X

Angel sat on the bed, staring into space.

Even though Bo had expected that Tommy had left her friend, the shock of seeing him tell Angel in such a brief and callous way felt like a punch to the gut. How cowardly to leave a note . . . not to face her and try to explain or give her any time to prepare. To run away . . .

'This is horrible. I am so sorry he's put you through this.'

'He didn't know the *Briar Rose* would get into trouble. He must have meant for me to find the letter,' Angel said.

'That's no excuse!' Bo shut her mouth quickly. She was making things worse, but what on earth could she say that wouldn't make things worse for Angel? The situation was appalling, heartbreaking, and she couldn't do a thing to help, apart from listen.

Leaving the letter on the far end of the bed, she sat down beside Angel.

'What does it mean?'

'I don't know, but I think you should stop worrying he's come to any harm. He must be staying somewhere.'

'With another woman, you mean?'

'I don't know, my love,' Bo said softly, unwilling yet to pile more misery onto her friend's woes.

'I suppose you think I should have seen it coming?'

'Not at all. It's obvious this has come totally out of the blue.'

'Why? I want to know *why*.'

'Of course you do. I'd be exactly the same, but you can't rush out now. It'll have to wait until morning.'

Angel hurled the ball of paper at the make-up box. It missed so she leapt up and threw the box on the carpet.

'That bloody Madame Odette! Saying I'd be with the love of my life by Christmas! I was so sure she meant me and Tommy. Now I'm wondering if dabbling in that kind of stuff has tempted fate and brought me bad luck!'

*   *   *

Bo woke in Angel's spare bed, in borrowed pyjamas with a Cath-Kidston-style print of the seaside. She lifted the curtains to find angry purple clouds marshalling over the distant horizon. The storm front was being blown away from Falford and calm had descended. The rear garden was littered with twigs and leaves, and two garden chairs lay upturned on the patio.

She didn't want to abandon her friend, but she had to go home, change and open up the café. She thought of calling a taxi but checked her phone to find a message from Ran, whom she'd texted while they were on the way to the port. She'd wanted to let him know, at least, that Tommy hadn't been on board and that she was staying the night with Angel.

The reply offered her a lift home if she needed one.

Bo went downstairs and found Angel already at the table.

'Any news?'

'No . . . I made you some tea.' She nodded at the mug on the table. 'I was going to bring it up.'

'Thanks,' Bo said, thinking of how kind Angel was, and how she was always thinking of others before herself. At work, at the dance club . . . She must have put people first her whole life. Bo's anger rose again. What kind of coward put his partner through the worry and misery that Tommy had?

'Angel. I need to go to work so Ran's coming to pick me up.'

'He knows about this?'

'Only that Tommy wasn't involved in the sinking. I didn't tell him anything else.'

'Everyone will know soon. I'll have to tell them. Everyone at work, all the neighbours, the customers, the Flingers . . . everyone in the village.' She rested her head in her hands. 'How will I face them?'

'You should phone in sick today,' Bo said firmly. 'If you don't want to do that, I'll do it for you.'

'Th-thanks. Would you?'

'Of course I bloody would. You need a couple of days off. I'll say you're unwell. You don't have to explain to Kelvin what's wrong or tell anyone until you're ready.'

'What about Ran?'

'He won't pry, though I can't think of anyone less likely to gossip.' Bo gave a brief smile and patted Angel's hand.

'You're right. Tell him if you like. Bo . . .'

'Yes?'

'I think Tommy must have gone off with another woman. I've lain awake most of the night wondering but I can't come up with any other explanation.'

'I fear that might be a possibility,' Bo said as kindly as she could. 'But you need to know for sure.'

'I keep wondering who she is and how long it's been going on for. He's been away at sea for decades so it could have been going on for years. How could she do this to me? Take another man's wife and go behind my back?'

'Maybe, if he is having an affair, the other woman didn't know he was married?'

'She can't have been local then,' Angel muttered.

'No.'

'I'm going to phone Abi. No, I'm going round their house to find out exactly what Skip knows. I'll make him tell me.'

'I can understand you want answers but why not hang on a day? The atmosphere's going to be pretty fraught at their house with him losing the *Briar Rose*. There'll be an enquiry and the salvage to organise. You might get more answers when they've had the chance to sort themselves out? Perhaps you

90

can arrange a time to see Abi. She might be able to prise the truth out of Skip.'

'Yes, that's a sensible idea. The trouble is, Bo, I'm not in the mood to be sensible.'

'I wouldn't be, either.'

Bo's phone buzzed. 'Excuse me.'

It was Ran, asking when she wanted collecting, and there was another message from Cade, saying he was running a bit late because the baby had been unwell in the night so he wouldn't be there to open up.

'You go,' Angel said in a firmer voice. 'You need to open up the café.'

'I do but I don't like leaving you.'

'It's your livelihood and, anyway, I'll have to be on my own sometime. I'll call in sick myself.' She squared her shoulders. 'And I'll call our Adam and Emma and tell them what's happened in case they hear about the *Briar Rose*. It's probably on the local news by now and I don't want them to find out on the telly or Internet and think their dad's been in danger. I'll have to tell them he's safe and that he's not coming home. I can't lie and hide away from the truth forever, even if Tommy wants to.'

Bo's heart went out to Angel but she was slightly heartened by hearing her ready to take some practical steps. The shock and confusion must be devastating and this was only the beginning of a very hard time ahead.

'I'll come back later, if you need me. I'm on the end of a phone too. Please let me know me as soon as you hear anything about Tommy.'

'Thanks.'

'I'll fetch my bag from upstairs and tell Ran to collect me.'

'OK. And Bo . . . you don't have to lie to Ran. You can tell him that Tommy's left me. I trust him. And anyway,' she heaved a huge sigh, 'I've got to start telling people sometime and maybe I'd better get used to being on my own. Though I still can't help thinking he might walk through that door at any moment . . .'

Chapter Ten

Ran picked Bo up in his van and drove her home. The storm clouds had gone, replaced with a grey sky and a stiff breeze. It felt as if summer had already fled, and today marked the start of the long but inevitable slide into autumn.

Tired and worried about Angel, Bo's spirits sank further, although she was grateful to see a familiar face.

'Thanks for coming out, though I could have ordered a taxi.'

'At this hour? In Falford?' He shook his head. 'It's no trouble to me. I was up before dawn anyway because I wanted to make an early start. We'll definitely be going ahead with the dive trips today. Besides, I'm guessing you had a rough night and might have wanted a friend to talk to?'

She didn't know how to reply at first, surprised and touched at his concern. 'Not as rough as Angel. I don't like leaving her but she's going to call her children so I hope one of them can come over and look after her.'

Bo relayed some of what had passed including the skipper's cryptic comments and Tommy's note.

Ran focused on the road, occasionally letting out a sigh or a quiet swearword.

'You haven't heard anything on the grapevine, I don't suppose?' she said. 'Not that you listen to gossip.'

'Normally, it's pretty impossible to avoid it entirely in Falford,' he said. 'Though I have a choice whether to take any notice. I hadn't heard anything about Tommy, if you mean in terms of him getting up to no good or having an affair . . .'

'But?'

'Nothing specifically about him, and this is only my opinion, but I thought Angel was . . . under-appreciated. The couple of times I've met her husband, I thought he took her for granted.'

'I've thought the same but they seemed happy enough. It's their thirtieth wedding anniversary on Christmas Eve, or was meant to be. Imagine it all going wrong after thirty years. How do you ever deal with that?'

'Maybe you don't deal with it,' he muttered.

His comment marked an end to the conversation. Ran drove through the ford faster than she would have, throwing up muddy water over the windscreen. The wipers swished it away and soon they were climbing the narrow lane that led up to Bo's cottage above the post office.

Finally Ran spoke again. 'Angel's a nice woman. She doesn't deserve this.'

'I'll call her later after I've got changed and opened up the Boatyard Café.'

He stopped the car. 'She's lucky she has a friend like you.'

'Thanks, but I'm not sure how much I can do in this case. I feel so helpless.'

'Just be there to listen. You're good at that, Bo.' He stared out of the windscreen. 'It matters.'

Bo didn't know how to reply, but his kind compliment gave her some comfort. It didn't lessen the concern she had for Angel, but it made her feel she at least could do something.

'Thanks.' Bo got out and was about to close the door when he leaned over the passenger seat. 'Let me know how she is and if I can do anything. God knows what.'

'I will.'

'With all the drama, we never finally decided on the music last night,' he said. 'Though it seems wrong to talk about that now. I suspect neither of us is in the mood for jollity and Christmas festivities.'

'No.' Bo heaved a sigh. For Angel, the season of goodwill was looking very bleak indeed, unless Tommy changed his mind and came back. How Angel would react to that, Bo had no idea – but it didn't seem very likely.

'Then again, music can be a consolation,' Ran said.

Or the opposite, Bo thought, remembering Hamish's expression as 'Blue Christmas' had played. He'd groaned and hid his feelings with a sarcastic joke at the time. In reality, he'd been overwhelmed by regret and longing for his ex. For the first time, Bo felt sorry for him. He'd used her to try and escape, and hurt her, but he probably hadn't thought he was doing anything wrong; maybe he'd genuinely believed he could simply sweep the loss away by hooking up with her and having loads of sex.

If only life was that simple, she thought.

'If you want to come over and discuss it, let me know,' Ran said. 'And not just the music. Last night must have been intense. I may not be your first choice of shoulder to cry on, but I'm always here if you need me, with a glass of wine and an unlimited supply of maudlin tunes.'

For the first time since they'd overheard that the *Briar Rose* had gone down, Bo laughed. She was surprised that he'd invited her at all, although even in the past half an hour, he'd revealed there might be much more beneath the cynical exterior.

She could refuse, of course, but after he'd made the offer, it would seem rude and standoffish. She didn't want to reject his first attempt at friendliness.

'I'll hold you to that,' she said, bidding him a farewell in front of the cottage. The postmistress was out walking her dog and stared. Even from this distance, Bo imagined her eyes were out on stalks at seeing Ran drop Bo off at such an early hour. Bo waved. 'Morning, Meera!'

The postmistress lifted a hand and muttered something inaudible.

'Oh dear. I think I've caused some gossip of my own,' she said.

His mouth lifted at the corners. 'Perhaps that's no bad thing. It will deflect some of the flak from Angel.'

Bo smiled, a little surprised he seemed so unperturbed at the prospect of creating a stir in the village.

'See you later,' she said, the image of his face lingering in her mind. It had been an image that had intruded, more than once, into her thoughts about Angel and Tommy, and had provided some much-needed light relief.

He drove off, leaving Bo contemplating the contrast between that smile and the bitter edge to his comment about never getting over the end of a long-term relationship. Still waters ran deep – definitely with Ran – but she wasn't sure she wanted to find out what lay below the surface if it meant getting closer to him.

Chapter Eleven

By the time Bo opened the shutters on the café at ten a.m., there were already half a dozen regulars waiting.

'What time do you call this?' the boatyard manager asked, only half-jokingly.

Finn Morvah was also waiting but not so blunt. 'Everything OK? Or dare I ask?'

'I'm fine but I stayed the night with Angel. Have you heard about Tommy since we spoke last night?'

'Only that he wasn't on board the *Briar Rose*. Does Angel know where he is?'

'Not yet. He left a note.'

The manager piped up. 'Are we ever going to get any breakfast?'

'OK. I'm coming! You'll have to be patient, though.'

Finn rolled his eyes. 'Want a hand?'

'D'you mind? You could turn all the power on and start up the coffee machine.'

Finn looked lost.

She laughed. 'Finn. If you can build a wooden sailing yacht from scratch, you can certainly work a coffee machine.'

He grimaced. 'Don't bet on it.'

Under her supervision, Bo set him to work and he managed to produce several cappuccinos and mugs of tea for the waiting customers. Some had left their orders and promised to return to collect them, which gave Bo a breather. Bo cooked up Finn's breakfast butties while he did a passable job of making drinks for the customers, all of whom he knew.

Bo wrapped the breakfast sandwiches in foil and put them in a paper bag while Finn put the takeout coffees in a carrier, ready to take them back to the boatyard.

Bo's assistant, Cade, eventually arrived, flustered and apologetic, so Bo was able to dispense with Finn's services.

Finn took off his apron. 'I have some news. It's Rose. She's pregnant.'

'Oh, really?' Bo hugged him. 'I'm so happy for you both! When is it due?'

'Early spring next year. We finally decided to announce it.'

Bo hugged him, delighted for Finn and his partner, Rose – an archaeologist who'd arrived in Falford the previous spring and eventually got together with Finn. She'd joined in with local events and become part of the community. Rose had also captured Finn's heart, much to the disappointment of many locals.

Bo had also dated Finn briefly years before and, despite him being totally gorgeous, neither of them had ever wanted to take their relationship beyond good friends.

'It's wonderful. I bet your mum's excited.'

'She's ecstatic. Joey's stoked about being an uncle too.' Finn was grinning fit to burst. 'I'll see you later. Better get these back to the boatyard. Unless you think I should consider a career change?'

'Thanks for your help,' Bo said. 'But don't give up the day job.'

Whistling, Finn left with an invitation for Bo to pop up to the boatbuilding shed to look at some wood and sails for her terrace when she had time. Bo made up more bacon butties for the rest of her regulars. Finn's news was wonderful but it had sparked off some troubling thoughts. A family? She could barely imagine it. How would she ever run the café? One day maybe . . . if it happened, but it was never going to happen when she didn't even have a partner. She'd begun to dare to think of Hamish as a partner and, occasionally, her thoughts had meandered further into the future . . . though to be honest, she'd envisaged him surrounded by a litter of unruly puppies rather than kids.

That made her smile to herself. She'd probably been subconsciously aware that he wasn't the family type; not with her at any rate.

'Are we ever going to get our breakfast?' The boatyard manager leaned on the counter, his voice carrying through to the kitchen.

'What? Sorry.' Bo slid the bacon and eggs onto the sourdough and topped it with the other slice. She had to stop wondering about what might have been or she'd have no customers left.

The morning whizzed by. Every so often her mind would turn to Angel and how she was feeling, but she had to carry on. Tourists and visitors turned up, bagging the few outside tables.

By afternoon, her late night was catching up with her. The sun had broken through the clouds and, after a few days of being kept indoors, the walkers were out in force. Bo and Cade were still turning disappointed people away at four-thirty, even though they'd stayed open later to make up for the early start.

It was with a sigh of relief that she pulled down the shutters and went outside to the terrace to empty the bin by the table area. The tide was coming in and the afternoon sunlight glinted on the water eddying around the channels and mudflats. Oystercatchers with bright orange beaks pecked at the mud. The sunlight had a mellow quality, a feeling that evening was close at hand. Autumn was coming.

'Hiya.'

Ran walked onto the terrace. He was wearing shorts, flip-flops and a dive centre hoodie. His hair was damp and, judging by the stubble, he didn't seem to have shaved that morning. There was something about his slightly dishevelled 'just tumbled out of bed' look that made Bo's stomach do a little flip – very similar to the way it had when she'd first started seeing Hamish. Was it because he'd looked more relaxed, less repressed – casually sexy?

She tried to pretend it hadn't happened.

She lowered the bin bag onto the terrace.

'Hello!' she said. 'What brings you here? We're closed but I might be able to make an exception for you.'

'Thanks, but I'm not here for a coffee, sadly . . . I wish I was.'

The downturn of his mouth set her on edge. 'What's happened?

'I think I might have an idea where Tommy Carrack is.'

Chapter Twelve

'I found out from one of the guys on the dive today. He works at a dive centre in Falmouth harbour and he and some mates were talking about the *Briar Rose* going down. They said that Tommy was holed up with a woman in Falmouth.'

'Oh God . . . That was what I was afraid of. Do you think it's reliable?'

'I didn't say anything but this guy's pretty solid so I think it's likely to be true and that the affair might have been going on for some time.'

'Poor Angel. He left her a note . . .' Bo said, feeling she could trust Ran's discretion. 'Why didn't he say he'd found someone else in his letter? Why leave her in suspense?'

'Who knows why men hide things – why *people* hide things,' Ran said bitterly. 'Cowards. Maybe he thought it would be kinder? Probably convinced himself it was better than telling her face to face.' He snorted. 'People can justify anything when they're guilty or can't face up to hard choices.'

Bo was thrust back to Christmas Eve and how Hamish had deceived himself, and perhaps she'd wanted to believe *he* was serious about her. 'I need to speak to Angel, unless she knows already.'

'If the news has reached me, she may well do. I'm sorry to be the bearer of bad news but please, be careful how you broach the subject. It may still be just gossip.'

'I will. Thanks for coming to tell me.'

'Not the happiest end to your day.'

'No.'

He nodded at the bin bags. 'Want a hand?'

She smiled. 'You're not the first man to offer to help with the café today.'

Confusion flickered in his eyes. 'Oh? Who was that?'

'Finn stepped in – well, he tried – to make the coffees after I opened up late this morning, until Cade got here.'

Ran seemed relieved, though she didn't know why. 'I've finished work and I can spare the time to shift a few bin bags. You've had a rough night, let me help.'

She nodded, though there wasn't much for him to do. Leaving him to empty the bin and stick it in the recycling and trade waste from the kitchen, Bo checked everything was safe and secure and locked up.

He hung around. 'Are you going to Flingers next Saturday night?' he asked.

'I was planning to.'

'I thought, maybe, that you'd like to come over to mine one night this week to discuss the playlist as we didn't get to do it last night.'

'Yes. Why not? That would be good,' she said smiling, but her heart still heavy with the news of Tommy.

It was with mixed feelings that Bo finally went home. She was looking forward to an evening out at the cinema later that week with a group of her non-Flingers friends but in a quandary about whether to pass on the rumours Ran had heard from his diving buddy. She didn't want to make the situation worse by sharing what might still only be gossip.

There was no word on Tommy from Angel for the next couple of days, and her son and daughter had visited so Bo was able to concentrate on her work. She'd arranged to go to Ran's on Thursday evening to discuss the music, but on Tuesday, she was off for her regular cinema night with the girls – some friends she'd grown up with in the village and who still lived locally.

Much as Bo loved her dancing companions, it was nice to get away from work and Falford for a few hours, even if she was asked the inevitable questions about her love life. She decided not to mention her visit to Ran's later in the week. It couldn't be called a date by any stretch of the imagination but her friends wouldn't believe that, no matter how much she insisted.

It was after eleven-thirty when she got home and remembered to switch her phone back on. There were several messages, including one from Angel:

I know where Tommy is.

'Oh no . . .' The text must have been sent while she'd been watching the film. Agonising over what to do, Bo eventually messaged back:

I'm sorry I didn't pick up your text earlier. Don't want to wake you now, but will call first thing in the morning.

She called as soon as she woke. Angel was understandably distressed. It appeared that Tommy was definitely living with another woman, though Angel still hadn't found out exactly where or who she was.

Maybe Angel would know more when Bo went to see her after work that evening.

Bo walked through the garden where the grass was long and the tubs needed watering. It had been Angel's pride and joy, yet another job to add to her list. Bo felt angry all over again at Tommy and, perhaps unreasonably, at Kelvin, Angel's boss, for making her friend's life harder than it needed to be.

Angel was at the back door. 'He called me last night. To think I gave him all those years!' she said the moment Bo arrived and before she'd had a chance to ask more.

Angel threw up her hands in despair, knocking a mug onto the tiles. Shards of china flew all over the kitchen.

'Oh, I'm sorry! Look at the state of me.'

'It's fine. Don't worry.'

Angel picked up the biggest pieces, while Bo swept the last of the shards of china into the dustpan and tipped them into some newspaper. Bo wrapped the newspaper up and put it in a paper bag by the bin. It smelled of curry but it would do.

'I'll take this out to the bin,' she said.

'No, leave it. The kids had an Indian takeaway last night. I couldn't face cooking for them.'

'Actually, I brought a few pasties with me, in case you hadn't eaten.' Bo placed a paper bag on the table. 'There are three, one each for you and the kids.'

'Thanks,' Angel said, but left the bag untouched.

She leaned against the counter and sighed. 'Sorry for bringing this to your door. You have enough going on.'

'It's fine. That's what friends are for. I'm sorry that when he finally called, it wasn't the news you wanted.' Bo was glad she was no longer in a dilemma over whether to share Ran's information.

'I feel like the past thirty years have been a sham. How do I know he hasn't been seeing her all that time? I bet she's younger than me.'

'Did he give you any more details?' Bo asked.

'No. He's probably too worried I'll go round and give them both a piece of my mind.'

'Do you know how long it's been going on for?'

'He said it was only the past few months but I think it's been longer, and even if not with *her*, I bet he's had other affairs. There's gossip about it. I've seen people pointing fingers when I went into the Co-op! And Kelvin wants me back at work tomorrow. He said I have to put my personal problems behind me. I took the last couple of days as holiday.'

'I loathe that man,' Bo blurted out.

'Me too. I hate him. I hate Tommy. I hate all men. They're all the same. Look at how that bloody Hamish upset you.'

Bo was shocked. Angel had never spoken to her about Hamish so bluntly. She'd seemed to accept Bo's story that they'd split up by mutual consent and that it had only been a fling. Perhaps Angel was merely being kind because other people must have suspected the truth: that Bo had been much keener on Hamish than she'd let on.

'I'm sorry. That was out of order. None of my business.'

'It's OK, and . . . you're right. He did upset me.'

'You put on a brave face like you always do but I could tell how upset you were. The life went out of you for a little while. I could see it in your dancing.'

'My dancing?'

'Yes. You didn't have your usual spark and sometimes, when

105

you didn't realise anyone was watching, or we were dancing to some romantic tune, I saw you biting your lip, trying to hold in how you really felt but then the smile was back. Hamish dimmed your sparkle for a while but it's back now. You're so strong, Bo, I wish I had your ability to bounce back.'

Bo was astonished. She'd no idea anyone had noticed how badly she'd been hurting. She'd simply carried on, grimly getting on with life, letting the pain out at home. That was replaced with confusion, a sense of being at sea and unable to trust her feelings any longer. Plus, she was nowhere near as strong as Angel claimed.

'Hamish wasn't what he seemed. He was still in love with his fiancée in Scotland.'

'He was *engaged?*' Angel said.

'Yes, I didn't tell anyone because I didn't want a big fuss or people feeling sorry for me. I am totally fine with it now. I've survived and I'm over it, though not ready to get involved with anyone yet.'

'And you never should,' Angel shot back. 'They're all liars. They let you down. You can't trust a single one of them! Bloody Hamish, bloody Tommy! Well, I won't be so trusting any more. From now on, I'm looking after number one.'

All Bo could do was listen and make soothing noises until Emma, Angel's daughter, arrived back from work so she felt able to leave.

She realised that Angel was at her lowest ebb, devastated and needed to be justifiably angry with and grieve for Tommy, even though he was still alive. Despite recent experience, Bo hadn't quite reached the point where she believed all men were liars or that it was an exclusively male trait to let people down.

Everyone let someone down sometimes. That was human

nature. However, Angel's experience with Tommy was another wake-up call for Bo. To love someone – to let them get close to you and trust them with your heart – was a very risky business, and the price of it was to endure a lot of pain when you lost them.

What Angel was going through was ten times worse than when Bo had split with Hamish. She wasn't sure she ever wanted to go through that or even risk it again.

Chapter Thirteen

'Oh, it's Thor.'

'Just step over him. He thinks he's a draught excluder,' Ran said, seeing Bo hesitate to venture out from the hallway. Thor was lying in the doorway to the sitting room, like a furry barrier repelling all invaders.

The cat opened one eye to check the visitor wasn't dangerous or edible and then went back to sleep. Ran, on the other hand, could hardly take his eyes off Bo. She wore a denim jacket over a dress with cherries on it and high-top baseball sneakers.

'I'm sorry I'm running late,' she said, lifting her feet carefully to avoid treading on Thor. 'I called in on Angel. I thought it was better to get on my way than waste time trying to message you. Then I was held up by a caravan that had a close encounter with a minibus. I would have messaged you but I didn't have any signal. Bet you thought I wasn't coming at all.' She seemed a little breathless and her cheeks were pink.

'It's fine. I guessed there was a hold-up,' Ran said, lying again. He'd definitely begun to wonder if she'd turn up at all and been taken aback at how disappointed he'd be if she didn't.

He realised it was the first time she'd been in his cottage. In fact, hardly anyone had been inside apart from the BT guy to repair the broadband.

'It's dim in here. Hadn't realised how dark it had got. I'll put some lights on,' he said, 'I'm afraid there might be some fur about, and I wouldn't want it to get all over your dress.'

'Don't worry, I can deal with that.' She lingered while Ran switched on the table lamps and flicked a switch that illuminated the underlighting in the bookshelves.

Her mouth felt open. 'Wow. When you said you had a "bit of a record collection" I never expected this. It's like a whole archive!'

'Oh. Yes. Slightly embarrassing, if I'm honest.'

'It's not embarrassing, it's fantastic.' She moved to the nearest shelf, peering at the spines of the album and singles covers.

'Is that Elvis's Christmas album you're playing?' she said.

'Yes. It's a first printing of a Canadian pressing from 1957 – the same year as "Jailhouse Rock".'

Bo ran her fingers along the record sleeves, making enthusiastic comments at the hundreds of albums from almost every era. There was swing, rock and roll, jazz, plenty of modern stuff going into the 1970s, prog rock, punk, right up to indie bands from the nineties. She also raised an eyebrow – appreciatively, he hoped – at the two record players, a vintage model and the latest Bose. Of course, he thought, she could simply be being polite and was secretly shocked by the extent of his collecting.

'I rented this place because of the shelves. Sad, isn't it?' It was strange to see his obsession through another person's eyes, even one sympathetic to the genre of music. It did look a little obsessive.

'Not if you needed the space,' she said. 'How many are there?'

'I've lost count. Into the thousands. I used to have more.'

'Wow. How long have you been collecting vinyl?'

'Since I was around fourteen. It wasn't cool then, especially when you were into the kind of music your grandfather listened to.'

'I'm hardly going to judge you, am I?' Bo said with a smile.

He loved the way the bandana on her hair framed her pretty heart-shaped face. She had a great figure too. Wow. The desire hit him like a punch to the gut. He'd swap his record collection for a kiss – and a whole lot more.

She was like a fresh summer breeze blowing through the dark cottage, even with autumn on its way.

'Um. They're not all from the rock and roll era,' he said, moving a little further away and picking out an album, just to give himself a distraction. 'There's everything from classical to contemporary, but most are from the fifties and sixties.'

'I'm surprised you want to collect the newer stuff,' she said.

'All genres of music have rare vinyl associated with them, even things like ABBA.'

She laughed. 'That's taking things too far.'

'You don't like "Dancing Queen"?'

She wrinkled her nose but there was laughter in her eyes.

'What makes a record worth so much?'

'Lots of things. Special limited-edition versions before the main disc is released wholesale. Or it can be something as simple as a very small number of original discs cut in the first place. Sometimes you get records by well-known artists – from the Rolling Stones to Pink Floyd – where the label on the B-side is wrongly shown as a copy of that for the A-side.' He smiled. 'Even though the record company would try to claw the wrong ones back and reissue them, inevitably some stay out there. Or it could be a Beatles record on which the label got the group's name misspelt – that kind of thing. They can go on to become priceless.'

'Priceless? Wow. There's nothing like that here, is there?' she said, resting her fingers on the edges of the covers, as if she might be unknowingly touching gold.

'Not any more . . .' he said. 'There are some worth hundreds, a couple might fetch four figures, if I was lucky with a following wind. I'd be living in a mansion if there was,' he added wryly.

'Good point,' she said, but he could see a flicker of puzzlement in her eyes. She might have guessed he was trying to deflect the question.

'How did you get into this?' she asked. 'Vintage music? I must say I'm surprised.'

He allowed himself a smile. 'Why are you so surprised? Because I'm cynical and taciturn and this stuff is sentimental and cheesy?'

He winced a little, remembering that's how Bo's ex, Hamish, had described it. Ran had thought he was a bit of twat who fancied himself as the local stud. God knew why they'd split up, but Ran hadn't known her well enough to pry – and even now, he didn't think it was any of his business. She'd acted as if it was fine, but he guessed it wasn't. His way was to retreat from the world and say even less than usual. He guessed hers had been to hide it under a veneer of activity and positivity.

'We both know vintage music isn't cheesy. OK, some of it's sentimental but some of it comes from a place of real pain and hardship. Look at the range of music here.'

'Hmm . . . Billie Holiday,' Bo said. 'There's nothing sentimental about her music or the woman herself. She was a genius and a legend but she had such a harsh life and upbringing.'

'True. She was a giant in music history. That's partly what attracts me: the history, the depth of emotion, the nuance in some of these old songs.'

'As well as the fun of course,' Bo said, with a small smile to lighten the mood. 'You said it wasn't cool to listen to your grandad's music. Is that where you got the love of rock and roll?'

'Yes, but I'd always loved music. I played the piano a bit when I was younger. I also learned to play the guitar very badly.'

'Don't say you were in a band . . .' Bo said.

'I'm afraid so.'

'Really?' Bo seemed highly amused.

'Only for a few months in the sixth form,' Ran said, half wishing he hadn't mentioned his youthful attempts. 'I'd much rather listen to real musicians. You see, from around the age of fourteen I was secretly listening to my grandad's records, though I'd never have admitted it to my mates. In an age of CDs and downloads, I thought they were beautiful, with the inners and the coloured vinyl. I guess I was as obsessed with the records themselves as I was with the music.'

'Go on. Tell me more,' she said.

'You might end up thinking I'm weird.'

She laughed. 'I doubt it.'

'OK, it started to get serious when I got my grandad to take me to record fairs . . . and then I started going on my own.' He smiled. 'I sneaked out to more than one fair, with cash I'd saved from my Saturday job. I didn't dare tell my school mates; they'd have taken the piss forever. My grandad bought me my first record player when everyone else had sound systems. When there was no one in the house, I'd dance around the living room to them. When I was at uni, I sometimes joined in at the rock and roll nights. Just casual stuff, messing around really.'

'I'd like to have seen that.'

'No way!'

'You *did* dance once, though . . .'

'I was young . . .' Ran thought of those days. Should he tell her why he stopped dancing? He knew the answer to that, but not why he hadn't started again.

'I'm happy behind the decks.' He looked at her. 'Now, your turn. How did you get into granny music?'

Bo burst out laughing. 'Originally? I was probably around twelve or thirteen. It started with me loving the style – the colours, the dresses, the hair and make-up. The music was secondary but when I saw people dancing to jive and swing and rock and roll, I thought: I want to do that! I wasn't interested in sport at school but I loved dancing so Mum encouraged me to take some lessons.'

'I'd like to have seen that too.'

Her squeak of horror amused and charmed him.

'No! I tried ballet and tap but they weren't for me so, in the end, I saved up to have swing and rock and roll lessons. We didn't live in Falford then, I lived near Truro. Back then I was training as a chef whilst working for a catering company and helping at vintage events. I met so many amazing people – plenty of crazy ones too.'

'Like record collectors?' he smirked.

'Oh, crazier than that. People who live the lifestyle all the time . . . Each to their own but I'm not sure it's that healthy to live literally in the past.'

'Some would say this,' Ran waved a hand at his shelves, 'is living in the past. I'm surrounded by it. It's all I listen to.'

'I don't believe that. You could say the same about me: look at how I'm dressed.'

'You look great to me,' Ran said, before clearing his throat. 'Right, enough about the past and back to the present. Would you, um, like a drink?'

He poured a small bourbon for himself and an elderflower cordial with sparkling water for Bo, and took them into the sitting room where Thor had taken up residence on the sofa next to Bo.

'You're honoured.'

Thor rubbed his head against her arm. 'He's a lovely cat,' she said. 'A big softy.'

'He's the Beast of Bodmin.'

'Oh, I bet you're not, are you, Thor?' She scratched the cat between his ears. He closed his eyes and purred.

'You wouldn't think that if he'd left a dead vole in your bed.'

'A vole in the bed?'

'Oh yes, but that's not the worst. You've no idea what I found in my boots as I was about to leave the house.'

Bo reacted with a mix of mock horror and laughter as Ran related some of Thor's 'catches' before thinking that it was hardly the best way of breaking the ice. If this had been a date, it would surely have been a cringe-inducing conversation opener. However, Ran reminded himself, it wasn't a date so maybe he should stop questioning his every word and simply play some music.

'Ranulph is an unusual name. What does it mean?'

'I'd rather not say.'

'Oh, go on!'

He pulled a face. 'Shield-wolf. I know. Don't ask more. It's slightly more common in Scotland. Apparently the Vikings introduced the name there in the Middle Ages.'

'Shield-wolf.' She arched her perfect eyebrows. 'Wow.'

She managed to suppress a giggle and Ran didn't blame her. 'You do know Bo is Scandinavian too,' he said. 'It's usually a man's name. It means dweller.'

'Really? I didn't know that. That would be very cool except, it's short for Bonita.'

'Ah . . .' Ran smiled. 'Bonita. Completely different origins.' A warm country, he thought: Spain. Vibrant, hot – it suited her but he certainly wouldn't make her feel awkward by saying so.

'Yes, it's Spanish. Inspired by Mum's holidays though it was shortened as soon as I was born. Only my aunts call me Bonita, or Mum, occasionally, if she's frustrated with me. Of course, it also happens to go very well with Boatyard.'

He enjoyed seeing the wry twist of her lips.

'Not very original, I know,' she added, eyeing the album spines.

'I think you're very original.'

'Oh?' She seemed taken aback. 'I've been called a few things in my time, but never "original".'

'I meant it as a compliment,' Ran said hastily, feeling awkward that he'd embarrassed her. 'I meant that you follow your own path, as if you're comfortable in your own skin. Your style, when you dance . . .' He hesitated, aware he was digging an ever-deeper hole for himself. This was meant to be a 'business' meeting, as much as social, and what he'd said was far too personal. 'Fancy a coffee and we'll play some more music? I've something a bit different I'd like to run by you for the Illuminations evening.'

She nodded, and Ran fled into the kitchen, keen to escape from Bo's rather startled face and kicking himself for his comments.

They had a brief word about Angel and then moved on to the choices of music. The dances hadn't yet been decided so they went through several different combinations of music to suit different styles and abilities – Lindy Hop, jive and slower tracks.

Not everyone in the Flingers was young or experienced, but they wanted to be inclusive so that as many members as possible could join in with the dance displays at the upcoming events.

Ran glanced at the clock then cursed himself because Bo caught him looking and must have thought he was hinting.

'I should be going. It's late.'

'Yes. I mean, you don't have to rush off.'

This was not a date and, even if it had been – even if he had wanted to ask Bo out, properly, not on the pretext of planning some dance playlist – there was little chance of her accepting now.

Until this moment, he hadn't realised that he *wanted* to put himself out there and ask her.

'I'd better go. Friday's always busy at the café and the weather's looking good. I expect we'll be run off our feet.'

'I'm leading a party to the *Schiedam* off Gunwalloe. She went down in 1684. You should come with me some time.'

She pulled a face. 'Thanks, but I'd rather be serving a busload of tourists.'

'And I'd rather take my chances under the water.'

'It's good we both know where we stand,' Bo said quickly. 'Thanks for the drink. I love the playlists. Can't wait to run them by the Flingers and we can start rehearsing some moves ready for the Illuminations. See you on Saturday night?'

It was on the tip of his tongue to ask her out properly and yet the thought of that letter in the kitchen held him back.

'I'll look forward to it. Might be a good idea to arrive half an hour before everyone else so we have time to get ready?'

'Sounds like a plan.'

He showed her out, waved her off in her van and went back into the kitchen where Thor waited for him, twitching his tail.

He shut the door and groaned. 'That went well. *Not*,' he said, running his hand over the cat's spine. Thor slunk away from his caress, as if to say: 'Don't expect me to comfort you.'

'Fine. It's not as if I feel rejected,' Ran said.

Utterly unimpressed, Thor trotted towards his food bowl.

Ran was torn with regret at not asking Bo out. He'd begun to nurse the hope she was enjoying his company and had genuinely enjoyed hearing about his music. He'd loved hearing more about her. They rarely had a chance to talk at Flingers, not one to one. Now he wasn't so sure. She'd seemed very keen to leave.

When he thought back over their conversation, perhaps she'd thought he was a bit obsessive and weird. Even though she loved vintage music, he'd babbled on about his obsession with vinyl too much. Living here alone with only a cat, not opening up to anyone . . . Or perhaps Bo had thought this was a 'date' and was disappointed that all he'd talked about was record collecting.

It had been a long time since he'd had female company and he was clearly useless at it. Was this fate's way of telling him he wasn't ready to see anyone yet? Or was it a wake-up call to move forwards?

Ran's gaze settled on the letter again. It was more like a small package, balanced across the empty fruit bowl, demanding to be answered. He'd opened it and read it, then replaced it. Like a lot of things in his life, he'd faced up to it to a degree but not taken the action he needed to.

'I know what you're doing, Thor,' he said, turning around to find Thor sitting on the kitchen table next to the bowl with The Letter. The cat stared at him reproachfully, but then Thor often stared at him reproachfully. He probably only wanted his dinner.

'Get down or there'll be no sardine and mackerel surprise for you,' he said.

Thor leapt onto a chair and then the floor, mewing by his bowl while Ran opened a pouch of his favourite food and added some kibble.

With Thor tucking into his food, Ran took the envelope into the sitting room. The cushion was softened into a small hollow where Bo had been and a trace of her perfume, a light floral scent, lingered in the air.

He sank into the armchair, pulled out the wad of papers and picked up a pen from the table.

Chapter Fourteen

'Hello! Are you there?'

Bo walked through the side gate that led to the garden behind Angel's house. It had been over a week since she'd last seen her friend, who hadn't turned up at Flingers on Saturday – not that Bo had expected her to – but they'd kept in touch on the phone and messaged each other.

On the Thursday following, after she'd closed up the café, Bo headed straight round in the late afternoon sunlight. She parked next to Angel's car but, having rung the bell and knocked on the front door and received no answer, Bo was growing concerned.

Angel hadn't been expecting her but even so .

She pushed the gate open with her bottom, because her arms were full with a box of treats for Angel and her family.

'Hello! It's meeee! Are you in the garden?' she called.

Angel's garden, like her house, was neat and beautifully kept in normal circumstances but today the grass was long and there were weeds pushing up through the patio. There was a shed painted pale blue, which looked like it had taken a battering in the recent storm as the roof felt was loose.

A piece of ragged bunting that had adorned the gable during the summer had come loose and was flapping around. Bo only had a tiny yard behind her cottage so she was no garden guru, and didn't want to judge, but it was unlike Angel to let her little patch go. She used to love showing Bo the 'not-quite-perfect' tools, pots and unsold seeds she'd rescued from the waste bins at the Country Stores.

Understandably, gardening was the last thing on her mind at the moment, and there was no sign of her outside. However, the back door was open and Bo was relieved to hear the sound of a sewing machine whirring away inside the kitchen.

She walked into the utility room and called over the frantic buzzing of the machine. 'Angel! Hello! It's Bo!'

'Oh bugger!'

Angel swore again and glared at Bo. 'Look at this! The seam's all wonky now. I'll have to unpick and redo it.' She pulled a strip of fabric from the machine and tossed it onto the kitchen table. There was material and wadding everywhere, piled up on the table and on the floor.

'I'm sorry I made you jump. I didn't mean to – I hoped you wouldn't mind me coming round the back. Argh. I've made you go wrong now.'

'It's not your fault. It's me. I'm all over the place.'

Angel pulled a piece of cotton from her hair which had been dangling in front of her eyes. She wore no make-up and looked worn-out.

'I brought some goodies from the café for you, but I can leave them and come back another time if you're too busy. It's not a problem, lovely.'

'Please don't,' Angel cried, scraping back her chair with a sound that set Bo's teeth on edge. 'I've been looking forward to seeing you; I must have lost track of the time. I've been trying to make some oven mitts but they're quite laborious.'

'It's like a regular production line in here,' Bo said, wondering where to put the box.

'I'm not getting very far. Here, let me take that box.' Her eyes widened. 'Is that all for me?'

'Depends if you want to share with Emma and Adam.' Bo smiled.

'Thanks, Bo. You're such a good friend. I haven't felt like eating much, even the lovely meals Adam and Emma have been cooking for me, but these goodies look wonderful.' Angel took the box and managed to slot it into a space on the worktop.

'It's only snack food. We made a bit extra in the café kitchen yesterday. There's a couple of slices of quiche and some pasties, and some Oreo brownies – help you keep your strength up. I've put a carton of couscous salad in too, in case you want to be healthy.'

Angel lifted the cardboard lid. 'Oh, it smells delicious. Thank you. Emma and her partner are coming tonight so we'll have that quiche and salad . . .' She paused. 'Tommy says "Real men don't eat quiche" and salad's only for rabbits. Mind you, working on the boats is hard physical labour. He always wanted a roast or a steak when he came home. Said he was sick of fish and chips on board. I don't blame him.'

Bo let her reminisce, once again thinking how impossible it must be to be without him after so long.

'I'll put the kettle on,' Angel said. 'And then I'll try one of these brownies. I've had no lunch. Been too busy.'

'I'll make the tea – you tuck in,' Bo said.

While they waited for it to brew, Bo leaned against the worktop, taking in the sea of fabric surrounding the sewing machine. The counter top was littered with Kilner jars full of coloured buttons, and a huge plastic sewing box was open on the tiles.

'What have you been making besides oven gloves?' she said.

'Oh, all sorts. Easy stuff, mainly. Tea towels, pot holders, aprons – kitchenware and the like.'

'What are they all for?'

'You know the animal charity Emma works for? She sells them to raise funds. I haven't been doing it long but she says they're very popular.'

'They're beautiful, but it looks like hard work on top of your job and the house.'

'It is but it's for a very good cause and it keeps my mind off Tommy.' Angel cast her eye over the table. 'I love sewing but I'm finding it hard to think as clearly as I used to.'

'No wonder with all the stress you're under. Are you getting enough sleep?'

Angel sighed. 'I used to lie awake wondering where he was when we were together – now we're not, it's no different.' She stretched her arms above her head and groaned. 'I've been sitting too long. Either that or I'm getting old.'

'Never,' Bo insisted. 'You look ten years younger than you really are, not that you're old anyway. I've plenty of friends younger than me who aren't half as fit as you are.'

'Thanks, love, but I feel I've aged a decade in the past two weeks since Tommy left.'

'Any more clues as to exactly where he is – or with who?'

'With this new woman, I presume. Abi says Skip claims not to know her name or where she lives exactly. He thinks Tommy's working with some bloke on a lobster boat now.'

'The gossip must be all over the quayside,' Bo said.

'Probably, but with the loss of the *Briar Rose*, the crew have had to find other work. Skip's too busy dealing with the investigation and salvage to try and find out more, according to Abi.'

'Tommy hasn't said anything to Emma or Adam, then?'

'They get the same message as me. He's safe and he "needs time to think", whatever that means. I'm not sure he's doing much bloody thinking. I'd say he was busy doing something else!'

'I'm so sorry, Angel.'

'Maybe it's best I don't know who she is or exactly where they're shacked up. I might be tempted to go round there with my pinking shears.'

It was encouraging to see Angel in feisty spirits. 'Probably not the best idea, even if he deserves it. I wish I could do something to help.'

'You already have. You listen, and you bring lovely food.' Angel scraped up a brief smile, the first Bo had seen on her face since Tommy had left. 'I've got the kids. I feel sorry for them. They may be adults but they're as upset as me at the split and angry with their dad.' She lifted her chin and hardened her tone. 'Unfortunately they'll have to face up to the fact that he might never come back, like I'm having to.'

'Will you be OK,' Bo said, 'I mean financially, if he doesn't?'

'The house has always been in my name, thank God. My great-grandma left it to me and she died a few months before I married Tommy. I don't know what would happen if he tried to get part of it.' She hugged herself. 'I shudder to think about it but I might have to. Who knows what's coming my way next?'

'I wish I had a crystal ball,' Bo said, then, 'Oh God, I'm sorry!'

'Don't be. I can't help thinking that bloody fortune teller has a lot to answer for. I know it's irrational but it's as if she tempted fate by telling me I'd be with the love of my life by Christmas.' Angel sighed, then set her mouth in a more determined line. 'Still can't face Flingers yet. Give my apologies to Sally and Hubert – and Ran, will you, and the others. Tell them I'm too busy at the moment, with everything going on?'

'Of course I will. We'll miss you terribly but take all the time you need and only come back when you're ready.'

'I don't know if I ever will be ready.' Angel's eyes were bright with unshed tears. 'They'll all know Tommy left me for another woman, whoever she is.'

'They won't. And as for those that do: they'll be kind,' Bo said and knew that most people at Flingers would only want to be supportive. However, there would be a few who would want to know all the juicy details. Any small community had its sizeable share of gossips and characters who were far too interested in other people's misfortunes.

'Did you – did you and Ran decide on the Christmas playlist?' Angel asked.

'We're getting there. As a matter of fact, he asked me to go round the cottage to listen to some of it last week but we're not totally ready to present it to the Flingers yet.'

'Ran invited you to his house?' Angel raised her eyebrows, intrigued. 'He must have a soft spot for you.'

Bo laughed. 'I doubt it. He probably wants a fellow obsessive to listen to music with him. Even if I were looking for a relationship, which I'm absolutely *not* after the business with Hamish, Ran would not be my first choice.'

'He's a dark horse, that's for sure. And maybe you're right: best keep well away from men with secrets.'

'I will.'

Bo steered the conversation back to Angel's children, asking how Adam was getting on in his job with the fire service. As Bo expected, talking to Angel about her family cheered her up. While they chatted, she helped her sort out some of the finished items into piles, amazed at the number of items she'd made over the past couple of weeks. There were dozens of pieces, in the cutest vintage-style prints, all beautifully finished, which was even more remarkable considering what Angel had been going through.

Angel put the machine away while Bo ran the vacuum cleaner over the floor to pick up the cotton and cast-off trimmings.

'Emma will be back here soon. Think I'd best have a shower, put my face on, and a nicer top,' Angel said. 'I'd made a new purple skirt to wear for the Christmas dances . . .' she added.

'I'd love to see it.'

'Thanks, lovely. Maybe some other time. I'm not sure I can bear to look at it at the moment. I can't imagine wearing it.'

Bo hugged her and Angel put on a brave grin. 'Thanks for coming. You have cheered me up, even if it doesn't seem like it. Say hello to everyone from me.' Her voice was full of regret.

'I will.' Bo took in the wonderful array of work Angel had produced. 'Do you have orders for all these gorgeous pieces yet?'

'I think Emma will take it into the charity shop and sell it on spec. She says people are always asking when there will be new stock.'

'Well, if you could spare a few of the tea towels and the pot holders, I need some new textiles for the café. These are so sweet and the vintage vibe is perfect.'

'Of course, you can have some. Let me know what you want, and I'll keep some back.'

'That would be great. Though I don't want to deplete your stock and overload you.'

'You won't. If I can get my act together, I love making them.'

'Great . . . Can I ask? Did you make the bunting that's on the shed?'

'Of course.' A spark of pride lit up Angel's eyes before she looked downcast again. 'I know it's come loose if that's what you mean. I haven't had time to fix it or the roof. Tommy was always going to repair it but never got round to it. Now I know why!'

'I can help you with the bunting now if you like, though not the roof,' Bo said. 'The reason I asked was because I need some new bunting for the café. It's waterproof fabric, isn't it?'

'Yes. I got a job lot in a closing-down sale at a fabric warehouse.'

'Then if – only *if* – you were thinking of making some more, I'll buy that too. Not for the charity, mind. I'll donate the money for the tea towels for those, but you should get paid for a special commission.'

'I don't know if I'd feel right about taking money. I'm not a professional seamstress.'

'No, you're much better than a lot of the stuff I see in vintage shops and online. It's been mass-produced thousands of miles away and it falls apart. I'd rather pay a bit more for things that are going to last and have a unique style.'

'If you really think so, I'd love to make some bunting for the café.'

'Tell you what. Let's work out a price, one that covers your costs and gives you some money for your skill and time. How does that sound?'

'OK.' Angel nodded.

Angel fetched a stepladder and they fixed the bunting back onto the shed within ten minutes. Bo helped her clear away the broken pots and soil and Angel said her son had offered to mow the lawn even though she usually did it herself.

Bo left, wishing she could do more than be a good listener and supply food. It didn't seem anywhere near enough.

Chapter Fifteen

When Saturday rolled around, Bo was enjoying an evening with the Flingers. In an ideal world, they'd always be dancing to a live band – especially when they were at an event – but for cost and convenience, they usually had to make do with recorded music, sometimes from streaming services but mostly from vinyl – which was where Ran came into his own.

He was behind the decks, headphones clamped to one ear, making sure the music sounded perfect. Bo thought nothing sounded as authentic and rich as a vintage vinyl played on a record player. With all its imperfections, and the aura of the original recording, the vinyl records gave a unique flavour and energy to the room.

She'd already danced with four different partners of all ages when Hubert asked her to join him in a fast-paced version of 'Boogie Woogie Santa Claus' by Patti Page. The switch between partners was a mental and physical challenge in itself, let alone trying different dances.

'Thanks, but I'll sit this one out,' she said, securing some escaped tendrils of hair under her ponytail. It was a mild autumn evening and the heat generated by a dozen couples bopping enthusiastically to some of the tunes from the Christmas playlist had turned the community hall into a sauna. It was a little strange to be dancing to Christmas songs so far ahead of the festive season though they had to start practising early.

'Not like you to wimp out, Bo,' Hubert said, grinning.

'Busy week,' she said. 'The café's been packed and I had two tour parties for picnic teas. I'm knackered. That's my excuse anyway.'

'Come on, I'm twice your age and I've not sat down.' Hubert's wife Sally joined them, rocking a musical note print skirt, with a blue top and matching underskirt.

'You and Hubert are professionals and you're much fitter than me. And besides, nothing would give me greater pleasure than seeing you two boogie woogie.'

'Next dance, then?' Hubert said.

Bo nodded. 'You bet!'

Sipping her water, she marvelled from the sidelines as Hubert took to the floor with Sally. Their energy was phenomenal as they boogied to the vintage track that had first been issued in the late forties. The turns, spins and changes of hands, the triple steps, the changing places were super fast – and they did it all with a smile on their faces.

Ran was jigging away behind the decks too, much to Bo's amusement.

They ended with a lift that drew whoops of delight from the rest of the Flingers.

'Whoa! Way to go!' Bo called and whistled.

Applause rang out and Hubert and Sally gave a bow.

The song ended and Ran announced a break before joining Bo. He'd shared the proposed playlists with Hubert and Sally and they all chatted about the music. Tonight was a 'taster session' of the music, to get people in the mood and to see the reaction to the music.

'I could do with a cold drink,' Ran said.

'Great idea,' Bo said, walking with him to the kitchen area off the side of the main hall. After they'd grabbed a drink, Hubert took him aside while Sally spoke to Bo.

'You were really rocking that last track,' Bo said to Sally who was a little pink-cheeked but hardly out of breath.

'Thanks. I love that one. I haven't danced boogie woogie for ages.'

'You could have fooled me.'

'Have you heard from Angel?' Sally asked.

Bo related a heavily edited version of her visit to Angel from earlier in the week.

Sally sighed. 'Hmm. I was wondering whether to ask her to help with putting together our costumes, or at least give her opinion. It would be great to have a festive theme and I thought it might help to take her mind off things for a while.'

'It's a good plan,' Bo said. 'I asked if she'd be coming back but she said she couldn't face it for now.'

'That's understandable,' Sally replied. 'I hope she'll change her mind eventually. I can understand she doesn't want to face a mass of people yet. It must be bad enough going to work every day and seeing the customers. I wish I could get my hands on that Tommy. I always thought he was a wastrel, but she worshipped him.'

'I think she might be coming round to a different point of view,' Bo said. 'It's tough when you realise someone isn't who you thought they were . . . Even tougher when they've been living a lie for so long, like Tommy has.'

Sally's eyes were on stalks. 'She knows who he's with, then?'

'No – though she's suggested a couple of names. They're mainly other fishermen's partners or exes, so they mean nothing to me.'

'Hmm. I've heard rumours but I've tried not to fuel them,' Sally said. 'And I'll keep it that way until Angel chooses to tell me more.'

When one of the other members called Sally away, Bo refilled her glass from the drinks dispenser before the music started again.

They danced some more and then Hubert called everyone together to make a final decision on the music. There was a brief but heated discussion and Sally said she'd email a poll so everyone could vote.

At the forthcoming Illuminations performance, four couples would be performing two dances each, so that no one had too many dances to learn. They weren't going to be coordinated like *Strictly* professionals. That wasn't rock and roll style, because every couple had their own way of dancing but they still needed to practise with their partners. One of the things Bo loved about rock and roll was that you didn't necessarily have to have the same dance partner all the time. While many duos were partners in real life, it was common to be asked to dance by any member of your group.

However, the performances had to be planned more carefully than the usual 'free for all' nights at the Flingers to avoid people bumping into each other during the more enthusiastic moves.

At the end of the evening, Sally found Bo again.

'The Illuminations are the second Saturday in December – that's still a couple of months away and, while it seems like we have plenty of time, we could really do with knowing who's dancing as soon as possible,' Sally said. 'We need to plan the programme and timing and make sure every couple who wants to has a chance. Angel's a great dancer and we want a mix of ages. I really hope she'll join in.'

'I'll ask her again but don't get your hopes up,' Bo said.

The Flingers began to drift away. Bo stayed to help restore the community hall kitchen to order while Cade helped Ran load his kit into his van.

Leaving others to lock up, she went outside. It was a fine night, the sky peppered with stars and a tiny sliver of moon hanging over the horizon. Ran was still by his van, chatting to Hubert. Bo's car was parked next to his. Hubert wished her a goodnight but Ran lingered by the van, waiting for her.

'How do you think it went?' he asked her.

'Pretty well. They seemed to like the music choices.'

'I'm glad I had your feedback. I might have gone for something a bit too obscure but now I see it was better to get them rocking in the aisles.'

She laughed. 'I thought we came up with a good mixture of classics and something different. That "Boogie Woogie" track is fantastic, though it's too fast for me – some of the others could do that one.'

'It's great, isn't it? First issued in 1948.'

'It's still a real corker,' Bo agreed.

'Though it seems a bit weird to be dancing to Christmas tunes in September . . .' Ran said.

'I agree but there are already Christmas puddings on sale in the post office,' Bo said. 'And I'm already trying out some recipes for the café and looking for new ideas at my suppliers.'

'I must admit Christmas passed me by in London,' Ran said. 'I was always too busy working.'

'What did you do?'

'I was an economic analyst for an investment bank – I won't bore you with any further details than that.'

'Doesn't sound boring to me.'

'Trust me, I'm glad to be out of it,' he went on briskly. 'I need to go to Falmouth on Wednesday to drop an outdoor amp off at the repair centre. I thought I'd call in at the vintage record shop – Coastal Sounds. I, um, wondered if you'd like to come with me? If you're not working?'

Bo was too surprised to speak, but Ran filled the gap.

'I thought it was your day off. I'm running a course first thing but I'm free by half-past ten. Obviously, I totally understand if you have a hundred better ways of spending your day off than mooching around dusty old racks of vinyl.'

He made it sound like a penance, even though Bo suspected it was Ran's idea of heaven.

'Mmm.' She pretended to give it hard thought. 'I ought to power wash the decking at the café . . .'

He nodded solemnly. 'Of course. Power washing trumps record buying.'

'Though I suppose I could do that another day.'

His eyes glinted as he realised she was, actually, teasing him. 'I could help you with the power washing another day, as recompense for coming with me?' he said. 'I don't want to put you on the spot though.'

'OK, it's a deal.' She wanted to spend more time with Ran even if it was what she'd promised herself not to do; but as with most things in life, temptation got the better of her.

'I did wonder if we could grab a bite to eat afterwards. There's a new café opening on Gyllyngvase beach – it's owned by an uncle of my boss at the dive centre.'

'Oh yes, I saw that in the local paper. Gylly Café? I didn't think it had opened yet.'

'Not officially, but they're doing a soft opening at lunchtime as a trial run. If you fancied it, we could drop off the amp, call in at the record shop and then have a spot of lunch?'

'That sounds . . . good,' Bo said, so taken aback by the invitation that she didn't have time to think whether she wanted to go or not.

'Great. Shall I call for you at eleven? Gives me time to change and come back?'

'Yes. Yes, OK,' she said.

'See you on Wednesday, then.'

With a nod, Ran walked off. She returned to her car, with a quick glance that showed him busy shifting the rest of the equipment to his van.

He hadn't looked exactly thrilled when she'd accepted – quite serious in fact. Maybe he was nervous about having asked her – expecting her to say no, and possibly regretting it? She was still in two minds herself. Of course, it would be good to know him better, but the alarm bells were very much still sounding, albeit muffled . . . like the Runnel Stone bell warning her.

Chapter Sixteen

Bo had a brisk day at the café on Sunday and she and Cade opened specially on Monday morning to serve coffee and cake to a group on a folklore shop tour.

She recognised a few of the party, as some were regulars, though others were clearly from further afield, judging by their accents. Oriel, the folklore shop owner and tour guide, planned to have coffee with them before leading them up to Cornish Magick where they'd hopefully spend some money. It made Bo smile to see how Oriel, who was only in her early twenties, had taken over the failing shop and turned it into a thriving business.

She was bouncing with energy as usual. 'Thanks, Bo,' she said, joining her behind the counter. 'That was awesome.'

'You're welcome. Thank you for the custom. Am I right in thinking that was the last tour of the year?'

'It was going to be but I'm doing a couple for Hallowe'en now, if you're up for it?'

'I'd love to. Do you want themed drinks and cakes?' Bo offered.

'That'd be amazing.'

'Great. I'll work on a menu for you.'

Bo surveyed the eclectic mix of tourists sitting at the tables comparing notes on the ancient sites they'd visited. Oriel spun a good tale about the legends associated with the stone circles and mysterious moorland pools, even if some of it was heavily embellished for the sake of entertainment.

'They look happy enough. Interesting mix, as usual.'

'Yeah. Had my hands full with a couple of 'em. One bloke's a retired history teacher and that woman in the purple hat writes erotic novels set in the Iron Age.' Oriel rolled her eyes.

Bo burst out laughing. 'Wow. Now that *is* niche.'

Oriel's grin melted and she frowned, counting under her breath. 'One of 'em's gone AWOL. There are meant to be thirteen and I can only see twelve.'

'I guessed someone hadn't turned up,' Bo said.

'Oh, they all turned up, but one of the women is missing.' Oriel shrugged. 'She got off the minibus. I'll go and check the public loos when I get this lot back to the shop.'

'Do you want a takeout box with a couple of cakes in it for her?'

'Great idea. Odd woman, kept herself to herself. She didn't seem that old, but she had one of them funny headscarves on. You know, like the old royals wear.'

Bo laughed and a vision of Madame Odette popped into her mind. A strange woman in a headscarf on a folklore tour . . . it had to be a coincidence.

'Um, this woman. Do you know her name?'

'I think it's Bunty or Binky something and she has a hyphen-ated surname.'

'You're joking?' Bo burst out laughing.

'I can check if you like after I've done the tour. Though I shouldn't really. Data protection and all that,' Oriel said solemnly.

'No need. I was only curious. You go and track her down.'

Oriel saluted. 'Will do!'

Oriel marshalled the rag-tag of tourists, ushering them along the lane to the footbridge that led to the other side of the estuary. While clearing up with Cade, Bo tried to spot the head-scarfed, double-barrelled mystery woman but soon gave up. The chances of it being Madame Odette were next to zero; she didn't even know why she'd thought it might be.

She closed up, relenting only to serve coffees to the Morvah Marine staff who were delighted to find her open unexpectedly on a Monday morning.

She spent the next day clearing mundane jobs like her accounts out of the way so she could enjoy her day out without any guilt. On Tuesday she also met up with her cinema friends again, resisting the temptation to mention she had a date. Could she call it a date? Mooching around a shop probably didn't count but lunch at a smart restaurant probably did.

She also had a message from Angel.

Might brave Flingers the Saturday after next. Miss you all. A x

'Thank goodness for that,' Bo murmured to herself. The prospect of Angel returning to Flingers was a major step in the right direction. That was simple.

As for Ran – that was way more complicated. Every time she realised how much she was looking forward to their outing, she reminded herself that she shouldn't be. She enjoyed his company and wanted to know more about him; more than was wise. If she hadn't accepted his invitation, she'd never know what lay beneath the enigmatic exterior.

But why did it still feel a dangerous thing to do?

* * *

'Bo! Glad I caught you.'

Ran sounded breathless on the end of the phone on Wednesday morning.

'Ran? What's up?'

'Nothing. Well, everything's OK now but there's a change of plan.'

'Oh?' She tried not to sound too disappointed, which made her realise just how much she was. So much for trying to curb her enthusiasm about their day out.

'We've had a problem with one of the dive students,' Ran went on. 'He's OK but he panicked underwater and had a bit of a scare. The paramedics have taken him for a check-up but I'm running late as a result. I'm still on the dive boat. Is there any chance you could drive over so we can get a head start?'

Instantly perked up, Bo readily agreed. 'That makes a lot of sense. The dive centre's on the way and I was going to suggest it when you first mentioned the trip.'

'Thanks, but I wanted to do the driving so you could enjoy a glass of wine at the restaurant. They're meant to have a great list. I'm sorry that things have worked out this way.' He sounded relieved.

'It's no problem. I can come over right away.'

She heard voices calling Ran.

'Sorry. Must go. See you in a mo.'

Having thought the trip was off, Bo wasn't at all disappointed to have to drive. She scooped up her keys and was on her way within a minute. It was only a ten-minute journey to the centre which was situated in a small cove by the side of the estuary. When she arrived, the dive boat was alongside the quay and Ran was talking to a couple of other people.

He spotted her and met her in front of the centre.

Bo took a long, deep breath.

His wetsuit was peeled down low on his waist and he was holding a pair of blue fins in one hand. She'd known he was lean and strong, but the full glory of that toned torso was almost too much to take. She should have realised that all the physical exertion of diving and the constant shifting of heavy tanks would give anyone a great body but . . . *wow*.

With the wet blond hair, a fading tan and a white line visible where the wetsuit ended and dangerous territory began, he made Bo's legs go ever so slightly wobbly.

'Hi there. Sorry about this.' He dropped the fins in a tank of water.

'It's f-fine,' she said, trying to focus on his eyes, which was a mistake because that cornflower blue was having the same effect as the bare torso. He had tattoos too, which she hadn't expected. A small compass design above his left nipple and one on his right bicep.

'H-how's the dive student?'

'He's OK. I think it was a panic attack. Extremely unpleasant for him but he'll be fine.'

'Good. Good . . .' Bo cursed herself. She was tongue-tied and realised she must be openly ogling his body.

'I'll have a lightning-quick shower to wash all the salt off so we can get on our way.'

'That sounds fantastic,' Bo said, unable to thrust the image of a naked Viking from her mind. She was in deep, deep trouble. 'I mean, good idea. I'll, um, wait here, answer a few emails while you get changed.'

'Excellent. Back in ten minutes.'

He went into the centre, treating her to a view of his broad shoulders – with another tattoo between the shoulder blades – and the tan line visible where the wetsuit was rolled down.

Bo tried really hard to scroll through her emails, though it was hard to concentrate on the messages from her accountant, the gas bottle supplier and the latest hygiene bulletin from the local council.

Ten minutes later, Ran came out dressed in jeans and a sweatshirt – much to her relief and, secretly, her disappointment.

'OK. I've let Luke, our centre manager, know you'll be leaving your van here and we can be off.'

She nodded, still shellshocked at her physical reaction to seeing him half-naked. She hadn't thought she could still experience such a powerful attraction to a guy. She'd thought Hamish had well and truly inoculated her against that. Clearly not.

'Damn. Left my van keys in the office.'

Bo hung about watching some of the other staff stacking tanks and throwing wetsuits into troughs of water. Another man, weaselly and dressed in a three-piece suit, walked onto the quay and stared at her. He had a document bag slung around his chest and looked very like the man from the council who'd come to inspect her kitchen. Same thin moustache like a caterpillar had crawled under his nose and decided to shrivel up and die there.

She had to suppress a snigger but she also didn't like the way he was staring at her.

Fortunately Ran walked out of the centre door.

'Ran!' A chestnut-haired man popped his head round the door. 'Can you take a call?'

Ran turned. 'Is it a matter of life and death?'

'No, someone wanting to know if you'll lead a night dive next week. I can put them off if you've other plans?'

'Thanks, Luke. I do,' he called back, shaking his head before joining Bo. He jangled his keys. 'OK, I think we're finally good to go.'

Relieved that they were ready to head off, Bo caught sight of the weaselly man with the caterpillar moustache, who was staring at them from the quayside in front of the dive centre. Maybe he was plucking up the courage to book a lesson, she thought, or just nosy. Either way, he gave her the creeps.

'Think it's a good idea,' she said. They'd set off along the quay to the car park when there was a call from behind.

'Can I have a word, please?'

Ran turned and the weaselly man trotted up, breathing a little heavily. Bo shuddered.

'You work here, don't you?' the man said.

'Yes,' Ran answered with a polite smile. 'Though if you want to book a dive, you'll have to make your way through to the centre. I'm off duty now.'

'I'm afraid I'm not here to book a dive.' He smirked. 'You *are* Ranulph Larsen of Creekside Cottage, Falford?'

'Yes, that's me, but . . .' Ran stared at him. 'Do I know you?'

'I work for Carnell's Solicitors in London. However, I have now identified you, Mr Larsen, and, due to your failure to acknowledge your spouse Phaedra Larsen's divorce petition, I'm obliged to serve the petition personally on you and advise you that if you don't return it within seven days, we'll start proceedings without you.'

Grinning broadly as if he'd just offered Ran a large bouquet of roses, he whipped a large envelope from his bag and thrust it into Ran's hands. 'Here are the papers. I note you've taken delivery of them. Have a very good afternoon, Mr Larsen.'

Chapter Seventeen

Ran had thought that the day Phaedra had asked him to leave the flat was the most humiliating moment of his life, closely followed by the day the record dealer had carted off his collection while his wife stood by him at the lock-up, face white with horror at the number of discs he'd managed to amass.

The look on Bo's face – shock and disgust – meant he'd topped those two lowlights by a long way today.

The process server had scuttled off like a centipede the moment Ran had the package in his hands. Clearly he was used to making a quick exit once his deed was done, in case of repercussions.

Ran was too stunned to have given any kind of response, and the guy, however odious he was, was merely doing his job.

It was entirely Ran's own fault; he'd started to fill the forms in after Bo had visited but then put off returning them.

He stared at the papers in his hands. Jesus, he should have responded sooner. He'd vaguely registered he had a couple of weeks to reply but he'd kept putting it off and somehow the time had flown by.

'I'm so sorry about that,' he said to Bo, who was staring after the guy as he jumped into his car and screeched out the car park, spraying up gravel. 'It was excruciating.'

'Can he even do that?' she said slowly.

Ran winced in shame. 'I think so. I guess he just did.'

'Fancy coming after you here, though – to your workplace in front of your friends.'

'Yes . . .'

She looked him full in the face, her dark brown eyes puzzled and, God forgive him, hurt. Even Bo, with her happy-go-lucky facade, couldn't hide her shock.

'I didn't know you were married,' she said simply.

'I should have told you.' His voice trailed off.

'You didn't mention a wife or partner. I suppose I assumed you were single.'

He sank lower, crushed with embarrassment. 'Technically, I am. We're separated. She lives in our flat in London.' He corrected himself. 'Her flat now, I suppose . . . I . . .' He faltered, unable to think of any simple way to say that he had spent a considerable chunk of their savings on things they couldn't afford. Unable to explain that he had probably suffered a mental breakdown but that was no excuse for the way he'd plunged headlong into a lifestyle that had made both of them miserable.

'It's complicated but I didn't want to leave Phaedra in debt. I, um . . . you know you asked me if I had any valuable records? I did have some rare stuff at one time, in fact I had far too many. It was that kind of expensive indulgence that got me into trouble in the first place. I had to sell anything really valuable to pay off my wife.'

Bo's lips were pressed together.

'So, I got rid of all the expensive stuff. Most of the vinyl you saw are bootlegs, barely worth the price of a coffee. I only pay pocket money prices now and I buy far fewer. Hoarding records I couldn't really afford was an addiction, the same as the expensive lunches, the clubs, the champagne, the weekends away . . . that's why I packed in my job in the City at the bank. It was making me ill and the way I behaved played a big part in wrecking my marriage.'

'I'm sorry. Sounds like you were under a lot of stress.'

'Yes but . . .' he swallowed hard, reminding himself that he had specifically invited her to go with him to buy records. How must that look when he'd just confessed to an addiction?

'I'm sorry,' he said. 'You came here for a fun day out, not to witness that bloody spectacle. There's nothing more tragic than some bloke moaning about his ex on a date with another woman – unless he's visited by a bailiff serving him with divorce papers, I suppose,' he said, going for humour, while dying of shame at the public humiliation of being hunted down by a process server and of having allowed the situation to get so far.

'You haven't moaned, and you had no idea that guy would turn up at your workplace,' she said. 'But I think maybe today isn't the best time for us to do this. You probably need time to sort this out. It looks like those papers are urgent. I'm sorry we can't make the restaurant. I hope your friend won't mind?'

By which she meant, he thought, that she wanted to get the hell away from a man with a problematic love life who hadn't been entirely honest with her about his situation. She definitely didn't need 'It's complicated.'

He also recognised he'd been too hellbent on keeping his private life private – or was his reluctance to be open with Bo, and to sign those papers, part of more serious issue: that deep down he still wasn't ready to accept his marriage was over?

'I'll deal with the restaurant,' he said, wondering what he could say to his mate, although it was the least of his worries. 'You're right, I don't think either of us is in the right frame of mind for a cosy lunch or a record-buying trip.'

'No. No.' Bo's smile was fleeting and awkward and he didn't blame her. 'Perhaps not today.'

She drove off, leaving Ran on the quayside, the papers in his hand, wondering how he'd found someone he cared about for the second time in his life and managed to balls everything up before it had even started.

Chapter Eighteen

*M*arried.
   Ran was *married*.

Bo still couldn't help thinking about the bombshell a week later as she checked the café after fierce autumn gales had caused them to remain closed on a Sunday morning. It had been too dangerous to open, with twigs flying about. The chairs and tables were intact, but only because she'd lashed them down under a tarpaulin with Cade's help the night before. Other businesses hadn't fared so well. The wind had blown some slates off the roof of Falford post office, narrowly missing the postwoman as she came to collect the mail. The plans to start refurbishing the terrace were on hold, although ironically, the weather highlighted the need for a sheltered space even more.

At least the turbulent weather matched her mood.

She hadn't seen or spoken with Ran since the disaster outside the dive centre. He'd sent her a message saying he'd cancelled the lunch reservation and apologising again, but nothing else. He also didn't turn up to Flingers on the Saturday evening, passing on a message via Hubert that he was busy.

She couldn't help wondering if it was an excuse not to see her because he was still embarrassed. Being honest, it must have been an excruciating situation for him, and yet.

He was *married*?

If he'd been straight with her from the start, she would have understood but she felt he'd been actively evasive and even secretive. She'd known him a year – even if they weren't close, he might have mentioned it.

Perhaps, more importantly, despite all his protestations, and the divorce petition, it was obvious that Ran was very much part of the relationship. Divorce was a tumultuous process and he still seemed very attached to his wife, otherwise why hadn't he responded to her divorce petition?

The situation had occupied Bo's mind far too much and yet she couldn't shake it off, and her mood wasn't helped by the thick grey clouds hanging over Falford with no intention of leaving anytime soon.

She decided to take herself off to see Angel at the Country Stores, which had been able to open. She planned to buy some hardier plants to replace the summer bedding at the café. The flower baskets and tubs had been trashed by the storm and she needed something fresh as autumn slid into winter. Her main motive, however, was to see how Angel was getting on and hopefully brighten both of their days.

On the way, she wondered if the process server's visit had been noted by anyone at the dive centre. Even if people had witnessed the weasel speaking to Ran, no one had been near enough to overhear, surely?

The Country Stores were located a few miles out of Falford, near a crossroads on the main road. It had started as a place for farmers and horse owners to buy animal feed and supplies but had evolved into a more general shopping destination that attracted as many holidaymakers as farmers. Angel's job title was administrator but, for all intents and purposes, she practically managed the place.

With the rain lashing down, Bo dashed from her car, across the yard area towards the large warehouse-like shed that housed the supplies and equipment. One side of it had a 'trade entrance' but Bo was heading for the 'posh bit', as Angel called it.

Here, the equestrian area stocked trendy outdoor gear from designers alongside the riding boots and harnesses. Several smaller concessions had also opened up, including a boutique stocked with country-themed gifts and cards and a small deli.

The garden centre was situated to the rear, sheltered by a covered area, which was fortunate as Bo's hair was already damp merely from the sprint from car to store.

A handful of customers were inside on this stormy day. A woman in riding gear was trying on a quilted jacket for size and a slender blonde in an oversized Barbour coat and matching hat was browsing the racks of cards. Angel was stationed at the main cash counter, which had an office with glass windows behind it where a few other staff worked. There was no sign of Kelvin, her boss, which was fine by Bo as it meant she could have a chat without him hovering nearby.

Angel's face lit up when she caught sight of Bo and she waved.

'Hello! This is a surprise!' she said when Bo reached the desk.

'I need some new plants and pots for the café but I thought I'd drop by to see how you are. I'm not disturbing you, am I?'

'No, no. We're quiet this morning. The rain's keeping the tourists inside, not that there are so many about now October's here. It's only the hardy regulars who've ventured out.' She nodded at the equestrian area on the other side of the store. The horsey woman had obviously decided against the jacket and was disappearing through the front doors. The card lady was still twirling the rack.

'Is *he* around?' Bo asked, referring to Kelvin.

Angel rolled her eyes. 'He said he was going to see his accountant in Helston but . . .' She lowered her voice. 'I think he was off to play golf.'

'In this weather?'

Angel smirked. 'He'll probably head straight for the nineteenth hole.'

'It's all right for some,' Bo said. 'I came to see how you are. Sally asked me how you're getting on.'

'Did she?' Angel sighed. 'I'm OK. The kids aren't round so much. There's still no word from Tommy.'

'I'm sorry.'

'I'm having to face up to the fact I'm on my own and there's nothing I can do about it.' She had to raise her voice as the rain pounded the roof as if a helicopter was coming into land.

'He can't leave you like that. Have you thought you might need to get advice?' Bo tried to keep her voice low.

'About a divorce, you mean?'

'Not necessarily.' Bo thought of Ran and the trouble he'd got himself into. She didn't want to frighten Angel but she was aware that Tommy might even now have seen a solicitor and it would be horrible if Angel suddenly received a letter like Ran had. 'I only wondered if you might like to get some guidance on where you stand . . . legally.'

'I have been thinking about making an appointment at the Citizens Advice Bureau. God, there's so much to do . . . mind

149

you, I'm used to dealing with everything myself anyway, with him being at sea for so long, but the thought that it is only me – for good – is terrifying.'

Bo nodded sympathetically.

'Oh, there's a customer coming over,' Angel murmured. 'I'd better deal with him.'

'OK. I'll go and choose my plants. See you in a minute.'

Rain drummed down on the polycarbonate roof of the covered garden area, swooshing off the roof and flowing down the drains. The wind drove sheets of water across the outdoor displays, and thick mist obscured the fields beyond the perimeter fence. In weather like this, with the days rapidly closing in, who wouldn't feel down? Even the thought of Christmas events couldn't cheer Bo up, with their past and present associations.

Normally, she relished the chance to do even fewer hours at the café and enjoy the breathing space after the busy summer. Now she almost longed for the breathless bustle of the peak season, no time to stop and think. Falling asleep the moment her head hit the pillow, body and mind completely spent.

This was no good . . . she found a trolley, and focused her attention on the bright yellows and violets of pansies, and the fresh green of trailing ivy. The café was her livelihood and it deserved some TLC. For a little while, she lost herself in choosing plants, pots and hanging baskets. Finally, with a trolley full of cheery colour, she returned to the counter.

'Oh, they're lovely,' Angel said, putting them through the till for Bo.

'I thought they'd brighten up the seating area by the waterside.'

'They'll be beautiful right through to March if you water them.'

'You think? I hope so. The café needs cheering up as the dark nights draw in.' *Me too*, thought Bo, but the last thing Angel needed was her moping and she certainly wasn't going to share what had happened at the dive centre.

She paid for her flowers and, as it still seemed quiet in the Stores, stayed for a longer natter.

'I've finished your bunting and tea towel order,' Angel said, chatting away while tidying up some petals from around the till.

'Wow. That was quick.' Bo could picture the piles of fabric and hear the whirr of the machine, Angel lost in a whirl of frantic activity.

'I enjoyed doing it. It takes my mind off all the other stuff. You can come and collect them any time you like. I'd have brought them in to work, if I'd known you were dropping by.'

'I'm happy to pop round.'

'Why don't you come one evening? I'll make you some dinner . . . give you a break from the kitchen.'

'I'd love to,' Bo said. There was still no one near the counter so she took her chance. 'Are you still planning to come to Flingers on Saturday?'

'I wanted to. Adam and Emma say I should. Now I'm not so sure.'

'We all miss you,' Bo said gently, trying to tread a line between encouragement but not pressuring her friend.

'I still feel awkward. People will ask so many questions and I don't have answers myself, let alone to them. On the other hand, I really miss Flingers, I miss my friends and the company and music. That's one thing. I can play "Rock Around the Clock" as loud as I want, whenever I want, with no Tommy to worry about. I always felt I couldn't listen to it when he was at home. He said he came home for a "bit of peace and quiet".'

'Oh?'

'I couldn't blame him. I wanted to talk to him and he needed a rest so I never played it when he was at home.' Angel had a wistful expression, then she said, 'But I bloody well play it now. I turned the volume up full and streamed it through the kitchen window when I was repairing the lock on the shed! He was always promising to "get round to it" and he never did so I had a go myself.'

'Good for you. Look, I'd never push you but you might like to know that we've all agreed a playlist for the Illuminations and the Christmas Spectacular. We used some of the songs you suggested and had a vote on it.'

'I bet some people moaned! I bet I know who.' Angel rolled her eyes.

'Of course.' Bo grinned. 'Obviously a few aren't happy but I think we've found a mix of songs everyone can live with and we're ready to rehearse.' Mentally she crossed her fingers, hoping Angel would take the bait.

'It sounds wonderful. Will you send me the playlist?'

'You can hear it yourself if you come on Saturday night.'

Angel hitched a tiny breath. 'True.'

She held her head high and set her mouth in a determined line that heartened Bo. However, a moment later her eyes narrowed and she whispered, 'It's Kelvin. I'd better get back to work.'

Bo turned to see Kelvin march in, golf umbrella in one hand, a phone clamped to his ear with the other. He shoved the umbrella in a stand by the door, before stopping by a wheelbarrow display, still barking into his mobile. His voice echoed around the warehouse space.

'Yeah, I can do you a deal, pal. I'll be giving it away, mind, but you're a mate so I'll do you a favour.'

He was wearing a Harris tweed jacket and matching cap, with red chinos and brogues, yet he was only Bo's age.

Bo picked up her flower pot but whispered around the side of it to Angel, 'Who does he think he is? Lord of the manor?'

'He says he needs to look the part. "The Gentleman Farmer" and all that, but his designer stuff is brand new. No real farmer would be seen dead in that kind of fancy gear. If it isn't full of holes and covered in dog hair, they wouldn't touch it.'

Kelvin was now on another call. 'Yeah, just sold him a shed-load of compost. He thinks he got it at cost but I'm making thirty percent on top. Some people are so gullible. Haw-haw. Yeah, mate, see you down the club tomorrow. Shame we couldn't get a round in. Thank God for the nineteenth hole, eh?'

He ended his call with a braying laugh.

'I'd better go,' Bo said hastily. 'Please do come to Flingers, won't you?' Her eyes telegraphed an appeal to Angel, who nodded and immediately started brushing soil from the plants off the counter into a bin. She clearly wanted to look occupied now her boss was on the scene.

Bo headed for the door, crossing paths with Kelvin who nodded at her flowers and grinned. 'Nice blooms, love,' he said with a grin.

Ignoring him, Bo sailed straight past, yet she could still hear him talking to Angel, or *at* Angel. 'Angel. You look like you need something to do. Get onto Mullion Feeds and tell them I want a new order of seed and I want a big discount. Don't let them get away with anything less than twenty percent. They're over-charging us . . .'

'But Kelvin, I already persuaded them to give us a bigger discount than any other customer they deal with and that's only out of goodwill because they know me – I mean, your uncle.'

Kelvin snorted. 'I keep telling you, my uncle's not in charge now. Mullion are taking us for a ride. You can do a lot better than that, from what I heard in the club – in my business meeting – this morning. If anyone calls, I'll be in my office looking at how I can trim some of the fat off this business – and I don't want to be disturbed.' He glared at Angel, as if to imply she might be some of the 'fat'.

Worried she might have to march back to Kelvin and give him a piece of her mind, Bo forced herself to focus on the exit. Luckily, the rain had eased so she managed to deposit the pot and plants into the rear of the van without getting too wet.

'Gah! That man is a Grade A git!' She slammed the doors, seething at Kelvin's treatment of Angel. With Tommy having left, the last thing her friend needed was her boss browbeating her.

Driving home, she thought again about how talented and capable Angel was, both at work and with her 'hobby' – and how unfairly life had treated her of late.

Bo hadn't asked about the extra help with costumes for the Christmas events. She hadn't wanted to add pressure to Angel and there hadn't been time before Kelvin had turned up. She'd sound out Angel when they had dinner together, though they hadn't actually made a date yet.

She drove home through weather that was in two minds about whether to unleash a downpour or let the sun come out. Patches of blue kept opening up and vanishing, with rain bucketing down even as the sun shone, and leaves blown down in the storm filled in the gutters. There was a rainbow over Falford as Bo approached the start of the twisty descent into the village.

Everywhere there were signs autumn was definitely here and local businesses had wasted no time in capitalising on that.

The farm shop was already advertising its Hallowe'en pumpkin carving workshops and urging people to 'Order Your Turkey'. A sign had gone up at the crossroads advertising the Christmas Illuminations at Trewhella House and Garden. The festive season was steamrollering its merry way towards her, whether she liked it or not.

She reached home and phoned her sister which cheered her up, followed by listening to messages from her cinema pals suggesting a showing of *Singing in the Rain*. Bo thought that would be just the tonic she needed. The dancing in that show was out of this world and if ever a movie was designed to cheer people up, that was it. One of the girls was going to book a minibus so they could have a meal and make a night of it.

Cosied up in front of her wood burner with a takeout from the local Indian restaurant, Bo counted her blessings and tried to think positive.

She'd almost nodded off in front of the TV when there was a knock at the door. Wondering who it could be, Bo answered it in a fluffy dressing gown and badger slippers which had been presents from her niece and nephew.

'Evening. Is it too late?'

Ran stood on the doorstep.

'Um, no, not at all. I just wasn't . . . expecting you,' Bo said, cringing at the fact she was wearing her dressing gown.

'I've been to the pub with a couple of the other instructors and I was passing and thought I might have a word with you.' Ran's eyes lingered on her footwear a moment too long and Bo's toes curled.

'Of course, come in,' she said, gesturing through into the hallway.

'If you're sure it's OK?' Ran replied. The damp figure with

his hands shoved in his jacket pockets was hard to square with the confident relaxed man who'd blown her mind at the dive centre – right up until the process server had delivered the unwanted 'surprise'.

'Yes, sure.' She led him into the living room, past a coffee table littered with Indian takeout trays. 'Sorry about the smell . . . I was meaning to put the leftovers in the fridge. I wasn't expecting visitors, hence my, erm . . . attire.'

'Please don't apologise. I quite like badgers.'

'So do I, but not on my feet. My sister's kids gave me them.'

'They have excellent taste in woodland animals.'

Bo laughed softly. He really was a very good-looking guy, which made it all the more frustrating that he was clearly laden with emotional baggage.

'I came over because I wanted to explain.'

'You don't have to.'

'I don't have to but I need to. I won't stay long but it's been driving me mad, wondering what you must think of me. I don't want to make excuses and I'm not looking for sympathy.'

There was a desperation in his eyes she couldn't ignore and, if she was honest, she was as keen to hear about what had led him to Falford as he was to tell her.

'You'd better sit down.'

'Thanks,' he said, dripping water on the sofa. It was the first time he'd ever been in the cottage and he looked awkward and out of place.

'I told you that I used to be an economic analyst for an investment bank, which sounds a lot grander than it actually was. It mostly involved sitting behind a computer, looking at business trends to help the bank make decisions about purchasing and investing.' He gave a wry smile. 'Occasionally,

156

they'd let me out to give a presentation to my bosses, and hope I didn't lose them millions of pounds.'

'Okayyyy . . . but diving and DJing – that's a big change from high finance, to say the least,' Bo said.

'You could say that. I thought it was what I wanted to do, or at least what I wanted to do until I'd made a load of money. I wasn't a hedge fund manager or a trader but I had a very healthy salary and there were bonuses too—' he broke off. 'I worked in Canary Wharf so I did a lot of corporate lunches and dinners with colleagues and clients. I wasn't paying, of course. Not always . . . trouble is, I carried on the lifestyle even when I wasn't expensing it. Phaedra kept threatening to get a lodger in because I was hardly ever home.' The comment was accompanied by a wry smile that faded as soon as it appeared.

He stared at the takeout trays as if they might hold an answer to a terrible dilemma. 'In the end, she was as busy as me. We hardly saw each other.'

'Did you have anything in common, for when you did have time together? Did she like rock and roll too? Or dancing?'

'You're joking!' He laughed out loud then apologised swiftly. 'Sorry, I didn't mean that to sound sarcastic. Phaedra had done some ballet at boarding school and she liked to attend the odd classical concert but that was as far as it went. She even joked about me being "as graceful as a rhino" when I trod on her toes at a work Christmas party. As far as she was aware – still is – my music was yet another pointless and expensive hobby that she didn't understand.'

'Surely she didn't really think that?'

'Almost, but don't get me wrong. I didn't blame her for feeling like that. I created a situation where she didn't feel I was reliable or deserved much respect. As I mentioned at the dive centre,

I'd been working longer and longer hours, trying to climb the greasy pole and staying out with my colleagues and clients most evenings.'

He examined his hands. 'I wasn't gambling but I spent the money as fast as it came in, including the rare records. I bought a fast car we didn't need and I insisted on booking holidays we couldn't really afford too. I thought it was what Phaedra wanted – what I wanted and she deserved.

'The good times came and went and the bonuses dried up. I'd borrowed on my credit card and we had a big mortgage. Phaedra was working hard in another bank's legal department but we were struggling and the bank merged with a much bigger one. They had a cull and started letting people go.' He shook his head. 'That's a better phrase than a "cull", isn't it? It meant the same thing. Anyway, the backroom staff were the first to get the chop and I lost my job, like hundreds of other people.'

Bo could see where this was heading, yet allowed him the time to gather himself again.

'I tried to get another job but no one was hiring. Although I realise I didn't try hard enough; I was burnt-out and spent my time lying around the flat listening to music, according to Phaedra. And she was right. It was the first time since leaving university and joining the bank that I'd had time to stop and listen. I also met up with some old friends from the diving club. We still had the debts and it became clear we'd have to sell the flat. That's when I decided I didn't want to go back to working in the City.'

He couldn't look Bo in the eye.

'Go on,' she urged softly, afraid he might clam up.

'I told Phaedra that I couldn't carry on as I was, and that I was going to retrain as a diving instructor. I said I couldn't stand the burden of the mortgage. She was horrified – rightly – because she was convinced I could get another job with a bank.' He looked really bad.

'And then I did something that finished off our marriage for good.'

Chapter Nineteen

Ran couldn't believe how much he was talking. After so long keeping silent about his private life, the floodgates had opened. Once again, he was pouring out his life story to Bo, almost as if he was deliberately scuppering any slim chance he might still have with her.

It was too late to stop now though – Bo's eyes were intent on him, her lips parted slightly, waiting for the rest of the story. Even in a fluffy dressing gown and badger slippers, he fancied her. In fact, the outfit only seemed to enhance how attractive she was, but that was irrelevant when he was about to tell her how he'd lied to his wife.

'Out of the blue, I was offered a job as an analyst with an investment company. It was almost the same salary and in the City. We could have managed the mortgage and I would probably have been promoted in time. We were still in debt and I knew I should have taken the job.' He stopped to reflect on the moment the phone call came from the head of the department, telling him he'd been successful, congratulating him.

He'd never felt less like celebrating in his life. Even now, his stomach tightened into a knot at the memory of it, the flood of panic at the thought of going back to that lifestyle.

'Ran . . .' Bo's voice broke through, bringing him back to reality. The new reality.

'I turned the job down without telling Phaedra. She didn't even know I'd been offered it. I couldn't face that lifestyle again, not the hours or the pressure – or the temptation to get into that mindset or position again. I was in my mid-thirties and I could see that treadmill stretching on endlessly until I was too old to actually enjoy my life. Phaedra wanted a family too – so did I – but I knew we'd both be working so many hours to support our kids that neither of us would have time for a proper family life. Not the kind I'd enjoyed at home with my parents.'

'I can understand that,' Bo said – very charitably, Ran thought.

'Perhaps, though at the time – and now – I look back on it as wholly selfish,' Ran went on. 'I still wonder if I should have taken the job, gritted my teeth and got on with it. Instead, I decided not to tell Phaedra about the offer and hit on a way of making it up to her. In my mind, I was doing the right thing for both of us by not accepting the job and paying off the debts I'd run up.'

He fiddled nervously with the set of keys he'd dropped on the sofa.

'How?' Bo said.

'You know I told you I'd got into rock and roll because of my grandad? Well, I also inherited his record collection. I'd always suspected some of it was pretty rare though I'd not registered how valuable it was. I found a dealer and sold the lot, plus my own expensive purchases. Together, I made enough to pay off the debts I'd run up and the surplus went a little way to making up the salary I'd turned down, for a few months at least.'

'So, you were back where you started?' she asked.

'Financially, almost, though not in other ways. The damage had been done. To be fair to Phaedra, she had mixed feelings about me selling the records. She felt sorry for me but was "proud" of me. I think she expected it to be the catalyst for a change of heart that would lead to the old Ran resurging, now that I'd had "a good break" and some time to enjoy my "hobbies".'

He laughed bitterly. 'Unfortunately, she couldn't have been more wrong and that made me feel even guiltier. I knew I'd never go back to my own lifestyle. I'd qualified as a diving instructor and started to get some freelance work that meant I could do a salvage diving course. I got fitter – I had to. Being in the water and doing physical work was what I loved, not sitting in some tower block for twelve hours a day, out schmoozing clients every night.'

He put his keys down on the table, between the foil trays. 'Sorry. This isn't painting me in a good light. Not that I've covered myself in glory lately.'

'I'd rather you were honest. Did you try to tell Phaedra how you really felt about work?'

'Occasionally but she tried to jolly me along, and would tell me I'd be fine once I got back on the horse, so to speak.' He sighed. 'In the end, I simply buried my head in the sand, carried on working freelance for the dive company and she assumed I was still looking for a proper job. I did try to persuade her to think about a change of lifestyle – moving down here or to Devon, for instance, where I could get a full-time job and maybe even set up my own business.'

'And?'

162

'She wasn't interested and I knew I wasn't being fair. She loved her job and she didn't want to move. And then the whole thing blew up.' He rubbed his hand over his eyes. 'Phaedra found out that I'd turned down the "dream job".'

'Ah . . .' Bo winced, as if she could picture the scene as well as he could. Phaedra thumping home, screaming at him. He'd taken every word like the blow he'd deserved.

'It's a small world and unbeknown to me she'd put the word out for me, asking if anyone had anything,' he told Bo, determined to hold nothing back. 'One day she had lunch with a client she hadn't seen for months. She asked if there was anything for me . . . it turned out the client was one of the HR people on the interview panel. She told Phaedra I'd turned a job down. I hadn't even told her I was being interviewed. I didn't want the pressure or to disappoint her.'

'Oh dear . . .' Bo let out a breath, 'I bet that was a shock to her.'

'You can say that again.' Ran's stomach turned over, recalling the moment that Phaedra had told him about the conversation, that she knew he'd lied and thrown away the chance for them to have a normal life, that he'd lost her trust, and hurt her more with his lies than with his refusal to get a real job.

He'd tried to explain that he hadn't wanted to let her down but he couldn't face 'a proper job and normal life', as she'd put it. He'd tried to suggest that there were millions of 'proper jobs and normal lives' that didn't involve hating every minute and selling your soul.

'I should have tried harder to help her understand how I felt. I should have been honest about turning down the job. But it was too late. I'd lost her trust, destroyed the last shred of her faith in me. That was the end.'

'I'm sorry this happened,' Bo said, rather mechanically. She seemed stunned and Ran didn't blame her. He knew he didn't look good in anyone's eyes, least of all his own.

'Me too. Our paths had diverged and there was only one way it was going to end. So, in February last year, I moved out. I decided to get as far away from London – from my old life – as possible.'

As far away from Phaedra too, he didn't need to add. Would Bo fill that gap in?

'Sounds like I ran away, doesn't it? I suppose I did.'

'You could look at it as making a fresh start.'

'That's very generous of you.'

'I'm being honest too. Do you regret moving away from London down here?'

'No. Not in most ways. I don't miss the stress; I don't miss the corporate lunches or the concrete . . .'

He didn't need to speak to fill the pause that followed. He could not say that he didn't miss his wife because he did.

He stopped, aware that he'd said more to Bo in the past fifteen minutes than he had to anyone since he'd left London.

Did it feel cathartic, this unburdening of his soul? It ought to, and yet it also felt self-indulgent.

'I've gone and done it again, haven't I?' he said, holding her gaze direct in his.

'Done what?'

'Ruined an evening with you.'

She shrugged. 'You needed to tell me and I'm glad you have.'

'I wanted to try and wipe the slate clean between us. I came here in the hope that if I was honest, brutally honest about what I did, you might start to trust me again.'

'It's not a question of trust, Ran. It's a question of me not wanting to be involved with someone who's still . . .' She was clearly measuring her words. 'Still, understandably, attached to their previous partner.'

'I've sent the papers back,' he said. 'I filled in the form that evening and sent it registered the next morning. There's no going back now. Phaedra can apply for the decree nisi and we'll be officially divorced by Christmas.'

'Oh. I am sorry – for you both.'

'Me too, but I have to stop feeling sorry for me and for Phaedra and look to the future. On that note, I've spoken to my friend at the restaurant and he says he'd be happy to invite us again on the same terms, though I insist on paying the full bill. It's the least I can do.'

Her smile was still full of hesitancy.

'I suppose what I really want to ask is, will you give me another chance?' he said. '*Please?*'

She sighed. 'Hmm. Will it involve record buying too?'

'Only if you want it to, though after what I've told you tonight, maybe we should steer clear of that.'

'Ran, I'm really not sure this is the right time for us . . .' she said.

He nodded, a lump forming in his throat. He had blown things.

'On the other hand, I respect the fact you have come over and cleared the air and that you've been honest with me. A fresh start – or at least a rewind – might be a good idea . . .'

'I do hope so. That's why I came, to be brutally honest about what happened and hope we can reset the clock.'

'I know what you mean . . .' She sounded wistful, hesitant. Ran felt he was teetering on a precipice. His fate was in her hands and he had to accept what she decided.

'OK.' She nodded and even smiled. 'If we never try, we'll never know. I'd like to give lunch another go.'

He just about managed not to punch the air and shout 'Yay!', contenting himself with: 'That's great.'

'Besides . . .' Bo added. 'There's a vintage boutique next to Coastal Sounds that I love. I think I should be there to keep you from buying up all the stock in the record shop.'

He laughed, mostly with relief at not being kicked out on his arse. He could barely believe he'd been given a second chance and coming clean about the past was a giant weight lifted from his shoulders.

'Sounds like a very good idea. Let's fix a time.'

Chapter Twenty

Ran's outpouring of emotion about his past and eagerness to make amends had left Bo a mix of moved and uneasy. Her head said she should walk away from this complex man but her heart had got the better of her. Didn't it always?

The following Monday, however, she was still on edge when he picked her up in his van from the Falford village car park. Unlike her own Citroën Berlingo, which was liveried with the Boatyard Café logo, the Transit was grey, anonymous, and spattered with mud and sand.

'Sorry about the mess,' he said, sweeping up a music magazine from the passenger seat and pushing it into the door bin.

'It's fine. Please don't worry.'

As she climbed in, she caught a glimpse of plastic buckets full of air tanks and breathing apparatus in the back. A couple of wetsuits and snorkels and masks were piled in builders' buckets. There was a strong whiff of neoprene, too. She hadn't really noticed before when he'd picked her up from Angel's. Maybe she was on the alert more now.

'How did you get into diving after working for a bank?' she asked, for something neutral to say.

'My dad was a professional diver. He'd been in the Navy when he was young and when he came out he went to work for a salvage company based in Plymouth. He took me diving from when I was in my teens.'

'Did you buy the van down here for your work?'

'I bought it when I knew I was moving here. It's practical for transporting dive and music gear. That's all I'll say for it. It holds all my diving gear and the amps of course, though I try not to mix the two. Salt water and electrical equipment are not great bedfellows.'

'I bet,' Bo laughed as they drove off. She hadn't known what to wear for record shopping and lunch at a swanky eatery that was a 'café' only in name. From what she'd read in the paper and seen on its website, the Gylly Café was the kind of place that would be heaving with the type of person dining on their company's expense account and driving a Porsche Cayenne – a bit like a couple of the smarter pubs round the Falford estuary.

Even so, dining in Cornwall was overwhelmingly a casual affair where the order of the day was wearing shorts and flip-flops while often paying an arm and a leg for fish and chips with a view.

It wasn't often she got the chance to check out somewhere as smart as this from a punter's point of view. She'd gone for smart jeans, ballet pumps, a Bardot-style jumper and a powder-blue swing mac she'd been dying to give an outing. It was breezy so she'd tied her hair back with her favourite scarf.

Then again, fretting over what to wear should have been the least of her worries – or maybe it was a distraction from the core dilemma: how close she could let herself get to Ran without getting burned again.

Ran turned on the CD player and the compelling intro to Nina Simone's 'Sinnerman' started. She wondered if he'd chosen it on purpose but said nothing. It was hardly sinful to avoid taking a cut-throat job that you hated, or to spend too much on records. Deceiving your partner then failing to be open with a friend . . . not sins, but not *great*. Then again, he was simply being human. Was she being too generous to him? Too harsh?

Nina sang about looking for absolution, and not finding it. Ran seemed lost in thought himself, or perhaps he was merely intent on the road ahead.

'Are you looking for anything in particular at Coastal Sounds?' Bo asked

'A couple of the Christmas records we considered for the playlist. I would love to get my hands on a decent copy of "Run Rudolph Run".'

She laughed. 'The B side of "Johnny B Goode"? I love that Chuck Berry track.'

'That's the one. Tyrone has a cheapo bootleg copy in stock. It's only four quid and he says it's in decent condition but you never know until you get inside.'

Ice broken, they chatted about music on the way and moved on to some of the dives Ran had been on over the past week. He dropped off the faulty amp at a commercial unit on the outskirts of town, before squeezing into a parking place at the top of the town.

Outside in the sea air, Bo inhaled and felt her spirits rising. Falmouth had a buzzing vibe that always energised her. She loved the sense of it being a busy working port as well as a seaside tourist town. There were pasty shops and pirate pubs, sure, and the derricks and cranes on the skyline gave testament to the fact that big ships came into the port for repair and even cruise ships occasionally docked there.

The top end of Fore Street gave a great view over the huge natural harbour of the Carrick Roads with its twin castles guarding the entrance. Bo remembered her dad telling her it was the third largest natural harbour in the world.

She could well believe it. Vessels of all kinds packed the marinas. Ferries criss-crossed their way to waterside villages like St Mawes and Flushing and took tourists up the Falford River itself to sleepy inlets like Frenchman's Creek.

Holidaymakers packed the long ribbon of Fore Street, browsing in the shop windows or queuing outside the pasty shops and bakeries. Gulls wheeled overhead and every so often there would be a gap in the shop fronts, and a short, steep lane leading to the quayside.

They passed bookshops, galleries, junk shops and quirky boutiques hidden away in cobbled corners which gave the town a quirky vibe, a place where enthusiasts and collectors – like Ran and herself – could disappear for hours.

Bo knew where they were heading, although she hadn't been inside for years. Halfway down the street, they turned into a small courtyard that was home to three businesses: a second-hand bookshop, the Vintage Threads Emporium and Coastal Sounds.

Stepping into Coastal Sounds was like stepping back in time. The walls were lined with CDs and cassette tapes on shelves. There was barely space to get round the tables in the centre, which were totally taken up with boxes of albums.

'The Drugs Don't Work' by The Verve was playing when they walked in. It seemed surprisingly modern to Bo but the shop wasn't a specialist vintage music store. Anyway, she reflected, it was probably over twenty years old now, something she'd heard on the radio a lot when she was a young teenager.

Tyrone was around Angel's age though not so well preserved. He looked like he'd 'lived a bit' – a phrase Bo's mum would have used. He was whip-thin with silver hair pulled back in a ponytail and rocking leather trousers and a T-shirt with a logo so faded Bo had no idea what it might once have read.

He was on his mobile, but broke off from his conversation and flashed them a grin. 'Hiya, Ran. Still after that Chuck Berry Rudolph thing?'

'You remembered.'

'Of course I did.' He flipped a thumb at the rear of the shop. 'It's in the back with all the singles. They're in date order – kind of. You probably know the place better than me. Shout up if you need any help.'

'I will,' Ran said.

Tyrone went back to his conversation.

Ran soon found the Berry single, but they stayed for ages, flipping through boxes of singles, oohing and ahhing at some of their old favourites from all eras.

'My grandad loved "Jingle Bell Rock",' Bo said wistfully, holding up a single by Bobby Helms. 'It's a shame he's not here for the Christmas Spectacular. He used to love seeing the Flingers perform.'

'When did he pass away?' Ran asked.

'A couple of years ago. My grandma's still alive though, and Mum and Dad are sure to bring her along.'

'My mother's parents are in Norway. It's their sixtieth wedding anniversary in the new year.'

Bo whistled. 'That's a long time to be married.'

'Yeah. They're doing better than me.' He gave a wry smile and Bo was pleased to see him in better spirits. Briefly on their journey, she'd wondered if he was regretting asking her out for a second time.

He bought another single, which meant his purchases added up to only a tenner, then they bid farewell to Tyrone and emerged into the soft autumn sunlight in the courtyard.

'Is there still time to pop into this place?' she said, looking at the Vintage Threads Emporium. 'You don't have to come in if you don't want to.'

What she really meant was she didn't want him to come in at all. Luckily he took the hint.

'There's loads of time. I need to phone the dive school about the trip tomorrow. I'll join you when I've finished.'

'You're assuming I'll still be in there when you've finished?'

'No. I mean . . .'

She enjoyed seeing him flustered – in a nice way. 'Once I get in here, you might have to send a search party for me.'

'Same with this place. Tyrone once actually made me a bacon sandwich because I'd been in since opening and it was dinner-time. It's only because we've got a lunch date and you're with me that I came out now.'

'Come and get me if you think we're going to run late.' Still laughing, she opened the door of the Emporium.

It was a mix of second-hand vintage clothing and new stuff by labels specialising in vintage style. Conscious of only having a short space of time, Bo gave the second-hand stuff a miss and went straight to the new dresses. Immediately, she felt a rush of excitement and could have bought half a dozen on the spot, imagining herself dancing in them.

Even with autumn here, she'd still opt for short sleeves

because jiving was warm work. Lighting on a white dress with a green and red holly berry print, she checked the label and discovered it was more than she'd have liked to pay. It had a circle skirt that would look great as she was being twirled around the floor by Cade or one of the other Flingers.

No, she couldn't justify it when she already had a lovely green and red dress that would be perfect too. She had a quick browse around the vintage housewares instead, comparing them to Angel's creations.

She spotted Ran peering through the window and then caught sight of a metal clock above the till.

'Wow. It's half past twelve. I have to go!'

'Like Cinderella?' the assistant piped up.

'Not quite!'

They made their way down past the port over to the promenade, with its elegant gardens and theatre. Gyllyngvase was a popular beach of pale golden sand and, on this fine autumn day, a group of schoolchildren were having lifesaving lessons.

'Wow, that's different,' Bo said when they reached the Gylly Café and looked down over the railing to the newly refurbished building on the beach. She remembered it as a wooden structure, with simple tables outside where people tucked into pasties and fish and chips. Its recent makeover was chic and eye catching. It had clearly been influenced by a vintage ocean liner and now had shiny porthole windows and a covered deck.

'I never saw the old one,' Ran admitted, pausing on the prom to survey it. 'What do you think? As someone in the trade, that is?'

'The building's out of the Boatyard Café's league, that's for sure, but I'm sure it'll go down like a house on fire with the clientele round here.'

Ran gave his name and the manager said he'd been expecting him.

'That's a relief. It would have been embarrassing if they'd thought we were trying to gatecrash,' he murmured as they waited to be shown to their table. 'Outside or in? Will you be warm enough?'

'I think so,' Bo said. 'Anyway, they give you fancy blankets if you're not.' She smiled, amused at the baskets of blankets, probably hand-woven, at the doors to the outdoor dining area.

They opted for a table for two on the deck which was screened by a glass wall that would protect them from the wind, but still afforded a fabulous view of the beach and the whole bay. A waiter took their drinks order and gave them a menu, but Bo was more interested in the view.

Vessels of all sizes sailed or steamed past on their way into Falmouth harbour and, on the horizon, tankers and container ships steamed up the channel from far-flung places.

'When I was little, I used to imagine where they were coming from and what they were carrying,' she said as they sat down.

'My great-grandfather was the captain of a merchant ship,' Ran said. 'Norwegians have always been a seafaring nation.'

'Wow. Do you get home often?' Bo asked.

'Not as much as I'd like. I became too busy.'

'What do you think of the menu?' he asked.

'Again, it's out of my league. I couldn't serve this from the café. I don't mind trying it though. It will be a treat to be cooked for and waited on for a change.'

She ordered hake with a piperade sauce and shaved serrano ham while Ran went for half a lobster with aioli mayo. The prices were eye-watering although Ran had said it was a soft opening and there would be a big discount. Nonetheless, she could have fed her pulled pork wraps – plus the drinks – to a family of four for the price of his half-lobster.

Sides were extra of course. Bo couldn't resist a wry smile as the waiter added skinny fries and house salads to the order. Shortly afterwards, their drinks and bowls of olives arrived.

'Are you used to dining like this?' she asked.

'Not these days. It's usually a pasty or a chicken baguette from the petrol station on the way to work. If I'm really pushed, I've been known to open a pouch of Thor's chicken broth.'

Bo let out a mock gasp, amused at his joke. Whatever Ran ate, it definitely hadn't done his physique any harm. The sight of him with his wetsuit rolled down sprang into her mind.

She shifted in her chair and picked up the wine list. 'Um. This is quite an exclusive wine list,' she said, trying to distract herself from an unbidden fantasy of him sitting naked opposite her. Despite it being well into autumn, being next to him was as good as sitting near a brazier.

A gust of wind blew a menu off a nearby table.

His fingers grazed hers briefly, full of concern, before he withdrew them quickly as if he was awkward about touching her. 'Are you warm enough?'

'Oh, more than warm enough,' Bo said. 'I mean, the sun's warm, even though it's so late in the year.'

'The joys of Cornwall,' Ran said. 'Remember the Falford fete? I nearly roasted inside that tent.'

'It was stifling,' Bo said. 'And all that incense and the joss sticks. I could hardly breathe at times.'

Ran stared into the distance as if he was back in the tent. 'You know, I still don't have a clue who she was,' he murmured.

'Nor me, and I hate to admit it but some of the stuff she told me hit a raw nerve,' Bo said.

'Mmm . . .' He laid his fork on his plate. 'That's another thing I'm not proud of. I told you that she told me a load of old rubbish. That wasn't strictly true at all. The letter with the divorce papers arrived the morning of the Falford fete. It probably wasn't the best day for me to visit a fortune teller.'

'Oh God. No. I can see why. You should have said. I wound you up and virtually called you a wimp. I'm sorry.' She cringed, understanding now why he'd been so cynical.

'No need to apologise. I could have told you . . . in fact, I should have been more honest about everything. Most of what she said was rubbish but some of it unexpectedly hit a bit too close to home. I didn't want to admit there might be something in what she said.'

'Oh? Don't tell me she said, "You'll meet a handsome stranger."'

'No. Not that.' He smiled. 'But she did say something weird. I thought it was cheesy and a total cliché . . .'

Her heart skipped a beat. 'Did it have anything to do with "being with the love of your life by Christmas"?' she said slowly.

'Yes. Yes.' He pushed his hands through his hair. 'Did she say the same to you?'

'Yes, and to Angel.'

He shook his head. 'So it was a load of old rubbish. Here's me thinking there might have been something in it.'

'What makes you think there was?'

'Only . . . Well, I don't know. Anyway, it's obviously the same line she trots out to everyone. Her cut-and-paste response.'

'Maybe it was but is that *all*? You were pretty agitated when you came out of that tent? Did she say . . . something else that disturbed you?'

'Like what?'

'OK.' She took a breath. 'I was almost as sceptical as you before I went in. I was mostly being kind to Angel by saying I'd keep an open mind and the whole set-up was so cheesy and ridiculous with the crystal ball. Then Madame Odette started talking about something – some *things* – that had happened to me last Christmas. Things she could only have known if she knew I'd split up with Hamish. It was really quite personal.'

'Yes.' He sighed. 'She had the same effect on me. She harped on about me being hurt and a broken relationship . . .'

'I did wonder if she'd upset you, but not until I'd had my turn. That was when I realised that she had a knack of getting under your skin.'

'I've thought back many times,' Ran said. 'I tried so hard not to give her any clues, and to see if I recognised her. Even though I didn't like what she said, and it was personal, she named no names. Nothing specific that could be tied to an individual. I still think she's like an angler, casting her lure to see if the victim bites. It doesn't take much to make us feel insecure.'

'So, there was absolutely nothing that gave you any reason to suspect that she knew you?'

'No . . .' he hesitated. 'The one specific thing she mentioned was too personal to share at the time. "I'm seeing a letter. The crystal ball is misty. It's fading in and out . . . Was it a P? I can't be sure. I suppose it could be an R too . . ."'

'That's still pretty vague,' Bo said, laughing at his imper-sonation of Madame Odette's strange accent.

'Yes, and I'm afraid I was pretty rude in return. I said: "I'm sure if you stare long enough into that ball, you'll get through the whole alphabet." I made to leave, then, but she asked me to wait and said, "The letters are becoming clearer and it's definitely a P."'

'A P? Oh, I see.' A tiny shiver went down Bo's spine.

'Yeah. Surprised it wasn't an F. Many people think Phaedra begins with an F.'

Bo laughed softly. 'Lots of female names begin with P and R.'

'Of course they do. I'm sure she was trying to provoke a reaction. At some point she'd have got to S and managed to hit on at least one woman I've ever met . . . What about you? How specific was she about you?'

'She also mentioned some initials and one of them was a H, though again it might have been pure luck,' Bo said. 'Whatever, she hit a raw nerve. As you say, that's almost certainly what she intended. She casts out her lures and once she gets the slightest whiff of a bite, she reels you in.'

'And then, you're well and truly hooked.'

Chapter Twenty-One

A rush of empathy filled Ran. Despite the fact Bo was making light of her experience with Madame Odette, it was obvious she'd been troubled by what she'd heard.

He and Bo were alike in one way, trying to keep their feelings under wraps and their personal lives exactly that; personal. Bo was a much warmer, more outgoing sprit than him, which was what attracted him to her so strongly.

And he was attracted very strongly. He'd had to try hard not to look at her too much, at her hair, the way her eyes lit up when she talked about dancing. She was vibrant, that was the word; so full of colour and life, and yet, he sensed a reticence too. Was that her experience with that tosser Hamish or was it because she wasn't anywhere near as attracted to him as he was to her? Or was it because, once again, he'd allowed the past to get in the way of the future? It was a stone on a chain he still carried around with him.

'She was very careful to hide her identity, wasn't she?' Bo said. 'That shawl and the lighting made it all but impossible to figure out who she really is.'

'I thought it was all part of the stage props.'

'True, though she was definitely trying to disguise her identity because I glimpsed her face for a brief moment and she very quickly covered it up again.'

Ran smiled. 'That could have been part of the act too. The whole woman-of-mystery thing.'

'Yes.'

The waiter arrived, asking if they wanted anything else.

'Do you?' Ran asked Bo, unwilling to cut their lunch short.

'No, thanks. I'm good.'

'Could we have the bill, please?'

'Of course, sir.' With a nod, the waiter left.

Bo pointed to a card on their table.

'Have you seen that? "Book for Christmas".'

'Never too early,' he said.

The bill arrived and he read it and took out his wallet.

After he'd paid, they took the steps back up to the prom. Ran checked his watch. Damn, why hadn't he put longer on the car park? He could have spent all day with Bo – and, he thought rather guiltily, he'd love to stretch that time into the evening. His fingers itched to take her by the hand, like so many of the couples they passed. He'd always thought that was one of the best things about being behind the decks: watching other people dance, surreptitiously, while looking as if you were totally engrossed in the music.

Lately, he'd spent more time watching Bo twirling around the floor with different members of the Flingers, laughing and smiling. Even though he knew they were only her partners in dance terms, he'd begun to feel envious and to wish he could take their place, if only for one dance.

They passed the Princess Pavilion with its palm-lined gardens and elaborate bandstand. Posters outside also declared it was time to book for Christmas parties, but a bridal party was still making the most of the late autumn sunshine, posing for wedding photographs. Several small bridesmaids were dancing around the elaborate bandstand, which looked like something from a golden age musical.

Bo stopped too, admiring it along with him. He had an inkling she didn't want the day to end either. 'Imagine dancing there,' he said.

'On the bandstand?' he asked.

'No. Inside the concert hall. It's huge.'

'Is it? I've never been inside.'

'That's a shame,' she said. 'I went to a rock 'n' roll festival here a few years ago. There were hundreds of dancers. It was amazing.'

'I bet . . .' He pictured her on the large ballroom floor, a queue of guys eager to ask her to dance. The urge to be one of them swept him up, like a wave, filling him with courage – or recklessness.

'I've been thinking,' he said.

'Always dangerous,' she joked. She turned and tilted her face up to his. He loved the smattering of freckles on her nose, the way the Cornish sun had bronzed her cheeks, the hair escaping from her ponytail.

Yes, it was dangerous to think, to dare to imagine he could move on from Phaedra. He guessed what Hamish had done to Bo and he mustn't lead her on if he meant to let her down but surely – surely – a dance would do no harm?

'I'm not a complete novice but it's been a long time since . . . since I danced.'

'It's difficult to start again,' she said. 'After you've stopped. Dancing, that is,' she added.

He hung on the threshold of asking her to teach him to dance again, and yet still held back. They both understood the other; the metaphors were heavy-handed but they both knew they were talking about more than dancing.

Her eyes sparkled with pleasure and Ran had an insane urge to take her in his arms and dance her along the prom. However, a second later, they widened in dismay.

'What's the matter?'

'There's Tommy Carrack. And I swear he's with Madame Odette!'

Chapter Twenty-Two

Ran whipped round. 'You're joking.'

'No. He's over there by the bandstand. With her, I'm sure—'

'I can't see them?'

Heart beating faster, Bo scanned the people milling around the bandstand. 'He's wearing a bright blue baseball cap and she's wearing the purple headscarf!'

'Bloody hell,' Ran said, craning his neck for a better view.

'There!' Bo pointed to the couple, slipping through the gates of the garden onto the prom. 'They're moving. Quick, let's go after them.'

Without a second thought, she grabbed Ran by the arm and urged him towards the gate. She let go quickly but he'd taken the hint and hurried after her out of the gardens and down the street.

'Where are they?'

'There, in that tatty cap he always wore on board. Angel hates it, says it's melted onto his hair. Hold on, they've turned down that alley.'

Bo practically ran to the corner of the alley, too narrow for cars, one of many that criss-crossed between the harbour and the town.

'Can you see him?' she asked Ran, who was able to see above the heads of people better than Bo.

'Er . . . no . . . oh, hold on. There's a bloke in a blue baseball cap at the far end.' Without asking, he jogged along the alley, with Bo behind. They had to make their way past pedestrians, some of whom gave them strange glances.

Ran was a few yards ahead and had stopped at the end of the alley which led onto a road above the port area. Bo caught him up, breathing heavily, more from excitement than rushing. 'Well? Can you see them?'

'I thought I saw him but he's gone.'

Bo scoured a sea of figures, frantically searching for Tommy and his companion. She *had* seen him. She'd have bet the café on that. She was sure he'd been with Madame Odette too. For a fleeting moment, she had a good view of the woman, who'd been merely a few yards away. She had been in the headscarf, and something in the way she'd laughed had struck an instant chord. She'd been flirting with Tommy, batting him on the arm with her hand, and her fingernails had been painted crimson red.

It was like those moments when you're trying to guess the voice on the radio or the mystery personality on a quiz show. That split second when a half-remembered feature or tone chimes with your senses and you know, without a doubt, who they are.

Without a doubt . . .

'There are quite a few baseball caps,' Ran said, moving forward down the hill. 'I did see the blue one go this way but now? I can't see the exact one, can you? Nor the purple scarf.'

Frantically, Bo scrutinised the backs of heads. There were plenty of men with baseball caps, but none looked exactly like the Tommy she'd spotted. What's more, she couldn't spot a matching Madame Odette at all.

The closer they came to the marina front, the more their quarry became flecks of foam on the tide, impossible to distinguish from the hundreds of people strolling, hurrying around the streets and the marina development, with its restaurants, shops and National Maritime Museum.

'No. It's impossible.' Bo groaned. 'I was so sure it was them. Him, definitely.'

'I agree and you should go with your instincts. I caught a glimpse of Tommy and, although I've only met him a handful of times, I'd say it was definitely him. After all, he *is* living here, we know that much.'

'Not with Madame Odette though. I must think I'm Sherlock Holmes, haring after them like that. Why would Tommy be with a fortune teller?'

'Stranger things have happened.'

'She is younger than him and I wouldn't have thought she was his type. I'm getting obsessed.'

'You could still have seen them *together* although it doesn't necessarily follow that she's the other woman. Mind you, I quite enjoyed playing Watson for a little while.'

Bo winced before she saw that his look was a gleam of amusement combined with the gentlest of teasing.

'It was definitely Tommy,' he said. 'And he was definitely with a woman, although I wouldn't like to swear it was Madame Odette. The question is: do you tell Angel or not?'

Chapter Twenty-Three

Well, *should* she tell Angel?

To say Bo had mixed feelings on the issue was an understatement, and she was still churning it over when Angel finally turned up at Flingers on the second Saturday in October. Bo had expected her the previous week, but Angel had phoned to say she'd wanted to come but her daughter had been ill, so she'd had to go round to look after her.

While Bo was delighted to see her friend feeling strong enough to return, she also felt guilty. She'd finally decided not to mention the Tommy sighting because she couldn't be one hundred percent certain it had been him – and was far less sure he'd been with Madame Odette. More uncertainty was the last thing Angel needed right now.

Immediately, Bo made her way to the door to give her friend a hug. After asking how Emma was doing, she mouthed a 'wow' as Angel shrugged off her coat to reveal a dress with a pattern of electric guitars and musical notes.'

'You look fantastic. That material's beautiful.'

'You think so? To be honest I didn't dare show it to Tommy. He'd probably have laughed. It's a bit OTT.'

'No, it's fabulous and fun,' Bo declared. 'Very rock 'n' roll!'

Angel swished her circle skirt, revealing a frilly scarlet underskirt that set off the dress's colours perfectly.

Sally came over and embraced her. 'Welcome back to Flingers. We've missed you.'

'Not as much as I've missed you.' Tears glistened in Angel's eyes but she took a breath and spoke. 'So, what are we dancing to tonight?'

'First go at the Christmas playlist for the Trewhella Illuminations.'

'I can't wait,' Angel said.

Ran was behind the decks with earphones on, intent on music no one else could hear. Bo kept sneaking glances at him, and once he caught her staring and smiled back. She'd really enjoyed their day out, despite her misgivings.

Hubert came over and asked Angel if she'd be his partner for the first few dances. Encouraged by Angel chatting and seeming happy to be back, other members arrived to welcome her. From what Bo could hear, no one mentioned Tommy or the situation – not for now at any rate.

Bo was paired with Cade and knew she'd have to be on her toes but on the upside was thankful to have a partner who knew what he was doing and would be happy to lead.

Music burst through the speakers and the chatter grew louder. 'OK, folks. Who's ready?'

The first dance started and the village hall rocked with the sounds of Christmases gone by. The foot-tapping set kicked off with the new disc of 'Run Rudolph Run' that Ran had bought from the record store, followed by 'Rockin' Around the Christmas Tree' and 'Jingle Bell Rock'.

Sally was choreographing from the stage. Ran was in charge of starting and stopping the music while they broke down the moves and began putting a dance together. It was chaotic, stressful, and fun all at the same time. Laughter, cursing and groans then simply music filled the room as people started to get to grips with the moves.

All of the dancers were au fait with the basic rock steps and a few of the more complicated moves but some were finding the turns and spins challenging, given that a few of the tracks were at a faster tempo than they were used to. Hubert and Sally were already adding lifts that made Bo breathless with awe. Ran was endlessly patient, constantly restarting the music so people could stop, take a break and practise tricky steps.

By the end of the first session, most had made progress and the music certainly had everyone energised and buzzing. Bo guessed they'd be sick of it by the time Christmas eventually came but, on the upside, they'd certainly have had plenty of practice.

'OK. Let's take a break!' Sally called. 'Well done, everyone. Grab a drink and have a breather.'

'I'm so glad the weather's turned cooler at last but I'll have to get fitter!' Bo said, joining Ran at the decks. She handed him a bottle of water.

'You looked good to me,' Ran said. 'I mean, you looked like you were keeping up.'

'Thanks.' Bo was suffused with pleasure even though she was sure he was being kind. 'Cade's so fit. He goes mountain biking and climbs.'

'I wouldn't like to imagine how I'd be after all this time . . .'

'You look fit enough to me.'

'Dancing needs a different kind of fitness to diving . . .' He glanced at the canteen where Angel was chatting and sipping water. 'Did you say anything to Angel about our Falmouth adventure?'

'No. I decided I couldn't be sure it was Tommy and that speculation like that would only make things worse for Angel.'

'Hmm. It's never a good idea to interfere when things are breaking down in a marriage.' His voice faded as Hubert, Sally and Angel headed in their direction.

Diplomatically, Ran changed the subject when they arrived.

'Have you checked out the ballroom at Trewhella House?' Ran asked. 'I've never been and I need to do a recce to see the set-up.'

'I went a few years ago and it's an impressive space,' Bo said. 'It's larger than here and there are big double doors at either end. I must have been the only visitor who was more interested in the floor that the paintings and treasures,' she added. 'It's lovely, beautifully laid wood and sprung. Perfect for dancing.'

'That's a relief,' Sally said. 'It would be very hard on my knees if it was concrete.'

'I'd love to see it too,' Angel said wistfully.

'We'll sort out a visit,' Hubert said. 'But it's time to crack on with the dancing now. Come on, no slacking!'

An hour later, everyone was hot and red-faced but still buzzing. Bo caught up with Angel at the end of the dance.

'How was it? Not too bad?'

'I was so rusty,' Angel said. 'But I did enjoy it. I've almost forgotten about – everything – for the past few hours. You can't concentrate on anything but the dancing and the music, can you?'

'No. It's the best form of escapism. Well done on coming back. It can't have been easy.'

'I've got to move on sometime. You went to Falmouth with Ran? How did that go?'

Bo was in agony over whether to mention their sighting of Tommy.

'Oh . . . It was good. He bought some records, we had a lovely lunch at the Gylly Café . . . I almost bought a new dress from the vintage boutique by the record shop.'

'Ouch.'

'I resisted. Seeing the beautiful pieces you make – it made me think twice about parting with my money.'

'The makers need custom, though,' Angel said.

'Yes, though I checked the labels in a few of the ones I liked. They were mass-produced somewhere thousands of miles away. I'd rather pay a bit more for a dress that's been made close to home by someone like you.'

'I'm no professional dressmaker and I'd find it hard to mass-produce anything.'

'I know.'

'The dresses would take ages but I've got better at the smaller things.' Angel smiled with pride.

'There were lots of things like that too,' Bo said encouragingly.

'Were there? Well, you've no need to buy them there. I've brought the bunting and tea towels with me tonight.'

'Great, I can't wait to see them!'

After the practice session, they went out to the cars where Angel opened her boot. 'Here you are. I hope they're what you were looking for.'

Even by the boot light, Bo could see the bunting was gorgeous, with bright colours of turquoise, cerise and yellow. 'Thanks. It will really brighten up the café over the next couple of months.'

'Good . . . And here are your tea towels. Half a dozen, OK?'

Peeking inside the bag, Bo let out a squeak of delight. 'They're so cute. I love the Cornish birds on them.'

'It's a new fabric, fresh in at the warehouse. To be honest, the woman who runs it wasn't sure it would sell so she was trying to encourage customers and I got it for a bargain price. I adored the little choughs and puffins.'

'It's gorgeous.'

'And, erm. I also made this for you. I know you didn't ask for it but I couldn't resist the material and I wanted to thank you for being such a good friend to me since Tommy left.'

She handed Bo another bag.

'Oh . . .' Bo pulled out another string of bunting, this time in rich reds, greens and gold. Some of the pennants had a holly and mistletoe pattern. 'It's Christmas-themed! Thank you so much, it will look so festive when we change to the new menu. Are you sure you won't let me pay you for it?'

'Not a chance.' Angel hugged her. 'I'm happy you like it.'

'I reckon people would buy these if I had some on display.'

'Do you?' Angel sounded amazed.

'Yes. I'm sure they would. With Christmas coming up, I could have a few on show.'

Angel hesitated before saying quietly: 'I've sometimes thought about having a little stall at the craft fairs, running my own business, but I didn't dare suggest giving up my job to Tommy. We needed the money – I still do. If it wasn't for Kelvin, I'd still enjoy my job.'

Bo snorted in derision. 'I wish that man would vanish in a puff of smoke!'

'Me too. I wish he'd leave but it seems as if his feet are firmly under the table. Old Mr Jennings doesn't want to get involved. He's owner only in name now.'

'Why don't you try and have a stall at the pre-Christmas craft fair at Trewhella House?' Bo suggested. 'I noticed on the website there was one scheduled for early next month and we could combine it with a recce.'

'Well, I'd *love* to see the ballroom but I expect it's too late for a stall.'

'It's worth a try.'

'I've never done anything like that before . . .'

'Do you have some stock you can sell?' Bo said, remembering Angel had been swamped by her creations the last time she'd called in.

'Oh, yes . . . I've done barely anything else since Tommy left, though I've no idea what I'm going to do with it all. I suppose I could contact the event organiser at the gardens. I expect I *could* hire a stall. Even if I only covered my costs, it would be good experience.'

'Exactly, and I'll help you if you like,' Bo said, feeling buoyed by Angel's positivity.

'Won't you be busy?'

'I don't open Sundays now autumn's here – it's not worth it – so I'll be free to come with you. We've agreed to scope out the ballroom anyway.'

'We?'

'Hubert, Sally, me and Ran.'

'Ran?' Angel said, raising an eyebrow.

'It's a group outing, not a date.' Even now the prospect of getting close to him again made her glow even more than the dancing had.

Angel smiled broadly. 'OK. In that case, I'd love to come. Haven't been anywhere apart from home and work for ages.'

Chapter Twenty-Four

It turned out it was, technically, too late for Angel to have a stall, but the organiser had had a last-minute cancellation and was only too pleased to let her step in.

Bo went over to Angel's after the café closed the evening before the fair and helped her gather together the goods she hoped to take and label them up, based on the prices they sold for in the charity shop. Bo told Angel she'd need cash and a float and loaned her a mobile payment terminal for the stall.

Apart from at Flingers, she hadn't seen too much of Ran, but that wasn't surprising. He was leading a week-long diving course at the centre and had been back to see his parents in Surrey for a few days. She'd been busy herself, looking after her niece and nephew for a couple of days during half-term. Her sister had been in hospital for a minor procedure so she'd been only too happy to step in, though by the time her brother-in-law had collected the children after his shift as a fire fighter she was more knackered than if she'd done a day at the café.

She'd also been at the Morvah Boatyard where Finn and Joey had prepared the sail and other fittings for her refurbished terrace. It would have to wait until after the half-term holiday, when families descended on Falford and she and Cade were busy dishing up Hallowe'en cupcakes and pumpkin soup to hungry families.

First, however, there was the visit to the craft fair at Trewhella house and the chance to check out the magnificent ballroom with Angel, Ran, Hubert and Sally.

Bo and Angel set off through the mists of a November dawn in Bo's van, arranging to meet Hubert and Sally later. Ran had a Sunday morning diving trip scheduled from first light so he promised to be along later.

Buoyed by a rising tide of excitement, they drove down the lanes to Trewhella. It was set on its own peninsular on the edge of the Falford estuary and, on this autumn morning, mist was rising from the fields. They'd been up at six preparing and were some of the first to arrive. Stewards showed them through the wrought-iron gates to the Trewhella Estate, where a large sign advertised the early Christmas Craft Fair.

'My stomach feels as if it has a million butterflies in it,' Angel said.

'It's exciting,' Bo exclaimed, determined to be positive while silently worrying that if the day didn't go well, Angel's confidence could be dented even further. 'We'll be fine.'

Glimpses of the estuary opened up at every turn on the drive to the house, with the famous woodland gardens sloping down to the water's edge. With the sun coming up and the mist burning off, the grass was dewy and sunlight dappled the drive. However, the trees were the real stars. Dressed in their autumn plumage, they were trumpeting one last hurrah before the gales stripped them of their finery.

The acer trees had turned glorious shades of crimson and

scarlet, while oaks and sycamore were painted an array of colours from ochre yellow to fiery orange. Bo put the elusive fortune teller to the back of her mind; the last thing Angel needed was any kind of worry or distraction relating to Tommy.

They were directed to an exhibitors' parking area near the house, a large mansion with a huge portico held up by stone pillars.

There was a queue and Bo had to wait in line to enter the exhibitors' area.

'Wow,' whispered Angel, in awe.

It was clearly meant to impress and Bo was *seriously* impressed, even though she'd visited before. She imagined pulling up there in a carriage or a vintage Rolls, and being greeted by a butler.

'Stallholders this way, love.' A man in a hi-vis jacket poked his head through the window. 'Make sure you tuck your van in tight to the vehicle next door,' he barked. 'We're packing 'em in, today.'

'Charming,' Angel said, twitchy with nerves.

Any thoughts of arriving by the main entrance, rather than the tradesmen's way, vanished. Some things didn't change, Bo thought, amused.

After squeezing out of the van, they unloaded their stock in bags for life. The craft fair was being held in a large marquee – more of a temporary building – to the side of the house. Lugging the stuff across wet turf was hard work but two trips did it and Angel's nerves seemed forgotten in the buzz of setting up. The organisers had been able to provide a table and screen, so there was no need for Angel to worry about that.

They were among the very first to arrive but, by the time they'd made their final trip to the van, the exhibitors' area was full. Angel must have been burning the midnight oil after work and on her days off, because Bo was amazed at the amount of stock she'd built up. Despite all her troubles, Angel had made a big effort, putting on a dress she'd made herself with a matching headscarf bandana.

'I slapped on loads of make-up to disguise the dark circles,' she joked when they started to arrange the goods on the stall. 'I blame all those nights I've spent sewing and finishing the stock. At least I'm not lying awake thinking about the future though . . . and I think it's been worth it.'

'You've done an incredible job.' Bo filled with pride at her friend's achievement when she surveyed the stall. There were kitchenwares in four different prints including one with berries and autumn leaves and a Christmas pattern of Cornish choughs in Santa hats that matched their red legs and beaks. Angel had hung a couple of her dancing dresses and some bunting over the folding screen behind them.

'I don't expect anyone to buy the dresses but I thought they'd draw people to the stall and be a talking point. People have made such an effort with their stalls. Some of them are like works of art!'

'Yours looks fabulous too,' Bo reassured her. 'The bunting is an inspired idea and I love the Christmas choughs.'

She flushed with pleasure. 'I found the fabric from a new local supplier and the Christmas one is exclusive from a new designer fresh from Penryn College – a friend of our Emma's. I paid a bit more for the fabric. That's my dream: to have my own design team and makers. You need a signature "look" to make it big.' Angel grimaced. 'Listen to me. "Make it big!" Anyone would think I wanted to be in Harrods or something!'

'There's nothing wrong with dreaming big,' Bo said.

'I know . . . I'd be happy just to cover my costs and make a bit of pocket money.'

'Would you ever give up your job at the Country Stores?'

'Until Kelvin took over, I'd never have even thought about it. The pleasure's gone out of it now though, and sometimes I can hardly face going into work. I knew I had to carry on because Tommy's income was so uncertain though he spent a fair amount down the pub. Unfortunately I need to keep working to pay my bills now and flogging a few tea towels can't replace a regular salary. Oh, blimey, the customers are arriving!'

'Angel. Chill. You've been in customer service for years and you're brilliant at it. I've seen you in action.'

'Yes, but this is different. The things I've made come from the heart. If people don't like them, I'll take it personally.'

'Please try not, my lovely, even though I do know how you feel. When you've put your heart and soul into creating something – anything – you want people to love what you do, and to know how hard you've worked. I do understand but try to take a step back. I've had to learn to do the same, or I'd have jacked the café in years ago.'

'Thanks.'

There was just time for Bo to grab coffees from the stable yard café and admire the view over the gardens to the sea, before returning to Angel ready for the opening at ten a.m.

The trickle of customers became a stream, some people heading straight for specific stalls, but most meandering around, browsing, and asking the odd question here and there. If she was honest, Bo's heart was beating a little faster, hoping that Angel's first experience of selling her makes was a positive one.

Business became brisker and Angel made her first sale. Her vintage costumes were admired and several people asked if she'd made them. Talking about dancing was a great icebreaker and a few of the older visitors bought the music-themed items and confessed they'd love to learn to dance.

Angel soon hit her stride and her experience at the Country Stores was paying off. She had an engaging, natural way about her that the customers liked. Bo was delighted when several returned after their tour of the other stalls and made purchases.

In the blink of an eye, the first hour had passed and Bo was busy restocking the tea towel display when Ran arrived.

'Hello! How's it going?'

Bo's heart skipped a beat. She hadn't seen him for a few days and was struck by how tall he was, standing out from the crowd of people.

'You look busy,' he said, nodding at Angel who was taking an order for bunting from a customer.

'We are. It's going well. We were worried we'd have no customers but we're nicely busy.'

'Nicely busy sounds the perfect kind of busy.'

'How was the diving trip?'

'Good. We saw a basking shark very close up. That was awesome.' His eyes lit up with excitement. 'Not so awesome is the fact I've had a call from Hubert and Sally to say they've been delayed – car trouble. That vintage Corvette of theirs can be temperamental. They'll try to make it but suggested we go ahead without them in case they can't get here.'

'Oh hello, Ran.'

'Hi, Angel. Looks like it's going well.'

'It is! Better than I hoped!' Angel sounded bubbly and was pink-cheeked with the thrill of selling her designs. Bo held back a smile. 'Can I tempt you to some lovely new linens for your kitchen? They'd go beautifully in your cottage.'

'Hmm . . . well, as a matter of fact, I need some new oven

gloves. Thor ripped the stuffing out of my old pair. He clearly thought they were prey. I found them on my pillow, as a present when I woke up, with Thor proudly standing over them with stuffing in his whiskers.'

Bo giggled at the image of Thor attacking Ran's gloves.

'In that case, I've got the perfect thing.' Angel held up a gauntlet with a pattern of cat silhouettes and musical notes. 'Matching tea towels and apron too, sir?'

'Perfect,' he said. Bo hid a further smile at Ran's attempts to look enthusiastic about tea towels. Actually, he wasn't doing badly. 'Definitely two gauntlets, they'll come in handy when I have to get Thor into his carrier for the vet's. I'll have two tea towels too but I think I'll pass on a cute cat apron for now. I'm not sure Thor would ever speak to me again.'

'I think he'd love it, and you can always come back if you change your mind. You know where we are. I'll keep these until you've been to check out the ballroom,' Angel said.

'Will you be OK without me?' Bo said. 'It's getting busier.'

'No. I'm fine! I can manage. Off you go,' she said, practically ushering Bo from behind the stall. 'I'll have a quick gander at the ballroom later.'

'That's us told,' Ran said, while they made their way past the people piling into the craft fair. 'Angel's doing well.'

'Yes, she's amazing, considering how she must be feeling.'

'Was this your idea?'

'I only suggested it. It's Angel's baby. She'd love to make a small business out of her hobby and I'm sure she could do it.'

Ran was thoughtful. 'If she hates her job and loves sewing, she should give it a go. I know how that feels.'

'It's not always practical financially, though, is it? Even though she can't stand Kelvin, she's always seemed to love running the

Country Stores. I understand that because I can't imagine giving up the café and leaving Falford.'

'No, it's the kind of place that seeps into your bones,' he said, sounding wistful.

She wondered if that meant he intended to stay long term. She was well aware he was self-employed and rented the cottage, so he could leave at any time. For all he said about never going back to his life in London, would that change if an opportunity arose?

Bo could not and would not ask him the question straight out. It would sound desperate and her vow remained never to let any man know her true feelings before she was sure of his.

For now, it was time to dive into the moment, which was an exciting one for anyone who loved dancing. While the gardens were open, the main house was off limits to the public during the craft fair. Bo had a word with one of the stewards at the entrance, explaining that they were part of the dance group and wanted to recce the ballroom. After name-dropping the house manager, who Bo had contacted earlier, the red silk rope was unhooked and they entered the grand hallway.

'It's like being shown to a VIP room at a big event,' she said.

Ran agreed. 'Even better because we have it to ourselves.'

'Wow . . .' Bo was filled with awe.

'Wow, indeed.'

The hallway was breath-taking with a full-height ceiling that had a minstrels' gallery at one end. The fact it was empty only made it seem larger and more imposing. She was glad to be wrapped in her coat, because the cavernous space was chilly after the heat of the crowded craft fair.

A stone fireplace dominated one wall, complete with a carved coat of arms above it. The wall was blackened by soot from thousands of fires although today the hearth was cold. Portraits of the ancestors of the Boscawens lined the walls, staring down at the two strangers who had invaded their home. Bo tried to imagine it full of life, activity and lavish celebrations, unlike today when it echoed to the sound of their footsteps and hushed voices.

'Spooky, isn't it?' she said in a hushed tone. 'Sad, in a way, that it's empty much of the time.'

'Hmm. Why are we whispering?' Ran murmured, a glint in his eye.

Her laughter echoed. 'I don't know. Perhaps because it still feels as if we've invaded someone's private home?' She spoke up, still feeling strange.

'Except we all own the place now, or rather the members of historic place trusts do,' he said. 'Remind me why they want rock and roll in a two-hundred-year-old mansion?'

'Because when Sir Richard Boscawen's daughters gave it to the trust in 1960, there was a scheme which meant you could gift a property to the nation instead of paying the inheritance tax. 1959 was the last time there was a dance held in the ball-room and the whole family spent Christmas together before it was sold off and they moved out.'

'But rock and roll?' Ran said. 'Why not waltzes and foxtrots?'

'The trust wanted to showcase the kind of culture that the locals and servants would have enjoyed, not simply the privileged few. Apparently, several boxes of rock 'n' roll singles were discovered in the attic rooms when they were renovated a few years ago. The events team decided it was a great time to highlight the great social changes taking place on the brink of the sixties.'

'I guess it fits with the way the Boscawens had to give up the house. The changing of eras . . .' Ran said. 'It's sad for them, though it means the house is open to everyone now, not just a privileged few. I'm glad the trust saved it from becoming a hotel or falling into ruin. There'd be no ballroom for us to dance in then.'

Bo shuddered at the thought of the house with its roof caved in and ravens circling above the open rooms. 'How horrible.'

They reached the elaborately carved double doors into the ballroom. She pushed it open and caught her breath.

'Wow. Look at that floor.'

The chandeliers were lit in the ballroom but they weren't what attracted Bo's attention. The magnificent wooden floor, polished to perfection, gleamed in the light from the sparkling crystals.

Ran whistled. 'That's one hell of a floor. It's sprung, I assume?'

'When I talked to the property manager about dancing here, she said the owners had it re-laid at vast expense. They used to throw glamorous parties and decided to install this floor in the mid-fifties to mark the end of all the post-war austerity.'

'A good way to celebrate. I approve.'

'Me too . . . and they expected to be dancing on it for years but, only a year later, Lady Boscawen became ill and the parties came to an end. She died a year after it had been laid and her husband, Sir Richard, was too upset to hold any more balls. He passed away barely a year after his wife. He was only in his late forties when he died and his daughters had to give the house away to settle the tax bill.'

Ran stared out across the empty ballroom. 'That's a pretty tragic story.'

'Very.'

'So, are the Boscawen daughters still around?' he asked.

'I don't really know. I didn't ask if there are any descendants. They left a wonderful legacy for everyone who visits now. To think we'll be dancing on that floor in a few weeks. I'm sure Sir Richard and Lady Anne would have approved.'

Ran gave a wry smile. 'Maybe – though not if we're playing Elvis and "Rock Around the Clock".'

'No, I think they'd have been more into waltzing and foxtrot but their daughters might have approved . . . and some of the younger house staff.' Bo pictured the servants sitting in the staff quarters listening to Bill Haley on a record player not dissimilar to Ran's, perhaps being told off by a stern-faced housekeeper for making a racket.

'Nothing changes; my mum says my grandad was disgusted that she played the Sex Pistols album over and over on her cassette player until the tape broke.'

Ran smiled. 'I approve. I've got *Never Mind the Bollocks* on vinyl.'

'I thought you would!' She laughed. She'd gone through a similar phase herself when she was fourteen or fifteen, trying to fit in at school. Her 'official' music, the kind considered cool at the time, had been stacked on CD racks ready to impress her mates when they'd come over. Secretly, she'd still preferred rock and roll and listened to that through her headphones while she was doing her homework.

'Of course, when we're here for the event itself, the dining room and sitting room are all going to be set up for a 1950s Christmas. Complete with all the decorations.'

'And a vintage turkey?' Ran asked.

She turned to him, amused. 'You're not taking this seriously.'

Ran rearranged his face into a solemn expression. 'I'll try harder.'

Don't, Bo wanted to say. She liked the new Ran that had emerged over the past few weeks. The more open Ran with whom she shared in-jokes and secrets – like the 'sighting' of Madame Odette.

Venturing onto the ballroom floor, Bo did a little turn to check how it would feel on the night.

'Listen . . .' Ran said and lowered his voice. 'Over there.'

Bo followed his gaze to a door at the side of the ballroom, music filtering in through it. The distinctive piano ending of 'My Baby Just Cares for Me' by Nina Simone.

'I think there's a radio on in that room,' Ran said.

They ventured a little closer and noticed the door was open a crack. The Nina Simone track ended and there was a muffled flurry of words from a radio DJ then a fresh intro.

Even before the lyrics began, it was instantly recognisable as Sam Cooke's 'Wonderful World'.

'Oh, wow. I love this one,' Bo said, unable to stop herself jigging around to the artist's distinctive voice.

'Me too. I love that movie too . . .' Ran said.

'You mean *Witness*?'

'Yes. Brilliant film.'

'Harrison Ford and Kelly McGillis are amazing in it,' Bo said. 'My parents said they went to see it when it came out. Have to admit, it's a great movie.'

Bo started humming along, recalling the scene in a barn where a young Harrison Ford, playing a tough but handsome detective, dances with the Amish woman who's saved his life. The longing looks, the forbidden love story, the sexual tension between them, all played out against a song that was now over sixty years old but still had the power to send shivers down her spine.

'That bit in the barn . . .' Ran murmured, as if he sensed the scene playing out inside Bo's head.

'Yes . . .' Bo held her breath.

He came closer, stepping and whistling along like Harrison in the film, closer to her and then moving away, humming the tune. Bo laughed.

He came closer again and held out his hand.

She took it. Before she had time to think that this was their first real physical contact or wonder at the sparks shooting through her whole body, he'd let her go.

She sensed what to do, letting him pull her closer, looking into her eyes and then breaking the contact. Coming closer again, reaching for her hand, she took the cue, let him turn her around. It wasn't just rock and roll, it wasn't just dancing. It was flirting, it was foreplay.

It was working.

'Oh!'

'Damn.'

The music had stopped.

She shook her head, embarrassed. Ran simply stood by, his blue eyes full of a fiery intensity she'd never seen before. A longing . . . for her.

The radio music started again. Another classic: 'Stand by Me' by Ben E King.

Ran broke into a grin. 'This one . . .' he said. 'Is possibly even better.' He reached for her hand again and this time they stayed together, swaying to the rhythm. Taking his cue, she twirled around and he pulled her back into his arms, much closer, face to face for a few seconds. Now she was back in his arms, allowing the music to carry her up and down, like floating in the sea.

The music ended but Ran still held her hands. The radio DJ chattered again, though she'd no idea what he was saying.

'Bo? This might be a crazy idea but remember what I said at the Pavilion Gardens about dancing?'

Her heart was in her mouth. She wasn't sure exactly what he was getting at. 'What did I say?' she murmured.

'That it would be difficult to start dancing again once you stopped.'

'I didn't mean to put you off,' Bo said hastily, knowing she'd been thinking of herself – and not of dancing but of daring to get close to someone again. 'Of course, you could start again if you really wanted to.'

'I do and as long as you're prepared to put up with someone with two left feet, and you haven't changed your mind, I'd love to take you up on it?'

'Um – I—' she stammered.

He let go of her hands. 'You're right. It's a bad idea.'

'No! It's a great idea. I'm a bit surprised, that's all. I thought your dancing days were over.'

'They probably should be.'

'No,' she said firmly. 'They should never be over.'

'I've been thinking that it would be a fresh start for me. Another thing I enjoyed but gave up.'

'A fresh start sounds good to me,' she said, aware he could only mean that dancing again would be another step on the road to his new life. 'I think I can handle it.'

'I'd like to keep our activities private. I mean, not in public – God, that sounds dodgy.' He smiled. 'Don't feel obliged.'

'I don't. I don't feel obliged to teach you.' But she did feel disappointed that he wanted to keep things to dancing alone, even if it was probably a good idea – one she ought to have suggested herself. 'Here's to being dance partners, then.'

He nodded. 'Here's to us.' He held out his hand. 'I hope you'll make allowances.'

Bo shook his hand gently. 'Same here. I'm not a dance teacher,' she insisted, already recognising the danger of what she'd agreed to . . . and yet the idea made her whole body tingle.

Ran kept hold of her hand. 'We'll muddle along together then . . .' he said in a low voice. For a moment, she thought he was going to pull her into his arms and that she might throw caution to the wind and kiss that mouth, trace her fingers along the stubble on his jaw, taste him.

'Have we interrupted an early rehearsal?'

Bo let go of Ran's hand as if it was hot lava and sprang back. 'Hubert!'

Ran was less ruffled, standing still, hands in his pockets.

Sally appeared at Hubert's side. Bo had no idea how long they'd been watching from the doorway. She hadn't even heard the door open. The radio was still on in the next room but Ben E King's silky voice had been replaced by heavy rock. They'd saved her in the nick of time from making a fool of herself.

'I didn't think you danced, Ran?' Sally said, walking over with Hubert, both of them with amused smiles on their faces.

'I don't. We were messing about.' A brief, cool smile. 'As you probably saw from my efforts.'

Messing about? That wasn't how it felt to Bo, whose pulse was still rocketing, her face glowing and, she suspected, as scarlet as the acer tree leaves outside.

'You looked pretty good together to me,' Hubert said. 'Great track. Sam Cooke. Hard to believe it's almost as old as I am . . .' he grinned. 'I've got a copy at home.'

'Lucky you,' Ran said.

The side door opened and a blonde woman poked her head around, as if wondering what all the noise was about. After giving them a polite nod, she closed the door again. The music had stopped completely.

'Who was that?' Bo asked, wondering how many other people had witnessed their private dance.

'The current Lady Boscawen,' Sally said. 'Though she's Jenna to her friends because she never uses the title. The trust allow the family to use a few rooms from time to time. That's the family sitting room.'

'The one that will be set up for the Christmas Illuminations?'

'Yes. Jenna's finding some old Christmas decorations from the fifties. Her family have handed them down over the generations,' Sally said.

'That's a lovely idea,' Bo said, thinking it would also be quite poignant for Jenna to see the end of her family's golden era, frozen in time.

'I see you've checked out this floor,' Hubert said, doing a spin on the wooden blocked surface.

Bo tried not to glance at Ran but he replied anyway. 'Yes, it's pretty cool.'

'We saw . . .' Sally raised an eyebrow.

Bo's cheeks warmed again. She made a show of checking her watch. 'Oh. I should be with Angel! I was only meant to be half an hour.'

'Time flies when you're enjoying yourself,' Hubert said with a sly grin.

Sally came to Bo's rescue. 'Don't worry, I lent a hand while she had a quick loo break a while ago, but then we decided to come and find you. We thought we'd check out the dance floor but it seems you beat us to it.'

Sally glanced from Ran to Bo and back again, a glint of amusement in her eye. It was like being caught out cheating by the teacher.

'Try it for yourselves if you like. I have to go back to Angel. See you later.'

Without a word to Ran, Bo hurried off, her heeled boots click-clacking on the wooden floor. It had been so unexpected, so wonderful to dance with Ran. It had felt natural to be in his arms, to take her cue from him, even if they had been playing around. Even now her fingers tingled at the memory of touching him, the moment they were up close, face to face.

It had been an intimate moment, shared by the two of them, not a performance. Dancing with Ran should be a private thing and the thought of people watching, even friends like Hubert and Sally – or a stranger like Jenna Boscawen   horrified her, even if it was probably best that the moment had ended.

Bo glanced at the door again. Was Jenna Boscawen a stranger? There had been something familiar about her keen eyes and the red nails . . . Bo wracked her brain, ducking past the red rope and outside, cool air fanning her hot cheeks.

Halfway down the grand steps, she froze, like a statue in the garden.

She'd just remembered where she'd seen Lady Boscawen before.

Chapter Twenty-Five

Bo rushed back to the stall where Angel was pink-cheeked with activity.

'Sorry I've been longer than I expected. We saw Lady Boscawen up at the house.'

She gave an 'ooh' of surprise. 'You mean Jenna Boscawen? She's a lovely woman. Good customer too.'

'Yes, she was in the Country Stores the day I visited you. She was looking at the posh jackets.'

Angel nodded. 'That makes sense. She runs a riding stables near Falford with her sister, Lucy. They're always really friendly. You'd never know they were aristocracy, though Kelvin is always creeping to her as if she was the Queen. Did you speak to her?'

'No. We only caught a glimpse. She was playing some music in a room next to the ballroom. She interrupted us.'

Angel's brow furrowed. 'She doesn't own the place now so I'm sure she wouldn't mind.'

'She didn't . . . but it was awkward. We were . . . dancing.' Bo decided to come clean. Hubert and Sally would find it too tempting not to share with Angel – and probably half the dance group. Better to act casual about it, as Ran had – even if the experience of being in Ran's arms was anything but casual. The memory filled her with excitement now, and she longed to take things further – much further.

'Dancing? You and *Ran*?'

'Kinda. Not a full-on routine. Lady Boscawen – Jenna – had the radio on in the family sitting room next to the ballroom. We were trying out the floor, messing around – you know.' Bo hoped Angel would put her pink cheeks down to the heat in the marquee.

'B-but, Ran doesn't dance.'

'He did once. At university, apparently.'

'Well, well. I'm surprised in one way though not in another. I've noticed him jigging away at the decks when he thought we weren't watching.'

'Really?'

'Yes, although I thought he was only getting carried away by the music. From time to time, the way he moved made me think he might have danced once. Do you think he'll join in at the club from now on?'

Bo laughed. 'I doubt it. He's far too shy and too happy hiding behind the decks. It was only a bit of fun. Anyway, I'm really sorry I'm late. Has business been going well? You look like you've sold quite a bit.'

'Mostly brilliant. I did have one woman who turned up her nose and said she could make "bits and bobs like this" if only she had the time.'

Bo rolled her eyes. 'I get the same. People telling me they enjoy making cakes and they'd "love to start a little café" when they retire or if they didn't have a full-time job – and telling me how they'd run it, the menu they'd serve, how I could improve the place. I'm all for taking customer feedback on board but often I just have to nod and smile.'

'I know exactly what you mean,' Angel said. 'Only it's my boss, not the customers, who make me grit my teeth.'

A group of eager-looking women approached so their conversation was cut short. Business was brisk until a slight lull around lunchtime when many people flocked to the Trewhella café to refuel. Ran turned up with packs of sandwiches and bottles of juice.

'Thought you'd be too busy to get some food.'

'We are!' Angel said.

'Thanks. We were starving,' Bo added, pleased at his thoughtfulness.

After wolfing down the sandwiches, Angel sold some pot holders to a portly man in a tweed suit and then started chatting to a familiar figure. It was Jenna Boscawen.

Ran exchanged a quizzical glance with Bo as if thinking the same thing: would Jenna refer to their impromptu dance?

He spoke quietly to Bo. 'I'll leave you to it. Hubert wants a word about where we're going to set up the sound system.'

Bo wondered if he was keen to leave because he was embarrassed about being spotted by Jenna.

Her customer-friendly smile back in place, Bo returned her attention to Angel who was putting Jenna's payment through the card reader while she tucked the tea towels and apron into a paper carrier bag for her.

Jenna's gaze settled on the dresses hanging behind the stall.

'Oh my, those are beautiful. That emerald jacquard one – oh my! My great-grandmother had a dress *exactly* like this, only in pistachio-coloured silk. The style is so similar and she had the stiff underskirt. My mother kept it for years and we used to try it on when we were children.'

'Really?' Bo said. 'Is that the lady in a green dress pictured in the great hall?'

'Yes. That's the one. It's from 1959. The last Christmas at the hall. Obviously, I wasn't even born and my mother was only a teenager. The underskirt had to be thrown out, it became so grubby and moth-eaten from being worn in the gardens . . .' Jenna smiled at the memory. 'I've no idea what happened to the dress itself.'

'That's so sad,' Angel said, handing Jenna's payment card back to her. 'Vintage pieces are very fragile. Not many survive even if they're not given away.'

'Your dress is so like my great-granny's, though.'

Angel positively glowed. 'That's nice of you to say so but this one is manmade material not silk. I'm sure your great-grandmother's was a haute couture design.'

'I doubt it. She probably had it made by a local dressmaker from Truro rather than London, to look like a couture piece. Even in those days the Boscawens weren't in great financial shape. This place was a money pit which is why my family were grateful the trust took it off our hands. We're lucky they let us use some of the rooms if we let them know in advance.'

'Do you stay overnight?'

'Very rarely these days. I was here discussing the Christmas Illuminations with the property manager and some of the volunteer team. I brought some of the original decorations and some personal items to try and make the setting look as authentic as possible. We are allowed to stay overnight but it can be rather spooky. I'd rather drive back to the stables to be honest than be all alone here.' She smiled. 'I prefer modern-day central heating too. The boiler system in here makes some alarming noises.'

'I wouldn't fancy it either.'

'I often volunteer – my name badge says "Jenna" and hardly anyone guesses my family used to own the house. It's fascinating hearing what people say about you.' She laughed. 'Actually, I've been asked to do the switch-on for Christmas Illuminations. Seeing that gorgeous dress of yours, I've had an idea . . . Imagine if I wore a dress like my great-granny's to do it! Is there any chance you'd take a commission?'

Angel's jaw dropped. 'I don't know . . .'

'I'm sure you could, Angel,' Bo chirped up, sensing a major opportunity for her friend. 'You're so talented.'

'Well, if you think . . .'

'It would be wonderful to wear a dress like the one Great-granny has on in the portrait in the hallway. Obviously, I wouldn't expect it to be silk. There's only five weeks to go. It's asking a lot because I know how busy you are at the Country Stores and with your family.'

Bo winced on Angel's behalf though her friend seemed calm enough in her reply. 'I'm not too busy to have a go. If you think I'd do a good job, I'd *love* to make it. I do have a week's holiday coming up and I was wondering what I was going to do with myself.'

'It's a deal then,' Bo cut in, hoping she wasn't interfering too much but desperate for Angel to accept the commission and boost her confidence further.

'I hope so,' Jenna replied.

'I'd need to take your measurements but perhaps I can come over to the stables for that?' Angel said.

'Perfect.' She beamed.

'I'd need to find the right fabric. I doubt we can replicate the original though I'll do some research and see what I can do.'

'Great.' Jenna clutched her bag of purchases to her chest. 'I'm surprised you don't have these on sale in the Country Stores. They're so sweet.'

'In my dreams. I'm not sure what my boss would think of that.'

Jenna pursed her lips. 'Hmm. Please don't repeat this but I wouldn't take much notice of Kelvin's opinion. All the customers – and the suppliers, from what I've heard – know it's you who runs the place.'

Angel flushed. 'I'm sure he tries his best. It's not been easy since his uncle handed over the reins over to him,' she added – with admirable diplomacy, Bo thought.

Jenna raised her eyebrows. 'Very charitable of you. Personally, I wouldn't hand over the reins of a Shetland pony to him.'

Bo giggled and Angel was struggling not to laugh.

'Whenever we've ordered feed or equipment for the stables and he's been in charge, something's gone horribly wrong. As you well know, because you've had to sort it out. Our hay man can't bear Kelvin and I absolutely loathe the way he calls me "Your Ladyship", all the time. I'm not "Her Ladyship" and never have been.' She shuddered. 'Ugh.'

'Kelvin's easily confused,' Angel said. 'I mean, he probably isn't aware of how you feel.'

Jenna patted Angel's arm. 'You're far too loyal to him. I'd not be able to bite my tongue if I worked for him.' She shuddered again. 'Odious little man, though, as you say, he is your boss. On a more positive note, do you have a card?'

'Um. No. I didn't have time but I printed off a few flyers with my number on.'

'OK. Great.'

Jenna added a flyer to her bag and exchanged numbers with Angel to be on the safe side.

She left, and Bo's mood was lifted for the second time that day. They packed away and loaded the stuff into the van, several boxes lighter after all the sales. Darkness was falling as they drove out of the estate and headed home through the Cornish 'mizzle'.

'Imagine Lady Boscawen wearing a dress you made at the Christmas Illuminations. What an advert for the business,' Bo said on the way home.

'The business? Phew, I hadn't thought of it like that.'

'You're more of a businessperson than Kelvin will ever be.'

Far from being boosted by Bo's comment, Angel let out a squeak of dismay. 'Oh, what have I let myself in for?'

'A lot of fun and some extra cash. And Jenna is right. You do need business cards. And maybe a Facebook and Instagram page.'

'I'm not sure about that. You don't think I'm getting above myself, do you?'

'"Above yourself"? You could never get above yourself! You're the loveliest, most modest person I know and one of the most talented, and you have every right to feel proud of what you do. As for the marketing, I'll help you. My customers love following the café on social media. It's how we keep them up to date with the new menus and keep them coming back for new treats. It's fun. You won't regret it.'

'I hope not.' Angel shook her head. 'Imagine if Tommy could see me now. Starting a new business, on Instagram and making dresses for Lady Boscawen. He wouldn't believe it.'

'Good!' Bo declared.

'I'm so glad I went. Thanks for dragging me out of the doldrums. I needed it.'

'I hope I haven't been too bossy. That's the last thing you need: someone else telling you what to do.'

'No. Not bossy. Encouraging. Persistent.' She smiled. 'I needed a gentle kick up the backside. I think I have to accept Tommy's not coming back.'

A fresh wave of guilt washed over Bo; however, now was definitely not the time to destroy the positive mood with her vague suspicions.

'While we're on the subject of kicks up the backside, do you mind if I say something to you about Ran?'

Bo gripped the wheel. That was the last thing she'd been expecting from Angel.

'No, though I've no idea what it could be.'

'Are you two . . . a thing?' Angel asked. 'If I've got the wrong end of the stick or I'm being too nosy, then you'll have to say. I've been wondering for a few weeks now. In fact, I thought you and he might have got together months ago.'

'You're not being too nosy.' Bo was glad she could keep her eyes on the road. 'I do like him and I think he likes me but no, we're not a "thing". We're still, as they say, "just good friends". Even if we wanted to take it further, the problem is we're both carrying enough baggage to fill a 747.' She felt guilty as hell about withholding the fact they were going to start dancing together but Ran had asked her to keep the lessons strictly private.

Bo bit her lip. After *that* encounter on the dance floor, getting up close and personal with Ran, keeping things 'strictly' anything was going to be almost impossible.

Chapter Twenty-Six

Ran paced the sitting room at the cottage, unable to decide what music to play for the lesson. It wasn't usually a problem for him but he'd been unable to concentrate on anything since he'd got home from a dive mid-afternoon – in fact, his mind hadn't been engaged on work for the past week, ever since his dance with Bo in the ballroom.

Now Bo was coming to give him his first lesson that evening and he was seriously worried he wouldn't be able to walk let alone dance. His legs were actually wobbly with nerves for the first time since he was a kid.

He was excited about rekindling his dancing days, even more excited about Bo being the one to light the flame. Also, already apprehensive. What if he was crap? If he embarrassed himself? What if he enjoyed it far too much and it led to him falling for Bo? Correction: what if it led to him falling for her more than he already had? He'd tried to hold back so far, avoiding being drawn in, and yet he was the one who'd asked her to his house, and now on this date.

'It's a deal,' he'd heard himself saying, like a man running back into a burning building even as the fire alarms rang in his ears, deafening him. 'I hope you realise what you've let yourself in for?'

Too late now. He heard her car pull onto the gravel at the side of the cottage. He put on a rock and roll mix tape, and turned the volume down low.

'Stop looking at me like that, Thor!' he ordered.

If Thor could have shrugged he would have, but instead he leapt into his radiator cradle and washed his paws.

'Hello!'

Bo breezed in on a cloud of light floral perfume, wrapped up against the autumn chill and wearing pattered Doc Martens.

He hung up her coat, inhaling the scent lingering on the wool before joining her in the sitting room. Was that creepy? He hoped not.

'You look nice,' he said, unable to find words to express how beautifully the blue swing dress showed off her figure.

'Thanks,' she said, producing her dancing shoes from the bag she took to Flingers every week.

Thor appeared, staring at him from the shadows, as if to remind Ran that he and Bo were there to dance. Nothing more.

She went ahead of him into the sitting room. 'I have to be honest,' she said. 'I thought you'd change your mind.'

Ran felt guilty because he'd been ready to chicken out at least half a dozen times over the past week. 'No, I haven't. Why would you think that?'

'Being caught together – in the ballroom. I wondered if it made you feel uncomfortable?'

'No. Not at all. I mean. OK, I felt like a bit of a prat.'

'Oh.'

Ran cursed himself. 'I enjoyed the dancing. I didn't mean that

I was embarrassed at being seen with you. It's only that it's been so long since I danced in public, or at all. I wondered if you were ashamed about being found dancing with an oaf like me.'

'You're not an oaf. You can still dance. You must know that?'

'Yeah. Maybe. I *want* to learn again and it hadn't ought to be a big secret but I'm not ready to go public yet.'

About the dancing or something more, he thought. *Was* there something more between them? With Bo standing right in front him, the need and desire he'd felt in the ballroom flooded back with a vengeance. He *wanted* there to be more between them. How could he dance with her, be so close, share the joy and emotion of the music without taking their relationship beyond dance partners?

He'd sent back the letter and the drawn-out divorce process was going ahead, yet he *was* still legally married. Part of him wondered if he still hadn't let go, psychologically. Surely he had to do that before he became involved with anyone else? Even then, the commitment scared him. His own feelings were fragile – how could he risk Bo's, so soon after she'd recovered from her break-up? Was it worth risking another crash to earth that might not be survivable for both of them?

'Ran?'

'Sorry, yes. I'm so out of practice. I've forgotten even the most basic steps.'

'Didn't seem like it in the ballroom,' she said.

'That was just messing about.'

'Oh.'

She looked hurt. He kicked himself for the flippant remark, designed to protect himself, really. 'I mean, it wasn't rock and roll. It was . . . fun.'

'Fun?' She smiled again but he knew he'd upset her. Fun and

messing about didn't describe the intense closeness he'd felt to her, the fizzing sexual tension and the sheer joy he'd experienced giving himself up to the dance. He'd only make things worse by apologising. He didn't have the words, anyway.

'The steps will come back to you,' Bo said briskly. 'Like riding a bike.'

'The last time I rode a bike, I fell into a ditch.'

She rolled her eyes. 'You won't fall into a ditch but it might take longer for some people. If you're prepared to put the effort in – not that it should be an effort, of course. It should be fun.'

Part of him wanted to tell her to forget the dancing completely . . . He wanted to experience the physical contact, the buzz of moving to the music – the adrenaline rush – but if he was perfectly honest, he wanted Bo in his arms more.

She cut into his fantasies. 'Shall we push back the furniture so we have more space?'

'There's no need. I thought we could dance outside. It's a fine night and not too cold.'

'Oh, that's a great idea.'

He opened the French doors. In the November evening a mist was rising from the river. He'd pushed the bench to one side of the terrace and switched on the string of lights around the trellis. It still hadn't seemed bright enough so he'd also lit a few of the garden lanterns he kept outside. The candlelight wavered in the whisper of breeze. He hoped to God Bo didn't think it was cheesy.

'Wow. This is lovely.'

An owl hooted from the trees, as it settled into its roost, and he thought he could hear rustling from the reeds around the mudflats.

'It's peaceful. That's why I like it. The stillness. We won't be

221

overlooked,' he said. 'Although I'm not quite sure what the local wildlife will make of it.'

'Do you listen to music out here a lot?'

'Sometimes on warm evenings.'

'It must be such a contrast with London.'

'It is.' He spent such a lot of time alone. The contrast with his and Phaedra's modern apartment in the middle of a bustling London suburb, his commute by Tube and the office tower filled with harassed, busy, important people couldn't have been greater. 'It's not a sprung dance floor. Those paving slabs could be hell on your joints.'

She laughed. 'We're not going to do anything too risky, are we? No lifts and throws.' Her eyes glinted. 'Not yet, anyway.'

'No.' The lighting threw soft shadows on her lovely face with its raised eyebrow. He caught his breath. This was going to be almost impossible. 'Nothing too risky.'

'What track shall we choose to start with? Any preferences?'

'Oh. Yeah.' He raked his hands through his hair. It was far too soon. Dancing had to come first: taking it slowly, seeing how it went – for both of them. They'd know soon enough if the dance would lead to more.

'OK. What about . . . a classic Elvis number? Something nice and slow to begin with so I can keep up . . . erm . . . I thought "Stuck on You" was a good start.'

He cringed. What a title, he hadn't thought about how Bo might take it, only that the tempo was gentle for a beginner like himself.

'You've probably got much better ideas.'

'No.' She didn't miss a beat. 'That one's a good choice for learning.'

'I've streamed the music from the smart speaker so I don't

222

have to keep cueing it in. We can start and stop it when I want.'

'Good move.'

Even though they'd danced in the ballroom, it had seemed like a public space and it had been impromptu. This was different: it felt private, intimate. Ran already wondered how he was ever going to get through a session without wanting to take things a lot further than holding her hand during the dance.

They cupped hands, lightly, never gripping, he remembered. Ran placed his hand in the small of Bo's back. At least he got that much right . . .

Her hand rested on his shoulder ready for the turns.

'Cue Elvis!'

The music started.

Remembering the different steps, that he was the leader and Bo was the follower – that was a joke for a start. Even the basic rock and back steps had him tripping over his feet and constantly apologising. Restarting the song countless times while Bo patiently offered tips and encouragement. The constant rejoining of hands, his fingers resting in the small of her back . . .

Thor sauntered outside, his eyes glowing in the dark, ever watchful and probably thinking: 'You've bitten off more than you can chew, human.'

An hour later, Ran was properly sweating, his feet were sore and he was breathing heavily. He was uplifted and frustrated at the same time. Dancing was simple but also complicated.

In contrast, Bo was fresh as a daisy, her cheeks were pink and glowing from the dance. He handed her a chilled bottle of Coke.

'I told you it would all come back to you, though I already knew that from the way you danced in the ballroom. You nailed the basics, and the turns.'

He shook his head. 'I'm sure I made lots of mistakes.'

'That's the beauty of it though, isn't it? As I'm following you, we both make the mistakes together and no one notices.'

'It's nothing to the jive you're doing at the performances. That was baby stuff.'

'You could jive if you wanted to.'

'Ha!' He tipped the Coke bottle at her. 'I don't think so.'

'You could. Have you ever done it?'

'A couple of times when I was at the uni club. It's tough.'

'You're fit. Fitter than me,' she said.

'Jive is a different thing to the basics we tried today.'

'We could practise – I need the extra practice for the performances so I can keep up with Cade and Hubert,' she said. 'When a man twice your age is putting you to shame on the dance floor, you need the help!'

Ran laughed. 'Hubert is a force of nature and, if it would help you, I'd be happy to learn some jive. But please, let's get the basics right first.'

He didn't only mean the dance steps. He'd enjoyed it all far too much but he had to take things slowly for both their sakes.

Chapter Twenty-Seven

'Steady. Joey, ready to secure the sail? Ran, you hold that end. Bo – OK?'

Finn Morvah gave his instructions clearly and directly on a crisp Sunday morning at the café. It was mid-November and Ran had heard about Bo's terrace project during their sessions and offered to help without being asked.

Admitting he'd no experience of carpentry, he seemed more than happy to be ordered about, and do the fetching and carrying. In fact, seeing him intent on the work, or sharing a joke with the Morvahs, Bo thought he looked quite at home in Falford. Or was that wishful thinking?

He'd already had several lessons and was a quick learner, attempting a couple of jive routines. It was a relief to Bo because the moves were so quick and demanding, they hadn't had time for any lingering looks. A loss of focus could mean both of them might fall flat on their faces – in more ways than one.

Today was all about the café, which was closed for the day so the sail could finally be fixed above the terrace. The Morvahs had already adjusted the large triangular canvas so it would stretch from the stone building on one side to sturdy metal poles on the other.

After much hammering, banging and lifting, Bo found herself surrounded by three sweaty hunks in their T-shirts, plus Dorinda Morvah, who'd expertly fitted the new wooden bar area along the side of the wall. The result was that the café now had twice as many tables under cover as it had before, plus four extra seats along the bar. Bo could now cater for twenty people at tables, or even more for a stand-up event with bowl food.

'Thank you so much, guys,' she said, handing out cool drinks to the team, despite the chilly morning. 'Those reclaimed timbers look fantastic as counter tops.'

Bo ran her hand along the old wood, which had been beautifully restored by Dorinda. 'And the sail is so perfect. So fitting.' She had a lump in her throat as she surveyed the terrace and imagined it full of customers, rain or shine. She might even have to take on another member of staff.

'You're welcome,' Dorinda said, sipping an apple juice.

'I've been able to take a booking for a Christmas cocktail party from Starfish Graphics, that trendy new design agency by the quay. They've created some new designs for some boat-builders and they wanted something different for Christmas. It's only a small start but we're doing themed canapés and drinks and we'll get the fire pit out. If it goes well, I should be able to book some more events in the spring.'

Joey Morvah pulled a sweatshirt over his T-shirt. Now the work was done, it was growing cold. He put his arm around Bo and kissed her cheek. 'Now, any chance of those brekkie butties we were promised?'

She saw Ran watching her.

'No problem. Sit there and I'll bring them over.'

'Want a hand?' Ran offered, joining her in the kitchen.

'Yeah. Why not?'

With Ran as kitchen hand, Bo soon had plates of sourdough topped with local eggs and bacon on their way to the new terrace where the cricket-loving Morvahs were engaged in a conversation about a match taking place in some exotic location on the other side of the world. Dorinda was on the phone but everything stopped once the food arrived. Ran came back for a tray of coffees and they all enjoyed breakfast together.

'Thanks for helping,' Bo told Ran when the Morvahs had gone and he helped wash and tidy up.

'It was the least I could do. Call it payment for my lessons.'

'You don't owe me anything,' she said.

'Oh, I think I do . . .' He reached up and caught a lock of her hair between his fingers then let it go and stepped back, hands in his pockets. 'Sorry. I have to go to work. My real job. See you for the next lesson?'

'Yes. Of course.'

He left, leaving Bo touching her cheek where his fingers had brushed it, wondering how long she could keep this up without breaking her resolution not to get too close to him.

With work, her dance sessions and helping Angel, the next couple of weeks flew by. The café was open Wednesday to Saturday but she'd also been busy with events, including an afternoon tea for a friend's baby shower and taken on a last-minute booking for a Christmas fair in the next village when the regular caterer had let them down. Cade had chalked up the Christmas menu on the A-board, and they'd joked that the 'low season' was proving to be almost as busy as summer.

Her parents and a friend had said she was looking tired, but no one knew that it was all the extra dancing – and the *extra* extra dancing – that was wearing her out, or how much she didn't mind.

Having encouraged Angel to branch out in business, she also felt she should offer extra support to her friend. The week before the Illuminations, she drove round to the cottage for the dinner they'd promised each other. They were both so busy, Bo called for a Chinese takeaway from the village en route.

'Here we go,' she said, looking for a space to put down the paper bag full of takeout dishes.

The kitchen was a sea of fabric and stock again.

'Sorry, sorry!' Angel cried, shifting her sewing box from the counter top. 'Pop that bag here.'

Bo put it down.

Angel shoved her hair out of her eyes, looking flustered. 'I had to use the kitchen table. I'd like to use the spare room but Tommy's junk and fishing gear is piled high. I'll get rid of that one day, though – imagine it as a proper sewing room complete with machines, ironing board, boxes full of patterns, fabric, equipment, books and lots of other stuff.'

'Lots of businesses were started from kitchen tables,' Bo said, helping to decant chicken chow mein and beef in black bean sauce onto plates.

'I know . . . and I'm scared.'

'Why? Of it being a success?'

'Of daring to dream – to let myself think – that I could be my own boss doing what I love, instead of working for Kelvin. I need the regular salary, that's the trouble.' She sniffed the air. 'This smells amazing. I haven't had time for a proper lunch.'

Angel carried her machine out of the kitchen to make room for their plates.

'Could you do this alongside your job?' Bo said when Angel reappeared. 'It's not easy starting again. I gave up a job as chef in a café to launch Bo's. I had a loan. It was scary.'

'I keep thinking I'm too old to start again and that there's been enough upheaval but now Tommy's gone . . . and I've survived . . . I keep wondering: what am I waiting for?'

'You need an outlet for your stuff. Not only craft fairs, but online – and retail. What about the Lizard gift shop? Of course the obvious place would be to have some in the Country Stores.'

They sat down and Bo offered Angel the bag of prawn crackers. She dived in, crunching one down before replying.

'Mmm. Half the time I feel determined and confident about starting my own business. The rest of it is overwhelming and I want to go back to the way things were.'

'That sounds totally normal to me.' Bo smiled. 'Do you want a hand clearing the spare room out some time?'

'Maybe.' Angel wrinkled her nose, and Bo took the hint that clearing out any of Tommy's stuff might be a step too far at this stage.

They tucked into the food and Bo steered the conversation to safer territory, asking about how Angel would go about recreating Jenna Boscawen's dress.

'I've got a collection of 1950s patterns. They're multi-sized and I mix and match tops and bottoms, so there can be lots of variations. I can adapt these to any requests for dresses. I think this is the best way for me to start out, before I move on to designing my own and having my own patterns.'

'I didn't know that's how patterns worked,' Bo said.

'Yes. The back of each pattern advises you on the type of fabric and how much to buy. You can order the material online but I prefer a mooch around the fabric shops if possible – I'll have to go and look for something to match Jenna's dress and maybe show her some samples. I don't have long to do it all though!'

'Is there anything I can do to help?'

'You've already done such a lot by getting me started.' Angel smiled. 'As for the patterns, I can print them out as a PDF. That's the easy part but there aren't as many haberdashery-type shops as there used to be. I remember my mum taking me to some when I was young and being fascinated by all the trimmings and ribbons. Sometimes they'd let me have little samples and I'd sew clothes for my dolls. Does that sound mad?'

'No, it's lovely,' Bo said, delighted to see the animation in Angel's face. 'I love hearing about it.'

'It'll be great to have a proper excuse to look at the fabrics. If I can, I like to buy from warehouses or local markets as the prices are really good and there's lots of choice. There's one stall in Truro pannier market that I can never resist.'

'Sounds great.' Bo sat back and patted her stomach. 'That was delicious but I can never eat it all. I hate wasting food.'

'I'll pop the leftovers in the fridge and have them tomorrow.'

Bo nodded.

'Have you heard from Ran lately?' Angel said, popping lids back on the uneaten dishes. 'You two seemed to be getting along at the craft fair?'

'I saw him the other night.' Bo laughed. 'Surprised he could walk afterwards.'

'Bo! Tell me more!'

'No! No, nothing like that.' Bo could have kicked herself. 'I popped round with a . . . um, a record he hadn't got. He almost tripped over.'

'Thor got in his way, I expect. Cats appear from nowhere.'

'Um. I think so . . .' Bo felt terrible, lying about the fact Ran had fallen over trying to lift her during a jive. She'd been OK, but he'd missed his footing and twisted his ankle.

'He's OK though?'

'Oh, yes. Only a bruise and hurt pride.'

'And you say you took a record round to him?'

'Mmm,' Bo said, feeling even worse by the minute. 'It was an, um, ABBA album.'

'ABBA! For Ran?'

'Mum gave it me. We thought it might be rare but it turned out it wasn't.' Bo reached for the last prawn cracker from the bag, even though she was already stuffed. She needed something, anything, to do with her mouth rather than have Angel scrutinising her expression.

'You know, you and Ran. If you're hanging on for the right moment or holding back because you're scared of being hurt, then don't. It's none of my business, of course, and I'm hardly one to talk, but life's a risk. You have to take it. Even if it might not work out,' Angel said.

Bo swallowed the last crumbs. 'I . . . it's complicated . . . for both of us.'

Angel nodded. 'I get that. I thought it might be but please, don't spend life waiting for everything to be perfect. Chances are there never will be a perfect moment and life will have passed you by.'

'Thanks, my lovely,' Bo said, on the verge of unexpected tears. 'I promise I'll bear that in mind.'

'Hmm.' Angel gave her a sceptical look but left it at that – much to Bo's relief.

Chapter Twenty-Eight

The Tuesday before the Illuminations had started well. It had been sunny but chilly in the December wind, a hint of winter hanging in the air even on Bo's newly sheltered terrace.

Everyone had gravitated to the covered area, devouring brunches and toasties, but by two p.m. the skies had turned leaden, rain had blown in and the wind had strengthened.

After taking the decision to shut the café early, Bo headed off to the Country Stores to buy extra lighting and decorations for the café to brighten it up for the festive period and the upcoming cocktail party. She wanted to pull out all the stops for the first business event, in the hope Starfish Graphics would recommend her to their clients and other businesses.

Angel was in the back office, so Bo contented herself with a wave, found a trolley and chose several sets of outdoor Christmas lights for the terrace. The Stores had some new wicker sculptures of sea creatures which she couldn't resist and would look fab, adorned with greenery and fairy lights. The Morvahs had also rigged up an old oar and suspended it from one end of the sail – that also needed some lighting.

Totting up the cost in her mind, she winced a little but looked on it as an investment.

Even if she wasn't looking forward to Christmas on a personal level, she had to look after her business and the lighting and props could be used for many years to come.

Pushing a bulging trolley, she returned into the main sales area where Angel was now on the till serving a familiar face.

Jenna Boscawen had a basket full of Christmas cards and a pair of jodhpurs.

'Hello there!' she said when Bo appeared. 'I guess we had the same idea.'

She nodded at Bo's trolley.

'It's for the café. We've refurbed the terrace and I've got my first corporate event coming up.' She held up crossed fingers.

'Oh, good luck!' Jenna declared.

Angel rang up all the purchases, and the three of them struck up a lively conversation about Trewhella and the Illuminations. Laughter rang out and Bo thought again what a nice woman Jenna was.

The doors to the building yard opened and Kelvin marched in.

Bo swore silently as he bore down on them.

'Chatting again, Angel? Are we not busy?' he said before turning to Jenna with a smirk. 'Good afternoon, Lady Boscawen.'

'Blame me,' Jenna cut in with a charming smile. 'I was here to buy some decorations and have a word with Angel about my dress.'

'Dress?' Kelvin sounded like it was an alien concept to him.

'Yes. Angel is making me a replica of one my ancestors wore for the Christmas celebrations at Trewhella House. I'm going to wear it for the Illuminations.'

'Right . . .'

'Will you be there? Angel's dance group are performing too.'

'Er . . . I hadn't made any plans. I'm not really into history. Or dancing.' He shot a pointed look at Angel that made Bo want to throw something at him. 'Or dresses.'

'What a shame. I'm sure you'd look divine in one.' Jenna laughed. 'Angel is a very gifted seamstress. Did you know?'

'Um. No.' Kelvin slid another glance at Angel. 'She's obviously a woman of hidden talents.'

'Really?' Jenna sounded amazed. 'I can't believe you've never seen some of the gorgeous things she makes. You should stock some of her homewares in here. They're the equal of any of the kitchen linens in your gift area. I'm sure the customers would absolutely love the chance to take home something that's been handmade in Cornwall, and by an employee.'

Angel seemed to shrink behind the desk.

'They're fantastic,' Bo said, adding to the endorsements. 'I have some bunting up at the café and some tea towels. She already sells some through the charity shops and they flew off the shelves at the Trewhella craft fair.'

'You have been busy,' Kelvin said.

'It's only a small business,' Angel squeaked. 'Just a hob—'

'Nonsense. You're brilliant,' Jenna declared. 'I'll expect to see them in here next time I visit, then?'

'You?' Kelvin glared at Angel. 'Make stuff to sell in *here*?' Kelvin barely hid his sneer.

Jenna cut him off. 'They would be an asset to your gift display and would fly off the shelves.'

Bo was shaking with anger, on the very edge of letting rip at Kelvin.

'I'm sure you have very good taste, Lady Boscawen,' he said, fawning over her.

'I have excellent taste, Kelvin, so do please take Angel's work seriously.' She flashed him a sweet smile, which Bo knew was backed with steel.

Kelvin laughed. 'I'll do my best, Lady Boscawen,' he said.

'I hope so and please, please, if you can possibly manage it, call me Jenna!'

Jenna left and poor Angel was on the verge of tears, clasping her hands together with anxiety. Bo didn't blame her. Kelvin was a vile bully who deserved someone to stand up to him. While she longed to be the one to sort him out, Bo thought it would make the situation even worse for her friend. She bit her lip as he held forth behind the cash desk, with the other staff staring through the back-office window, their faces pale.

'That bloody woman,' he sneered. 'Lady la-di-dah. Thinks she owns the place.'

'Jenna's lovely,' Angel shot back. 'And a very good customer!'

'Yeah, don't I know it – but if she weren't, I'd have told her where to go. You might think the sun shines out of her jodhpurs but you're living in cloud cuckoo land if you think you can make a living from a few tea towels. Lady Boscawen might think it's OK for you to have a little hobby, but I know better. Besides, when are you going to find the time to make all of this stuff? How are you going to market it, do your books, speak to suppliers, go out and sell it to the customers? How d'you propose to do that and hold down a job here?'

Bo held her breath, a heartbeat away from flying to Angel's defence. She had an insane urge to throw a flower pot at Kelvin.

Angel was rigid, her fingers clenched around the oven glove. 'You're right,' she murmured.

Bo trembled. She couldn't let this happen to her friend. She had to sort Kelvin out and she was bloody going to!

'You're right,' Angel repeated. 'How can I market my business, do the books, speak to the suppliers and deal with the customers? How could I?' Her voice rose with every phrase. 'I'll tell you how I could, Kelvin. I could because I already *do*. I already run this place while you're off playing golf and visiting your fancy woman. I already sort out the mess you create, keep this place afloat so your uncle doesn't lose what's left of it!'

Kelvin's jaw dropped. 'You what?'

'You heard me!' Angel declared. 'I've been running this place for ages so I'm damn sure I can run my own business.'

'B-but how will you have the time?' he stuttered. 'You work for me.'

'Correction, Kelvin. I *did* work for you.'

Angel ripped off her name badge and threw it on the floor at his feet. 'But as of this moment, I don't any more.'

He'd turned puce. 'B-but you can't quit! You have to give notice.'

'I think you'll find that you never checked my contract. I only have to give a week's notice and I have three weeks' holiday owing so I'm starting it now. Goodbye, Kelvin. I'm sure you'll have no problem running this place on your own as you're such a brilliant entrepreneur.'

'Oi! Wait a minute!'

'I've wasted far too many minutes here already.'

Leaving Kelvin open-mouthed, Angel strode right past him and joined Bo at the door.

For a few seconds there was absolute silence in the warehouse but then the space erupted. Applause and cheering rang out from the office and around the store as several customers emerged from behind the pet food section and the equine sundries aisle. A spaniel started barking and snarling at Kelvin.

'Serves you right, you horrible little man,' the dog's owner declared. 'And I'll be finding a new place to get Tilly's food from, now Angel's gone.'

'You can forget about any help from me either.'

Reg, a white-haired man, abandoned a trolley full of compost bags. 'I've wanted to retire for ages. I was only staying on to help Angel, and without her, you won't have any staff left.' He ripped off his apron and threw it at Kelvin's feet. 'There's a load of manure just arrived in the yard, which you ordered and we don't need. You can sort it out yourself, mate, because you're full of it. Oh, by the way, everyone for fifty miles thinks you're a complete tosser.'

'Thanks, Reg,' Angel whispered.

Reg patted her arm. 'It's OK, love. It was worth staying on just to see you tell him to shove his job up his arse!'

With her lip wobbling, Angel nodded but then turned and almost ran out of the shop.

Bo went after her, struggling to keep up.

They were out in the yard by Bo's car before Angel slowed down.

'Angel!'

'Oh God, what have I done?' she wailed.

'Exactly what you should have done and what Kelvin deserved.'

'I don't have a job!'

'Correction. You don't have a job you hate and where you're treated like crap.'

'I know, but I need the money.'

'Yes . . . we can sort this. You could probably do him for

237

constructive dismissal. If he hasn't been following employment law, bullying you, not doing appraisals, et cetera, et cetera.'

'I don't want to do that. I don't want to work here.' Angel put her face in her hands. 'I've burned all my bridges.'

'You burned one rickety, shitty bridge. It's a shock but it'll turn out to be the best thing you ever did. I promise,' Bo declared although she was under no illusions as to the total bewilderment Angel must be feeling. 'Everyone knows what a great manager you are, how you ran this place. You could get a job with any of the suppliers or the garden centre – or the craft centre. Or you could take this as the moment to start your new business.'

'It's not going to be that easy, though,' Angel said. 'I'm not young and confident. I'm not even coming to terms with Tommy leaving yet, let alone starting a new business. I've had the whole foundation of my life swept away from under my feet!'

Bo flinched but stayed silent.

'Why did I ever even think I could run a business? Make a go of it? I must be out of my mind. I'm Angel. I cook, I dance, I have a little hobby just like Kelvin said. I'm a sad, nice older lady from the Country Stores whose husband left her. Now I don't even have my job.'

Chapter Twenty-Nine

'I feel responsible for this,' Bo said the moment Ran answered the door when she went round for their scheduled dancing lesson later that evening. She'd gone back to the café and couldn't resist setting up some of the lights and trying them out in different configurations as darkness fell. With Angel on her mind too, she'd forgotten the time and had to drive straight to Ran's.

'Come in and tell me about it.'

'How is she now?' he asked as they walked into the living room.

'God knows. Devastated. She drove home. I was so worried, the way she left the car park, wheels spinning and all. She drives like a demon at the best of times.'

'Angel?' He raised an eyebrow.

'Yeah. Always has. Don't know why unless she takes out her frustrations on the road.'

Ran was obviously trying not to smile.

'It's not funny!'

'No, it's not.' He put on a serious face although the amusement was there in his voice. 'I'm simply trying to square the idea of Angel as Lewis Hamilton with the woman we know and love.'

He gestured for her to sit down. From the open door to the kitchen, the aroma of spices hit her senses.

'That's the thing, though. Do we really know her?' she said. 'The Angel we see has been holding back her real self, how she feels, the pain, the frustration for so long. She's put herself last, and been devoted to her family and sticking at a job that's become a misery for her. Now, she's lost everything and she must be wondering what the hell it was all for.'

'Yes. She probably is. We all go through that. I do know what it's like . . . to lose your job and your partner,' he said. 'In my case, it was self-inflicted. Still, I understand a little. You question the basis of everything; what have you done with your life? Have you wasted precious time on stuff that was never worth it? Time ticking by . . . hurrying . . . and you chose wrongly. In my case, drinking, spending, living some life that I thought I ought to live, a cool life, a work-hard, play-hard life.'

'Angel probably feels the same – what have those years been for?' Bo said.

Thor leapt onto the sofa next to her and curled up, nose to tail.

'Ah. A kitty croissant,' Ran said. 'He must feel comfortable with you.'

'I'm glad someone does. Ran . . . I don't feel much like dancing tonight. Or at least, not until I've unwound a little.'

'That's fine. Shall we just chill? Would you like a coffee?'

'That would be great – thanks.'

Ran brought mugs from the kitchen and sat down on the armchair.

'I've been thinking,' he said. 'Maybe Madame Odette was a

catalyst. We don't know exactly what she told Angel or how she might have sowed the seeds of change in her mind, however subconsciously. She made us all question what we were doing.'

'That's true . . .' Bo said, remembering how disturbed she'd been by the encounter, and how it had made her question her whole life.

'Oh, we didn't think she had. We dismissed her and laughed at her . . . but she has influenced us and that's why I didn't want to go into that bloody tent. I didn't want her to hold up a mirror – a bloody crystal ball – to my sad life, to my past deeds, the stupid, reckless, pointless things I did. I didn't want her to show me any kind of glimpse into the future, in case I didn't like it.'

What about Phaedra, Bo thought. Did he mean her? Was he still clinging to the past?

'What will Angel do now?' he asked.

'She has three choices, I suppose. Get another job. Start her own business – or a combination of the two. There's no way I'm letting her go back to work for Kelvin.'

'I'm so relieved you said that,' Ran said, curling his lip. 'I don't think I could stand it if she ended up having to beg that tosser for her job back.'

'I'm with you,' Bo agreed. 'Yet . . . it's not our lives – or livelihoods. It's Angel's decision and if she wants to make peace with Kelvin, should I really try to stop her? I already feel I've caused her enough trouble.'

'I think . . .' Ran began gently. 'And God knows, I'm no person to dish out career advice. I don't think Angel will go back. Not now she's glimpsed a way out. You should support her to make a new life away from that bastard. I'll help if I can, though I don't know how. Everyone at Flingers will.'

'You think so?'

'Yes.'

He showed a lot of empathy yet offered no certainties. It was a lethal combination. Lethally attractive and very dangerous, Bo thought.

'I'd love to offer you something stronger than coffee. A glass of wine, maybe, but you're driving.'

'I know.' She'd love to have one, and stretch out on his sofa. Thor had already made himself comfortable, creeping closer to her so his furry back was warm against her leg.

'Of course, I could always walk you home afterwards . . .' he said.

'To Falford?'

'Yes. Have you had dinner?'

'No . . . but that's a lot of trouble for you and I'd have to collect my car in the morning.'

'True, though I'd be happy to collect you and bring you back here for your car. As for dinner. I've made a lamb tagine in the slow cooker. Nothing fancy . . . you can probably smell it.'

Her nostrils twitched. 'I can. It smells delicious.'

'I'd hold off on the judgement until you try it.'

Bo was running out of excuses not to stay. The waft of spices, the warmth of Thor, the cool fire in Ran's eyes and his soothing words were a seductive combination . . . They wound around her, filling her senses, impossible to resist.

'It's only a tagine,' he said. 'And a glass of wine. It's no trouble.'

'OK. It would be lovely not to have to cook and it's been a very long day. I was at the café early, doing some baking, and then all that business at the Country Stores . . . and then I tried out the new lighting I bought.'

'No wonder you're knackered,' he said.

'I guess so. OK, I'll walk home later. Thanks for the offer to give me a lift to get my car in the morning.'

'Great. I'll open the wine. Now relax. Look, even Thor insists.'

Thor purred loudly next to Bo.

'In that case, I'll take his advice,' she said.

A few minutes later, Ran came in from the kitchen with two glasses and a bottle of red wine. He poured Bo a glass and sat opposite her in a leather armchair. Turning up the music a little, he rested one jeaned leg over the other. The worn denim tautened over the muscles in his thighs. Bo tried to focus on his face, not those long legs, which was a mistake.

She'd always thought he was an attractive man, even when Hamish had been around, although she'd never allowed herself to truly notice him. Why would she, when she'd been dazzled by Hamish?

Lately, she'd found herself obsessing with every tiny feature of Ran. The hint of stubble, the faint lines around his eyes and the sun-kissed skin, still tanned from a summer outdoors. She couldn't imagine him working in an office, in a suit.

Music drifted from the speakers. 'Sea of Love', an old R&B love song with a seductive melody. Thor rubbed his chin against her hand and purred.

Glass of wine? Dinner with a friend? No trouble? Bo thought. Maybe not to Ran. Bo, on the other hand, was in big trouble.

'Oh God, what time is it? Ow!'

Thor leapt off Bo's lap, digging his claws into her thighs at the same time. She blinked at a blurry image of Ran who was standing a few feet away.

He showed her his diving watch. 'One twenty-three.'

'Past one o'clock? You let me fall asleep . . .'

'I went to make us coffee and when I came back, you had your eyes closed.'

'Oh . . .' She hoped she hadn't snored. Hamish had teased her about it and she still wasn't sure if he meant it or not.

Still wobbly, she made a half-hearted attempt to get up off the sofa. 'I have to go home.'

'OK. I'll walk you if you like but it might be more practical if you stayed here for now and drove home in the morning. I've got to be at the marina for seven-thirty so I need to be up early and I'm guessing you do too?'

'Um . . . I suppose, I could try to get a taxi.'

'Yes, of course, if you like,' he said.

Bo smacked her head against the sofa cushion. 'We both know that there's no way any local taxi firm will come out here to drive me a mile back to Falford and I'd have to come back for my car.'

'I'm sorry, I should have woken you. I didn't know what to do for the best. You said you'd had a long day, so I thought you might need the rest.'

Had he engineered things so she would have to stay the night? If he had, did she care?

It would be so, *so* easy to stay . . . to stay in his bed?

'The spare room's made up. I keep it ready – not that I've had anyone to stay other than my parents and a couple of dive buddies lately.'

'Oh. I—' Bo flushed, ashamed of her own thoughts that he might automatically assume she'd share his bed. The flush went deeper, a rush of tingling warmth from top to toe.

Thor rubbed himself against her legs and gazed up at her.

'OK. That sounds like the perfect solution. I'm sorry I fell asleep. I promise it's nothing to do with the company.' She

244

smiled. 'It's just been a hell of a day.' She got up, eyeing the half-drunk coffee on the table.

'Please don't worry. I've an en suite off my room so the bathroom's all yours, too. I've got some of those business-class travel kits somewhere.' He rolled his eyes. 'A relic of a different life.'

Bo eased herself out of the chair and followed Ran up the narrow cottage stairs.

He pushed open an old oak door. 'This is the spare room.'

The small room had sloping eaves and contained a double bed pushed against a wall under the window, a chest of drawers and an alcove made into a bookcase, bulging with books about music.

Ran opened a drawer. 'Here you go.' He handed her a small leather toiletries bag. 'It's a guy's but there's toothpaste and a toothbrush . . .'

She took the washbag. 'Thanks. I never expected this.'

He opened another drawer and pulled out a folded T-shirt. 'There's this if you want too.'

Bo put the wash kit on the bed and shook out the T-shirt. A giggle burst from her lips when she saw the slogan: 'Divers Do It Deeper'.

Ran rolled his eyes. 'Christ. I'm sorry. It was a secret Santa from the instructors last year. It's never been worn and I don't own pyjamas, I'm afraid.'

The fizzing desire seized her again. Why didn't she simply tell him now to forget the T-shirt and the spare room and take her to bed?

That's what she wanted – or at least, her body did. She was pretty sure he wouldn't say no, and yet she didn't trust her instincts. Dancing wasn't a substitute for a relationship. It was choreography.

Her blush was fiery, approaching Mount-Etna level, but Ran bade her a quick goodnight and, after a trip to the bathroom, she climbed into the bed wearing his T-shirt. She thought she heard Thor miaowing outside her door then all the lights went off. The darkness was so thick, she felt as if she could scoop it up with her hands.

She lay awake, staring into it. All she could think of was Ran, lying naked beneath the sheets in the room next door, and what might have happened if the exhaustion and red wine hadn't overcome her earlier. She was pretty sure she wouldn't get a wink of sleep now.

Chapter Thirty

Despite all Bo's expectations, sleep had come and in the morning, with a quick coffee for breakfast, she'd driven off home, showered and gone to work. Cade stayed later to help her finish the lighting display and decorations on the terrace. The customers were appreciative and she felt it was now looking more like a fun, festive place to hold a cocktail party for Starfish Graphics. With mulled cider and hot canapés around the fire pit, and a playlist of vintage Christmas tunes, she was confident it would be a quirky, fun evening they would all enjoy.

On the Wednesday evening, Angel's kitchen worktops had vanished under a sea of fabric and trimmings when Bo dropped by to see the progress of the dress. A basket on the tiles next to her overflowed with small fabric items, which Bo realised were Christmas decorations.

She scooped up a red bell and a green heart and held them by the ribbons. 'These are adorable. New line?'

'I made them with offcuts. To be honest, my daughter helped

me. We thought we'd put them out at the Illuminations and ask people to donate to Emma's charity.'

'They're lovely. I'll buy some for my mum and sister as stocking fillers.'

Angel's harassed frown melted into a smile. 'Thanks, Bo. Fancy a cuppa?'

'You look like you need one. Shall I put the kettle on?'

'If you can find it.' Angel held her hands up to her face and groaned. 'I really need more space if I'm going to be making stuff. I need to make a start on clearing the spare room. I had a quick look and it's full of manky old fishing rods, tackle and boxes of lures. I even found a box of maggots in there last summer!'

'Maggots? Oh my God.'

'Yes. Tommy'd forgotten about them and left them in a tackle box then went to sea. The smell soon let me know and I chucked them outside. Some had hatched and flew off over the garden like something from a horror film.'

Bo felt queasy. 'Eww. I'll make the tea.'

'I'll finish this last dec and then I can show you the dress.'

'That's what I'd hoped – I can't wait to see it.'

With the whirr of the machine and the rumble of the kettle, conversation was out for the next couple of minutes, but once peace had descended, Angel cleared a space at the table and Bo joined her with the mugs.

'The dress is in the sitting room. I don't dare have it in the kitchen in case I drop something on it.'

They went into the lounge and Bo noticed there were still photos of Tommy and Angel's wedding on the dresser. She wondered if her friend had even realised they were still there, or if they'd become an unnoticed part of the fixtures. Perhaps

Angel simply couldn't bear to take them down – after all, there was still a possibility Tommy would come back and that they'd patch up their marriage.

'Here it is.'

Angel unhooked the dress cover from the top of the door frame and laid it on the sofa to unzip it.

Bo was almost as excited as Angel when Angel removed the dress on its hanger and shook it out.

'There you go.'

The sight of the dress, so beautiful and lovingly made, brought an instant lump to Bo's throat. The colour was sumptuous – a delicate pistachio green that reflected the light. Bo could imagine Jenna wearing it, possibly with a string of pearls like in her great-grandmother's portrait.

'It's got a concealed placket front,' Angel explained. 'See, the style is called a princess line and it's meant to shape your bust and flatters the tummy area, not that Jenna needs it.'

'All that riding and mucking out must keep her fit,' Bo said. 'I love the way the skirt flares at the hips.'

'I added a net underskirt but nothing too voluminous so it doesn't stick out as much as a dancing dress. It's meant to seem elegant and restrained but still make a statement.'

'It's simply stunning.'

'It was the most difficult and stressful thing I've ever made. There was so much to go wrong.'

'I can imagine, but it's perfect.'

The shirt-dress style looked simple and elegant but Bo suspected it had been incredibly complicated to make, with its button-through front, three-quarter turn-back sleeves and stand-up collar.

'Can I touch it?'

Angel smiled. 'Course you can.'

Bo lifted a piece of the hem with her fingers, afraid to leave the tiniest mark on the dress but desperate to feel the cool, smooth fabric under her fingertips. 'Is it silk? It looks like real silk but you said you wouldn't be able to get any.'

'I did find some. I phoned one of my favourite haunts and they said they had some left. Jenna agreed to the price – don't ask – and they sent it. It was a risk because I hadn't actually seen the fabric but I trust the man at the warehouse. So then I was working with the most expensive piece of material I've ever had on the most complicated style. My hands were shaking at times.'

'How did you design it?'

'I took some photos of the portrait at the event and Jenna had an old photo of her great-granny wearing it. I adapted a pattern that I found on a vintage site online. Obviously, Jenna came round for some fittings.'

'Has she seen the finished article?'

'Not yet. She's only seen it in parts or pinned together. In fact, I am going round to the stables tomorrow afternoon if you'd like to come with me? For moral support?'

'You don't need moral support but yes, I'd love to.'

Angel let out a huge sigh. 'Great. Even though she's been happy with it as it's been going along, I won't rest until I know she likes the final result. I can't tell you how many times I wished I'd never said I'd make it.'

'I can guess,' Bo said, thinking of the times she'd committed to doing things she thought were beyond her – like setting up the Boatyard Café.

'It's the emotional weight that comes with this dress, isn't it? The fact that it's for Jenna and her grandmother wore it and it will be on show at the launch of the Illuminations.'

'Yes, and that makes it even more exciting. I promise you, she'll love it. And I must confess, I've always wanted to see the stables.'

'It's a lovely place but definitely not that posh. Jenna and her husband live in the farmhouse – a big, rambling house. Her sister lives down the lane in a modern bungalow apparently, but they own the stables business jointly.'

There was a pause. Angel chewed her lip and seemed twitchy. 'I've something else to tell you . . . Tommy's called me.'

'Oh my God, Angel. What did he have to say?'

'He admitted he's living in Falmouth with someone. He won't say who with but he's promised it's not anyone I know.'

'Do you believe him?'

'After what he's done?' She shrugged. 'I don't know what to believe.'

'Has he asked to meet you?'

'He said he wasn't ready to so I told him we had to sort things out, like the house and what was going to happen in the future.'

'And?'

'He said he'd make arrangements to see me but he couldn't face it now. I can, though.' Her tone hardened. 'I'm going to see a solicitor and I'm going to ask for some advice. First of all, though, I'm going to throw all his crap out of that spare room. It's time I had a proper place for my business!'

Bo whizzed straight to the stables after the café had closed the next day, leaving Cade to lock up so she could arrive in daylight. She waited in the van for Angel, in a small parking area by the house. The farmhouse was a sprawling double-fronted granite affair with numerous outhouses and sheds, some of which were quite dilapidated. The stables, yard and menage were modern and beautifully kept, however, and it was clear that horses came first in the Boscawen family.

Angel pulled up alongside Bo.

'Hello,' she said, a little out of breath. 'Sorry I'm late.'

'Don't worry, I've only been here a few minutes.'

'I managed to get through work but I can't stop thinking about Tommy's call. I phoned him back and told him I want a divorce. There's no future for our marriage and I want out. I've told the kids and they were upset. I think they'd still hoped we could patch things up but I'd already accepted it was over between us. There's no coming back from that.'

'I am sorry it's ending but I think you're doing the right thing. At least you've got them to support you.'

'Yes. They'd both called their father to try and get him to at least see them but he won't. Too guilty or worried about getting an earful from them. He won't give them the name of his fancy woman either.'

'He'll have to sooner or later,' Bo said.

'Yes. I guess so. I don't want to think about it now.'

'Quite right.' Bo smiled. 'Have you remembered the dress?'

Angel laughed. 'Yes, but I did almost pull away without it. I'd hung it on the door in the hall and taken a call from Kelvin. He can't work the accounts system and it's time for the VAT return.'

'The bloody cheek of him!'

'I told him he should have spent more time learning the system instead of swanning off to the golf course. He moaned that it was my job so I told him to open his wallet and pay someone else!'

'Oh, Angel, you're magnificent.'

Angel sighed. 'Maybe not magnificent but I am quite proud of myself. I'll never let anyone walk all over me again. Now, enough of useless men. Let me fetch this dress.'

Carefully, almost reverently, she retrieved the dress in its carrier from the rear seat of the car and they walked towards the house together. Horses were peering out of stable doors and two were being saddled in the yard.

Jenna Boscawen was talking to three riders when she saw them. With a wave, she strode across the yard, smiling.

'Oh help! Is that it?' She nodded at the suit carrier. 'I can't wait to see it! Let's go inside the house. I am clean,' she joked. 'It's only my wellies that are covered in muck.'

She led the way towards the granite farmhouse, chattering. 'Oh, you've just missed Lucy, my sister. She's off on a hack with a couple of pupils. That was her I was chatting to.'

Bo had only seen three riders who could have been any gender or age but listened politely.

'She's looking forward to seeing the dress too.'

'Will she be at the Illuminations?' Angel asked.

'Oh no. I have asked her but she's too shy. Not her thing at all. Says she'll leave me to hog the limelight.' They reached the house and Jenna pushed open the door. 'In we go. Please excuse the mess. Angel's used to it by now, I hope. Still, shame Lucy isn't here for the big unveiling.' She beamed. I can't wait to see it! I feel we should be drinking champagne.'

Angel unzipped the cover. 'I do hope it's a champagne moment . . .'

She uncovered the dress and held it up on its hanger.

Jenna's mouth opened wide. 'Oh my . . . oh my . . .' she kept saying, then covered her mouth with her hand.

Angel's smile faded. Jenna seemed stunned.

'There's still time to alter it a little if you don't like it . . .' Angel said.

'Oh, my dear! No!' Jenna took the dress and stroked it lovingly. 'I'm quite overcome, that's all. It's *so* like Great-granny's. If my mother were alive, and saw me in it, she'd think she'd seen a ghost.' She held it up against her slim figure. 'It is beyond beautiful. Thank you so much, my dear. I can't wait to wear it to the Illuminations. And I can't wait to show it to Lucy!'

Chapter Thirty-One

Bo was almost as stunned herself when Trewhella House loomed in front of her on the day of the performance. She and Angel had travelled to the event together in Bo's van where they were meeting up with Ran, Hubert, Sally, Cade and the other Flingers.

'Wow. Just wow,' she said when they caught their first sight of the mansion.

It was only three o'clock but the house was already lit up. Green, violet and pink lights highlighted the magnificent facade, with each pillar picked out in a different hue.

'Look at the tree!' Angel wound down the window for a better look at a huge fir tree, adorned with twinkling lights, that stood proudly at the front of the house. A queue of people snaked back from the door and down the steps, eager to get their first glimpse of the interiors.

If Trewhella had been spectacular by day, the magical transformation as dusk fell made Bo catch her breath. She could only imagine how it would look in full darkness with the windows of the house blazing out in all their glory against the night sky.

It was easy to imagine the awe, and perhaps envy, of the guests turning up for that final Christmas before the family were hit by tragedy. Her heart was already beating a little faster at the prospect of dancing in such a grand setting, in front of the audience.

She parked the van in the staff area and she and Angel took in the house in amazement.

'I am so nervous,' Angel said.

'I must admit I am too,' Bo said. 'I love dancing but I always feel on edge when we do a demo and especially in a huge mansion like this. What if I trip up or land on my bum?'

'What if my mind goes completely blank?' Angel said.

'Firstly, it won't, and if it did, you're dancing with Hubert so you'll be fine,' Bo said. 'That's what I love about rock and roll, you can just make it up and still look like you know what you're doing!'

Angel and Bo unloaded bags containing shoes, make-up and other 'essentials' from the boot. Angel had also brought some of her dresses and a small 'exhibition' of photographs and samples showing how she had made Jenna's dress. She'd decided she wouldn't have time to sell her own products too so she'd just made a few Christmas decorations, with an honesty box where people could leave a donation to the Fisherman's Mission.

'It isn't only the dancing that's making my stomach tie up in knots. I'm excited about seeing Jenna in her dress. I wonder what the reaction will be?'

'You already know she absolutely loves it.'

'Yes, but I haven't seen her in all the finery and she'll be on full display. I wonder how she must be feeling with the house decorated for her family's last Christmas and wearing a replica of her great-grandmother's dress.'

'I thought the same. It's pretty sad that all this grandeur was so soon to melt away and that house must have felt empty and cold the following year.'

'After his wife's death, Lord Boscawen couldn't bear to spend Christmas there alone and took his daughters to one of their other houses.'

Angel was silent.

'Are you OK? It's been a hell of a week. Working so hard on your stock and the dress and hearing from Tommy.'

'Yes. Well, no, but I have to move on. If I hadn't had the dress to focus on, I don't know what I'd have done to be honest. I've told him I've called my solicitor. He was gobsmacked. I think he thought my life still revolved around him.' She set her chin determinedly. 'Now, do you think we can move all this in one go or are we going to have to make two trips?'

They were saved from a decision – and the double trips – by Ran turning up.

Between them, Ran, Angel and Bo managed to carry all their kit to the rear of the house, through to the old servants' hall which was being used as a green room for the Flingers. It had sofas, chairs and tables and was lit by a cheerful fire. They'd helpfully set up tea- and coffee-making facilities and there was a cloakroom where the dancers could change if they needed to.

They left their stuff and went for a quick look around the house before the public were let in.

'Isn't it fabulous?' Angel said as they made their way up a flight of stone stairs into the grand hall.

Bo totally agreed. The house had been transformed from the deserted and rather melancholy space at the autumn craft fair. A showpiece Christmas tree in the great hall almost touched the ceiling, and there were others in the drawing room, morning room and dining room, each decorated with vintage decorations.

Plump wreaths of evergreens decorated with baubles and scarlet ribbons adorned the doorways, along with seasonal floral decorations on tables. In the drawing room, someone was playing traditional carols and Christmas music of the era on a grand piano. Fires blazed in the hearths behind the fire-guards.

The ballroom had been divided to give space for the Flingers to dance, and also allow several rows of seats. They were doing one half-hour session and the audience could book tickets on arrival to watch the demo.

The dining table was laid with a snowy-white cloth and fine china and more cutlery than Bo had ever seen.

'Just like our house at Christmas,' Angel said in a low voice that made Bo giggle.

'We always booked a restaurant and met friends for Christmas dinner,' Ran said. 'With only the two of us, it seemed pointless to cook and clear away.'

Bo thought of her own family; her mother would have considered it almost sacrilege not to have her brood around her on Christmas Day. She'd expressed her disapproval in no uncertain terms on the occasions that Bo had had to work on the day.

'I've worked in restaurant kitchens a couple of times over Christmas,' she told Ran.

'Ouch.'

'I survived but it's absolute mayhem. Some of the staff wanted an excuse not to join in the whole family thing and I was OK with it when I was starting out but not now. I'm quite happy to let someone else cook . . .'

She suddenly wondered what Ran would be doing on Christmas Day. Would he go to see his family in the South-East? Or maybe even go to Norway? He wouldn't be spending it with his wife, that seemed clear enough. She'd love to invite him to hers on Christmas Day if he didn't have any other plans – she hated the thought of anyone being alone at Christmas – but there was no way she was going to ask, putting him under pressure and risking a rejection as she did with her declaration to Hamish.

'My kids and their partners are coming,' Angel said.

Bo thought that it would be a very strange time for Angel. She was brave to come along at all and face the full-on festivity at the event.

'Hello!' Jenna joined them.

'Oh my,' Angel cried. 'You look incredible!'

'Your *dress* looks incredible, my dear. It's all your doing.'

'It's beautiful,' Ran said.

The pistachio dress had a lustrous sheen and fitted Jenna like a glove. Teamed with pearls, evening gloves and pointed stilettos it made Jenna look like a fifties movie star.

'Just like the portrait . . .' Bo said.

'I could never match up to Great-granny but I hope I've done her justice.' She smiled. 'Would you like to see the sitting room?'

'Yes, please.'

Jenna led the way through the ballroom to the door at the side where the radio music had been playing. Even now, Bo experienced a thrill at the memory of the moment they danced and what it had led to. Ran was making great progress though, sooner or later, Bo was wondering if they'd take things further. Perhaps Angel was right and she *should* take a risk.

The sitting room was hung with brightly coloured paper

chains looped from the picture rails and wall lights, with foil decorations in the shape of bells and stars. Though large by any normal family's standards, with the fire burning and the homemade decorations, it seemed surprisingly homely.

'They used to be made by my mother and her sister,' Jenna explained. 'Everyone had them in their houses, and if money was tight, they might make the chains from strips of newspaper.'

As in the rest of the house, there were vases full of festive greenery from the gardens and holly sprigs pushed behind the pictures on the wall. The centrepiece was a tree was covered in tinsel and glass baubles and topped with a Christmas fairy.

'I brought the fairy,' Jenna said. 'It's been handed down through the family. When the Illuminations are finished, I'll take it home and put it on our own tree at home.' Her phone rang. 'Oh, I'm sorry. I must take this.'

Before any of them could offer to leave, Jenna had exited the room and closed the door.

'Oh my God, look at this,' Angel said, lingering by a hefty wooden display cabinet. 'That's a bit creepy,' she said.

Ran and Bo joined her.

'That's weird,' Bo said.

They all stared at the object in the cabinet: a crystal ball very like the one Madame Odette had used, apart from one major difference: this ball was set on a gilded stand, with moulded animals. Not the cute kind, but rather creepy creatures like goats and rams with curled horns and staring eyes.

'The ram's head symbolises the occult,' Ran said. 'They've always been associated with witchcraft and Satanism.'

Angel shuddered and goosebumps popped out on Bo's arms. 'How do you know that?'

'A friend was into folklore,' he said.

'It's a long way from Madame Odette's fairground predictions to witchcraft and the occult,' Bo said.

'Even so, I wish I'd never gone to have my fortune told.'

'Me too.'

'Do you think it's worth a lot of money?' Angel asked the same thing that had been going through Bo's mind.

'No idea.'

When she returned, Jenna took Angel off to a small exhibition area about the house and the dress, leaving Ran and Bo alone.

'I'd love to take a look around the gardens if there's time,' Bo said.

'We still have over an hour until the first dance. We could have a quick look round and be back in the ballroom in time to set up,' Ran said.

It was far too tempting an invitation to be turned down. 'OK. Let's go for it.'

Dusk was falling and the garden was starting to move from its daytime existence to a glamorous night-time mode. That's how it felt to Bo, as the sky deepened to a dark blue.

'Look up!'

Her eye was drawn up and up to the canopy of trees, lit from below by coloured uplighters. It was incredibly effective, the colours reflecting off their pale trunks – pinks, greens, blues and violets. The lighting showed the lace-like tracery of the branches, some still with a few leaves clinging to the twigs. It lit up the gnarled trunks of the older trees with their twisted branches and spiky twigs like witches' fingers. Yet also there were also late and early flowers out on the shrubs and bushes.

'It's absolutely spectacular,' Bo said in wonder, making her way along the gravelled walkways. They came to a long metal arch – more of a tunnel – which had been covered in a net of fairy lights.

'Spookily magical,' Ran said.

'You're teasing me.'

'No, I'm not. It is a spectacular place.'

They meandered along the trails, not following any particular route, simply choosing interesting ways, or so it seemed to Bo. She was no real gardener but recognised azaleas and mahonias. Their shiny leaves were brighter in the lights and the silhouettes of spiky palms and monkey puzzle trees created an exotic backdrop.

It was the camelias that were the stars, their rose-like blooms rich shades of scarlet- and coral-coloured petals. They shone like jewels against the dark green foliage.

'I love the camelias. It's like finding a patch of summer in the middle of winter.'

'I have one in the garden at Creekside. Nothing like this, of course. It puts my weedy specimen to shame. It's magnificent . . . I don't miss a London winter . . .' Ran said. 'And the extra daylight here. Almost half an hour. It makes a difference for it not to be dark by four o'clock.'

'London at Christmas must be exciting. The shops, the parties, the buzz and the Christmas lights. Cornwall can't compete with the vibe of a big city.'

'Well, I wouldn't go near Oxford Street for at least two months. London is a great place – but as for Cornwall not competing. I wanted to get as far away from competition as possible. London became a place I didn't feel I could breathe in.'

'I can understand that but don't you find it so small here, so confined and claustrophobic?' She was playing devil's advocate, she knew, but she had a strong need to tease out how he felt about staying, longer term – even if the answer might not be one she wanted to hear. She'd never asked Hamish's plans, never thought about them – or was it that she'd assumed he would stay? Assumptions were bad things. So were questions but it was too late now.

'I wanted to hide away here, I suppose. A cottage concealed under the trees in the most remote offshoot of an inaccessible river valley.' He smiled. 'You can't really get much more hidden than Creekside.'

'Then why join the dance group? Why come out into the light and colour and sound? You chose to be sociable.'

'Maybe I was only hiding from one person in particular,' he said. 'But the plan's failed spectacularly. I'm so glad I did join in – or I wouldn't be here now.'

There was no time to walk down the hill to the estuary beach at the bottom of the estate but Bo sensed that Ran, like herself, wasn't ready to return to the house yet. There was a tranquillity and magical atmosphere in the gardens that made you want to linger – or maybe she only wanted to linger with Ran.

Even as they walked, the sky was changing: turning from sapphire to indigo as night rolled in from the west. They came out of the wooded garden area and onto open lawns that sloped gently down to the Fal estuary. Fewer people had ventured out here, most transfixed by the showier sights in the main gardens.

'Wow.'

Ran echoed her thoughts as they stopped on a terrace that marked the boundary of the formal lawns. They'd found it by walking through a gap in a wall and down a short flight of stone steps. It felt as if the terrace was hidden from the main house. It was lit by some sunken lights set into the wall, but far more discreetly than in the rest of the garden, and Ran and Bo were completely alone.

It wasn't large but very private, edged by a stone balustrade and urns. A small clover-shaped fountain stood at the centre, with a fantastical fish sculpture.

The spot gave a great view of the Fal estuary which was silvery in the moonlight. Lights glimmered along its banks, and in the far distance you could see Falmouth town itself on one side with boats lit up in the port and the fishing village of St Mawes on the other. Further out to sea, there were tankers on the horizon. Bo imagined the Boscawen family taking tea there in the summer, gazing over the river as it opened out into the shimmering sea. What a life . . .

The sky darkened. Clouds hid the moon and Bo felt a splash of cold moisture against her skin. 'Uh-oh, I think that was a raindrop . . .' She peered at the pond, trying to detect the tell-tale ripples. 'Or am I imagining it?'

'I felt it too . . .'

'We'd better be getting back. I don't want to get wet,' she said, wracked by a reluctance to leave. Yet her hair would be ruined, and it wouldn't take much for her dancing dress and tights to be soaked.

A cold gust of wind blew and more droplets spattered her face.

'Now that *is* rain. Let's get back to the house sharpish,' Ran said.

The squall of rain was a grey sheet that had already obscured the seaward end of the estuary and was heading for them, driven by the wind.

'Shall we make a run for it?' Bo asked and turned. Already she felt the rain against her hair and pulled up her hood.

'I think it's too late. We'll have to shelter,' Ran said.

'Where?'

'There. By the steps!'

Bo could only see a mass of ivy but Ran took her hand and they dashed forward.

He hurried with her to the rear of the terrace and she saw what she hadn't noticed when she'd scurried down the steps before. There was an alcove in the wall beneath the double flight of stairs. She'd been so transfixed by the view, she hadn't looked behind her.

Seconds later, they were huddled inside.

There was a wooden bench at the rear of the alcove and they sat down on it. The rain lashed the terrace, drops bouncing off the flagstones and hammering into the pond. Water already dripped off the tendrils of ivy hanging down in front of them. The wind whooshed and fresh waves of rain blew in like chilly veils.

Bo shivered. The temperature had plunged and night had fallen properly. The lights of Falmouth were no longer visible, and the terrace lamps glowed feebly through the mist created by the rain. She drew her feet under the bench to keep them dry. Ran put his arm around her, pulling her closer.

'I don't know how we're going to get back to the house without getting drenched,' she said.

'I wish we didn't have to go back to the house.'

Even with the low light, she was so close to him she could see his face. She tensed, half-afraid she hadn't heard him correctly. Every nerve ending was alive, even in the cold with the rain hammering down.

'We have to,' she murmured.

'I know we have to but if we *didn't*,' he said.

'If we didn't, then I could stay here all night with you.'

His arms encircled her, and a moment later, his warm mouth was against hers. His lips were soft, the kiss was gentle yet hungry too. Bo's body responded, relaxing into the embrace, enjoying the sensation of his lips on hers. Her eyes were closed and everything was gone: no rain drumming on the steps, no breeze blowing from the sea, no chilly winter shower; only the warmth of Ran pulling her even closer and her melding against him. He was right: it was too late to go back now.

Chapter Thirty-Two

'Bo!' The call came from above them.

She let Ran go, still breathless and almost dizzy from the kiss. 'That sounds like Sally,' she said.

'I think it is.' His voice was ragged too.

'Bo, where are you?' The cry was urgent.

'Something's wrong,' Ran said.

Bo jumped up. It was still pouring down and, now she wasn't in Ran's embrace, she felt very cold.

'Here!' she called and a moment later a figure appeared in front of the alcove. Ran stood up too.

'Bo! Is that you? Ran?'

Sally's face was pale in the moonlight. She wore wellingtons and a large mac and was sheltered under a golf umbrella. 'Thank goodness we found you! We've been trying to phone you but the signal is terrible round here in the river valley so you probably haven't even realised.'

'Oh. I . . . I hadn't even checked my ph— um, no, I haven't *heard* any calls. We were, um, literally on our way back to the house to get ready when this storm blew in so we sheltered here.'

'*Literally* on our way back,' Ran said smoothly. 'We still have plenty of time before we start. Is everything OK, Sal?'

'Not really. It's Cade. He's twisted his ankle. He was so busy looking up at the illuminated trees that he tripped and fell.' Sally shook her head.

'Oh, poor Cade! Is he OK?'

'The first aid team are with him. It's probably only a sprain and he's refused to go to the hospital to get checked out. Hubert's stayed with him but I came to try and find you when we couldn't get an answer.'

'Bugger. That doesn't sound good,' Ran said.

'He's still insisting he can dance,' Sally said mournfully.

'Typical Cade.' Bo was mortified that she hadn't taken the call and worried about her partner. 'I'll come now and see how he is.'

'We can share the brolly,' Sally said. 'I'm afraid you'll have to get wet, Ran.'

He turned up his collar. 'I'm used to that,' he said, with a glance at Bo that she didn't dare return.

They squelched over the lawn before regaining the main path. Bo hadn't realised quite how far they'd wandered from the house itself. Rain dripped from the canopies, and the buzz of chatter grew louder. The sound of a generator and scents of hot food reminded her they were here for a public event.

The squall was passing and the rain had eased a little. By staying close to Sally under the umbrella, Bo kept reasonably dry but a soaking was now the last thing on her mind. She was still stunned by the kiss with Ran but also concerned about her partner. She had to put the kiss to the back of her mind for now and focus on Cade.

'He's in the family sitting room,' Sally said. 'Jenna insisted he go in there for some privacy.'

They crossed the ballroom where Ran's decks and sound system were already set up. He hesitated. 'It might be better if I stay out here. I'm sure Cade's being well taken care of without me adding to the audience. Let me know how he is and if you need me, and if I can do anything at all to help. I'll be right here finishing the set-up.'

'That's a good idea,' Sally said. 'Someone needs to organise everyone while we're looking after him.'

'Leave it with me. I'll call through to the green room and give them an update and tell them to carry on.'

'The show must go on,' Sally said. 'Thanks, Ran.'

Sally turned away but Bo finally met Ran's eyes full on. He shared a look that told her just how much he'd enjoyed their moment, and the rush of desire flooded back, tugging deep inside. She'd suppressed so many feelings for Ran until now, but after that kiss, they were fizzing out and spilling over.

Dragging her gaze from him, Bo joined Sally in the sitting room.

A small fire burned in the hearth. Cade was sitting in an armchair with his leg raised on a footstool. Hubert was standing next to him, a first aid kit in his hand.

By the flickering firelight, Bo could see straightaway that her normally livewire young partner was subdued and pale. She patted his shoulder. 'Oh Cade, you poor thing. How are you?'

'OK. People are making a fuss.' He glared at his mother. 'I went for a walk to look at the lights and tripped down a step. I'll be OK in a minute.'

'There's been too much wandering off around the grounds,'

Sally shot back. Bo cringed, wondering if she was referring to her and Ran, as well as her son.

'Are you sure you're fit to dance?' she said, venturing nearer to Cade who was grimacing. His ankle was already puffy and showing signs of bruising. 'That ankle looks nasty.'

'Someone's gone to fetch some ice from the restaurant,' Hubert said. 'But you won't be dancing on that tonight, my lad.'

'I will!' Cade pushed himself out of the armchair and put his foot down on the rug. 'Ow!' He collapsed back into the chair. 'That feckin' hurts.'

Hubert tutted. 'I warned you. It looks like a bad sprain to me.'

'Maybe you should go to hospital to get it checked out in case it's broken,' Bo said gently.

'No.' Cade groaned. 'I don't want to let you down. We've been rehearsing for months.'

'I know, but you'll damage your ankle even more if you try to dance. If you rest it now and take care of yourself, you'll be fit for the Christmas Spectacular.'

Sally crouched beside him. 'Bo's right, son. You can't even walk on it.'

Cade sank back into the chair and closed his eyes before muttering under his breath, 'Why was I not looking where I was going?'

'Hello!'

Jenna arrived with a bag of frozen peas and a tea towel. 'The café team gave me this.' She winced when she saw Cade's ankle. 'I wouldn't let a horse out with that injury.'

'I'm not a horse.' Cade sounded indignant but Bo hid a smile.

'Jenna's right. You can't dance. Stay here and rest.' Sally wrapped the peas in the tea towel.

Leaving Sally to minister to her son, Bo took Jenna on one side. 'Thanks for getting the frozen peas. Is that one of Angel's tea towels?'

'Yes,' Jenna said. 'She popped back to see how the display stand is and was almost swamped by people asking questions. I grabbed the towel on the way back.'

'I'd been wondering how she was. I've, um, been for a quick look round the gardens and got caught in the rain.'

Jenna's mouth twitched in a smile. 'I noticed Ran was looking a little damp when I came through the ballroom.'

Bo's hand automatically went to her own hair. 'I haven't even had time to check mine.'

'You look fabulous,' Jenna said. 'Although you might want to remove that from your ponytail.'

'Leaf?'

'Petal. Camellia Gloire de Nantes, if I'm not mistaken.'

Bo felt the bow securing her ponytail and pulled out a soft pink petal. 'Oh—' She winced. 'Thanks for warning me. I must get back to the green room and tidy myself up. It's almost time for the performance—' She cut herself off, remembering that she wouldn't be dancing.

'I'm sorry, Bo. After all that hard work too.'

She met Ran by the decks, an armful of singles in his hand. Visitors were already peering round the main doors to the ballroom, probably hoping to be let in early so they could nab their seat for the performance.

Ran glanced up and his eyes lit with pleasure that made Bo's pulse beat faster. He hadn't regretted the kiss, then. That made her ridiculously happy – and more scared than ever. She'd fallen for him. Done the thing she'd vowed not to do barely a year ago. Only this time, fallen harder. Much harder.

'How's Cade?' he asked.

'He won't be dancing. He's sprained his ankle badly and can barely stand up. We're going to have to manage with three couples.'

'That's a shame. I know how hard you've worked,' Ran said softly.

'It can't be helped,' she said, although she was terribly disappointed.

He hesitated. 'I ought to go to the green room and help people get ready. We only have half an hour before they start letting the audience in. It's a shame because the performance would have looked better with four couples in this big space.'

'I know,' Bo said. 'But the show must go on!'

'Bo . . .' Ran touched her arm. 'I was going to suggest something but it's probably a stupid idea.' He laughed at himself. 'Forget I said anything.'

'No. What?'

'I, er . . . look, this is probably *the* worst idea in the world but I could dance with you.'

'Do you mean it?' were Bo's first words after a moment of stunned silence.

'Wouldn't have offered if I didn't. But think before you say yes. I've barely started learning.'

'You're really good. You can dance, you could before. You were a bit rusty, that's all.'

He laughed. 'Rusty's one word for it. I don't want you to miss out. Even if I only do one dance with you, at least you won't have wasted all that hard work for nothing.'

'I'd love to dance with you. Don't get me wrong. I'm surprised to be asked.'

'Call it a one-off,' he said.

Bo had to think on her feet. 'OK, OK. What about the last one of the set? "Rockin' Around The Christmas Tree"? I know that one well. We're basically improvising anyway.'

Ran hesitated. 'I love that one but it's a fast pace, and we'll have no time to rehearse.'

'You'll be great,' Bo replied, still amazed he'd offered to dance with her. 'You already know all the moves. How will you manage the music?'

'Let me worry about that. I have an idea.'

She glanced around her then brushed her lips across his. It might only be a dance but it felt like a new beginning. She might even start to look forward to Christmas again.

Chapter Thirty-Three

What the hell had he done? Half an hour later, Ran was more nervous than he'd ever been in his life – far more than before a big presentation to his bosses or a client meeting. He'd fed off the adrenaline then, thinking he enjoyed the dubious 'excitement'. It was only after he'd been made redundant that he'd found the idea of all that stress – the nervous energy – scared him. It had all been to prove a point and ultimately make money for corporate entities who already had billions.

The nerves he felt now were good nerves. Butterflies in the stomach, a kind of fizzing in his limbs. It was because he wanted to do his best – for Bo, for his fellow dancers and for himself.

He'd come to Falford to hide and inch by inch emerged – been coaxed – out of the shadows. To the point where he'd exposed himself to the full light today: dancing with Bo, kissing her.

Man, it felt great. He felt more alive than he had for years.

The Flingers were all around; the three remaining couples and other members of the group who'd come along to help shift kit, with costumes and setting-up. Angel was dancing with Hubert. Sally with a younger guy. Everyone gathered at the side of the decks. Word had clearly got round, to Sally at least.

'Ran. What's this I hear about you dancing?' she asked. 'Is it true?'

'Yes, I didn't want Bo to miss out.'

'That's very noble of you. Hubert and I caught a glimpse of you at the autumn craft fair but I didn't think it was serious.'

'I was in the rock and roll club at uni and Bo's been giving me some lessons over the past few weeks. I enjoyed it when I was young but then life got in the way. I never intended to go public.'

'I think it's a bit late for that now.'

There was definite innuendo in Sally's voice but he pretended to ignore it.

'I'd hang on with the congrats until you've seen me strut my stuff in front of an audience,' he said wryly. 'Maybe you'll be begging me not to dance again after that.'

Ran wasn't about to tell her there was more between him and Bo. He wasn't even sure himself yet, though if that amazing kiss had been anything to go by, he hoped so. Man, he hoped so. Once this dance was over, they could find out. Would she come back to the cottage with him tonight? Was it too soon? The night he'd spent in his bed – alone – knowing she was in the next room, had been on his mind ever since. He'd lain awake, hoping she'd come to his bedroom – fearing he wouldn't be able to say no to *anything* if she had.

For now, dancing and the Flingers were his immediate priority. Cade was taking things hard but Ran guessed that helping with the music might be a welcome distraction.

'Hey, buddy. How's it going?' he said.

Hubert and another dancer had helped Cade limp across the floor to the decks where Ran had set Cade up on a chair and explained how to cue in the final record or restart the music if anything went wrong. It was no substitute for actually dancing but Cade had brightened up a little when Ran had asked him to help out. He and Bo had managed around five minutes of practice, with Cade watching on, before Ran had to get ready.

With the room filling with visitors, his pulse quickened. He put some Christmas swing on low to set the mood, nothing too fast-paced yet, just mellow oldies.

He was saving the lively stuff for the performance. Fuelled by mulled wine and the festive atmosphere, more people filed in, laughing and chattering with their friends. They were a largely older audience but by no means all. There were plenty of under-forties, some in vintage gear themselves. Ran recognised a few faces from the local dance and vintage scene and a few were actors hired to add a touch of glamour to the event. There was also a couple in the front row who must have been pushing eighty, and were wearing full rockabilly gear – a sticky-out skirt for the lady and the old guy in crepe-soled shoes and a rock and roll jacket.

'It takes all sorts . . .' Bo said in his ear.

Ran couldn't help thinking of Phaedra's less charitable remarks about 'saddos' and 'weirdos'. He still couldn't blame her but he thought it was great that they had such a spread of characters in the audience, all united by wanting to have some fun and enjoy a bit of glamour or nostalgia. Not everything had to be cool or complicated.

'The room's packed! Look at them,' Angel said in a low voice. 'I'm not sure I can do this.'

'Of course you can. You know the routines and Hubert's a great partner.'

Angel visibly puffed with confidence. 'Thanks, lovely.'

'Come on, guys. I think we're ready to start,' Ran said. The only vacant chairs were a few at the front with 'reserved' cards on them. He could feel the nervous tension from his friends. They were breathing more deeply, and there was the odd muttered swearword, followed by Hubert's calming encouragement:

'This is going to be awesome. It's not a competition and no one will even notice if you go wrong. Enjoy yourselves and remember: we're here to share our love of the music and dance.'

'OK?' Ran mouthed and Hubert nodded and stepped onto the floor, with Sally at his side.

'Ladies and gentlemen! Welcome to the Falford Flingers Christmas dance party. I hope you're all in the festive mood and ready to rock 'n' roll!'

Bo was behind the decks with Cade. The other couples took to the floor and Ran cued in the first track. The set opened with one guaranteed to get people's feet tapping by Brenda Lee, followed by a Chuck Berry classic and 'Sleigh Bell Rock' by Chuck Blevins.

All the nervous energy exploded into dynamite on the dance floor and Ran savoured the reaction of the audience. From not quite knowing what to expect, they were soon smiling, tapping their feet and jigging around in their seats. Some were finding it impossible not to sing along and Ran was half-tempted to cut the sound to hear how many people were singing out loud.

Bo was next to him, swaying along to the music. She looked gorgeous in her red dress with cherries on it, patent dancing shoes to match and her hair in a ponytail. There was no way he was going to leave her on the sidelines when she'd been looking forward to the event so much. Besides, he *wanted* to dance with her, even if he made a prat of himself in the process.

Hubert told people the name of the song after the track and introduced the next one. Halfway through the track, Bo mouthed to him, 'It's us next. Ready?'

'As I'll ever be.'

The track ended and Hubert took the mic again. Ran was amazed as ever that he didn't even seem out of puff. In contrast, Ran, thirty years younger, was taking a discreet breath, and his heart was pounding. All eyes were on Hubert, and, in a few seconds all eyes would be on the dancers. He could only pray they were focused on Bo, not him.

Her hand closed around his. What the hell had he done?

'You'll be fine,' she whispered in his ear.

Cade took the headphones and Bo stepped forward with Ran. It was his job to lead, to decide the turns and steps. His brain had scrambled but it was way too late to back out and, anyway, he'd never let her down.

'Ladies and gentlemen. We've come to our final track for this evening . . .'

Bo squeezed his hand. Ran knew the track started almost instantly with no intro. His heart pounded. Adrenaline pulsed through his veins. 'Enjoy it. That's all that matters.'

Hubert spoke. 'The Falford Flingers will be dancing to a classic by Brenda Lee . . .'

'"Rockin' Around the Christmas Tree",' Ran murmured at the same time as Hubert announced the track.

They took to the floor and Ran exchanged a glance with Bo. He only had eyes for her, pretending that she was the only one in the room, and that there weren't hundreds of eyes upon him

– just Bo and him, exactly like on the cottage terrace or in the gardens. Just the two of them.

Her pulse raced too, he could feel it.

'You'll be great,' she mouthed then. 'Smile.'

Cade started the track. They were off.

He had no time to think and tried to lose himself in the music. Dancing had been tricky on his terrace but now he was in the full glare of the spotlight. Admittedly there were three other couples on the floor, but he still felt so exposed.

And he was supposed to lead. Never had it felt so archaic that the 'gentleman' was supposed to direct the dance, when Bo was so much more experienced than him. The upside was that he was holding both or one of her hands for virtually the whole time. If he faltered for a microsecond, she guided him, expertly and discreetly.

The audience were clapping along and the endorphins had kicked in. In a matter of moments he'd hit his stride. He felt confident, he spun Bo, he turned with her. He not only smiled, he grinned, he felt joyful even though his heart was hammering and he was breathing harder than he had for years.

'Rockin' around the Christmas tree . . .'

Final chord.

It was over.

From whirling around the floor, they were stationary, still holding hands, still connected, with the audience clapping and whooping. Whistles of approval came from the Flingers in the front row.

He'd done it. Danced in public. With Bo – and most miraculous of all, he'd loved every second of it.

'Take a bow!' Bo hissed in his ear.

Ran did as he was told, and a few seconds later he took her

from the floor to the side of the decks area – though he was so stunned he'd actually survived without falling on his face, he felt she was leading him.

She flung her arms around him and hugged him, squeezing out what was left of his breath. 'That was amazing!'

Ran held her. 'N-no. Y-you were amazing.'

'We both were. Thanks for stepping in.'

'It was an absolute pleasure . . .'

'Ran!'

'Well done, mate!' Cade slapped him on the back, and the rest of the Flingers added their congratulations.

'That was fantastic!'

'You dark horse!'

'Thanks, but I didn't know what I was doing. Really.'

'No way. We'll expect to see you on the floor at every meet-up from now on.'

'No. Please don't. It was a one-off.'

Hubert kissed Bo on the cheek. Ran thought she looked radiant. Like Ran himself, she was a little breathless but he'd never seen her so bubbly. He thought back to the previous Christmas when she'd walked into the pub with that bloody vet. That was the last time he'd seen her so truly happy.

Was it simply the adrenaline of the dance that had done that? Or was it dancing with *him*?

'I must thank poor Cade and see how he is. I'll be back in a moment,' Bo said and flew off to Cade, who was sitting behind the decks, a smile on his face despite his accident.

Ran smiled. Typical Bo to think of others, even when she was so excited though he longed for her to return.

'Well, well . . . who would have thought it?' Sally patted Ran on the back. 'You should have danced all the songs!'

'One was more than enough. It was short. I winged it, but only because of Bo.' He looked around for her and saw her hugging Cade.

'I'm sure she'll be desperate to have Cade as her regular partner,' he said.

He was being polite because he had loved it and half hoped the same.

'You were great, lad,' Hubert said before he and Sally were whisked away by a group of people from the audience wanting to know how to join the Flingers.

Ran wandered back to the decks where Cade was hobbling around, trying to put some records in a box. Bo wasn't with him, much to Ran's disappointment.

'Don't worry, I'll do that. You be careful,' Ran said. 'Do you know where Bo's got to?'

'She went to the loo, I think,' Cade said. 'I expect she'll be back in a minute.'

'OK,' Ran said, starting to clear the records as Cade hobbled over to his parents. There was now chaos in the room, with excited people filing out, and a dozen or more milling around the decks wanting to chat about how they could learn to dance or reminisce about music.

'I remember that track from my days at the Princess Pavilion.' An octogenarian from the front row came up to him. His wife joined him.

'You did well, young man, but she's a great partner. Makes it a lot easier, eh?' the older lady said.

'We saw Heinz and the Wild Ones at the Pavilion once. Brilliant. Mind you, that was in the sixties, before your time.'

It was before his parents' time, Ran thought, laughing politely while desperate to find Bo.

A moment ago he thought he'd spotted her with Angel and a group of performing arts students from the local college. He'd give anything for a glimpse of that ponytail. The older couple were still chatting to him and he didn't want to be rude.

'Remember when Rikki and The Layabouts were there in '65? There was a bit of argy-bargy that night.' The old lady giggled.

'Sorry, I *have* to find my partner,' Ran said, detaching himself and hurrying towards the door where people were flowing out like water down a drain. He cursed under his breath. The ballroom was rapidly emptying and still there was no sign of her.

Chapter Thirty-Four

Bo soared, high as a kite in a breezy autumn sky. What a night!

She didn't think she'd ever come down from being whirled around the floor by Ran. The exhilaration had left her head spinning. Dancing was fabulous, but dancing with someone you had a real connection with was the most joyful thing in the world.

All she'd wanted to do was find him and tell him again how fantastic it had been and relive every moment. Actually, what she *really* wanted to do was drag him home and, finally, carry on where they'd left off in the gardens. There was no way she would be sleeping in the spare room tonight.

However, the moment the applause had died down, her thoughts had been for Cade, sitting it out on the sidelines after all his hard work. With all the excitement, she'd also needed the loo, though she hadn't wanted to share *that* unromantic fact with Ran. She now had to politely fight against the tide of people flowing out of the ballroom to reach him again.

She smiled, seeing an old couple who had Ran almost pinned to the decks It was manic.

She found herself at the edge of the melee and finally, *finally*, the older couple had left and Ran was talking to Hubert.

'Hello! It's Bo, isn't it?'

A blonde woman, around her own age, approached her. 'Yes, yes, it is.'

'I hope you don't mind me saying but you looked fantastic out there. All that energy, the coordination. I don't know how you do it!'

'Thanks,' said Bo, wondering if she was supposed to know the woman. She didn't recognise her but she could be a customer of the café. 'Excuse me, but have we met?' she said, smiling.

'No. Not at all but I know your name.'

'I see . . . you're a fan of the Flingers, are you?'

The blonde laughed. 'Gosh, no! Quite the opposite. Whoops. I didn't mean it to sound so blunt – but no, rock and roll isn't my thing. I really enjoyed the show, though.' She held out a leather-gloved hand and smiled. 'I'm Phaedra Larsen. You were dancing with my husband.'

Bo felt as if the dance floor had been cut from under her.

'I'm sure he's mentioned me. I *hope* he's mentioned me.'

'Yes. Of course . . .'

'We're separated at the moment. I expect he mentioned that too?' Phaedra arched an enquiring eyebrow, a tinge of amusement in her voice. Bo had never felt less amused in her life.

'Um. Yes but – Ran keeps his personal life private,' Bo said, at a loss what else to say.

Phaedra tutted but her fixed smile was instantly back. 'Typical Ran, although I must admit he has somewhat come out of his shell since I last saw him. The last thing I expected was to find him strutting his stuff in public.'

'He hadn't planned to,' Bo said, still in shock to be accosted and at a loss as to why Phaedra was at the event at all. 'My partner, Cade, hurt his ankle so Ran stepped in for the final dance.'

'So I saw. He told me he'd joined a rock and roll group down here but I thought it was only because of the music. He never mentioned taking part himself.'

'Like I say, he really wasn't going to dance until an hour ago.'

'And yet you two looked like you'd been partners for years.'

Bo's hackles rose. 'Rock and roll is an improvised dance form. That's the beauty of it. You only have to know the basic moves to be able to dance with any partner.'

Phaedra scrutinised her.

'So anyone can learn?' she said.

'Yes. Yes, of course. Anyone can learn to dance.' The lump in her throat, the dread. 'If they really want to.'

'That's good because now I've seen how much fun it looks, I might take your cue and learn myself. In fact, that's really why I'm here. I heard that your group was performing and I wanted to see Ran so I thought I'd surprise him.'

'I'm sure it's a big surprise,' Bo said, as the future she'd dared to imagine crumbled to pieces before her eyes.

'It would be if I told him I was going to learn to dance and how you've inspired me.'

'Yes . . .'

Phaedra rolled her eyes. 'He'd laugh, of course. After me saying I'd never do it.'

'I don't think he'd laugh,' Bo said, dying a little more inside. She was cold now the effort was over and the ballroom had almost emptied.

'It wouldn't have to be *this* kind of dancing. Not necessarily.

We could do salsa classes, or the tango.' Phaedra laughed. 'A different kind of dancing, but still dancing.'

'Different but still dancing . . .' Bo echoed.

Having spotted Bo – and his wife – Ran was on his way over. She had to get away.

'He's coming over. I'll see you later, I'm sure?' Phaedra said.

'Yes.'

Turning her back on Phaedra and Ran's shocked face, Bo walked out of the ballroom. That magnificent dance floor felt like shifting sand beneath her feet and it was all she could do not to scream. Bo could have been rude or stood up for herself but she could not and would not stand in Phaedra's way.

She'd had her first and last public dance with Ran – with his wife watching. His not-yet-ex-wife. His not-yet-ex-wife who had, if Bo's instincts were right, made up her mind that she still wanted to dance with her husband – and not only for one night but forever.

Chapter Thirty-Five

'Where's Ran? You two were absolutely amazing together. I'm quite happy if you want to go home together.'

Angel was hyper while they loaded Bo's van with her samples and their dance costumes. Bo's emotions were ripped in two such different directions. She was ecstatic for her friend, yet shattered by Phaedra's appearance – and her blatant warning to keep away from Ran.

'Why would I want to go home with Ran?' She tried to keep her tone as light as possible, all while her heart was crumbling into tiny pieces, bit by agonising bit. 'I'd rather we were together. I'm dying to hear all about how you got on.'

'Oh, it's been fantastic!'

Luckily, Angel was so excited, she jabbered on. 'I can't believe this. I have so many enquiries and commissions for dresses and the other stuff, I don't know what to do with myself. I don't know how I'll cope.'

'That's brilliant. I'm so happy for you.'

'Jenna had her photo taken for the trust website and possibly for their national magazine. Imagine that: one of my dresses in a magazine. And I've agreed to have a stall at the Lizard Craft Centre Christmas fair. Oh, I'm glad we made all those Christmas decs now. I'll have to get cracking on some more kitchen stuff though. I'll ask Emma to help me. She's a good little seamstress herself. You know, one of the students from the art college asked me if I'd think about working with her on some vintage fabric designs – think of that! They'd be exclusive to us. I can't believe it.'

'It's wonderful.' Bo's knuckles whitened around the wheel. It had started to sleet and she had to put the wipers on. She had to bite her lip to stop the road ahead blurring. No windscreen wipers would help with that.

'I *need* to hear more about you and Ran. You'd better keep him away from that blonde woman. Like a queen bee around a honey pot, she was! Still, I don't blame her. He is gorgeous and a great dancer – though with you teaching him, I'm not surprised. You kept that quiet.'

Word was out now. She and Ran had been dancing, and there was no way the rest of the Flingers – and probably beyond – would believe there was nothing more to their relationship.

'He wanted it kept quiet. He never meant to dance tonight and if Cade hadn't had an accident, he never would have. Tonight was probably the last time I'll dance with Ran, though.' Bo's hands tightened around the wheel. 'The queen bee. The blonde woman. That's Phaedra, his wife.'

'What? I thought he was divorced?'

'No,' Bo said tightly. 'Not yet.'

'Oh. But I thought you and him – we all thought . . . when you were dancing. It was such a shock yet you looked so good together. So perfect,' Angel added.

'We're friends. He wanted to learn to dance again. He used

288

to when he was young and it was meant to be a bit of fun. He was embarrassed about it so asked me to keep it quiet. You know what he's like.' Bo gave a little shrug and a smile, even though she was dying inside.

'OK. So either you taught him well or he was good to start with. Probably both. Did you have any idea his wife was going to turn up tonight?'

'No. It was a surprise. Apparently, she knew he'd joined the Flingers and saw we were going to be at the Illuminations. She decided to come along. She didn't expect him to be dancing though.'

Angel squeaked. 'Wow. I bet she had a shock when she saw him with you.'

'I think you could call it that. Ran too.'

'Oh, Bo. Here I am rattling on about the dresses and your evening has ended like this.'

'It's fine. I'm fine,' Bo said tightly, choked with emotion. Angel's sympathetic words were the key that would open the floodgates any moment. They'd reached Angel's cottage and the sleet had turned to rain.

'You don't have to pretend,' Angel soothed. 'You've been such a support to me, and I know how it feels to put on a front. Even tonight, even though everyone was being so nice to me, raving about the dress and wanting to know more, I still couldn't help thinking: I wish Tommy was here to see this. However much he's hurt me, I would rather go home to him, complaining he had to eat a cold dinner or moaning, than an empty house.'

Bo's heart went out to Angel.

'I understand that. You've been with Tommy for thirty years. I've known Ran five minutes in comparison. If he wants to get back with his wife, there's nothing I can or should do about it.

I've a great business, loads of friends and I don't need a man to make my life complete.'

'That's true. You've helped to show me that. It's early days but I can see a chink of light at the end of the tunnel. I do see I can make a life without Tommy, no matter how much I loved him – and I still do, despite everything. You shouldn't dismiss your feelings for Ran. If you're falling for him and he's going to be snatched away from you, you have every right to be hurt and upset.'

Upset *again*, Bo thought. She could hardly bear the reminder of her double disappointment – let down by Hamish and Ran – or the truth that Angel was telling her.

'I won't stand in their way. They were *married*, and I've known him five minutes in comparison to that.'

'It doesn't matter that you've only known him – well – for a short time. He's a good man. He's twice the man Hamish is – anyone can see that. But I understand what it's like to be scared – and scarred. I don't think I'd trust any man completely again either.'

'You're right,' Bo declared, gripping the wheel tightly. 'After my experience of romance over the past year, this is the final nail in the coffin for me.'

Chapter Thirty-Six

'This is a sweet little place. I can see exactly why you wanted to hole up down here.'

Phaedra cast an approving glance around Ran's sitting room. He'd flicked on the lamps and the light glinted from her honey-blonde bob, which was still perfect despite the rain. She was still beautiful, with pale skin dusted with freckles that she'd always hated but he thought enhanced her delicate looks. She ran a lot so she'd always been slender but he thought she was even thinner than the last time he'd seen her. That had been over a year ago.

'Plenty of room for the vinyl too.'

'That's why I chose it,' he said more gruffly than he meant to.

There was a thud from above.

She looked upwards. 'My God. What was that?'

'Probably Thor. If not, a ghost.'

'A ghost?' She pulled a face. 'Don't say this place is haunted!'

'Only by the Beast of Bodmin.' He sighed. 'Thor is my cat.'

'I thought you didn't like cats.'

'We had cats when I was a boy . . .'

'I didn't know that.'

'I don't think I ever told you. Anyway, Thor found me, rather than the other way around. A friend said he needed a home and I could provide one. He seems to have settled in.' He smiled wryly. 'Plenty of mice for him to chase round here.'

Phaedra wrinkled her nose. 'Not inside the cottage, I hope?'

'Not on Thor's watch. I'll make us a drink. Tea or coffee?'

'Coffee? Don't you have anything stronger to go with it? It's been a hell of a journey.'

He nodded. 'Sure. Take a seat. I'll sort something out.'

Making the drink was as much for his benefit as Phaedra's. The sight of her talking to Bo had rocked him to the core. He'd been too stunned to even move for a few seconds but then he had rushed over to them – but Bo had left the ballroom before he could say anything. He hadn't seen her since then, and he'd had no choice but to pack up his kit, with the help of some of the other Flingers.

During all of this, Phaedra had retreated to the Trewhella café, leaving Ran to wonder why she'd turned up – and how Bo felt about her sudden reappearance. He'd no idea how long the two women had been in conversation, and God knew what had been said.

Ran had led the way, with Phaedra following. It was a good job she'd arrived in her own car because he didn't think he'd have had room for her, with all his diving gear and sound system and records. There was also sand in the footwells and probably cat hair somewhere too.

He drove far more cautiously than he normally would, aware she was unused to the twisting narrow lanes with their high 'hedges' that were actually hard as stone. It was dark and intermittently sleeting. Every so often he'd lose sight of her car headlights in the rear-view mirror and pull over to check she was still behind. She had a satnav but they weren't always totally reliable down here and he still wanted to make sure she reached Creekside Cottage safely.

After the initial shock of seeing her in the ballroom had left him dumbfounded, he was determined to stay calm. She'd so far refused to explain exactly why she'd sought him out until they reached the cottage, but he knew her too well to think she'd made the long journey without planning to stay over with him for the night. The spare room was ready, but he felt guilty that he hadn't changed the sheets since Bo had stayed. He hadn't expected to have another guest in there so soon.

He made a cafetiere of coffee, thankful he still had some decent stuff in the back of the cupboard, then feeling annoyed with himself that he was so bothered about impressing Phaedra. He took a bottle of Armagnac from the cupboard, too, and some amaretti biscuits that he couldn't even remember buying.

There was a clean, unchipped mug for Phaedra but everything else was in the dishwasher so he made do with one that had the dive school logo on it. She noticed everything of course.

He lingered a second in the doorway and watched her eyes darting everywhere, assessing the cottage, his possessions – his new life. He felt naked under her scrutiny and regretted not chucking instant coffee into a mug.

He sighed. Why did she have the power to make him feel like a soldier during an inspection parade?

Why the hell was she here, turning his life on its head when the past, with all its pain, was vanishing in the rear-view mirror?

Why now when he'd finally allowed himself to fall for Bo – and worse, had let her know how he felt?

He watched as Phaedra hugged herself. She hadn't taken off her coat.

He put the tray on the coffee table and picked up a fleece blanket from the back of the chair.

'Here, have this. The heating hasn't been on and it's a raw night. I could light a fire but the heating will be quicker.'

The sitting room door opened and Thor sauntered in. He stared at Phaedra but kept his distance.

'He's wary of new people,' Ran said.

'I can't think why. He looks like he can handle himself.'

Ran handed her the blanket.

'Thanks.' She took off her coat before draping it around her shoulders and tucking the blanket around her knees. She rubbed her hands together. 'I thought Cornish winters were meant to be mild.'

'If you mean we don't have much snow and ice yes, but it can be damp down here by the creek and it seeps into your bones.'

'You can say that again. I'm turning blue.'

He poured her a black coffee and added a slug of brandy, before handing the mug to her. 'The brandy and coffee will help but I'm afraid you'll have cat hair on you from the blanket. I haven't had time to vacuum. I wasn't expecting guests.'

'I thought about warning you but I was worried you might try to persuade me not to come.'

'Why would I do that?' he asked, attempting to hide the sarcasm that laced his question. The mac had hung off her frame and, under the careful make-up, he thought she was tired. She'd probably been working far too hard and perhaps been worrying about the end of their marriage and the fact he hadn't dealt with the legal aspects to end it as swiftly as he might have. A bolt of guilt struck him but it was too late for regrets.

'Because I wasn't sure of the reception I'd get. Because you'd wonder why on earth I'd have come all the way down here when I've been badgering you to sign the divorce papers for so long. Because . . .' She took a sip of her coffee and sighed in satisfaction. 'I'm still not certain that I should be here. Even when I crossed the Tamar, every minute of that damn interminable journey, I wasn't sure. Even when I drove up here to Trewhella, I still wasn't convinced.'

'And yet you came.'

'Yes. I came because I have to know. Are we doing the right thing?'

Unease stirred in the pit of his stomach. 'I'm not sure I understand . . . This was what you wanted,' he corrected himself so he didn't sound so confrontational. 'We are doing the right thing.' He might not have wanted a divorce at one time but he'd come round to the view it was the best thing for both of them. 'Surely it's too late to back out now. I signed the papers ages ago and sent them back. Your brief did get them?'

'Yes, my lawyer got the papers.' She brushed cat hair off her arm.

Thor stared unrepentantly and flicked his tail.

'Even so . . . I can't help thinking about what we had, and how good it once was, and wondering if we could make things work for us again.'

'We've been through that.' Ran almost wept in frustration. 'So many times. We agreed that we'd grown too far apart to salvage our marriage.'

'I know. This may sound mad but the situation's changed.' She held his gaze. 'You've changed, Ran.'

'I haven't changed. I've changed my job and the place where I live but I'm still me.' He touched his chest where his heart was. The heart that was beating faster than he liked. Phaedra still made that happen. She was still beautiful, still clever and intriguing. Still exciting. Still turning his world upside-down, even though he'd tried to hide away from her.

'Will you hold me? It's cold.'

The breath left his body. How many nights had he longed to hear her say that? How many nights when she'd slept on the furthest edge of the bed, turning her back on him? How many nights had he regretted that he couldn't take the way he'd been living? In the end, the only solution had been to leave London and live apart. A few months later, she'd asked for the divorce and, after several fruitless attempts to persuade her to change her mind, he'd reluctantly agreed.

'Ran, haven't you missed me? We were both so busy, under such a lot of stress. I've done a lot of thinking since then.' She reached out her hands and took his. They were freezing. 'I still love you.'

Those words caused him physical pain, a tightening in the chest that actually hurt. 'I still love you too, Phae. I always will, no matter what happens.'

'No matter what happens? I'm not sure I like the sound of that.'

She squeezed his hands, gazing up at him. 'I'm glad I came.'

Ran didn't know how to reply but her unflinching gaze, the one that used to make him want to carry her off to bed, unnerved him. Her tongue flicked over her lips before she yawned and patted her mouth.

'I'm tired, but at least I'm warmer. Must be the brandy.'

'Probably. I'll get your overnight bag in from the car if you let me have your keys.'

'*Overnight* bag?' She laughed and pushed the rug off her

knees. 'Oh, you are funny, Ran. I wouldn't schlepp all the way down here for one night. I've got a bit of holiday to use up so I brought two suitcases. I'd better help you carry them up to our room.'

Chapter Thirty-Seven

'Are you sure you're OK?' Angel asked as they drove through her village towards her house.

'Yes, I'm fine,' Bo lied. 'I need to go home and collapse into bed.'

They turned into the drive and Bo helped her friend unload the items she'd taken to the Illuminations. They went round the side of the house and paused.

'Oh my God, the kitchen door's open!'

'Did you leave it open?'

'I left it unlocked. I always do. Most of us do in the village . . .'

'Oh, Angel!' Bo was horrified. 'Maybe it blew open in the wind.'

'There's no wind . . .' Angel said. 'Maybe the catch has gone. I'm being silly.'

Bo was more cautious. 'Let's be a bit careful.'

Angel opened the door and flicked on the light. It was tidy, with the washing-up stacked on the drainer. 'It's OK,' she said.

Bo let out a sigh of relief too, but a moment later, there was a crash from up above.

'Oh God! What was that?'

'Shit,' Angel whispered. 'I think I'm being burgled.'

Bo grabbed her arm. 'Get out of here now. I'll call the police.'

Abandoning their bags in the kitchen, they fled out of the back door and into the garden.

In her panic, Bo dropped her phone on the terrace and scrambled around for it in the darkness. 'Bugger.'

'Look! The light's just gone on in my sewing room!' Angel said, clinging to her arm. 'What if they're stealing my machine? I can't manage without it. It's my most treasured possession . . .'

'They're probably looking for cash and jewellery. Let's go back to the car and I'll call the police.'

They rushed around to the front of the house and opened the car door quietly. 'Get in and lock the doors while I call,' Bo said.

Before they could climb inside, another light went on in the hallway.

'They're coming out! Quick! Lock the doors,' Angel cried.

Bo leapt inside and slammed the door as a dark figure emerged from the front doorway.

'Oh my God!' Angel said, stunned. 'Give me your phone, Bo.'

Chapter Thirty-Eight

'Mulled wine, sourdough toast, mint hot chocolate topped with clotted cream, turkey and cranberry pasties with winter slaw . . .'

Angel was on her knees outside the café, carefully writing on the menu board with the chalk pen a few days after the Illuminations. 'How will anyone be able to resist those?'

'Hopefully they won't,' Bo said, already spotting a few regulars peering at the café while working on their boats. Angel was helping out, working on the till and taking orders while Bo was cooking. Cade was taking a few days' holiday.

At such a quiet time of year, Bo couldn't justify giving her a permanent job – not that Angel wanted to work in a café. Despite Kelvin's influence, she'd been earning far more working at the Country Stores. Old Mr Jennings had been a much fairer employer than his nephew, and valued her. The fledgling textile business was no match for a full-time salary, but at least it was a start.

It was still mild enough to sit outside, and Angel was a natural at serving the customers. Coloured lights now decorated the covered area, and on dull days they attracted visitors and walkers like moths to a flame.

Angel got to her feet, marker pen in her hand. 'Thanks for giving me the shift.'

'You're welcome – and it's me who should be thanking you! I can't manage on my own and Cade's still in no fit state to be on his feet all day.'

'I wanted the company – especially after what I came home to on Saturday night.'

They went inside the kitchen area to start prep for the lunch service, chatting about the shock of seeing a figure walking out of Angel's front door a few nights before. Once they'd realised that the figure was Tommy, Angel had gone to confront him. They ended up arguing inside the house, and Bo had waited by the car for a while before sending a message saying she was going to head home but would be ready to come over if need be.

'So, Tommy's new woman was the ex of one of a crew from another boat based out of Falmouth. He met her down the pub when he was out with a bunch of mates in the summer. He admitted they started seeing each other in June!' Angel said.

'The bastard. I'm so sorry, Angel. It must have been so hard to hear that.'

'Thanks. It was tough. I was so mad I almost threw something at him, but at least I've been put out of my misery. I've been wondering who she was for so long. I think I met her a couple of times, way back, when she was married to one of the other skippers. She's been divorced for years.'

Angel's words answered Bo's remaining doubts about the woman she and Ran had spotted Tommy with in Falmouth. It couldn't have been Madame Odette, or Angel would have recognised the fortune teller back in August.

'He's definitely gone for good, then?' Bo said, stirring mulled apple juice on the hob. The small prep area filled with spicy aromas and steam wafted out.

'Yes, he's gone.'

'Back to this woman?'

'No. She's kicked him out.'

Bo dropped her spoon into the pan. 'Ha!'

'He's admitted he's now living at his mum's,' Angel went on, 'though the cheeky sod asked if he could stay with me.'

Bo fished the spoon out of the warm juice. 'I can't believe he had the nerve!'

'I said no, of course. I told him that I could never trust him again and it was my house and if he thought he could disappear like he had and let me think he was dead and lie to me, he wasn't the man I thought.'

'Good for you,' Bo said gently, while aware of the toll it must have taken on her friend.

'That night he broke in, he'd been upstairs to find something from the junk room. I told him I'd chucked his stuff out and sold it to an angling shop! He wanted to know why the room was all set up with my sewing kit. I told him I was running my own business and that I'd left the Country Stores.'

Bo almost burst with pride at Angel's bravery. 'You absolute star.'

'He said he thought I was mad and that I'd chucked a good job away. I called him a rat and threw him out. You should have seen his face . . .' Angel folded her arms.

'I wish I had.'

Angel let out a huge sigh. 'I cried my eyes out after he'd gone.

I regretted telling him to go, questioning whether I'd done the right thing. But when I woke up this morning, I phoned the locksmith, who came straight round to change the locks.'

'Good for you! I'll help in any way I can. Have you heard any more from Kelvin, by the way?'

'Not yet. He was meant to send my P45 certificate and I've asked twice but he hasn't done it yet. I might have to go to the Stores and demand it.'

'He's treated you like dirt ever since he took over that shop. I despise that man,' Bo said.

'Me too, though I admit it's not only the money I miss, it's the rest of the staff. The team at the Stores are lovely apart from Kelvin and I never minded the hard work. Still, at least I have time for my sewing, but it's one thing having a pastime as a hobby. The pressure's on when it's your job.'

'I understand. It's always on your mind but there's nothing like being your own boss, and you're passionate about it so I know you'll succeed.'

'It still feels like a pipe dream that I could make it full time. Once Christmas is over, orders will drop like a stone and I'll have to work super hard. Making dance dresses is great but it's not financially viable. I'll have to focus on the gifts and homewares. I must do a proper business plan.' She smiled. 'Anyway, enough about me. It's *your* business that matters today.'

'I can see Finn Morvah and his girlfriend wondering if we're open yet,' Angel said with a nod towards the slipway.

Bo waved at Finn and Rose and beckoned them over. It was time to be Bo the cheery café owner again, no matter what turmoil was going on in her personal life.

For the rest of the day, she and Angel kept busy. It was a mild December day, and the Cornish sun still had the strength to make sitting outside a very pleasant experience. Bo did provide blankets on her new Under Sail terrace but they weren't needed today as people tucked into her festive fare. She hoped for a similarly fine evening for the Starfish Graphics do.

Around two-thirty, the shadows were already lengthening and she and Angel closed the kitchen. They served a few more cakes and coffee before rolling the shutter halfway down on the kiosk.

'Shall I help you close up?'

'No, no – you get on home.'

'Are you sure?'

'I'll be fine.'

'Thanks. I want to finish the dress I'm altering for Sally for the Christmas Spectacular. It's racing up on us and I've also got stock to make for the Lizard Craft Centre fair.'

'Blimey! You'd better be off then.'

Angel left, chattering away on her mobile to her son. Bo's spirits were lifted by her friend's enthusiasm. It was great to see the transformation in her from someone bullied by her boss – and in some ways by Tommy – to a budding businesswoman. Yet Bo was also under no illusions. Angel missed her husband terribly and the loss of her job was causing her major financial worries.

While working and chatting with Angel, Bo had been focusing on something other than her own troubles. Once she was alone in the gathering dusk, they descended on her like a pall. A chill settled as the sun sank and the winter sky turned crimson, reflecting in the waters of the creek. She switched off the Christmas lights and the covered area was plunged into shadow.

She went out to collect the menu board, ready to store it inside.

'Turkey and cranberry pasties? I thought it was sacrilege to use anything but meat and veg? Won't you be run out of Cornwall for serving that?'

Her heart flipped at the arrival of Ran. 'Well, we've sold out and most of the pasties went to people from the boatyard. Even sold one to Frank Cardew.'

'Frank? Cornish-for-thirty-generations-Frank?'

'Yup. And he didn't bat an eyelid.'

There were smiles on both sides but the banter couldn't defuse the tension.

'That's a beautiful sunset,' he said. 'It'll already be dark in London.'

'Yes, I guess it will.' She put the board inside the café kiosk.

'Bo. I know we haven't spoken since the Illuminations but I wanted to see you in person.'

Her pulse soared. This was it, then.

'I didn't expect you to call.' She turned off the lights in the kitchen.

'I guess you know that Phaedra's been staying with me? I hardly had any choice but to let her and I had absolutely no idea she'd rock up to the Illuminations. It was completely out of the blue – out of character too.'

'I'd worked that out by the look on your face,' Bo said, almost amused at his awkwardness. It would be funny, if it wasn't so sad.

'She said she wanted to surprise me,' he added.

'That's what she told me on Saturday night, too,' Bo said. 'She said she'd had a quick chat with you.'

Bo bit back any response. She had no idea what Phaedra had shared with Ran, though she suspected Phaedra might have decided not to reveal she'd none-too-subtly warned Bo to back off. There was no way Bo was going to say a word against his wife. It was beneath her dignity. She would not be dragged into a fight over a man.

'She's staying with me for a week,' Ran said.

'That'll be nice . . .' Bo almost said before realising that any response might sound sarcastic. She could only manage, 'Oh?'

'She's taken some leave she was owed and I think she's feeling burnt-out after a big project at work.'

'Maybe Cornwall will work its magic on her?' Bo said, no longer able to keep the sarcasm out of her voice and angry with herself for showing she cared.

She felt Ran's hand on her arm. 'Please. Be patient with me. This is an awkward situation.'

'Yeah. I bet.' She ushered him out of the door. 'Do you mind? I need to lock up and get showered and changed.'

'Going anywhere nice?' he asked gruffly.

'Drinks, dinner, cinema.'

'Right . . . I wouldn't want to make you late for a date.'

Bo set her jaw, too frustrated at the situation to correct him. She watched him march off, then let out a cry of frustration before taking a deep breath, hardening her heart, and heading home to get ready for the Christmas party night with her cinema girlfriends. *It's a Wonderful Life* had never looked less appealing in her life.

Sometimes, there wasn't a happy ending. Not even at Christmas. Especially not at Christmas.

Chapter Thirty-Nine

Never had five days seemed longer to Ran. Never had his cottage felt smaller. Even Thor was feeling the pressure of having Phaedra in the house.

'I swear that cat's deliberately hiding from me!' Phaedra moaned when Thor had studiously ignored the gourmet reindeer cat food she'd bought for him from the Country Stores.

'That's what cats do,' Ran had said when she'd had to tip it in the bin. 'They don't like strange people in their territory.'

Phaedra had treated him to a laser stare. 'What's that supposed to mean?'

'That Thor's wary of visitors. He's taken ages to even tolerate me.'

'Humph!' Phaedra had leaned against the worktop. 'Have you thought of building him a catio?' she'd asked. 'Then he wouldn't have to be inside the cottage and you wouldn't have to clear up the cat hair all the time. I'm sick to death of emptying the vacuum cleaner.'

'I'm not building him a catio. He can stay inside.'

Phaedra had taken herself off in Ran's van, returning a few

hours later with a load of shopping bags and moaning that a wall had sprung out and scraped the side of the vehicle.

Ran had shrugged. One more scratch wouldn't be noticed. Besides, he was too worried about Bo's reaction to him at the café when he'd called to see her. She was hurt and he didn't blame her. He knew what he *could* have said to reassure her – that he wasn't going to revisit the past with Phaedra, that she was staying in the spare room, that he couldn't stop thinking about Bo – but their conversation had ended so abruptly, and he wasn't sure she would have believed him anyway.

The next day was Friday. Having exhausted the charms of Falford and complaining the paths 'were ridiculously muddy' and the van was 'totally impractical' for the Cornish lanes, Phaedra was pacing the cottage like a caged tiger. Despite it being the off season, Ran still had to go into work so he couldn't spend time ferrying her around, even if he'd wanted to.

She'd ordered an eye-wateringly expensive wine from a merchant in London for dinner, along with some oysters from Kev's Seafood Shack. At least they were local, Ran thought, though in all honesty he'd have preferred a steak. His only consolation was that her stay had to end soon. She'd be leaving on Sunday, or so he assumed, as there had been no mention of her going back to work on the Monday.

Finding her sitting on the terrace, wrapped in a blanket with a glass of wine, he softened. This wasn't her territory and she would surely be happier in London. He decided not to mention that the blanket was the one he used to cover Thor's carrier on his vet's visits.

'Phae. We need to talk.'

She burst out laughing. 'Ran. Please. No one says that in real life. Only in TV soaps.'

'OK. We need to have a big row? How's that?'

'It's original, I suppose. I always liked you when you were fired up.'

'I don't think rows are amusing.'

She tugged the blanket closer around her. 'OK. Let's "talk".'

'I'm not sure this is going to work. You staying here. Us spending so much time together again.'

'I beg to disagree,' she said. 'But you're going to have to put up with me for a while longer.'

His flesh grew cold. 'Why? I thought you were leaving tomorrow – or Sunday?'

'*We* are. You and me. I've made an appointment at the solicitor's in London for us next Thursday.'

'Thursday! Why do I need to come?'

'I've decided to sell the flat.'

Ran was in despair. 'I thought you were hellbent on staying in London? We've already sorted out that you can have the flat. I'll admit I'm surprised you're selling it but you don't need me to deal with it, surely?'

'You still, technically, jointly own it, even though you agreed to let me live there as part of the settlement. I'll be honest, Ran, I've already got a buyer . . .'

'Bloody hell, that's quick.'

'Not really, we've been apart for so long . . . Look, let's go inside. It's so damp out here!'

He followed her in and closed the French doors to the terrace.

She paced around. 'A lot has happened in that time. I've found a private buyer and instructed a solicitor. It's Carl Amfo . . . he works for my brother-in-law's firm in Camden. You have met him several times at dinner parties, Ran, don't say you've forgotten.'

Ran remembered the big, smiling man who seemed too jolly to be a lawyer. 'Yeah, I like Carl.'

'Good. Well, we need to go and see him in person for a chat and to do the identity checks. I've made an appointment.'

'When?'

'Next Thursday.'

'But there are solicitors here. And Zoom meetings.'

She laughed. 'I'm sure he'd prefer to see us in person. And as for using a local firm, you don't think I'd trust some provincial junior fresh from their legal diploma at the local college.'

'They could still handle checking our passports, Phae. They're not incompetent!'

She pouted. 'I want to see Carl. Not only for the check . . . as I have a buyer lined up, I'd really appreciate you helping me box everything up ready for the removal men. It's not only that I need your help physically . . .' She spoke softly, touching his arm. 'It's going to be a very emotional process. It's so final, isn't it? Packing away our lives?' Her eyes glistened with tears. She rarely cried and he was shocked.

Ran hesitated, torn in half. He didn't want to go back with her but she seemed to have finally abandoned any ideas of them getting back together. Even though she'd instigated the divorce, she'd clearly been on more of an emotional rollercoaster than he'd imagined. She was simply better at hiding it than he was.

'Please come with me, Ran. It'll only be a flying visit. I'd hoped you could spare a few days off. You're freelance, aren't you? How much diving do you do at this time of year?'

On that point, she was right. There wasn't much in his diary until well into the new year. Perhaps, helping her pack away their possessions would help them both achieve closure and, finally, be able to truly leave the past behind. That would be good for Phaedra, for Ran himself – and, more important, for Bo, in the long run.

'I'd have to talk to my boss at the centre . . . you seem to have it all worked out.'

'That's why you asked me out in the first place. You said I was the "most together person" you'd ever met.' She moved within kissing distance, gazing into his eyes. 'And the sexiest.'

He laughed to disguise his unease at her proximity. She smelled of frangipani flowers on hot summer nights in cloudless climes. It was the perfume he'd gifted her on their wedding day . . . ludicrously expensive, filling his senses. He'd come home late some nights to find her between their white sheets, wearing only the perfume.

Her fingers lingered on his cheek. He hesitated, the scent of perfume clouding his thoughts.

She sighed. 'What am I going to do with you, Ran?'

He enclosed her hand in his, lowering it gently. 'This isn't a great idea, Phae. I thought we were packing away the past.'

Her laughter echoed around the cottage. 'Don't look so terrified. I was only going to do this.'

She raised her hand again, plucking at his collar.

'Cat hair,' she said, holding a few strands of white fur between her fingertips. Her eyes sparked with amusement. 'On your shirt.'

He shook his head, smiling, mostly with relief that she hadn't tried to take things further between them. It had been awkward enough telling her she was sleeping in the spare room, not sharing his bed. She'd laughed at him for that but said she'd go along with it, if it made him feel better. She'd obviously decided he wasn't in a serious relationship. You couldn't call a kiss a relationship – but when Bo had insisted they kept things to friends, she'd evidently been wise to do so.

With Phaedra in Cornwall again, in his house – and if she'd had her way, in his bed – he dare not rekindle the spark with Bo. She would do well to keep away from him . . .

'Look,' he said, feeling stifled by the heat from the fire and the cloying perfume. 'I'll think about whether I can spare the time to come back to help you sort everything out for the move. It's stuffy in here, I . . . need a walk to clear my head.'

'But it's getting dark!'

'I need some fresh air. And I need something more than oysters for dinner.'

She grimaced. 'And you're not leaving so you can avoid the conversation?'

'Give me some credit,' he said, uncomfortable with his fib.

Her eyes narrowed to slits. 'Hmm. How long will you be?'

'About an hour by the time I've walked to the post office and back.'

She pursed her lips. 'OK. See if they have any lemons and some of that saffron mayo to go with the oysters. Some sourdough wouldn't go amiss.'

'I'll do my best,' Ran said, thinking she'd be lucky if he returned with a microwave lasagne and bottle of ketchup from the post office shop.

As he walked into the dusk, at the back of his mind, a plan of his own began to form . . .

Chapter Forty

It was growing dark by the time Ran reached the footbridge over the stream at the end of Falford Creek. He paused on the bridge. One side of the stream led left to the main village where the post office stores and many of the cottage windows were brightly lit. Turning right would lead him to the opposite bank, home to the yacht club, the boatyard – and of course, the Boatyard Café.

Ran paused, puzzled. The café should be shut now but, instead, the fairy lights adorning the new terrace were glittering and the kitchen light was on. Bo must be working late . . . then he remembered. Tonight was her Christmas party event. Her big night!

Why did he feel he ought to be part of it?

Well, he could pop in now. There was plenty of time and he'd love to see how the café looked bedecked in all its finery after the refurb. It could do no harm to wish her luck before he went to the post office shop. Besides, he needed more time to think.

As he grew closer, he started to worry. He'd expected it to

be a hive of activity, with Cade and Angel buzzing around the terrace, getting it ready, but there was no one to be seen.

'Bo!'

He went to the back door and literally bumped into her. Unfortunately she was carrying a tray of glasses.

'Oh!'

The tray wobbled and the glasses fell onto the deck with a crash and shattered at their feet.

Bo let out a little squeal of shock. 'Oh God, what else can bloody go wrong!'

'I'm sorry! I didn't mean to startle you.' He could have kicked himself.

'No – it's OK. It's just I didn't expect anyone to be here.'

'I was on my way to the shop and saw the lights on; I came to see how you were getting on.'

'I'm not getting on! That's the point. The water's been off until around five minutes ago so I'm way behind with the prep. Cade's had to babysit because his wife's mum has been taken ill and I daren't call Angel because she's got an urgent commission for a dress and I know she'd drop everything to help when she definitely doesn't have the time.' She glanced at her watch. 'And the guests will be here within forty-five minutes.'

'You should have called me,' he said gently.

Bo stared at him as if he'd suggested she ask Gordon Ramsay to help. 'I didn't want to disturb you,' she said tartly.

'Well, you should have. Look, I'm here now. I can help.'

She eyed him suspiciously. 'I thought you said you were only popping to the shop.'

'Look Bo, you need a hand. I'm here to provide it. Beggars

can't be choosers.' He tried a smile and she pouted then heaved a big sigh.

'You're right. If you can find the broom and dustpan in the staff cloakroom to clear up the glass first, that would be great. And after that, the fire pit needs lighting. The wood and fire-lighters are already in the bowl. Matches on that shelf up there. Then you can help me in the kitchen, Cinderella.'

He grinned. 'That's more like it.'

'Don't sound too enthusiastic. You might regret it.'

'I doubt it.' He laid a hand on her shoulder. 'Will you do one thing for me in return?'

'What?'

'Don't forget to breathe.'

She exhaled and laughed. She looked gorgeous with her hair piled on her head – admittedly half of it had escaped the bow – and a sparkly green Christmas jumper under her blue apron.

'You need an apron,' she said, perhaps catching him admiring her.

She handed him a sky-blue affair with 'Bo's Boatyard Café' on it. 'It's just your colour,' she said, obviously amused.

'Thanks.' He rubbed his chin. He must look scruffy for serving guests. 'I wish I'd had a shave now.'

'The stubble suits you.'

'Really?'

She seemed embarrassed. 'There's no time for compliments. Get to work!' she ordered.

'I hope you're not going to go all cheffy, throwing pots and pans around.'

Hands on hips, Bo treated him to a stern look that was even

315

sexier than her smile – before he remembered that his wife was waiting at home.

'Only if I catch you slacking.'

He laughed and went to fetch the broom. Sooner rather than later, he needed to tell Phaedra he wouldn't be home with the ketchup, let alone fancy mayo – and why.

Chapter Forty-One

The whole day had been a series of unfortunate events for Bo, with problems on and off at the café most of the time they'd been open to the regular Friday crowd. A couple of brief but annoying power cuts earlier in the morning had left her continually on edge, then, minutes before they'd closed in the afternoon, Cade had been phoned by his wife to say her mum had been blue-lighted into A&E with chest pains and he'd had to rush off to babysit their little one.

He'd been devastated to let her down, so Bo had lied and said she would call Angel to help, even though she knew she'd have to manage on her own. Coping solo would have been a challenge, though do-able, until the problems with the water supply topped off a nightmare day. They'd been caused by some work at the boatyard office next door, and had eventually been fixed as darkness descended. Even so, Bo hadn't been able to use the kitchen for almost an hour, which had slashed her prep time further.

It was rare that she ever admitted defeat but she'd been at her wits' end and she'd considered cancelling rather than make a gigantic hash of the event.

Ran was the last person she'd have called upon to be her guardian angel. She had no time to worry what Phaedra might think of him 'popping out to the shop' and ending up at the café all evening. The fact he *had* offered to stay gave her heart and yet she was acutely aware that his not-quite-ex-wife was waiting for him at the cottage.

But there was no time to worry about it tonight.

While Ran cleared up the broken glass and lit the fire pit, Bo tackled the mulled wine and worked through the list of tasks in her mind so she could meet her guests in a calm and festive frame of mind. Thank God she and Cade had made the canapés earlier. They were chilling in the fridge but she still had loads to do and not much over half an hour to do it in.

Ran stuck his head around the kitchen door. 'Glass cleared. Fire underway. What's the plan?'

Bo turned away from the stove where she'd been adding spices and cinnamon sticks to the red wine and brandy mix.

'OK. We have twenty guests for canapés and cocktails. There's mulled wine and a non-alcoholic pomegranate option. The canapés are a mix of fish, veggie and two vegan options. I've put them all on separate platters and they're covered and waiting in the fridge.' She took a breath. 'Afterwards, we're doing mini festive brownie bites and vegan brownies plus hot chocolate with the option of Cornish clotted cream rum for those who aren't driving.'

'Sounds delicious. I wish I was a guest.'

'We'll be too busy to enjoy ourselves, I'm afraid,' she said, butterflies still fluttering at the prospect of the important event going ahead with a novice assistant. 'I'll need you to hand round the drinks and canapés and tell guests about the ingredients if they ask. I'll have my hands full with the food and keeping everyone happy. I want to have time to do a bit of schmoozing with the design company. Then I'll need a hand to serve the hot drinks. You can go after that . . . I can clear away myself.'

'I'm not leaving you until the whole event is finished.'

'You may be desperate to escape by then.'

'I doubt it. Shall we have some music to get us all in the mood?' he offered.

She nodded and took his advice to breathe a little more often. 'Great idea. Thank you.'

Soon after, a festive mix tape was playing from his phone via the smart speaker in the kitchen. The Pogues, Wizzard, Slade, Pretenders . . . It was only a small thing but it was amazing how the sounds of Christmas favourites made her feel better.

'Smells great,' he said. 'I've cleared up. What do you want me to do next?' he said.

'Well, they'll be here in fifteen minutes so could you prepare cocktails and mocktails, please? It's fizz, cranberry and orange liqueur and the pomegranate juice is in the fridge for the mocktails. Glasses are on the shelf above the microwave and those ruby glass jugs are for the drinks.'

'No problem.'

Ran set to work with the cocktails while Bo laid out plates and serviettes on a side table. Angel's festive bunting was stirring gently in the breeze and she thanked her lucky stars that the weather was calm. It was cool, obviously, but the fire pit on the terrace was now glowing warmly and Ran was humming away to Madonna's version of 'Santa Baby'.

Bo spotted headlights at the boatyard gates and her adrenaline level spiked.

'I think they're here! Oh wow . . . I hope it's going to be OK.'

Ran touched her hand. 'It's going to be more than OK. It's

going to be fantastic. It's a cool place for a Christmas party and, with the sail and the decorations, it looks really special.'

'Thanks.' Her pulse was racing and her stomach whirling. It wasn't only the café that looked magical. She was struggling to ignore her feelings for Ran. The way he made her feel as if the stars were shining a little brighter . . . . this was crazy.

She moved away from him and his hand dropped to his side. 'There's something missing . . .'

'Candles?' he offered.

'Yes! The tealights are in a box in the storeroom.'

Ran grabbed the box as the first cars were parking in the boatyard car park. People clambered out, laughing and excited – and expectant.

Bo was like a demon, popping tealights on the tables and helping to light them at superfast speed. They'd just finished the last one when the MD of the design company reached the terrace. Bo hurried out to greet him, her biggest smile in place. You'd never know she'd been dreading Christmas, or that she thought the event wouldn't go ahead an hour ago, or that she was very afraid she'd fallen for a man once again who was destined for someone else.

Despite Ran working alongside her, or perhaps because of it, Madame Odette's prediction that she'd be with the 'one she loved' at Christmas had never seemed further away.

Chapter Forty-Two

'Went well, did it?'

Phaedra was sitting on the sofa with her feet up when Ran finally got home around ten p.m. She didn't even look at him as she spoke, simply flicked through the TV channels.

'I think so. Yeah.' He stood in front of the TV, blocking her view. 'I had no choice but to stay. Bo was on her own. Her assistant had to rush off and she'd had problems with the water and power.'

'You had no choice?' She turned off the TV and threw the remote on the coffee table.

Irritation stirred. He was knackered, and certainly had a new respect for anyone who worked in hospitality. It had been non-stop, serving people while smiling and being upbeat and charming. He'd been way out of his comfort zone, though he'd never have let on to Bo.

'OK. I did have a choice. I chose to help a friend when she needed it and I'd have done the same for anyone round here. That's how it works. We pull together. I let you know straight-away and I knew you'd be fine.'

He collapsed onto the sofa next to her.

'Ran . . .' Her voice softened. She leaned forward and picked up his hand. 'It's OK. I can see you've been drawn into this community, that the place has got under your skin. You needed to help a friend.'

A friend . . . Ran swallowed.

'Thanks for being so understanding.'

'I hope you're not being sarcastic?' she said, doubt in her voice.

'No. No, I'm not. I'm knackered, that's all. It was bloody hard work.'

'I'm sure . . . but you know, you said you knew I'd be fine here on my own.'

He turned sharply. 'You are, aren't you?'

Her eyes glistened. She might have been crying.

'Has something happened while I was out? *Are* you OK?'

'Yes. Physically, I'm fine. The rest has done me good.' She glanced away nervously. 'I'm not fine in other ways. I haven't been for a few days, in fact for weeks. Ran, I can't believe I'm saying this but I have to level with you. I don't want a divorce.'

'What?'

Ran was knocked for six and let go of her hand. He'd thought she was moving on – she was in the process of selling their flat.

'I can see that's come as a shock. It did to me, though I now realise my doubts really started when you finally sent the papers back. Seeing the finality of it, the end of our marriage in black and white. It was so cold and stark. Such an admission of failure.'

'Failure? I thought deciding to split was the best thing we could do for each other. You told me that often enough!'

'I know and I'm sorry, but Ran, we loved each other so deeply once and we shared so much. I suppose you could say I have a classic case of wanting what I no longer have.'

He groaned. 'Phae. You can't do this now.'

'I'm sorry, except I'm not. I'd be sorry if I waited to tell you until we were officially divorced so I'm telling you now. So please, come home to London.'

'It's not my home.' He shook his head, kept on shaking it. 'And don't tell me I've had my escape and I should go back to reality because I can't do it.'

'I wasn't going to say that at all. The opposite, in fact. I understand now. I've seen how happy you are – how at home you are here. I want to suggest a compromise, a way we can both live the lives we want and still be together.'

'That's not possible.'

'The dancing, the sea – you look so happy, so at ease in this place. I've been thinking, maybe we can make this work for us. We didn't try hard enough. We could find a place by the sea . . . where you can work. There must be diving jobs you could do but be based in London? Surely you know that? You learned there so I know it's possible.'

'There are jobs I could do there . . .'

She beamed. 'You see, this isn't so hard . . . and I could learn to dance too.'

'You? Learn to dance?'

'Yes, Ran. *Me*. I could learn to dance. Don't look so amazed.'

'I . . . I know you could do it. You'd be brilliant but you've never said you wanted to before. You don't like the music.'

She laughed. To see her beautiful green eyes shine with pleasure had always made him happy, yet the feeling of unease seeped into his bones.

'It doesn't have to be your kind of music, necessarily, of course,' she went on. 'It can be something new. Salsa, tango, bhangra, oh I don't know . . . something cool and sexy would be fabulous. Of course, we could do lessons in any kind of dancing in London.'

She'd made him an offer that she made sound so tempting – she'd always been good at that; good at getting her own way.

'When you come back to London with me, you'll realise it might not be the horror show you remember. You may have a different perspective now. On London. On everything.'

'I'm not sure I can do that.'

'Why? Because you're afraid that if you do, you'll want to stay? Going back isn't always a bad thing, Ran. Reassessing your life – you can change more than once. Maybe moving here was a firebreak. The time you needed – that we both needed – to find out what we really wanted from life. It's certainly made me realise you're the love of my life.'

He gasped. 'What did you say?'

'The love of my life.' She laughed. 'Sorry, that is *so* cheesy but you know what I mean. What matters to us. What makes our hearts sing, and makes us get out of bed every day.'

'Yes, OK.'

'You'll come back with me, then, and see Carl – see what you've been missing?'

Ran hesitated, conflicted again. He was determined not to let Phaedra walk all over him and think they would ever get back together but, also, her words had echoed what Madame Odette had said. He'd been so sceptical, in denial even, and yet . . . was this a sign it was a path he should follow? And what about Bo's reaction if he went to London now? She was so upset with

324

him, and he mustn't risk letting her down. Whatever he did, he had to be sure.

No decision was simple, nothing perfect . . .

Phaedra meanwhile seemed very certain of what she wanted. 'At least email your boss at the scuba centre or whatever you need to do, so we can confirm our appointment with Carl.'

'Where did you say his office was again?' Ran asked, his mind working overtime on his course of action.

She frowned. 'Camden? Why?'

'Oh, nothing . . . I thought they were south of the river.'

'He moved offices when he was made senior partner. Like I said, a lot has happened while we've been apart. It will do you good to catch up.'

He nodded. 'Like I said, I'll check my diary and see what I can do.'

She clapped her hands. 'Hurrah! He's coming round to the idea.'

'Well, Carl's a good solicitor.'

He didn't want to hurt Bo. She was still scarred badly by what happened with Hamish and he didn't want to mess her around. Yet he still felt guilty about how he'd acted in his marriage.

'I knew you'd see sense,' Phaedra said. 'I presume that old van is in a fit state to transport you home?'

Was there a slight emphasis on the word 'home' or was he imagining it? Ran thought of the permanent tang of neoprene in the van and the cat hair on the seats.

'It'll make it as far as London,' he murmured.

Having hung on to the divorce papers, the least he could do now was behave respectfully and kindly towards her, no matter how difficult the situation was. He could hardly pack her into her car and send her back to London. He cared too much about her wellbeing for that. By going back, he could do his duty by helping her with the move and show her, finally, that he no longer belonged in the City, or as part of her life.

More importantly, the idea he'd been churning over on his way to the village earlier that evening began to crystallise further in his mind.

Chapter Forty-Three

'Morning! Can I get a double espresso, please?'

Bo's heart sank like a stone when Phaedra walked up to the counter with a broad grin on her face. She'd still been buzzing from the success of the Christmas party the previous evening. The customers had loved it, saying it was exactly right for their clients: fun, different and informal. They'd already booked a summer event and would be recommending her to other clients. Ran had been great, his dry sense of humour going down a storm with the guests. Bo could only imagine how his turn as a waiter had gone down with his wife.

'Mornin',' Bo said cheerfully. 'Is that to go or to drink here?'

'Oh, drink here, of course. It's so mild. You'd never know Christmas was less than two weeks away. I love the festive bunting by the way.'

'Thanks. My friend Angel made it.'

'It's sweet. Ran told me how good the place looked last night. How lucky that he turned up just in time to act as a waiter.'

'He did more than waiting,' Bo said, then reminded herself not to rise to Phaedra's bait in any way. 'He was a big help,' she added.

She had to turn her back to make the coffee, yet Phaedra lingered by the counter.

She glanced over her shoulder and forced a smile. 'I'll bring your drink over to the deck if you like.'

'No problem. I don't mind sitting here.' Phaedra slid onto a bar stool.

It was probably her imagination but Bo could feel the woman's eyes burning into her while she tamped the coffee grounds into the basket.

'This is a nice little place you've built up. Ran tells me you started it almost from scratch.'

'Not quite. We had a loyal clientele at the old café. I modernised things a bit.'

Bo put the basket into the machine head, fumbling with the portafilter – and yet she'd done it thousands of times before. She hoped Phaedra hadn't noticed. Steam curled into the air and the machine gurgled. The aroma of coffee filled the little kiosk.

'Don't put yourself down . . .'

She whipped round. 'Sorry, I didn't hear that. The machine's noisy.'

'I said, "Don't put yourself down." This is a nice little business. You've done very well. I know Ran's impressed.'

'Really? That's kind of him.' Bo handed over the espresso, hoping Phaedra would then make her way home.

'He's a nice man. Always willing to help a friend in their hour of need. Of course, he's had his fair share of problems but haven't we all? They're over now.' She inhaled then sipped.

328

'Hmm. Great coffee. I'll go a long way to get a better one when we're back in London. I know Ran will miss it too.'

'What?' Bo dropped the portafilter on the worktop. 'I mean, sorry, I didn't quite catch that.'

Phaedra smiled sweetly. 'Ran and I are going back to London.'

'Oh. I . . . you mean for Christmas?'

'Possibly. Probably. We've some business to sort out . . .' Phaedra lowered her voice. 'I won't go into it and I'd rather you didn't mention I'd told you about it – you know what a private guy he is – but I should think he'll be staying until the New Year.' She lowered her cup onto the saucer. 'At least.'

So, he was leaving . . . and, even allowing for Phaedra's interpretation, Ran must have agreed to go back to London. Phaedra wouldn't lie about something like that. Why would she?

Only now did Bo realise she'd nursed a hope that she'd be spending Christmas with Ran. No matter how hard she'd tried not to nurture that tiny spark, to snuff it out, it hadn't worked. And now Phaedra had chucked a bucket of icy cold water over those hopes.

She was right about one thing, though: Christmas was almost here and Bo couldn't stop it. With or without him, she had to accept it was coming and try to embrace it for the sake of her family and friends. She hated moping, and her instinct was to throw herself into the action.

After work, she went to Flingers – Ran gave it a miss of course – and Bo spent late Sunday afternoon hunting down all the presents she'd squirrelled away. The sitting room looked like Santa's factory on Christmas Eve – if the elves had gone on strike. There were rolls of wrapping paper that had unfurled from the sofa like a waterfall of Christmas trees. Snippets and off-cuts of paper, sticky tape on various surfaces.

She'd dragged her old tree from the loft and decorated it, smiling at the rock 'n' roll themed decorations that Cade had given her the previous year and leaving a tartan heart from Hamish in the box. She and Cade had made several fresh batches of Christmas brownies and kept a few back which she intended to take to the Spectacular refreshments.

She hung 'Elvis' complete with Santa hat on the tree.

The cottage now looked like Christmas and smelled like Christmas, but Bo felt as if she was just going through the motions. Even the usual excitement and anticipation of the Spectacular had been dimmed. Her mood was like faulty Christmas tree lights – just about holding on, but dimmer than usual and flickering as if they would plunge into darkness at any moment.

Bo abandoned her wrapping to take a call from her dad about stocking-filler ideas for her sister – at the last minute, of course – before ending the call.

'Oh no. Not again!'

She really hadn't been taking much notice of the TV, which she had on mute after answering the phone to her dad, but in a scramble to retrieve the wrapping paper before it crashed onto the floor, she'd finally noticed the screen. *Love Actually* was on – and Bo had had enough of it to last a lifetime.

Worse, it was the scene in which Emma Thompson's character realises Alan Rickman has been having an affair. Bo couldn't bear to watch the moment when Emma breaks down, quietly, in her bedroom, before heading downstairs with a smile on her face, one more time.

She floundered for the remote . . . where was the bloody thing?

'Argh.' It could be Easter before she found it at this rate. She lunged for the TV's power button and tripped over her box of bows and ribbons.

'Ouch!' She stubbed her toe on the TV stand and knocked a load of cards off the shelf in the process. 'I hate Christmas!' she screamed.

'Bo!'

A man's face loomed in the window. Cursing her throbbing foot, Bo limped over, wishing she'd closed the curtains. It was Ran, face pressed up to the glass.

'Are you OK? I heard you shouting.'

'I'm fine,' she said through gritted teeth. Why did he have to turn up now?

'Can I come in?'

She nodded and hopped to the front door, cursing the raised pulse rate that made her toe throb even harder.

Ran stepped inside. He was wrapped up in a smart waxed jacket she hadn't seen before and had a chunky scarf tucked around the neck.

'You've walked?'

'Yeah. I needed to get out of the house – I mean, I needed the exercise. Both, in fact.'

'Oh. Well, I'm afraid the place is a tip. I've been baking and wrapping presents.' Bo couldn't ask him to sit down, the sofa and chairs were covered in paper.

'It smells great.'

'I've been making some Christmas brownies to freeze for this week's rehearsal. I guessed we'd all need the energy,' Bo said.

'Good idea . . . I'll be sorry to miss it. Cade's DJing instead. I've told Hubert.'

'Oh? It's our last chance to rehearse before the big night itself?'

'It's not really Phae's scene.'

Bo's faint hope that Phaedra invented the London trip was dashed. 'Really? She told me she'd like to learn to dance.'

He frowned. 'Did she? She says a lot of things.' He glanced around. 'Is it OK if I sit down for a few minutes?'

'Um, if you want to clear a space on a chair, I can make us a drink.'

'No, thanks. Normally I'd love to – and maybe pinch a brownie – but I can't stay long.' He gave a crooked smile. 'That's partly what I came over to tell you. I'm leaving for London early tomorrow morning.'

Despite every resolve not to be upset, Bo's stomach lurched. 'I know.'

'What?'

'Phaedra dropped by yesterday morning to inform me.'

'I'm sorry. It's only for a few days, but I need to go back with her . . . some legal stuff to do with her selling the flat and . . . for all kinds of reasons. For me, for Phaedra – for all of us.'

Bo hated the way her heart was racing, the sick feeling in her stomach. She thought she'd been on her guard, but all she'd done was sleepwalked into having her heart broken all over again.

'Did you know you were going to London when you helped out at the party on Friday night?'

'I hadn't finally agreed,' he said carefully. Bo had the impression he was bottling up a lot of emotions, though she wasn't sure if they were guilt or anger.

'I see. You don't have to say any more. In fact, I'd rather you didn't.'

'Yes, but I *wanted* to tell you. I can't explain, not yet. I only wanted to ask you to hold off judgement on . . . everything, until I come back.' His voice had a weary, resigned edge.

'I respect that and I'm glad you came to tell me, but I need you to understand something too. I like you, Ran.' She hitched a breath, walking a tightrope between telling him how she really felt – how *much* she felt for him – and protecting herself. 'I like you a lot, but I can't put my life on hold or place my happiness into anyone's hands again. I did that last Christmas, with Hamish.'

'I'm not Hamish! God, I bloody hope I'm not Hamish.'

'No. You're definitely not Hamish,' she said with a smile that was meant to hide her heart, dissolving all over again. Ran was ten times the man Hamish was but that didn't mean he still wouldn't break her heart. 'You're married for a start.'

'Yes . . . but we're getting a divorce,' he said mechanically.

Bo wasn't convinced. 'In that case, I really think you need to tell Phaedra that because it seems to me that she's forgotten you're splitting up and I don't want get stuck in the middle.'

Ran hesitated, his expression anguished, before nodding and getting up, ready to leave.. 'I understand,' he murmured, 'I wouldn't want that either. I *will* be back for the Spectacular,' he said. 'Believe me.'

Bo just nodded, and murmured something about seeing him soon before closing the door behind her.

Lingering a moment in the hallway, she realised that was exactly the problem with Ran – with her love life in general – she didn't know quite what to believe any more.

Chapter Forty-Four

'Bo! Hello! Oh, mind the boxes of stock in the doorway. I've already brought them down to price up for the Lizard Craft Fair on Sunday.'

Buzzing with energy, Angel showed Bo into the kitchen on the following Wednesday afternoon. She'd gone round to collect some altered costumes for the Christmas Spectacular rehearsal that evening.

Driving over, she'd been unable to quell the thought that Ran and Phaedra had been in London since Monday and there'd been no word from him. For now, she was determined to put it to the back of her mind and concentrate on Angel.

The kitchen was almost back to normal, with the surfaces free of sewing paraphernalia, although the machine still stood on the kitchen table with its cover on and Angel's workbox was perched on a chair, albeit closed.

'It's great having my own workroom where I can keep my stuff tidy but I missed working in here,' Angel explained. 'I like to look over the garden . . . and it seemed strange locking myself away upstairs.'

'Too many changes at once?' Bo said.

Angel nodded. 'Something like that.'

Bo understood. The past few months had been a roller-coaster ride for all of them. She retrieved a cardboard cake box from her bag. 'I bought these.'

'Oh! Let's see.' Angel lifted the lid and gave a happy sigh. 'Brownies! And they smell divine. What's in them?'

'They're a Christmas recipe. They have mixed spice and brandy-soaked cranberries in them. We served some at the launch party and they're flying off the counter.'

'I'm not surprised. They smell and look delicious. Did you make them?'

'Cade and me. We get some of our patisserie and bakes from the Dolphin Bakery in Helston but we make some of our own too if we have time.'

Angel made coffees and they sat down to enjoy the cakes.

'How did the party go? I wondered how you and Cade got on.'

Bo knew she couldn't lie, as news would reach her friend soon enough. 'It went really well. The design agency people loved the outdoor space and the food. One of the guys mentioned the bunting.'

'Really?' Her eyes lit up.

'Yup. I told them I'd had it custom-made by a new business. "Made by Angels".'

'You like the name?'

'It's perfect . . . This is nice coffee . . .' she said, noticing Angel had brought out a cafetiere and realising she didn't need to mention Ran or get into a difficult conversation.

'Yes . . . I bought it from the Lizard Craft Centre yesterday. Jake's organising it. He runs a gourmet tea and coffee stand at the centre now and he gave me some samples. I've had that cafetiere for years. It was a Christmas present from my sister but Tommy only likes instant so I've never used it.' She filled a mug for Bo. 'This winter blend is perfect for cafetieres.'

Bo added some milk and inhaled the spicy aroma. 'It's lovely coffee.'

Angel nibbled a cake and licked her lips. 'It goes well with your lovely brownies.'

She moved the talk on to Christmas shopping, how busy everyone was, and plans for Christmas Day.

'Have you thought about what you'll be doing for Christmas?' Bo asked. There were only crumbs on both their plates now.

'It'll be strange. Emma has invited me and Adam's asked me for Boxing Day. It will be weird without Tommy. He's still at his mother's . . . I bet they're driving each other mad. She was never the most tolerant woman at the best of times and I can only imagine what it's like with him under her roof.'

Bo was quietly thrilled with the idea of Tommy being driven mad by his mum.

'What about you?' Angel asked.

Bo was ready with her answer; she'd already given it half a dozen times to other friends.

'I'm off to my mum and dad's as usual. My sister and her brood will be there too. I keep finding presents for them hidden in cupboards and the back of the wardrobe. I must have squirrelled them away throughout the year. We'll all probably sink under a sea of wrapping paper.'

'Well . . .' Angel shifted nervously in her seat. 'Talking of presents, I've got something for you. I know we don't normally exchange gifts but you have been such a great friend to me always – and I know I'm seventeen years older than you.'

'When has that ever mattered, you daft thing!'

'You've never made me feel old, though I have a few times lately. Fifty-three is hardly decrepit and I'm lucky to be fit and healthy but I was beginning to wonder what I'd done with my life. I love the kids to bits and I've enjoyed being a home-maker – though that's not fashionable – and I loved my job until Kelvin came along . . .'

Angel's eyes were suspiciously bright and Bo's heart went out to her for all she had lost in the past few months.

Angel blew out a breath. 'But enough of looking back. You've made me see the light at the end of the tunnel and actually get my arse into gear.'

Bo laughed. 'I've been worried that I've bullied you into doing things.'

'Bullied me? No chance! I love my sewing. It's terrifying but I don't think I'd go back now. And on that note, you wait here while I fetch your present. Oh, I hope you like it.'

'Angel! You're really naughty, spending money on me. You shouldn't have.'

'I haven't spent much . . . that sounds awful, doesn't it? Oh, wait here. I'll be back in a tick and all will be revealed.'

Angel virtually skipped off, leaving Bo alone in the kitchen to reflect on the conversation about Christmas. She hadn't heard from Ran and, as things stood, he was the last person she should be spending Christmas with. It was madness even to be wishing for that, considering her vow not to get involved with anyone who was on the rebound.

It was dark outside and the wind was keening around the cottage. It seemed a very long time since that hot August day when the three of them had stood outside Madame Odette's tent, with no idea of what was in store.

She'd no detailed idea what the fortune teller had actually told

Ran, and her forecasts about 'being with the love of their lives' for Angel and Bo herself were way off the mark. Bo didn't even know why she'd given a shred of credence to the predictions.

'Here you go. Oh, I hope I've done the right thing.'

Angel held up a hanger, on which hung the most beautiful dancing dress Bo had ever laid eyes on.

The swing dress was in berry red with a large black velvet bow in the middle of the sweetheart neckline.

'It's detachable,' Angel said. 'So you can dial the glamour down a little for other occasions.'

There was a contrasting black trim at the neckline and on the cuffs of the elbow-length sleeves and a cute PU belt through black belt loops that gave the dress more shape. The full skirt was gorgeous, flaring down from the waist. Bo could picture it twirling round as Ran sent her into a spin.

She checked herself: it would be Cade or one of the others dancing with her at the Spectacular. Her throat was scratchy with emotion. The pent-up dam threatened to burst. The contrast between her disappointment at Ran, her crushed hopes she never should have nurtured. They contrasted with the kindness of her friend, already working so hard and battling so much in her own life. Yet she had found the time and generosity to make this beautiful dress.

Angel's beaming smile faded, into doubt. 'I hope it fits . . . I have your measurements already but . . .'

Bo lost it. The tears had found her voice. 'I l-love it . . . I love it so m-much, I can barely speak. The bow, the skirt, the colours. It's divine.' She dived for the kitchen roll and ripped off a handful to stem the tears rolling down her cheeks.

'Oh, Bo. Please don't cry!'

Bo flapped a hand in front of her face, mortified by such a

display of emotion. 'They're happy tears,' she said, only half lying. 'It's so gorgeous. I can't wait to wear it. You must have spent ages when you're so busy.'

'It was easy compared to Jenna Boscawen's dress. The hard part was wondering if you'd like it and if I'd put you in a difficult spot. Please, please be honest with me. If you don't want to wear it, or need me to alter it, I promise you I won't be offended.'

'It's perfect. Perfect.' Bo wiped her eyes and got a grip of herself. 'Can I try it on now?'

'Of course.' Angel's eyes danced with delight. 'I also got you these from the charity shop. They're brand new . . .'

She handed over a box and inside were the sweetest earrings, with red berries hanging from them.

Bo dug her nails into her palms, fighting back a fresh wave of tears. 'They're perfect too. Where shall I get changed?'

'In the sewing room? There's a full-length mirror in there. There are a couple of tulle petticoats hanging up if you want to try one underneath. I know you've got your own at home. I thought the colours would work with your red dancing shoes.'

Bo flew up the stairs with the dress and into the sewing room. It was unrecognisable from the junk room it had been. It looked much bigger and the shelves were neatly lined with boxes of stock and fabric, see-through shoeboxes and recycled jars of buttons, trimmings and threads.

A bookshelf was packed with patterns and there was a sewing table with accessories for the machine, Bo presumed. An ironing board was stacked against a wall, next to a full-length mirror. On the wall was a large corkboard with lists pinned to it, presumably of Angel's commissions, and some cuttings of dresses, skirts and tops which she must use for inspiration.

Bo slipped out of her jeans and jumper and into the dress, with its cleverly concealed side zip. She dreaded it not fitting and having to ask Angel to alter it, but soon realised that it had truly been made to measure.

The moment she had it on, she felt like dancing and stood in front of the mirror, swishing the skirt to and fro. She even did a little twirl. Who cared that she'd been catapulted back to being a kid again? This was her style, the style that made her feel comfortable in her own skin. She could hear the Christmas playlist and the beat.

Then she remembered. It wasn't likely to be with Ran again. Despite being determined to enjoy the Christmas Spectacular, she was looking forward to it about as much as a trip to the dentist, even with a stunning new dress to wear.

'Stop it!' she said out loud.

She fastened the earrings on and went downstairs in the dress and bare feet.

'You will knock 'em dead!' Angel clapped her hands in delight.

'It's a lovely dress, Angel. I feel like dancing already.'

'Give us a twirl.'

Bo did a little routine on the kitchen tiles, ending in a spin.

'What are we like?' she said.

Angel burst out laughing. 'Having fun? Life's too serious not to. I am so happy you like it.'

'I adore it and I can't wait for the dance now.'

She sat down.

'It's nice to see you smile again.'

'Really? Haven't I been?'

'Not enough. Not since that Phaedra woman turned up.'

'Hmm . . .'

'I don't know why she's here at all. Hubert said she cut him dead when he wished her a good morning outside the boat-yard . . . and I had a message from Sally that Ran's not doing the rehearsal because he's gone to London. Something to do with the sale of their flat. Did you know?'

'Yeah. I did. I'm trying not to interfere.'

'But you like Ran, Bo, and he *really* likes you. She's a troublemaker, I can tell, but I guess we might find out more when he comes back for the Spectacular.'

Bo rested her hand on the skirt of the dress, focusing on its berry-red richness. '*If* he comes back.'

'Ran would never leave us in the lurch for the Spectacular!' Angel declared. 'I'm sure of it.'

'I hope not,' Bo murmured. 'But sometimes we don't know people as well as we think we do. Sometimes, we don't know them at all.'

Chapter Forty-Five

Ran couldn't believe he'd been in London for a matter of days and yet it was as if the past eighteen months had never happened. He guessed Phaedra wished they hadn't, and at one time, Ran would have gladly wound back the clock. Perhaps even as far back as the day he, Bo and Angel had stood outside Madame Odette's tent.

Walking into the flat on Monday morning, he'd set down the cases on the oatmeal rug, a solitary rectangle of comfort on the ash blond floor. 'Wow.'

Despite the dishrag skies of a London afternoon, the white light inside the open-plan room had dazzled him. After living at Creekside Cottage amid the clutter of vinyl, cat paraphernalia and someone else's furniture, the minimalism was a shock. There was nothing on the surfaces – tables, counters – that hadn't been carefully chosen for its aesthetic appeal, from the shiny espresso machine to the smooth, white abstract sculpture on the lamp table. Three hardback books were perfectly aligned on the coffee table, all too pristine to ever have been read. There was precious little sign of stuff being packed up, but that was one of his reasons for being there.

Phaedra had laughed at him. 'You're shocked? Is it because the place looks different to how you expected?'

'No. Because it looks the same.' So sterile . . . a thought he buried deep inside, not wanting to hurt her even though he was already wishing himself back in Falford.

She pursed her lips. 'Is that supposed to be clever? Ironic?'

'I'm surprised you want me in here.'

She shrugged off her coat and folded it over her arm. 'Don't be silly. Now, sit down. I expect you're tired after that long drive. I'll hang up our coats and make us some decent coffee. By the way, I've booked a table at Rascal's tonight. I thought we deserved some decent food. It's at eight p.m. Hope that's OK. We were incredibly lucky to get in at such short notice but I said it was a special occasion.'

'There. That wasn't too painful, was it?' she said when they stood on the pavement next to the painted railings on Thursday morning.

Phaedra linked her arm through Ran's once they'd stepped out of the front door of the law practice into the street. The shiny navy door closed behind them. Over the past few days, he felt as if he'd been swept along in a current that he couldn't escape no matter how hard he tried to swim against it. Phaedra, on the other hand, seemed cock-a-hoop.

'No, though I still don't know why we had to be there in person. Still, at least you can go through with the sale of the flat now,' he said. 'And we can start some serious packing. Have you got a place to go to yet or are you still planning on moving in with your sister for a while? How was that house in Wimbledon you viewed?'

'I haven't made a firm decision yet.' Her eyes glittered with annoyance. 'Come on, let's get home.' She squeezed his hand but he pulled it away.

His stomach clenched. He dreaded what she might have to say. 'You go home. I've a few places I need to go myself.'

'Like where?' Her eyes bored into him.

'Pub. I arranged to meet an old friend for a quick pint.'

'Who?' she demanded.

'An old diving buddy,' he said. 'You met him once when he called at the flat.'

She rolled her eyes then brushed his lips with hers. 'Typical. Well, I suppose it's nice to see you reconnecting with old friends. You've been pacing around the flat like a caged animal since you arrived. Now you can see being back in London isn't all bad. Don't be too late home!'

'I won't . . . and I'll help you sort out your stuff as soon as I get in!' he added but she was already on the kerb, hailing a cab.

He strode off in the other direction, turning up the collar of his jacket against the cold. It had been a painful few days, but the thoughts he'd arrived with had gelled further over that time. It was time for a decision, and whatever way he went, he was certain to hurt someone. However, one thing he'd learned over the past couple of years was that shying away from hard choices was the worst of all the options.

Hours later, Ran stepped out of the pub into the street. He felt guilty about the little white lie he'd told Phaedra earlier about meeting a diving buddy . . . still, he consoled himself, he'd only misspoken one word of the 'lie' and he hadn't wanted to set her antennae twitching.

It was dark at four but you'd hardly know it. Darkness was a relative term here. It wasn't the syrupy blackness of Falford. The sky above was orange, while street lights blazed and neon billboards rolled around with a stream of adverts. Pedestrian crossings flashed, releasing hurrying throngs of people with laptop bags and shopping bags.

The traffic roar was constant, punctuated with sirens and horns hooting – mind you, he thought with a wry twist of the lips, you got that in Falford. Some of the locals weren't that tolerant of people who couldn't reverse.

Ran looked up and from the orange sky a few wispy flakes of snow fell. He closed his eyes and felt the moisture on his face. He stuck out his tongue, tasting the snow.

'Hey, mate!'

A drinker, pint in a plastic cup, knocked into his back and he realised he'd been blocking the pavement outside the pub. The endless flow of people – like the river – hurrying on, never stopping, ducking and diving around him or angrily glaring at him.

Phaedra wanted him to stay. It was her territory, and that was fine.

Crammed onto the Tube, he felt more alone than ever. Alone and confused. Was he doing the right thing? Had he made the right choice? Whatever he decided would hurt someone.

You couldn't avoid it, no matter how hard you tried to run away and hide. Madame Odette had told him that. He'd never shared that part of her 'wisdom' with a soul.

Maybe it was his fate to hurt someone.

Emerging from the bowels of the Tube and out through the

station, he dawdled on his final walk to the flat, past workers enjoying drinks around braziers on the waterfront, wrapped up against the wispy snow which probably wouldn't stick here in the city. Christmas parties were in full swing, loud music blaring out of the bars and restaurants. It was probably the only occasion he'd ever hear 'Rockin' Around the Christmas Tree' from a trendy bar . . . the Christmas classics were acceptable here only as a novelty.

He entered the apartment block and took the lift to the fifth floor, inexplicably weary, with legs like lead.

He put his key in the lock and pushed it open, noticing immediately how loud the TV was blaring – or more likely a radio play or audiobook, given the dramatic scene that was playing: a man and woman arguing.

He shut the door behind him and strained his ears.

The couple arguing weren't actors. The voices were Phaedra's – and that of a stranger. His heart banged like a drum roll.

Jesus Christ! An intruder had broken in.

'Phae!'

Ran launched himself through the door from the lobby. He didn't have time to think, lunging at the man holding Phaedra by the elbows.

'Get the fuck off my wife, you bastard!'

Her scream was almost as loud as the man's cry as Ran brought the man crashing to the floor.

'Call the police!' Ran yelled, sitting on the man. 'Call the bloody police now!'

'Get off me!' the man shouted, flailing at Ran with his fists.

Ran seized his lapels, ignoring the blows. 'No chance. Call the police!' he shouted again.

'Leave him alone!' Phaedra tore the back of Ran's jacket. 'Get up, Ran! He's not an intruder.'

'Who the hell is he, then? The bloody gas man?'

The man glared up at Ran, his face red. 'I'm her boyfriend. I came to get my stuff. Get off me!'

Phaedra dropped to her knees next to Ran and the man. 'Ran, please! You'll hurt him.'

Ran let go of the man's lapels and got up. His heart was pounding, he felt sick . . .

'Your boyfriend?'

'Ex-b-boyfriend,' the man muttered, catching his breath before struggling to his feet.

'Hugo. Please.'

'We split up two weeks ago,' Hugo growled, keeping a safe distance from Ran. 'You could have crushed me.'

'Shut up!' Ran spat. 'And don't come near her. Phae, what's going on here?'

'We were going away before Christmas to the Maldives but we had a row and . . . and . . . Hugo had paid for the holiday so he went with a mate.'

'That's gallant of him.'

'Well, I wasn't going to pay for her to come with me,' Hugo said with a sneer.

'And you were left with nowhere to go?' Ran directed his attention to Phaedra.

'I had two weeks' leave,' she said. 'I would have been alone in the flat and I wanted to see you. Like I said, I wanted to see if we could start again.'

Hugo exploded with a snort of contempt. 'That didn't take you long.'

Ran silenced him with a glare. 'Get out.'

'You can't tell me to get out. You don't live here.'

Ran folded his arms. 'My name's still on the deeds though.'

'My stuff's here!' Hugo whined.

'Where? I never saw it.'

'It was in the cupboard in our bedroom. Phae's room,' Hugo corrected himself.

Phaedra grabbed Ran's arm. 'Darling, Hugo came to clear a few bits and pieces out but things turned a little heated.'

Ran flipped a thumb at a sports holdall on the rug. 'Is that your junk?'

'Yeah,' Hugo muttered.

'Then take it and get out.'

Hugo curled his lip. 'I haven't finished my conversation with Phaedra.'

'It didn't sound like a conversation to me. It sounded like you were harassing her.'

'Oh, Ran!' Phaedra said, trying to pull him further away from Hugo. 'What's the matter with you? I don't need your protection.'

'You're right. But that doesn't stop me wanting to make sure you're OK, and not being threatened by scumbags like this.'

'Ran!'

'Don't worry, I'm leaving.' Hugo poked a finger at Ran. 'You're a nutter, mate!'

He grabbed the bag, scuttled off and slammed the door.

Phaedra collapsed onto the sofa. 'Well, that was embarrassing.'

'Embarrassing?' Ran stared at her.

'Also, rather magnificent.' She whistled. 'I've never known you to be jealous before. You went the full Viking warrior.' She smiled.

He ignored her joke. He wasn't in the joking mood. 'I'm not jealous. I'm worried for you. Worried about you hanging around with him, about him laying hands on you. Most of all, I'm flabbergasted that you didn't share with me the fact you only came down to Cornwall because your boyfriend had dumped you and you had two weeks at a loose end.'

'It wasn't like that, I promise.'

'Wasn't it? It looks like you came because I was a convenient shoulder to cry on, not as glamorous a location as the Maldives, but still, a place to escape to when life got shitty.'

'Like you did?' she shot back.

She'd taken his breath away.

'Yes. Like I did. And I am sorry for the way I behaved, the hundred ways I disappointed you. You have every right to see who you like, though personally I think you're better off without Hugo.'

Phaedra pouted. Her eyes were mutinous.

'I came back because I think we can make things work. I told you.'

'No. It's too late. It's been too late for a long time. I'm going to Cornwall.'

She curled her lip. 'To Little Bo Peep?'

He shook his head. 'That's beneath you, and I think you know it.'

'You can't leave now. It's late. It's a long drive. It's snowing!'

'All the more reason to set off now. I don't want to be snowed in here and miss the Christmas Spectacular.'

'That's not until tomorrow night,' she said, her expression hardening.

'Like I said, I don't want to miss it. The Spectacular is the event of the year. It means a lot to the Flingers.'

'The Flingers?' she scoffed. 'The only thing spectacular about that lot is what fools they are.'

Ran took in the bitter, angry person he'd once loved and felt desperately sad for her and what they'd once had, yet also more determined and surer of what he wanted than ever before.

He retrieved his overnight bag from behind the sofa, thanking his lucky stars he'd already packed it that morning.

'I hope you'll be happy, Phae. I mean that, and with someone who truly loves you and won't let you down. I'm sorry but it can't be me. Goodbye.'

'Wait!' She clutched at his arm. 'Don't leave me on my own at Christmas. Not in this flat.'

Her eyes were wild, her voice edged with desperation. A pang of guilt hit him like a punch to the gut.

'I still love you. You feel the same, don't you?'

How could he tell that desperate face that he didn't. It would be a lie. He *did* love her, if caring for her deeply and wanting her to be happy was love. Nothing more.

'Ran. *Please*. For the sake of everything we had together. I'm begging you to stay.'

Chapter Forty-Six

'Tonight's the night,' Angel said, almost skipping into the community hall with Bo an hour before the Christmas Spectacular was due to start.

Angel was glowing, she'd had a new colour on her hair; a glamorous auburn that looked fabulous with her emerald-green dress and reminded Bo of a 'bombshell' star of the fifties.

Carrying her dancing shoes in a bag, Bo walked with Angel past the rows of chairs towards the stage. They could already feel the buzz of anticipation in the hall which was alive with last-minute activity. At the rear of the hall, an electrician was busy checking the lighting with his helper and Hubert was in deep conversation with some of the Flingers next to the stage.

The community hall was decked out with streamers and tinsel, and its walls were covered in paper snowflakes made by local children's groups. A disco ball hung from the ceiling, shooting shards of coloured light across the room. Laughter filtered through the doors of the canteen area to the side of the room, where volunteers were lining up mince pies and refreshments for sale in the interval.

Bo recognised so many faces from the village: Dorinda Morvah, Oriel Stannard and her auntie Lynne. Her parents and her nan of course too, which brought a little lump to her throat. The clatter of voices seemed louder than usual and she realised why: there was no warm-up Christmas music playing from the speakers because Ran wasn't here . . .

Angel peered at the side of the stage where the decks and sound system should have been. 'No Ran yet?'

'Doesn't look like it,' Bo said, her stomach flipping.

'Have you still not heard from him?'

'Not since he went to London.'

Angel chewed her lip nervously. 'I'm sure he will . . . Ran wouldn't miss the Spectacular for the world.'

'No . . .' Bo refused to acknowledge how much she'd been anticipating Ran's return, even if it might bring bad news. At least she'd be put out of her misery.

'I'm so nervous, even though I normally love it. Did you know Jenna's coming tonight, and some of the guys from the Country Stores and the Lizard Craft Centre? Jake organised a group!'

'That's great,' Bo said, happy to hear that Angel was making new friends. Jake seemed to feature a lot in their conversations lately.

'You look so gorgeous. Ran doesn't know what he's missing.'

Bo had also changed at home and had to admit that her own 'couture' dress looked even more beautiful than when she'd tried it on in Angel's sewing room. She'd put her hair in a ponytail secured with a glittery bobble and done her make-up with extra care so it would stay in place for an evening of energetic dancing.

'Thank you, Angel. That's down to the dress you've made me. You look like a Hollywood movie star.'

Angel flushed. 'Oh, I wouldn't go that far! But . . . I do feel happier than I have for a long while. More confident. And I want to thank you for that.'

They gave each other a little hug, laughing about being careful not to leave make-up on each other.

A beaming Hubert and Sally joined them. 'All the tickets have been sold. That'll swell the coffers!' Hubert declared.

'Brilliant,' said Bo, feeling deflated again. All those people . . . except the one she'd most like to be there. The gap to the side of the stage where the decks should be was conspicuous. A vital piece of the jigsaw was missing.

Hubert followed Bo's gaze. 'Where's Ran? Shouldn't he be here by now?'

'He was supposed to be back from London by now, wasn't he?' Sally asked Bo.

'As far as I know. I haven't seen him for a couple of days.'

'Of course he'll come back,' Angel said. 'There's no way Ran would miss the Spectacular.'

'Well, I wouldn't be too surprised,' Hubert said. 'Creekside Cottage is going to be sold.'

'What?' Bo said. 'Where have you heard that?'

'Imelda Cronk told me. She works for the solicitor's in Helston. She probably shouldn't have said anything but it slipped out. It's very early days apparently but they've been asked to start all the legal stuff though she doesn't know the details.'

Bo's stomach lurched. 'That's news to me.' Her mind fled to the thought that Ran might be left homeless if the cottage was sold and be more tempted to stay in London. Even worse, the cottage might be being sold because the tenant had given notice.

'Imelda Cronk is a gossip and shouldn't be sharing private

information.' Sally shot a warning glance at her husband. 'She might have got it wrong, Hubert.'

'Maybe . . .' he said, looking worried. 'That's what I heard.'

'I'd have thought if he'd told anyone, he'd have told you, Bo,' she said kindly. 'You seemed very close.'

'We're good friends . . . but we were only dancing.'

Sally's eyes clouded with confusion. Bo remembered that she wasn't supposed to reveal Ran had been having private lessons.

'At the Illuminations, I meant. We're only friends and we've both been busy lately . . .'

Sally patted Bo's arm, her eyes telegraphing sympathy. It was obvious she thought Bo had been kept in the dark by Ran over his plans, and probably left in the lurch – again.

'I expect it's been awkward while his wife had been staying,' Sally said.

Summoning her best customer-friendly face, Bo smiled. 'He's probably been held up.'

'Hmm. I heard they've had some snow upcountry,' Hubert said.

Bo had seen the weather forecast too and heard there'd been some snow in the south-east. However, Ran would surely have called if it was only bad weather preventing him from returning to Cornwall. The fact he hadn't been in contact made it seem like there was a much more serious issue.

'Maybe I should give him another call,' Sally said.

'You do that, honey,' Hubert said. 'I'll sort this lot out. Time's flying by! Can I have your attention, guys?' He climbed the steps to the stage but everyone was too busy chattering away to take any notice. 'Hello!' He clapped his hands, then bellowed, 'Oi! Listen up, Flingers!'

Nervous laughter rippled through the group. Gathering everyone together, Hubert addressed them. 'OK, everyone, it's finally the Christmas Spectacular! Make sure you know who your partners are for each dance.'

There were groans from Cade and a couple of the dancers. 'We know, Dad.'

'Then check again, to make sure. We don't want a scrap over partners in front of the audience, do we?'

Cade rolled his eyes.

Hubert added a few words of encouragement, ending with his usual 'Let's rock and roll, guys!' and a cheer followed before the Flingers dispersed to make last-minute touches to make-up and outfits, and do some stretching.

The hall was strangely silent without the warm-up music that Ran usually played to put everyone in the mood while the audience arrived. Bo kept her smile fixed while putting her dancing shoes on, yet unease swirled in her stomach. Her eyes constantly scanned the entrance to the hall, willing Ran to appear, yet dreading it too. Minutes ticked by and the clock showed only forty minutes to the start.

People would be arriving any moment – in fact, she could hear voices growing louder in the foyer. A couple of people drifted through the doors, making a beeline for the refreshment area to get a glass of wine. What if something had happened to Ran? An accident? It was a long drive on dark winter roads to Falford.

She checked her phone again and started a text to him to check he was OK. The signal was so patchy in the lanes it must have arrived late.

Sally threw her hands up. 'Hallelujah! He's here!'

Before Bo had finished her message, Ran strode in through

the doors, arms full of a box of vinyl. His mouth was set in a line.

Cade met him and Bo wasn't far behind, flooded with relief that he was safe, followed swiftly by wondering where he'd been – and what would happen next.

'Where've you been, mate?' Cade demanded. 'We thought you were never coming and I'd have to step in.'

'Sorry. Sorry for everything but I'll tell you later. Can someone give me a hand getting the kit from the car?' Ran said, his voice edged with tension. 'Bo, would you and Cade help me set up in here, please?'

He exchanged glances with her, the most fleeting of smiles that could have meant anything.

Hubert weighed in between them. 'About time! I was going to send out a search party.'

With more early birds arriving, nabbing seats and queueing for refreshments, there was no time for explanations and all hands to the pumps – or rather, decks. Bo had a reasonable knowledge of the set-up but Cade was really into it since his stand-in duties at the Illuminations. Between them, they were able to get a head start while Ran and his helpers brought the rest of the kit and more vinyl from the car.

Bo crouched down to help him plug in the electrics. His eyes were bloodshot and he had a dark mark on his cheek.

'What happened to you?'

'Don't ask . . . Bo, I'm so bloody sorry,' he said. 'I couldn't leave London until first thing this morning. I wanted to leave last night but there's no time to explain why I didn't, now. Then when I finally *could* get away, the roads were a nightmare and there was a pile-up.'

'Have you been in an accident?'

'No.' He rubbed his cheek. 'This is something else. I swear I'll tell you more after the Spectacular. Not here, in public.'

She got up. 'I need to get ready for my first dance. It's almost time.'

'Bo . . .'

Hubert bounded up. 'Oi! Bo and Ran. We've only got half an hour. People are already queueing at the doors.'

She sped to the dressing room, fielding questions from Angel about Ran's late arrival. With Cade helping, the equipment was set up. The hall was half-full of people with glasses in hand and, a minute later, Christmas tunes started playing softly over the speakers. Immediately, the volume of chatter in the room swelled, and the excitement built.

The stage only held four couples on at once, but the Flingers were going to do two dances in each half and take it in turns so that everyone who wanted to could perform. Bo was opening the first half and dancing the finale of the show after the interval.

'Places please!'

Sally's shout had them all hurrying up onto the stage. Bo's heart thumped wildly. Familiar faces waved from the audience; her parents, sister and brother-in-law . . . her niece and nephew wearing sparkly Christmas jumpers.

Oh no, she was going to cry . . . her mascara would run.

Hubert was the MC and took centre stage. Cade, Bo, Sally and the rest of the Flingers waited, big smiles on their faces. The show must go on . . . just like life.

'Ladies and gentlemen, welcome to the Christmas Spectacular! The Falford Flingers are ready, the music is ready, but are you ready to rock and roll?'

'Yes!' voices shouted back from the audience.

The lights dimmed, a spotlight came on, and the glitter ball spun, showering the audience with coloured rays.

Cade took Bo's hands and her beaming smile was ready. This was rock and roll, high-energy, joyous. The dance floor was a place to leave your troubles behind for a few minutes. No time to worry or think.

Focus on the beat, the music, your performance.

Ran cued in the first track, 'Santa Claus Is Coming to Town' by the Crystals. It had a spoken intro that had the audience smiling in surprise then suddenly the music kicked in, with sleigh bells and a superfast upbeat tempo that got the show off to a flying start.

Bo knew people would be tapping their feet and, when the song ended, there was clapping and cheering and some whoops from the front row.

Cade and Bo took a bow and left the floor. Finally, Bo could breathe.

'How's your ankle?' she murmured while another set of Flingers took to the floor, and Hubert did his patter about the next track, 'Run Run Rudolph'.

'It'll be fine,' he said. 'Don't worry about me.'

Warming up with every song, the audience were soon clapping along and some were singing too. With her initial nerves quelled, and Cade's ankle holding up, Bo threw herself into the next two dances of the first half set. In her breaks, she cheered on the other Flingers. There was no time to speak to Ran, and she avoided even looking at him. She owed it to her fellow dancers to give everything to the performance; her personal life could go on hold a little while longer.

The final song of the first half finished and the lights went up. Bo was taking a bow when she suddenly saw a familiar figure leave the end of a row of chairs.

'Oh my God!'

'What's up?' Cade asked.

'Nothing . . . I thought I saw someone I know . . .'

She wanted to run after the woman but she had to keep smiling and move off-stage with the rest of the dancers. She hurried down the stairs at the rear of the stage and into the small backstage dressing room. The noise level in the room and from the main hall meant she had to raise her voice to be heard.

Maybe she'd have the chance to slip out into the hall, but Angel found her immediately. Her face was glowing with effort and excitement. Bo hadn't seen her so happy for a long time.

'Here you go!' Angel handed her a glass of water from the table.

'Thanks!'

'Wow. It's warm in here.' Angel fanned herself. 'That was fantastic, wasn't it? I think the audience are enjoying it. How do you think it's going?'

'Great . . .' Bo was distracted, having caught sight of Ran on the other side of the room, talking to Hubert.

Angel spotted him too. 'What a relief that Ran made it. I was getting worried. He was held up by the snow and an accident, he said, and his phone had packed up.'

'Yes . . .' Bo said, guessing Ran had been economical with the truth so far. She turned away to refocus on her friend. 'My dress is so gorgeous to dance in. So many people have said they love it. Thank you, Angel.'

Angel positively glowed. 'You're most welcome. People have been so nice to me too and Jake wants to talk to me. He says

359

there's a unit becoming vacant at the Lizard Craft Centre and would I like it.'

'That sounds exciting.'

'It is.' She grimaced. 'It's a big decision because it would add to my costs, but it would give me year-round customers and I'd be able to work alongside other craftspeople again. I miss that so much.'

'When do you have to decide?'

'Not until after Christmas. For now, I can just relax and enjoy myself.'

Bo was so happy for her friend, she forgot her troubles and decided against trying to find the woman-who-probably-wasn't-Madame-Odette among the audience. She'd been on one wild goose chase too many in pursuit of that elusive woman – and what would she say if she did meet her?

'You're a fake and your predictions were totally wrong. Angel's split up with the love of her life and mine's going back to his wife'?

Soon they were being called back on stage for the second half. Fuelled by wine, beer and mince pies, the audience were well up for some fun. Bo danced two more dances with Cade and Hubert and then it was the finale. She danced with Cade again and the audience erupted, demanding an encore.

No one had expected such a reception but it was a happy local crowd in the festive mood and Hubert was determined to make the most of it. He mouthed: 'Shall we go again?' to the dancers. There was some confusion behind the stage smiles. Bo was ready to dance again, one last dance to put off the moment when she might have to hear what Ran had to say.

However, she found Cade leaving her side and Ran climbing onto the stage. The two men had swapped places.

Bo's stomach did somersaults.

Ran held her gaze. 'You dancing?' he said, those blue eyes burning into her.

Cade was already announcing the final track. The intro would start at any moment.

'And now we come to our finale! The Elvis classic, "Santa Bring My Baby Back To Me"!'

Every rational fibre of her begged her not to take his hand, keep her distance. Her head told her not to dance with him, but her heart won.

Bo took his hand. 'If you're asking, I'm dancing.'

Chapter Forty-Seven

The spotlight bathed Bo and Ran in a pool of dazzling light. Every eye in the hall would be on them, yet she only had eyes for one person in the room.

A moment of sheer terror seized her, that she might not be able to move, then the music started and instinct and adrenaline kicked in. She remembered all those nights on the terrace. All the practice. Starting. Stopping. Laughing. Swearing. Tripping over their feet. Trying again and again.

'You can do it, Bo,' he mouthed, his eyes bright with the same excitement as hers.

'Santa bring my baby back to me.'

They were off.

Rock step, back step, change hands, turn . . . finally, gloriously, they were dancing together, knowing instinctively what the other was going to do before they even did it.

It was such a great track. So playful, pacy and foot-tapping with Elvis's smoky voice and the Jordanaires' backing vocals, Elvis pleading for his girl to come home for Christmas. The other dancers were a blur of colour and light around them but Bo could hear whoops and cheers as Hubert lifted Sally. The audience were singing along, clapping and tapping their feet. The whole hall vibrated to the joyful rhythm of people coming together to perform, to dance and sing and share the experience.

'Oh!'

Ran tripped over his feet, stumbled, almost fell.

Bo steadied him with her hand, and he regained his footing. 'Keep going!' she murmured, guiding him into the next turn.

'Santa bring my baby back to me . . .'

Elvis had ended on a high note and Bo was soaring too.

Ran held her hand tightly, and the audience erupted.

They took a bow, basking in the cheers and clapping as Hubert thanked everyone for coming and the lights went on. They were still holding hands, breathing heavily, unable to tear their eyes away from each other.

'I c-can't b-believe we just did that,' he said. 'In front of everyone in Falford. And I almost went flat on my arse!' he said, laughing.

'But you didn't.'

'Thanks to you. Bo, about my trip to London, please listen to me . . .' Ran began.

'Wow, you two! That was amazing!' Sally bounded up, slapping Ran on the back.

They both turned to her, letting go.

'I got through it,' Ran said.

'And you enjoyed it! Don't say you didn't. We could tell!'

Bo forced a smile at Sally's teasing while longing to get Ran on his own.

'Yeah, I'll admit it was great but that was down to my partner.'

Sally arched an eyebrow. 'Wow. Look, we'll clear up here and then we can all have a party. It's Christmas!'

Sally flew off, congratulating the other Flingers while the audience streamed out of the hall.

'Let's skip the after-show party,' Ran said. 'Please come to the cottage with me. I've a lot I want to say to you. If you'll hear me out.'

Bo hesitated.

'It's not bad news, Bo. At least I hope you won't think it is. Please give me a chance?'

After that dance, how could she refuse? Then again, a dance wasn't a relationship. Sexual chemistry wasn't everything – if Hamish had taught her anything, it was that sexual chemistry was not nearly enough.

'OK. I'll come and hear what you have to say.'

His shoulders slumped in relief. 'I'll get my kit packed and meet you there?'

Bo went off to have a word with Sally and Angel and tell them she was giving the party a miss to talk to Ran. Neither seemed surprised and she returned to help Ran pack his car with Cade's help. He set off first and after a few words with Angel, who wished her luck, Bo followed on after him.

Never had the short drive around the twisting creeks seemed so long, but she made it and found the cottage lights on and his van on the drive. The front door was open a crack, presumably for her, so she pushed it open.

Thor was miaowing from the kitchen and his cries and her footsteps echoed strangely on the hallway tiles. He brushed against her legs, curling around them, and she stroked him. 'Hi, Thor. I've missed you. Ran!' she called. 'It's me.'

There was no answer so she walked into the sitting room.

'Oh my God!'

Now she knew why the cottage had sounded so hollow. The shelves had been stripped bare and every surface, from floor to sofa to table, was covered with cardboard packing boxes full of records. Thor jumped onto one of the boxes, settling down on top of a Chuck Berry album.

Footsteps thumping down the cottage stairs were followed by Ran bursting into the sitting room. He was shirtless and had a towel around his neck. 'I wanted to jump in the shower before you got here. I've had a rough day.'

Bo's eyes flickered from his naked torso to the empty shelves and boxes. 'I heard the cottage has been sold. You're leaving?'

'You heard right about the sale but I'm not leaving.'

'What? Then why all these packing cases full of records?'

'I've sold them to a dealer in London,' he said. 'I'm waiting for a courier to come and collect them.'

'The whole lot?'

'Ninety percent of it. He didn't want the rest.'

'I don't understand.'

'The reason I stayed in London – part of it – was that I decided to sell my collection to help fund a deposit on this place. The owners have wanted to sell for a while and they gave me first refusal.'

'I thought you said they weren't worth anything?'

'Like I told you, all the expensive stuff was sold ages ago to repay the debts I'd run up when I lost my job and make sure Phaedra could stay in the flat. I didn't ask for the flat when we arranged the divorce settlement.'

'That was generous.'

'I owed it to her for the way I'd lived the high life in the past . . . but she's decided to move out of the flat herself and accepted a new job with a practice outside the city.'

'So, you're not moving back in with her?' Bo said, unable to believe that the scenario she'd dreaded wasn't happening after all.

'Absolutely not.' Ran gestured to her to sit down. He sat by her on the sofa, his hair still damp from the shower.

'I'm staying here, buying this cottage,' he went on. 'I've got some savings but not quite enough, so I visited a dealer friend and he said he'd take most of the rest of my collection. Luckily, I'd catalogued them. I didn't have much else to do when I first came here, hiding away from everyone.' He gave a rueful smile.

'I can believe that and you do – did – have a big collection.'

'There are over two thousand . . . most worth less than a tenner as I thought. I never expected that some would fetch so much. Prices have rocketed lately. There was a special edition Beatles EP in a cardboard box that a builder friend found in a skip and gave to me. I hadn't even had a chance to look in the box. I've told him about it but he's minted and he said I need it more than him.'

Bo looked around her at the empty shelves. 'Even so, it's so sad you're getting rid of your music.' She meant it.

'I've more important things to spend my money on.'

'But your DJing . . .' she said, unable to believe he'd got rid of his precious collection so he could stay in Falford.

'I only DJ for Flingers and I still have a tiny handful of the records that I really can't bear to part with. The ones that truly mean something to me. This cottage – Falford – suits the person I am now, not the one I once tried to be.'

He lifted her hand and held it in his, yet she still wasn't quite sure.

'So, you went to see your solicitor and to sell the records. You could have told me.'

'I wanted to give you certainty: a fait accompli. You deserve nothing less. I was already sure I was coming back to Cornwall to stay, though I wasn't a hundred percent *how* I was going to do it. I didn't know if the record sale would raise enough for the deposit, even though I'd agreed to the purchase price. I thought I'd have to borrow some money from my parents and I didn't want to do that and the sale of this place couldn't go through until I could prove I have the funds.'

'Ran. I have to level with you. I'm surprised Phaedra agreed to let you come back.'

'She didn't want me to, and I'll level with you too,' he said. 'She told me she was having genuine second thoughts about the divorce and I tried to make her understand that it didn't make any difference and that I only agreed to go back to London one more time to help her pack up the apartment and to sell the records and help her realise that I didn't want to go backwards. She thought I'd change my mind when I got "home".' He mimed inverted commas around the word.

Bo swallowed a lump in her throat. She'd been convinced Phaedra's powers of persuasion would win the day; now she knew she should have given Ran more of her trust.

'I'm so glad you didn't.'

He pulled her into his arms. 'I *never* would have changed my mind and, in the end, I was misled even about her genuinely wanting to get back with me. I came back from seeing my dealer friend to find her boyfriend – ex-boyfriend – rowing with her in the apartment.' He winced. 'It didn't end well.'

Bo touched his cheek, feeling the tender skin. 'Is that where you got the bruise? I'd thought you'd been in a car accident.'

367

'No. The guy was getting heavy with her when I came home and thought he was an intruder so I tackled him.'

'Wow. That *is* heavy.'

Ran closed his hand around her fingers and lowered her hand, keeping it in his.

'Phaedra seemed to enjoy the drama but only because she'd been left in the lurch by the boyfriend and enjoyed having me come to her rescue.' He heaved a sigh. 'It turns out that she was only here because they were meant to go away for Christmas and he'd let her down. She was upset and desperate when she turned up in Cornwall.' He sighed again. 'He'd dumped her and her pride was hurt.'

'I know how that feels . . .'

'Me too, and I do feel sorry for her, but we have separate lives now. I was literally about to leave the flat to come to Cornwall very late on Thursday night but she was in a terrible state and begged me to stay. I was genuinely worried she might do something serious so I had to stay and make sure she would be OK. I managed to get her sister to look after her.'

Bo almost felt sorry for Phaedra. 'Did she?'

'She managed to come over early on Friday morning but by then the snow was covering the streets of London and it was absolute gridlock. The police were advising people not to travel. You see, I'd had this big idea of whizzing down here like a knight on a white charger, knocking on your door and explaining everything face to face, but it all went wrong.'

Bo laughed. 'I don't need a knight!'

'I know. I'm an idiot. Anyway, once I did get away, the journey went from bad to worse. Much worse. The snow created chaos and I crawled most of the way from London. I'd decided to finally call you and explain myself, even though I wanted to do it in person, but then I ran out of fuel in a blizzard on Bodmin Moor.'

'Oh, Ran!'

'I'm a complete prat. I'd been so worked up and the van was using so much fuel, crawling along with the heaters on, that I hadn't noticed the gauge. Eventually, I had to walk three miles in the snow to find a can of diesel from a service station. I couldn't charge the phone until I was on my way again.'

'I didn't get your voice message . . .'

'Don't worry, I'll tell you now what I wanted to say. That actions speak louder than words . . . what I mean is that you deserve nothing less than me *showing* you I want to stay – how desperately I want to be with you. Phaedra and I have been on different paths for a long time, diverging further and further away from each other. She thought I'd be tempted back by seeing our old life but it only made me realise how much my heart has taken root here.'

'In Cornwall?' Bo said.

'Cornwall is a county. A geographical boundary. A line across a map.'

Bo gasped in mock horror. 'Don't let the locals catch you saying that!'

'I love seeing you smile. I've made you frown far too often. I hope I haven't made you cry.' He held her face in his.

She turned her face away, not wanting to look at him. 'Stop this. I refuse to cry over a man ever again.'

'I know you've been let down and you deserve better than Hamish – better than *me*. But, Bo, I'm ready to try to be the person you deserve. I'm just angry I spent the first six months I was here wishing for the past and the next few trying to let go of it. You were already in my life – I wish I'd let you in sooner.'

'I wasn't ready to let you in either. We were both pushing at the door, trying to keep it shut.'

He smiled. 'It's a miracle we're together now.'

'You don't think . . .' Bo said, then shook her head, laughing at herself. 'No.'

Ran wasn't going to let that go. His intense gaze was unwavering. 'I don't think *what*?'

She wrinkled her nose in embarrassment but knew there was no getting out of it. 'This is ridiculous and you'll laugh at me but you don't think that Madame Odette . . . that her predictions might be coming true, do you? For us, anyway.'

'Ah, Madame Odette . . .' he replied seriously.

'I sense a sarcastic reply . . .'

'No. I've wondered the same myself and, also, I think I saw her at the Spectacular tonight.'

'Me too! I spotted her – or a woman I thought might be her – slipping out of the back row of seats in the interval. I was going to go after her but we were too busy and then later, everything happened.'

'I thought I saw her too, when I was packing away after our dance. Everyone was putting on their coats to leave and this woman was walking out of the door. She was wearing a headscarf but I glimpsed her face and I *knew*.'

'I had the same thought. It must have been her yet we're still in the dark. Short of asking around if anyone knew her, we might never find out her identity.'

'No, and perhaps we're not meant to. Maybe we're meant to let it go and enjoy our fates,' he said.

Bo shook her head again. 'You don't believe in fate.'

'Do you?' he asked.

'Mmm . . . perhaps. I haven't decided. What matters is that

I'm happy with the outcome.' She planted a soft, delicious kiss on his mouth.

It turned into an embrace and a much longer series of kisses, followed by a collapse onto the sofa and the shedding of clothes more rapidly than was wise.

A mug fell off the coffee table onto the floor, causing Thor to let out a yowl and shoot out of the sitting room in horror.

'I didn't want him watching anyway . . .' Ran said raggedly, unbuttoning Bo's blouse.

Then, in silence underneath the lamplight, they celebrated Madame Odette's prediction finally coming true.

Ran was whistling 'Winter Wonderland' and making coffee when Bo wandered into the kitchen the following morning. The tiles were cold under her feet, in contrast to the rest of her body, glowing with very recent activity.

She was wearing Ran's dry robe and very little else.

He turned and gave her an approving nod. 'I like the new look.'

'I found it on the bathroom door.'

After feeding Thor, they took coffee and croissants into the sitting room and Bo sat with her bare feet in his lap. The boxes were still there, and the empty shelves seemed even drearier in the grey light of a December morning.

Bo laid her hand on his arm. 'What's the matter?' she said.

'I was thinking that this place looks a bit sad. I suppose I ought to get a Christmas tree . . .'

She was reminded of the evening he'd visited her while she was wrapping presents and the hollow sense she'd felt about decorating her own tree.

'They sell them at the Country Stores . . . I think they might have a few left. Angel said Kelvin over-ordered . . . and I need a few last-minute gifts though I hate to give him my business.'

'The dealer's van is coming shortly. When I've helped him load the stuff into it, I think we should get out of here and find a tree.'

Despite their misgivings, the Country Stores was close by and, as Bo had hoped, had a few trees left. Ran chose one from outside, carrying it into the main shop. Entering the place gave Bo mixed feelings. It was beautifully decorated for Christmas, which Angel had organised weeks before, of course, though there were far fewer customers as Bo might have expected on the final Saturday before Christmas. Carols were playing from the loudspeakers.

'Joy to the world . . .'

They took the tree to the cash desk but before Bo got there she saw two familiar faces chatting by the giftware. Angel saw them too and waved frantically, and her companion, Jenna Boscawen, smiled a greeting.

'It's Angel and Jenna,' Bo said in delight.

Yet Ran didn't reply.

He was too transfixed by the cash desk where Kelvin was standing with his arms folded and a mutinous glare on his face.

Looming over him, a furious look on her face, in her trademark silk headscarf, was Madame Odette.

Chapter Forty-Eight

Whatever it was that distracted Madame Odette, Bo wasn't sure, yet she met their eyes and Bo was certain in that moment she knew they knew who she was.

However, she was too busy dealing with Kelvin to give any explanations yet.

'We'll continue this later, Kelvin,' she barked.

'No, we won't!' Kelvin swore, causing the other staff to peer out of the glass-windowed offices. 'We won't because I'm not standing for this. My uncle must be out of his tiny mind. I always thought he was going senile and now I know. Well, I'm not staying here, you interfering trout!' He pointed a finger at Angel. 'And if you think I'm working for *you*, you can sod off!'

With that, he marched from behind the counter, straight past Bo and Ran, cursing under his breath. When he reached the door, he aimed a kick at the Christmas manger and the figures went flying into the air.

'Kelvin!' Angel called after him but he was out, leaving the door swinging back and forth.

Madame Odette met Angel halfway to the counter. 'Don't

you take any notice of him. Horrible little man. He can't do a thing now.'

Bo exchanged a look with Ran who shrugged. Other customers were craning their necks to see what was happening and muttering to each other. The Christmas music tape ramped up a notch in volume, probably to try and overcompensate for the recent display of anything other than Christmas cheer. Ran leaned the tree against the counter.

'Um . . .' Bo said. 'We've obviously missed something.'

'I thought he'd kick off like that,' Angel said.

'I was hoping he wouldn't,' said Madame Odette.

Angel sighed. 'I could have told you,' she said.

'You were right but I only offered him a job as deputy manager out of respect to his uncle. Now I wish I'd simply got rid of him. I suppose he's given me the perfect excuse.'

'It would be really great to know what's happened,' Bo cut in.

'Lucy's bought the Country Stores,' Angel said. 'Haven't you?'

Lucy . . . Bo peered at Madame Odette's face. There was no doubt it was her and the squeeze of her hand from Ran told her the same.

Her headscarf framed her features, although this scarf was a silk affair with a horsey print, rather than purple with jingly coins. Those piercing dark eyes were unmistakeable. It had been Lucy Boscawen who Bo and Ran had seen at the Christmas Spectacular.

'Angel, would you like to come into the office? And your friends – Bo and Ran, isn't it? I think we could all do with a nice strong cup of tea after that. If it wasn't the middle of the working day, I'd add a nip of whisky from my hip flask, but we'd better wait a few hours more for that.'

After a few calming words to the rest of the team, Lucy

closed the door to Kelvin's office although, as she explained, it wasn't Kelvin's office any more, it was hers.

'Mr Jennings has sold the Country Stores to Jenna and me,' she said. 'We've known him many years although I rarely come in here myself. As you know, Angel, Jenna is in charge of ordering for the stables so you won't have spoken with me. I spend more of my time with horses than people. Present company excepted, I tend to prefer them to most humans.'

Ran had a knowing smile on his lips.

'What made you decide to take over this place?' Bo asked.

'Mr J mentioned he was thinking of selling it to Jenna and we were both aware of the problems the place has been having. We've always been loyal customers and had excellent service, until Kelvin took over. Obviously, Mr J wanted to help his nephew's career, but Kelvin's clearly not cut out for this life and I've now no qualms in letting him go. Mr J wasn't happy with the way the business was being run. It was losing money and Kelvin was upsetting customers and hounding loyal and experienced staff . . .' She cast her eyes on Angel. 'Like you, Angel.'

'I never deliberately set out to get Kelvin the sack, for all his faults,' Angel said.

'I know that but he's brought this all on himself. His uncle has decided to make a clean break and we offered to take over. We're not the only customers who've been upset by the way Kelvin has mismanaged it and been horrible to the staff.'

'I'm not surprised,' Angel said. 'He doesn't care who he hurts.'

'I heard a lot of the goings-on from Jenna of course. She's the sociable one, the face of the stables, who gets about all over the county, but gossip spreads like wildfire amongst our horsey set. Kelvin's name is mud with everyone, the owners who stable their horses with us, the staff and the customers . . . even the vet's.'

She shifted her focus to Bo.

'The vet's?' Bo said. 'You mean, Hamish's old practice?'

'Oh, yes. I'm close friends with the people at the vet's, as you can imagine. Shame that Hamish left so suddenly, although perhaps it's not such a great loss. He's a handsome young chap though I'm not sure he was as wonderfully popular as he liked to imagine.'

Bo opened her mouth but caught Lucy's glance. She wasn't ready to share all that had passed between them in the tent. Lucy must have heard the gossip about her and Hamish at the practice. It sounded as if Bo herself hadn't known Hamish as well as she'd thought.

Ran touched her fingers discreetly. 'I suppose you have clients at the stables who like diving as well as riding, do you?' he said wryly.

'Only one . . .' Lucy said, 'though he does love a gossip and I'd rather not say his name. Look, can you forgive me? I've already apologised to Angel about my, um, performance at the festival. It was insensitive of me, given what transpired.'

'You're forgiven and you were very good,' Angel said. 'You had us all fooled.'

Bo let that pass. While Madame Odette did have them fooled about her identity, Bo still wasn't quite certain about being duped. Ran caught her eye again and Bo revised her opinion: perhaps it hadn't turned out to be an unpleasant piece of subterfuge.

'I never intended to play Madame Odette but then Harriet Polbean persuaded me.'

'The fête organiser?' Ran said.

'Yes. She and I are very close. Very close . . .' Lucy said, a glint in her eye. 'We were looking at ways of raising money and

376

she knows about my interest in this sort of thing. We thought it was the perfect opportunity to drum up extra cash at the fete and have a bit of fun. I never meant to hurt anyone. I was already having second thoughts when I started the readings that morning. I realised I could easily upset someone or tip them over the edge if they were feeling vulnerable. I did try to be positive.'

'You were. You didn't say anything frightening,' Angel said.

'Even so, I knew your thirtieth wedding anniversary was coming up from Harriet. I made assumptions and I am so sorry that I was wrong.'

'It's OK. I was confused and later I was angry but not now. I forgive you and, in fact, I think I found a different love of my life: my sewing, if that's not mad.'

Lucy seemed relieved. 'No, not at all and I'm thrilled for you. I only wish we'd had the chance to buy this place and get rid of Kelvin before you left.'

'I might never have taken my business so seriously if you had.'

'True. So, I knew enough about you and Bo to give my "readings" some credibility,' Lucy said. 'Ran, however, was the most difficult. I knew almost nothing about you, you made sure of that, and I almost let you walk out of the tent as you so clearly wanted to do. Can you forgive me?'

An amused expression hung on Ran's lips. 'I'm glad I stayed. What you said made me think very hard about the situation I was in. It was uncomfortable though it triggered me to, eventually, make some decisions I'd been putting off. And actually, Madame Odette, you were right. You said I'd be with the love of my life on Christmas Day.' He squeezed Bo's hand. 'Or at least I hope I will be.'

A warm glow of happiness filled Bo up.

'So, you just made up your forecast based on a mix of guess-work and psychology,' Ran added.

'Nothing supernatural at all?' Angel's voice was hopeful.

'I'm afraid not. Although . . .'

'Although *what*?' Ran jumped in.

They all perked up, leaning forward, waiting to hear what came next.

'When you went to Trewhella Illuminations, do you remember the crystal ball?'

'Yes!' Bo exclaimed. 'I remember that.'

'Well, Jenna told me you'd seen it and asked about the history behind it and I was slightly worried you might work out the connection.'

'I thought Jenna was Madame Odette for a while,' Bo admitted.

'I'd have recognised her if she had been,' Angel said.

'That crystal ball is mine, or rather, I inherited it,' Lucy said. 'It was my great-aunt Matilda's. She took an academic interest in the occult and wrote several books on the subject. They're in the library but her hobby was rather frowned upon by the rest of the family.'

'Oh, what a shame,' said Angel.

'It is. She had a wonderful collection of tarot cards as well as that crystal ball. Actually, it's recently emerged she used to conduct secret readings for the servants and a few trusted friends. In fact, I borrowed the ball for the fete.'

'We thought you'd bought it online,' Angel said.

Lucy laughed and Bo and Ran exchanged an amused glance, recalling their conversation about it coming from a website.

'No. I took it off the elaborate stand. I thought that might be a bit of a giveaway . . . and in fact, that's where Ran's prediction comes in.'

He sat up straight. 'What do you mean?'

'While I knew very little about you, when I looked in the ball, I did see *something*,' Lucy said, her voice lowering, almost as if she didn't want anyone to overhear. 'It was an indistinct picture, fuzzy, like TV interference.'

Bo noticed Ran had let go of her hand and leaned forward a little, intent on Lucy's words.

'I saw you . . . I saw you dancing.'

Angel let out a squeak.

Ran burst out laughing.

'I know, it sounds crazy. But that's what I saw.'

Bo wanted to laugh too, at the look of disbelief on Ran's face.

Angel stared at him. 'Well? That came true!' she said.

'You can't deny it,' Bo added.

'No – no, that much did come true . . .' He nodded, thoughtful – or maybe simply stunned. He didn't try to explain away her confession. Like Bo, he must have accepted that she was sincere.

'Will you ever forgive me for deceiving you?' Lucy said. 'I'm not a real fortune teller.'

'I think so,' Bo said, still amused by Ran's stunned expression. He either didn't believe a word of the crystal ball story or was freaked out by it. 'Everything worked out in the end.'

'Ran?' Lucy said, holding out her hand. 'Am I forgiven?'

Ran took it. 'Of course, Madame Odette.'

'That goes for me too,' Angel said, remaining in her seat while the others got up

'I need a chat with Madame Odette,' she said with a wicked grin. 'She's made me a proposition.'

Chapter Forty-Nine

'Happy Christmas, Bo.'

Bo woke in Ran's bed, wearing nothing but the afterglow of a very steamy night. They'd spent the day after their visit to the Country Stores putting up the tree after buying some decorations in Falmouth. With Christmas hastening towards them, and visitors arriving in Falford for their Christmas holidays, Bo had had to tear herself away from Ran's – and her own – bed to open up the café.

However, finally, she locked up the shutters once again on a crisp Christmas Eve and joined the Flingers in the pub. This time she was with Ran, who had his arm very firmly around her, much to the delight of Sally, Hubert, Angel and Cade. What a contrast, Bo thought, with the previous year. With Ran by her side, she was ready to burst with happiness. It felt so right to be with him.

Angel looked happy too, a miracle considering what she'd been through. Despite being offered her old job back by Lucy, Angel had decided to stay being her own new boss. She was going to rent a new unit at the Lizard Craft Centre and have her own display at the Country Stores.

After Christmas gifts were handed over in the pub, the two of them had walked home to Creekside Cottage, as the bells of the village church heralded in Christmas Day.

'What are you thinking?' Ran asked her now, as she woke up.

'Do I look as if my brain's whirring?' she said, propping herself up on one elbow and looking into that handsome face so close to her, with its tousled morning hair.

'You were miles away.'

'Not for long . . . I was only thinking about this time last year. If only we could have foreseen how different things would be now.'

'I'd have been delighted to know you would be lying here with me and not that bloody vet.'

'Ran!' She gave a mock gasp. 'Really?'

'I fancied you a lot, though I'd never have tried to come between you and I'd never have wanted you to be unhappy. If he'd deserved you, I'd have accepted the fact, but he didn't.'

'And you do?' she teased.

'I'd better not answer that.' He threw back the covers, stood up and stretched. His rear view, like the front, was honed and muscular and made her want to reach out and touch him.

She heard a faint click as he stretched his neck. 'Jeez, I'm not used to this much exercise.'

Ever since the day she'd glimpsed him half-naked at the dive school, it had been impossible not to want to touch him, explore his body and have him explore hers. Two nights in his bed had only fuelled her desire to know every inch of him.

'Rubbish. You're super fit.'

Turning, he raised an eyebrow. 'You think?'

'You know very well you are. You only wanted to make me say it.'

He laughed.

Sex with him hadn't sated her, simply left the burning embers a fire that seemed as if it could never be quenched, and that flared into life now, in every fibre of her body.

'Do you have to get up?' she murmured.

He was already slipping between the sheets again. 'We don't have to do anything.'

Light was filtering through the voile curtains when Ran finally climbed out of bed again, to shower in the bathroom. Bo lay in bed, still marvelling at the turnaround in her life.

After her shower in pine-scented steam, and smelling of the same masculine fragrances he had, she followed another luscious scent downstairs.

Ran was at the stove, making scrambled eggs. Slices of dark rye bread were on plates on the table, with a platter of smoked salmon next to them.

'What's cooking?'

He left the stove to plant a kiss on her lips. 'A special Norwegian breakfast. Take a seat – it's ready.'

He scooped the eggs onto the rye bread and topped them with the salmon. A pot of coffee was already on the table so they sat down to tuck in.

'I hope it's up to Bo's Café standards.'

'Anything that I haven't had to cook will be wonderful.'

'I'd hang fire until you've tasted it . . . Norwegians normally eat lightly at breakfast but this is a Christmas Day tradition when I visit my family.'

Bo swallowed a mouthful and sighed with pleasure. 'It's a tradition I approve of. What would you have for Christmas dinner?'

'My grandparents – Mum's parents – will probably have pinnekjøtt. It's a lamb rib, salted and dried and boiled on top of birch twigs. And it wouldn't be Christmas without lutefisk, which is fish fermented in lye and made into rolls. And sometimes we have smalahove.' He gave a sigh of pleasure. 'That's a burnt sheep's head. My grandmother always smokes and boils ours herself.' He smacked his lips. 'Yum.'

Bo's eyes grew wider at the list of Nordic festive 'delicacies' and he must have caught her slightly bemused expression. 'I promise you they're way more delicious than they sound.'

She wrinkled her nose. 'I'll take your word for it.'

He grinned. 'Unfortunately, the supermarkets here were all out of sheep's heads this year so turkey will have to do.'

'It doesn't sound quite as appealing as this delicious breakfast, I must admit.' She popped another forkful of smoked salmon into her mouth.

A faint miaow emanated from somewhere near Bo's feet and warm fur brushed her bare calves.

'What a surprise,' Ran said, as Thor appeared from under the kitchen table. He sat down and gazed up solemnly at his human.

'He can probably smell the smoked salmon,' Bo said.

'He'd smell that if he was in Truro.' Ran dangled a morsel from his plate in front of Thor's whiskers. 'There you go, you beast. Happy Christmas.'

After a brief sniff, Thor was on the salmon like a helpless rodent, wolfing it down in two gulps.

'His breath will stink,' Ran said mournfully.

Bo laughed. 'He's happy, that's all that matters. I wonder how Angel's doing today? It must be emotional.'

'She has some big decisions ahead.'

'I'll message her later. She'll be with her family today, of course.' Ran had already been invited to spend the day with

Bo's family. 'I warn you they always over cater by a country mile. I'm only warning you it could be a baptism of fire.'

'I think I can handle it, though I may want something in return.'

'What?'

'Apart from the obvious of excessive amounts of sex, I'd planned on going to Norway for New Year. There's a family reunion for my grandparents' sixtieth wedding anniversary. If you can leave the café, I'd love it if you came with me.'

'I always close at New Year. There aren't enough people around to make it worthwhile. I'd love to come.' She'd have closed anyway, she thought gleefully.

'I warn you, it will also be a baptism of fire. And very cold. They live near Tromsø – they can lend you some gear.'

'I've a better idea. You'll have to keep me warm.'

'I've got some aquavit here. It's a spicy potato liqueur that's a lot nicer than it sounds. Goes perfectly with all the rich festive foods. It'll blow your socks off, mind, and on that note, I'll drive us to your parents and back; it'll be too late to arrange taxis given it's Christmas Day.'

'Well, Mum and Dad do have a spare room where I normally sleep so we can both stay over . . . if you'd like?' Bo made the offer tentatively as she wasn't sure he would be happy with a full overnight stay. 'I'll give them a quick call to warn them I'll have a guest.'

'If you're sure they won't mind having me, I'll bring two bottles of aquavit, one as a contribution and one as a gift.'

'They'll love it!'

'Hope so.' He fiddled with his fork nervously. 'I also got you something.'

'Oh, no!'

He looked crestfallen. 'Have I misjudged?'

'No, not at all . . .' She shook her head. 'It's just that I didn't get *you* anything. I wanted to, but I stopped myself . . .' Buying him a gift had felt way too much like tempting fate, and then when all had seemed lost when he returned to London, she was glad she'd held back. Now she regretted it again.

'It doesn't matter. I have everything I need.' He reached across the table and squeezed her hand. 'Anyway, I bought your gift in London. In fact, it's still in the boot of the car. Don't get too excited!'

He was back in half a minute with a bag bearing a label of a record dealer in London.

She pulled out the vinyl disc. 'Oh, Ran. It's the Elvis we danced to last night.'

'When I bought it, I planned to be at the Spectacular and I hoped you'd let me dance to it with you . . .'

'I love it – thank you!' Bo said. 'Shall we put it on now?'

'Is it too early to dance?'

'It's never too early to dance.'

Ran put the record on the player and pulled her into his arms. Barefoot and wearing a dry robe, she giggled. Neither of them tried to rock and roll, despite the tempo; they both wanted to hold each other and simply be together.

'Hmm,' Bo said, listening to the lyrics and thinking of Hamish's cutting words – and the contrast with the warm-hearted, gorgeous man she was with now. 'It's not cheesy, is it? Dancing along to the songs our grandparents loved?'

'No, it's not and who cares what anyone else thinks,' he declared. 'We're old enough and wise enough to know all that matters is being ourselves.'

'That's so true . . . Last night, Angel said something about

Madame Odette's predictions. This year has shown me exactly what it means, for all of us.'

'What?'

'She said that as well as her sewing and her business, she'd also found the real love of her life – herself. That she's finally learned to put herself first, after years of giving up her own dreams for the sake of Tommy and Kelvin.'

'I'm happy for her and she's right. A weight has been lifted from me and I feel at home here, being part of the Flingers and Falford. There's something else too. Madame Odette might not be a real fortune teller but she was right about one thing: I am spending Christmas with a very special person.'

Bo hesitated, but only to take in the words, like someone drinking deep of cool water in a desert. She didn't need a man, she never had, but she wanted to be with *this* man. There was no shame in that, and no need to deny it. She also knew, instinctively, that he wasn't demanding anything in return, and yet she did want to give him a gift. One that cost nothing apart from her trust and her heart.

Silently thanking Madame Odette, Bo looked into his eyes, which were shining with pleasure and the happiness of having found his place in the world, as she had.

'So am I, Ran,' she said. 'And it's going to be a very special Christmas.'

Acknowledgements

This is my third book written in 'unusual circumstances', those being that we were under a lockdown while I wrote most of the first draft. This meant that my experience of rock and roll dancing was confined to my living room and lots of YouTube videos. Luckily I had three fantastic people on Zoom who shared their passion for vintage music and dancing with me. It would have been impossible to write this book without Richard Tew who is actually a Northern Soul fan and told me all about the world of record collecting. He also introduced me to Bridget and Seamus Doyle, who are now, I hope, able to take to the floor again to enjoy their rock and roll dance club.

To Bridget, in particular, I send a huge thank you. Imagine my delight when she mentioned she makes her own dance outfits. I'd already created the character of Angel but Bridget enabled me to bring Angel's hobby/business to life in a way I couldn't have dreamed of.

The setting was inspired by a visit to Cornwall in Christmas 2018 when we visited Trelissick Gardens. Trewhella House is an imaginary version of the wonderful house and illuminated gardens. As I couldn't go back last year, I asked a Truro-based gardener, Liam Shoesmith, for his advice on what flowers might be in bloom at 'Trewhella' at different times of year.

Readers, I love you for buying my books in your droves and making my previous two titles bestsellers. It's due to the indefatigable Team Avon that the finished copies make it to your e-readers and the bookshelves, and to Becci Mansell and Ellie Pilcher that you hear all about them in the press and online.

I've worked with two amazing editors on this book, Rachel Faulkner-Willcocks and Katie Loughnane, so I want to thank them for their help and expertise in making my story shine so much brighter than it would without them. At the last stages, my copy editor, Rhian McKay, adds a final touch of magic.

There's also a hidden team behind all my books, who are the rocks of support and encouragement. They include my author buddies and friends, The Coffee Crew, The Party People and the Friday Floras.

I have now worked with my agent, Broo Doherty, for sixteen years and the reason is that she is the best in the business, supportive and professional and a dear friend.

This year, more than ever, we have needed to escape and fiction has provided that in spades. So to all the booksellers, and book bloggers who share their passion for reading, a big thank you – particularly my bookseller friend, Janice Hume.

Finally to my parents, John, Charlotte and James. As ever, ILY x

If you loved *A Special Cornish Christmas*, why not go back to where it all started in Falford?

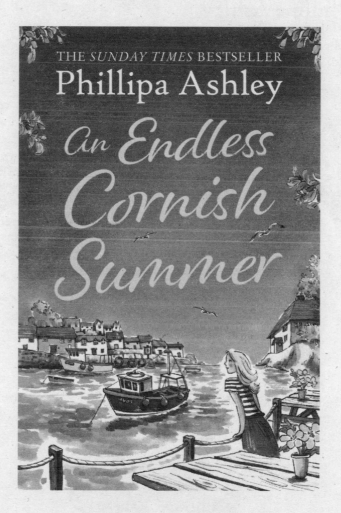

Discover Phillipa Ashley's glorious Porthmellow series . . .

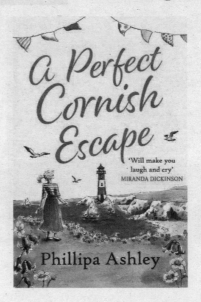

Escape to the Isles of Scilly
with this glorious trilogy . . .

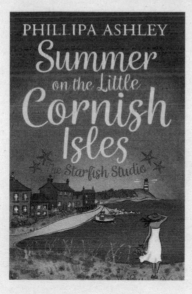

Discover the wonderful
Cornish Café series . . .

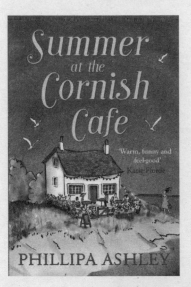

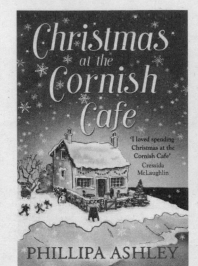

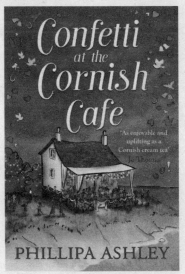

Escape to the Lake District with Phillipa Ashley's stunning Christmas story . . .

A
Surprise
Christmas
Wedding

'Warm, funny and feel-good'
Katie Fforde

Phillipa Ashley